# Don't Play With Those Kids D Street

By

Rudolph Whitcomb

# Contents

# Dedication

Well yes, this all started out to be just about my boyhood pal, my best friend who for the purposes of this book will hereinafter be called "Timothy, Timothy Schmitt." That is a fictitious name and so far as I know there isn't anyone with that name.

If so, this isn't about you.

And there are others who must be given credit for their part in all this, large or small, direct or remote. Those "others" who had something to do with or were touched by what happened to "Timothy Schmitt."

Those names are fictitious also, and if there's anyone with those names, this isn't about you either.

From Torrance and Hollywood, California to Hartford, Connecticut to Manhattan, New York to Hamilton, Bermuda.

Movie stars and mobsters, cops and conmen.

# About the Author

Rudolph Whitcomb enjoyed, and I mean enjoyed a career dealing with the financial exposures of the world's largest corporations. This career involved extensive travel from Hawaii to Italy. Hard decisions made by interesting and powerful people, decisions that resulted in actions that changed the world. The author has drawn on his experiences and observations of events that took place during that career.

# Prologue

*Jim Miller*

*August 16 1965*

*Torrance, California*

Sergeant Tom Larson was in his 50's and working traffic when I was partnered with him in the summer of '65.

I was just twenty-three that year. After a couple of semesters at El Camino College and a year on the beach I was lucky to get on the force. Jobs in the refinery or one of Torrance's two steel mills were scarce. This was a real break for me, even if it meant working with the fearsome Sergeant Larson.

Until shortly before I came along, Sarge had been Torrance's only motorcycle cop and he still longed to be back on the bike. I remember one day we had to respond to an accident involving a car and a motorcycle. The accident resulted in a fatality and the scene was as gruesome as you might imagine.

After the ambulance left, Sarge and I walked the street kicking out the flares. On our way back to our car we passed by the tow truck with what was left of the bike on its lift. Sarge stopped to look at it, hanging there all twisted and broken like a dead animal. He reached out as if to touch it, then stopped.

He shook his head and said gruffly, "There's nothing like the feeling of freedom you get riding a motorcycle. Damn me, I'd do it again in a heartbeat."

I didn't say anything. I'd always believed that anyone who'd ride around on a motorcycle all the time was nuts.

It was only a few months later that Sarge and I were taking a break, sitting in the squad car under the trees that lined Torrance Park.

It was very hot that day. Sarge was behind the wheel and I was slumped in the passenger seat fiddling with the handle for the spotlight mounted outside. I'd found that when I adjusted it just right, I could see my reflection in the spotlight's chrome.

We were in one of the city's two brand new black and whites, a 1965 Ford Fairlane sedan equipped with air conditioning. Although it was mid afternoon and nearly 100 degrees, we were cool and comfortable, almost cold in the idling police car. Sarge was watching some kids running through the sprinklers and playing on the grass, but we could barely hear their laughing and shouting through the car's closed windows.

Down the street at the other end of the block I saw a guy I thought I recognized. The guy paused at the intersection, glanced up and spotted us. He looked back down at his feet and kept shuffling along.

Nothing much ever happened around here and that made being a cop in Torrance a pretty good job. The town was so quiet and peaceful that people still talked about a ten-year-old murder case in the next town as if it were big news. A night manager in a cheap motel had been shot to death, probably in a failed robbery attempt.

But things like that never happened in Torrance. Giving out traffic tickets had turned out to be the biggest part of this job.

For me, the toughest calls were for family or business disputes. I wasn't comfortable with that duty. Confrontations bothered me. Since I grew up in Torrance, I usually knew the people involved, at least slightly. I didn't like being drawn into their private lives. Sometimes I'd run into them afterwards, and there it would be, they knowing that I'd seen them at their worst.

That day we sat there in the car next to the park for half an hour without saying anything, Sarge and I. Truth was, I didn't much like talking with Sarge. Like most people, I was intimidated by him. Although I never saw him lose his temper, I thought of him as being like a caged animal, ready to break loose at any time.

The racket from a garbage truck passing by drowned out the radio just as it crackled to life. I didn't hear what the dispatcher said so I was startled when Sarge suddenly yanked the Ford's gearshift lever into drive. He slammed his foot down on the accelerator and flipped the switch for the flashing lights on the roof.

Tires spun in the dirt, then with a screech found the asphalt. In a heartbeat we were barreling down what had seconds ago been a very quiet street. He slammed on the brakes as we approached the intersection. I grabbed the armrest to brace myself as we made a screeching right turn.

With lights flashing, but no siren, traffic was slow getting out of our way. We weaved from lane to lane passing cars and trucks as we headed south on Cabrillo toward Sepulveda.

Over the roar of the engine he yelled, "Let them know we're responding to the call."

I fumbled with the mic, pressed the button, and said loudly, "10-4. We are code 2," without any idea what call we were responding to. I set the mic back in its cradle. With my free hand, I cinched the seatbelt tighter. I gripped the door's armrest as we made a skidding left turn on Sepulveda. The radio came alive again. "Go to tach 2 to back up two LAPD units responding-" Screeching tires drowned out the rest of the message.

The car became airborne when we hit the railroad tracks. I sneaked a glance at Sarge. His expression was especially grim. We returned to earth with a bone shattering crash, then another skidding turn. We were now southbound on Western, heading directly into the sun's glare. Sarge pressed the accelerator to the floor.

Ahead of us, approaching from the south were the flashing red lights of two LAPD black and white's, the lead car's siren screaming. We were over the line into Los Angeles territory.

The two LAPD cars were about a quarter of a mile away when they abruptly turned in front of us. Crossing our path, they churned up the dirt and dust of the unpaved median and bounced into a trailer park. We followed them.

Less than a hundred yards into the park they skidded to a stop. Sarge slammed on the brakes but rammed into the rear of the second LAPD car. If it weren't for the seatbelt I would have been thrown against the windshield.

I was shaking from that wild ride. What was going on? The two officers in the lead LAPD car got out of their vehicle. One of the officers was carrying a shotgun. He took cover behind the car.

"Oh Christ!" I whispered, trying to control my panic.

The driver, somewhat out of my view since he was on the other side of that car was crouched down and yelling ahead toward one of the trailers.

I couldn't see the cop who drove the lead car. But I could hear him yelling something, something I couldn't understand. The officer driving the second car recovered from being rear ended, got out of his car and joined the two officers from the lead car. Directly in front of me the fourth officer opened the passenger side door and gun drawn, scrambled on his hands and knees, taking cover behind the nearest trailer.

I tried to steady my hand enough to open the door and get out of the car.

# Chapter One

## Schmitt Household on Beach Street, Torrance California

## September 1954

Marcia Schmitt stood back from the fogged old mirror on top of the dresser in her bedroom and adjusted the lavender cloche, the flapper hat that her mom kept in a box on the top shelf in her bedroom closet. The helmet-shaped felt cap was a remnant from her mom's youth and because it had been tucked away in the box all these years, it was still almost new. It was a light, dusty lavender thing, and wearing it Marcia looked very coquettish and very, very beautiful.

She adjusted it first one way, then another. She pulled it down so that her eyes were just visible beneath its narrow brim. She moved it a little more to the left, then to the right.

She was trying to decide what to wear next Saturday to the City of Torrance's *1954 Factory Frolics Celebration.*

Marcia enjoyed experimenting with different looks and different clothes and wasn't above trying on her little brother Timothy's cowboy hats and his little vest with the imitation leather fringe.

It seemed to her that she looked great in practically anything.

She was wearing a black oriental silk robe with a big dragon sewn in thick gold thread on the back. It was another one of mom's hand-me-downs, a souvenir that someone, an uncle maybe, had brought back from Japan after the war.

She untied the belt and did a little wiggle. The robe, with a rustling sound, slipped off her shoulders and fell to the floor.

Now she stood naked in front of the mirror wearing only the lavender cloche.

With a half-turn to the left she struck a pose. She was pleased with what she saw. At fourteen years old, almost fifteen she was starting to fill out, becoming a woman.

She smiled. *"No more stuffing Kleenex in my bathing suit next summer."*

She cringed hearing her father coughing and wheezing in her parents' room at the back of the house.

Her mom hurried past Marcia's closed door.

Marcia had lots of girl friends and usually there'd be a gang of them here in her room. They would giggle and talk about boys or movies and stuff.

But lately her dad had been off work, sick in bed, so her mother had asked that Marcia not have her friends over until he got better.

Sunshine streamed through her bedroom window. She was anxious to be outside. She slipped into her panties and bra. After trying on five different combinations of skirts and sweaters, she settled on a brown skirt and a cream-colored blouse.

She had a fair complexion, big brown eyes, and thick chestnut hair. She wasn't too short, and she wasn't too tall. She definitely wasn't fat. Her mom was a little heavy, but Marcia did not seem to be inheriting that trait. She was slender, like dad, and maybe just a little tall for a girl her age.

She left her bedroom and walked down the short hallway past her brother's room, into the living room.

Through the drawn yellow shades, the light from outside made everything look sickly and dark, depressing.

And there was a new smell. Like something rotting. She was used to the odors of her family living in the small house: yesterday's dinner, laundry soap, stale cigarette smoke.

But this smell was different. She was afraid it might have something to do with her father's illness.

Marcia *had* to get out of the house into the fresh air and sunshine.

What she *really* wanted was to see Gavin Keller, the boy that lived down the street. His family had lived there for years, but for some reason it was only recently that she'd become so conscious of him. He was a year or so older, maybe sixteen. He had a dark complexion, deep brown eyes, and brown hair. Everything about him seemed fascinating, mysterious, and maybe even a little dangerous.

She thought about him almost all the time.

Now that she was in high school, she saw him once in a while on campus. It was all she could do to keep herself from talking about him to her friends or asking her little brother Timothy about him.

She couldn't do that, of course. Then everyone would guess she had a crush on this guy she didn't even know. All she did know about him was that his parents worked and that he had an older sister named Valerie, or Val.

She'd only seen Val a few times. Very beautiful, taller than average, slender and dark like Gavin.

Marcia's older brother Dick was sprawled on the couch thumbing through a car magazine.

"Tell Mom I went out for a while. I'll be back before dinner."

"Tell her yourself," Dick snapped without looking up. "I'm not your secretary."

She didn't say anything but just walked on past him and out the front door.

Her two brothers were so different from one another. Dick was mean and obnoxious. Her little brother Timothy was really a nice kid.

Beach Street was lined with tall beech trees and all the homes were similar to hers, modest and well maintained.

At the far end of the block, a few houses past Gavin's the street ended in a small ravine that had been cut for railroad tracks. Now that she'd become aware of him, she had to fight the temptation to walk past his house hoping to see him. But since there was nowhere else to go in that direction there was no reason. Her motive would be only too obvious.

She stepped outside and was momentarily blinded from the glare of the afternoon sun. Timothy's friends were running madly across the lawns, hiding behind trees and bushes playing cops and robbers with toy guns and she almost tripped over her brother crouched behind the hedge bordering the porch.

"Timothy, if mom asks, tell her I went to the store."

"Aw jeez," he said. "You gave away my hiding place."

"I'm sorry Hopalong, I wasn't thinking."

Timothy's freckled face broke into a grin. "I'm the police, can't you tell? Here, see my badge?" he said holding the little metal badge that had come in a Wheaties box. "Randy and Danny are the bad guys."

Her little brother was bright, always happy, and had plenty of friends. Some of her girlfriends had little brothers, too and they were always going on about what pests they were.

3

Marcia couldn't say anything bad about Timothy.

Something novel had come to Torrance. It was a big new grocery store, a "supermarket," and it was only two blocks away from Marcia's house. This market was much bigger and much more elaborate than the town's little corner grocery stores. It had different departments, box boys to help customers, shopping carts and even a "snack bar."

That was where Marcia was headed. Since her dad was sick and the house was off limits, Marcia and her friends had been meeting at the supermarket snack bar for cokes and gossip.

When she turned the corner, she saw ahead of her that someone, a boy in a t-shirt and jeans, was standing waiting for a break in traffic. Getting closer she saw it was Gavin himself! Bashful as she was, she couldn't stop and wait till he went on ahead, she'd look like a fool. She had to walk right up beside him to wait for a chance to cross the busy boulevard.

As luck would have it, traffic was particularly heavy.

She stood right there near him for what seemed like hours thinking, "Well this is awkward."

After a moment he turned, smiled down at her and said, "I've been hoping for a chance to meet you."

Startled, she looked up at him. "You have?"

"Well, yes. I'm Gavin, Gavin Keller. I live down the street from you."

"I'm Marcia Schmitt," she said, holding out her hand.

He took her hand in his just as there was a break in traffic. Still holding it he said, "It's now or never," and started running across the boulevard, pulling her behind him.

Was her heart beating because she was running, or was it more because she was running with him, her hand in his, as if they were together?

When they reached the other side, he didn't let go, he still held her hand as they walked along the sidewalk toward the store.

He was talking to her, saying something. What was it? His hand was so warm, so firm but gentle that she wasn't paying attention.

She only wished the store were further away, that this moment could go on.

"Would you like to go out sometime?"

4

"What?"

"I asked if you'd like to go out sometime?"

"With you?"

"Yes, with me." He stopped at the edge of the parking lot, turned to her and smiled. Up close, he was even better looking.

"How about this Saturday? Maybe we could go see a movie?"

She bit her lip. As much as she wanted to say yes, in Torrance going to the movies wasn't that attractive an idea. The town's only theater had two seating choices. A balcony or "loges" where all the kids went to make out, smoke stolen cigarettes and throw stuff over the railing onto the audience below, or sit in the audience below and be subjected to a rain of juju bees and who knew what else.

When she hesitated, he added, "We could go into Hollywood and see the new Cinerama movie."

She'd only been to Hollywood or Los Angeles a few times, and that was with her parents. Would they let her go? Would they let her go on a date at all? It was all happening so fast, his sudden entrance into her life, his interest in her.

"Yes," she blurted. She could skip asking her parents, just tell them she was spending the day with her friends at the "Factory Frolics" Celebration. They'd never know she had a date, never know she'd gone off in a car with a boy, gone to Hollywood.

Thinking quickly, she said, "My dad's sick. Could we meet here in the market, at the snack bar?"

# Chapter Two

## Sergeant Tom Larson

## September, 1954

It was Sunday, day two of Torrance's 1954 Factory Frolics Celebration. Sergeant Tom Larson sat in the back row of the briefing room sipping coffee, half listening to Watch Commander Coleman preparing the shift. After going over their schedules and positions around the fair, Coleman reviewed an incident from the previous night, a complaint of a possible prowler or peeping tom.

"This is the eighth peeping tom complaint in the last month," he concluded.

Torrance was a quiet town, seven miles from the beach and twenty-five miles south of L.A. There were only two main roads leading in and out and since it was primarily a blue-collar factory town, visitors were rare.

"Not being on the way to anywhere, people rarely just "pass through" on their way someplace else," one of the officers volunteered.

"That's an important point," Commander Coleman said. He straightened the papers and put them on his desk. "It means we'll presume the prowler or peeping tom or whatever he is must be a local. Everybody, just work your areas today and keep your eyes open. There will be a lot of people around the park and on the streets downtown. We don't expect any trouble. This prowler or peeping tom is more likely a problem for the night shift anyway." Pausing to take off his glasses he added, "But just in case you do see something, or some citizen brings it up, now you know about it."

The morning, as expected, passed without incident. By mid afternoon, Larson was sitting on his motorcycle relaxing in the shade near the *1954 Factory Frolics Celebration* banner.

He was absently tapping his fingernail on the bike's gas tank. From this vantage point, between the fair and downtown he could keep an eye on things. Couples, parents with their children and just kids on their own were lounging on the grass, playing the carnival games, riding the merry-go-round and window-shopping along Cravens Avenue and El Prado.

Tap tap tap. From the dull sound his fingernail was making on the metal he thought the bike's gas tank must be almost full.

Overhead, the fair's banner, strung between two trees stirred a little in the afternoon breeze.

Larson thought it must be about two o'clock. He checked his watch. Sure enough, it was five minutes after two. A little breeze from the ocean blew into town every afternoon at about this time.

He could practically set his watch by it.

He took off his helmet and rested it on his lap, propped it against his holster that held the .38-caliber police special.

The gun felt light on his hip, like a toy. Not like the weight of the Colt .45-automatic he wore when he was an M.P. during the war. Now that was a gun. When you fired a .45 you really felt it. Hell, the kick of a .45 could break a small man's wrist. Larson figured that was why the Army issued .45's to the Military Police. A person thought twice about pulling the trigger. Since the primary job was to maintain order among our own troops and not kill them, the army wouldn't want an M.P. to be trigger-happy. Larson had little call to fire his .45 while in the service. Sure, there were three or four times, but Larson was a big man, and he was usually able to establish his authority because of his size.

He took off his leather gloves, draped them over his helmet and looked down at the small scar on the palm of his left hand.

In '42, when he returned to California from Fort Myers, he'd quickly joined a unit and shipped out. As soon as they left Long Beach they ran straight into a violent storm. The old tub they were on pitched and rolled all day and all night. Almost all the guys were seasick, crammed into that old ship. Fear and seasickness and the stench of diesel and vomit made each day of that voyage seem an eternity.

The ship's crew tried to make the best of it for them. Merchant Marines were a pretty good bunch. What was the name of that damned old tub? The Lane something? Lane Crusader? Lane Triumphant? Christ. Only ten or twelve years ago but he couldn't remember the name of that damned ship from hell.

He did remember nearly every other detail of that voyage.

He shifted his weight on the bike and scanned the strollers on El Prado.

Yeah, Merchant Marines were pretty good guys, but there was always the exception.

Chief Petty Officer Sweeny.

The guys called him Sweeny the Weenie and he was the exception. Chief Petty Officer Sweeny the Weenie was a bully through and through. He was a big guy, 5'11" or 6 feet, almost as big as Larson. Sweeny was always taunting the guys, telling them horror stories of the front and the wounded, the maimed that the ship brought back on its return trip to the States. Sweeny would drop in on the men at mealtime when everyone was already sick from the smell of backed-up toilets and the roiling sea. He'd give graphic descriptions of the mutilations and the disfigurements the war they were headed for had inflicted on young guys just like them.

On the fourth day out, Larson had the midnight to four a.m. watch. Even as late as it was and as nasty as the weather was, some of the soldiers were up on deck trying to gulp down enough air to keep from puking.

He'd gone down a gangway to check below. Sweeny was coming through a watertight door a few feet down the passageway on Number Two Deck. Larson saw one of the soldiers in his unit, Billy Prewitt hurrying up the passageway behind Sweeny. Larson had been watching out for this kid because he was really young. The kid had probably lied about his age to get in the army and seemed panic-stricken from day one. Even taking into account the greenish hue cast by the blackout lights in the passageway, it was obvious from the boy's pale face that he was hurrying to get topside to throw up.

Billy put his hand on the watertight doorway just after Sweeny had passed through. Larson knew Sweeny saw the young soldier, knew he was there.

Sweeny slammed the heavy steel door shut on the soldier's hand anyway, severing four of the kid's fingers.

The clang of the door slamming, and Billy's scream echoed through the passageway.

Grinning, Sweeny turned. He looked surprised when he saw Larson. He shifted his eyes, looked away and muttered, "Oops, sorry. I didn't know anyone was behind me."

Larson pushed Sweeny out of the way and moved to reopen the steel door. Blood was splattered along the bulkhead. The kid was huddled on the floor of the passageway holding what was left of his hand. His eyes were wide and his face pale as a sheet. He was breathing in short, rapid gasps

8

and seemed to be going into shock. Larson picked Billy Prewitt up as if he was just a child. Pushing past Sweeny, Larson carried the boy back through the narrow passageway and hurried up the gangway to the infirmary to awaken the medic and get some aid for the kid.

Then he went back down below looking for Sweeny the Weenie.

All that had happened ten years or more ago. Torrance was a world and a war away from that night. But it all came back to Tom Larson as if it had only happened last week.

Larson took off his sunglasses, carefully wiped them with a Kleenex, and put them back on. He looked around the crowd to see if anything had changed while he had been lost in thought.

No, all was quiet at the Torrance Factory Frolics Celebration.

That was what he liked about this town. Nothing ever happened here.

Larson adjusted his position on the bike and let his thoughts drift back to that voyage and the feeling they all had, the ominous feeling of foreboding, of being trapped in an endless nightmare that was only going to get worse.

The passageway leading to the crew's quarters on number two deck was empty and almost dark, lit only by the dim green bulbs of the blackout lights.

Slipping past the bulkhead door Larson saw a glow at the far end of the passageway.

He moved quickly, quietly.

He reached the cabin where the light was and looked in.

Sure enough, it was Sweeny the Weenie, calmly sitting on his bunk polishing his shoes.

Startled, Sweeny jumped to his feet.

But Larson was across the small space in an instant.

He slammed the heel of his booted foot down on Sweeny's bare toes.

At the same time, he grabbed a handful of Sweeny's t-shirt at the neck and twisted the fabric so tight Sweeny's howl of pain was lost in his throat.

The little scar on Larson's palm was a reminder of that night. Sweeny's dog tags had caught in the cloth and cut into Larson's hand.

Palm up, Larson hit Sweeny under the jaw as hard as he could.

Sweeny's head snapped back, his neck broken.

The crack of Sweeny's neck breaking in that dark steel passageway all those years ago sounded a lot like the sound Larson was making with his fingernail, tapping on his bike's gas tank.

Wrenched back to the present, he stopped tapping and looked around the park.

Nothing had changed. People were still walking around, looking and talking.

Ordinary people. Peaceful, ordinary people.

But once Larson began reliving that night on the Lane Whatever-the-hell-it-was, he always had to see it through to the end.

Larson had grabbed Sweeny's t-shirt, tried to keep the limp body from falling to the deck.

The shirt tore.

Larson let Sweeny drop.

He bent and grabbed Sweeny by the ankles, started dragging him down the passageway toward the gangway to the engine room below decks.

The whole incident couldn't have taken more than a few seconds.

Larson opened the watertight door to the engine room.

Pulling Sweeny's body behind him, he stepped through and stood for a moment on the steel mesh landing.

Below, in the noisy machinery filled space, the sweaty faces of two black boiler men looked up at him.

Their eyes moved to the feet Larson was holding.

They quickly looked away, as if there was something very important that needed their attention at the other end of the engine room.

Larson started down the gangway stairs dragging Sweeny's body behind him.

He could still hear the thump Sweeny's head made as it banged on each steel step; still remember the feeling of detachment he'd felt all those years ago.

He dragged Sweeny across the engine room to one of the ship's boilers. A short-handled shovel was leaning against a safety rail.

He grabbed the shovel, knocked the latch on red-hot boiler door open and propped the shovel against it to keep it from swinging shut.

The two black seamen standing only a few feet away kept their backs turned the whole time as if they didn't even know he was there.

Larson fed Chief Petty Officer Sweeny's body into the blazing boiler furnace feet first. He'd had a little trouble getting the body all the way through the opening.

Chief Petty Officer Sweeny the Weenie's shoulders were too broad. Larson had to turn and twist the body sideways.

Because of the searing heat he'd had to step back, use the shovel to jam Sweeny the rest of the way through the opening.

He used the shovel to re-latch the door, and then put it back where he found it.

During the whole time Larson was in the engine room the two black seamen had not turned around.

No one ever said a word about the missing Sweeny.

Maybe he fell overboard.

It happens.

A popping noise from a burnt-out light bulb on the string hanging over the bandstand brought Larson's attention back to the park, the carnival games and the present. The power for the fair had failed and the merry-go-round slowly came to a stop. Barkers at the booths looked up curiously and the crowd milled about as if waiting for directions as to what they were supposed to do. The lights came back on; the merry go round started again. The public address speakers emitted a screech. Mayor Talbot announced that they were able to get electricity from the generator of the car on display near the grandstand, a modern looking white boat-tailed Buick convertible that actors Cary Grant and Constance Bennett had driven in the movie *Topper*.

Larson covered a yawn and rubbed his face.

Factory Frolics.

Doesn't really seem to be a very festive title for a fair and celebration, but the Chamber of Commerce was very proud of the fact that this little town was the most industrialized city for its size in the United States.

Almost every face he saw in the crowd was familiar to Larson.

Ordinary people.

Peaceful, ordinary people.

He viewed his place as a law enforcement officer in Torrance as being the "local constabulary" and not a "crime fighter." There really wasn't any crime around here. People in little towns like this lived by rules and within boundaries. Larson felt his job was to stand aside, see that everyone pretty much obeyed the rules and not get too close to those boundaries.

The late-night prowler, the peeping tom came to mind.

He figured that the peeper was a younger person and almost certainly an unmarried male. Of course, this whole thing could have just been imaginations triggered by a possum or a cat on a fence. Open fields surrounded Torrance in all directions and there was still plenty of wildlife, varmints like skunks, possums, raccoons, and even the occasional rattlesnake.

But eight complaints were a lot. Larson was pretty sure there was more to it than just varmints.

That afternoon, as he was checking out at the station he heard about another incident, the victim, a fourteen-year-old girl with "gorgeous, long slender legs," according to Tony Giuliani's partner, Charlie the rookie.

"Fresh out of the shower, standing naked in front of the bathroom mirror brushing her long blond hair before going to bed."

Larson thought this was a bit more information than was necessary. He wondered just how long Charlie was going to last on the force.

Giuliani turned to Larson; "Joyce Peterson. She's a freshman at Torrance High, an "A" student and an only child. Her father works at the bank. The family is well-to-do. She thought she heard a noise at the bathroom window. She said she turned quickly and was pretty sure she saw a face but wasn't certain. It was dark outside, so the glass reflected her own image, too. But she was fairly sure she got a glimpse of someone. She grabbed a towel and ran to the living room to tell her father. He ran outside to see."

"Did he see anyone?" asked Larson.

"Nope, but he thought he heard footsteps running down the alley."

"Do you think she was telling the truth?"

"Oh yeah" Tony replied. "She was really spooked."

Charlie added, "It was no wonder someone was peeping. The kid is stunning."

12

Larson caught Giuliani's sidelong glance. He guessed this was the kind of wise-ass comment Giuliani had to put up with from Charlie all the time.

That would get old real quick.

# Chapter Three

## Marcia Schmitt

## September 1954

Marcia's friend Jill was going on and on, yelling above the din and confusion in the line for the cafeteria. She was saying something, some darn thing or other about Joyce Peterson.

Marcia didn't even try to follow whatever it was she was blithering about. Her thoughts were only of Gavin. He was all she thought about, all she wanted to think about. She wondered where he is right now, what he's doing.

She scanned the slight hill that led from the cafeteria area to the main school buildings, hoping to catch sight of him in among the milling crowd of students.

There.

There he was, coming down the path toward the cafeteria, toward the crowd at the door and around the tables.

Toward her.

Was it just because she had this major crush on him or was he really an island of calm, of beauty in the tumultuous sea of students trying to make the most of their lunch break?

The sight of him made her heart beat faster. Were students clearing a way for him? Like Moses parting the Red Sea, was Gavin parting the students on his way to her? Does he have this effect on all these others? Was it her imagination or were the girls sneaking glances at him and the boys looking at him in awe and admiration?

While her friends moved forward in the line, he stepped next to her, bent and whispered, "Are we still on for miniature golfing this Saturday?"

She nodded that they were.

She didn't think she had ever been this close, this connected to anyone in her life. Sneaking off to Los Angeles last Saturday, the date, everything went so perfectly.

And her parents never suspected a thing.

That night in bed she'd thought about Gavin and all she knew about him. She didn't know much of anything about his family, had never met any of them. But for that matter he hadn't met anyone in her family either.

Just as she was dropping off to sleep, she'd heard a noise outside her window. Probably just the wind, she'd thought.

Saturday arrived, another beautiful bright sunny day. The sky was an intense blue that set off the white clouds floating on the cool gentle breeze. A perfect day for miniature golf.

She slid across the front seat of his parent's big Hudson to get closer to him, but not too close. When he leaned forward to start the car, he brushed against her leg. Was it an accident? Well, too late to do anything about it now. She was committed, so to speak. A move had been made, a bridge crossed. Who initiated it? Her, by moving closer, or him by touching her?

It was her first time miniature golfing. Gavin stood close behind her, reached around her to show her how to hold the club, touched her.

That night in bed she again thought she heard a noise outside her bedroom window. When she got up and looked, she saw nothing.

# Chapter Four

## Dick Schmitt

## September 1954

Good jobs were hard to come by in Torrance, but when Dick Schmitt graduated from high school his father put a word in for him at the steel mill. Dick was hired as a welder's assistant on the swing shift, four o'clock in the afternoon till one in the morning.

This suited Dick just fine. The family was asleep when he got home, and since he slept till mid-morning, he could avoid his brother and sister and his parents.

The cool, quiet darkness and the almost deserted mill at night suited him and the drive home through Torrance's empty streets in the early hours matched his sense of aloneness.

Dick had weekends off. Like everyone else, he looked forward to the weekends, but since he had no friends and never had anything to do, he usually spent both days just killing time.

He was sprawled on the couch reading a car magazine when the screen door banged open and pain-in-the-ass little Timothy came charging in.

"Hey, Mom!" he yelled, running down the hall, "a train fell off the tracks. Right at the end of the block!"

Curious despite himself Dick got up from the couch and went to the porch. Neighbors and their kids were hurrying toward the shallow ravine cut for the railroad tracks at the end of the block.

Dick decided to take a look. When he got to there, he saw that three boxcars were partially off the tracks and tilted at odd angles. The door on one of the boxcars had opened, dumping several boxes of chrome automobile door handles on their way to the Ford assembly plant in Long Beach. A gang of kids, boys mostly, were excitedly gathering as many as they could carry and clambering up the slope. Several of the neighborhood moms were yelling for their kids to be careful and stay away from the derailed train cars.

Dick made his way through the weeds toward the front of the train to see what else there was to see. This took him toward the alley that ran behind the houses on the other side of the street from his parent's home.

16

Although this alley was only a block or so from his home he hadn't been over here for years, not since he played around the neighborhood as a little boy.

Satisfied that there was nothing else about the wreck to interest him he started down the alley to head for home.

Where the alley intersected the cross street there were garages for the three old clapboard rental units. Parked almost at the alley entrance was a 1936 Auburn four-door sedan in wonderful mint condition and backed into one of the garages was another Auburn, its huge radiator grill and big headlights staring haughtily as if it knew it belonged in better surroundings.

The one parked in the alley was the most beautiful car Dick had ever seen.

It was tan with chocolate brown trim, chrome spoke wheels, and white sidewall tires. Big chrome supercharger pipes came out of the side of the hood and ran down under the car's running board. The spare tires were mounted in wells in the fenders.

"Really something isn't it?"

Dick turned. It was a good-looking kid, a boy about his age, maybe a little younger.

"I have never seen anything like this before in my life."

"Belongs to Mr. Johnson," the boy said. "He has three of them." The kid extended his hand. "My name's Gavin, by the way."

Dick rarely shook hands with people. It made him feel open and vulnerable, but without even thinking he shook Gavin's.

"I'm Dick. I live just around the corner, and I've never seen these cars before."

"Well, Mr. Johnson has lived here for as long as I can remember," Gavin replied, "and he's always had these cars. Of course, he does usually keep them in the garage."

It was completely unlike Dick to feel so relaxed around another person, but here he was, actually enjoying this conversation.

"You know, there's a junk yard over on Main Street that specializes in these old luxury cars. There are Packard's and twelve-cylinder Cadillac's, Cord's, and big old chauffeur-driven limousines, all kinds of stuff. You want to go over there some time and look around?" Gavin asked.

"We can go right now if you want! I'll go get my car and be right back."

The two drove to the junkyard and explored the old cars for hours. By the time they were ready to leave, Dick felt like he had known Gavin for years.

Gavin mentioned the auto show the following weekend in Los Angeles. Dick always avoided crowds, but this time he surprised himself. "Wanna go?" He was actually eager to hang out with Gavin again.

"Sure. How about 11 o'clock next Sunday morning?"

"I'll swing by and pick you up at your house."

# Chapter Five

## Timothy Schmitt

## September, 1954

It was Saturday night and Timothy just could not get to sleep. He knew that the harder he tried, the less likely sleep would come. He always played hard all day, so he was usually out like a light as soon as he went to bed.

Tonight though, it was after 10 o'clock and he was wide-awake, tossing and turning. His blanket had fallen on the floor twice and his sheets were wrapped around his legs.

Timothy and his older brother Dick shared a bedroom. The house only had three bedrooms and Timothy's mother and father got the largest down the hall.

His sister Marcia had her room all to herself, although Timothy wasn't clear why. He thought it would be much better if he could share a room with Marcia.

She was nice to him, and Dick wasn't.

Dick had rigged up a divider using a tall dresser and a blanket strung from the ceiling. This gave him some privacy and left Timothy with what amounted to half a bedroom of his own.

Timothy wished he had someone to talk to, even if it was Dick.

That afternoon Timothy and two of his friends had gone downtown to see a movie, *The Mummy's Ghost.* In Timothy's mind that was scariest movie ever. His friend Randy kept his hands over his eyes through the whole thing, but Timothy, to show how brave he was, watched it from beginning to end.

To avoid the crap thrown from the loges they'd chosen seats way down in front and by the time the movie was over Timothy had slumped down so far, he could barely see the screen over the back of the seat in front of him.

Now, alone in his bed he couldn't shake the image of the dark forest, the sinister trees and in the moonlight the mummy relentlessly, remorselessly, stalking its terror-stricken victims.

Timothy wondered why the victims, all young, healthy and able to run, climb walls, and jump fences were unable to escape from the clumsy, lumbering mummy. But then he wasn't too clear on just what a mummy was anyway. Why was it wrapped up like that? Maybe that had something to do with the mummy's ability to catch people who were clearly faster than it was. And what did the mummy want with these people? What was the mummy going to do with these people once it did catch them?

Restless, hot, he got out of bed, went to the window and looked out.

The cold glass felt good on his forehead. He looked over the rooftop of the house next door. The night sky looked just like the night sky in the movie. The moon, occasionally hidden by luminous clouds was bright enough to silhouette the rooftop and the trees.

The house next door to Timothy's belonged to a policeman, Tony Giuliani and his wife. The light through the drawn shade on the Giuliani's bathroom window outlined the top of the fence.

Timothy shivered and looked to his right, out toward the street that passed in front of his house. A lone streetlight cast long shadows. Dew on the lawns and on the cars parked along the curb sparkled like tiny diamonds. The branches of the tall beech trees lining both sides of the street met to form a canopy overhead, a dark, ominous tunnel.

He had lived all his life in this neighborhood, played on the sidewalk and lawns all up and down the street. He knew everyone that lived here, knew every fence, every gate, every bush.

But tonight, the silent street looked alien, threatening.

He was sure it was quieter than usual.

Too quiet.

Timothy turned and looked to the left, toward his backyard.

In the dark it looked to him like someone was right there next to the house, crouched outside his sister Marcia's bedroom window, barely visible next to his mother's big chrysanthemum bush.

The figure was so close that if the window's glass and the screen hadn't been in the way Timothy could have reached out and touched whoever it was.

At first, he couldn't believe it. He rubbed his eyes and looked again, thinking that what he was seeing must be a trick of the shadows and moonlight.

A noise from Marcia's room must have startled the figure. It suddenly jumped back from the window, turned and ran silent as a ghost across the wet lawn through the back yard toward the gate that led to the alley.

Who the heck was that?

20

Without stopping to think, Timothy hurriedly pulled his pants on over his pajamas. He slipped his bare feet into his shoes, opened his bedroom window, and undid the screen as quietly as he could.

He climbed out the window and into the chilly night.

He ran past the chrysanthemum bush, across the cold wet grass to the narrow space between the garage and the fence and climbed up on the gate so he could look out into the alley.

To the left, three houses down, where the alley intersected with the street, a streetlamp lit the entrance.

There was no movement other than a cat, slowly, cautiously making its way across the empty street. Timothy figured no one had passed that way or they would have frightened the cat.

Looking to his right, four or five houses away, maybe halfway down the alley, a bare bulb was suspended. It cast long, dark shadows of garbage cans, telephone poles, the neighbor's closed garage doors.

On the opposite side of the alley, the Robinson's dirty old blue Plymouth was parked up close to their garage.

Timothy peered into the darkness for a long time in both directions. Nothing moved.

All was still in the alley.

Suddenly he sensed a movement just above his head. A figure swooped down on him from the roof of the garage.

Petrified with terror, Timothy was suddenly living his nightmare, the nightmare that he was being chased like the victims in the movie.

But he could not run, couldn't move at all. He couldn't even scream, no matter how hard he tried.

A cloth covered his nose and mouth, a smell like a doctor's office and everything went black.

The next thing Timothy knew, he was back in his room on the cool bare hardwood floor below his open window. His memories of all that had just happened, seeing the figure next to the house, running through the back yard, all were fading, drifting away like wisps of smoke from one of his father's cigarettes.

He shut his eyes tight trying to stop his head from aching.

He was so cold.

Why was the window open?

Why was he on the floor?

Where are his pajamas?

He rolled over and got to his knees. Shaking, he felt around in the dark and found his pajamas on the floor next to him.

What were they doing there?

His head ached. Trying to concentrate only made it hurt worse. He couldn't make himself think, couldn't force himself to even try to remember why the window was wide open, why he was naked. His knees and face were scratched and dirty. He was very sore. His crotch and bottom felt wet, sticky.

Gripping the windowsill for support he struggled to his feet. His bottom really hurt bad, hurt like nothing he had ever felt before.

He was scared.

What was this? What had happened? What's wrong with him?

Crying, he stumbled through his dark bedroom and down the hallway to his parent's room. A sliver of light showed under their closed bedroom door.

Timothy opened the door and peeked in.

His mother was sitting in a chair reading by the light of the little cut-glass lamp on the nightstand next to the bed, his father propped up on pillows.

Was his dad asleep? The lamplight made his dad look old, grey, and shrunken, like he was dead.

Timothy shivered. With the back of his hand, he wiped a tear from his cheek.

Startled, his mother looked up from her book.

Clutching his pajama bottoms, he burst into the room, ran crying to her. He tearfully tried to explain his condition, hoping she would say everything was all right, tell him why his bottom hurt, why it was wet and sticky.

She took him in her arms and tried to calm him. "There, there now," Timothy. "I don't know. Dr Beeman will be here in the morning to look in on your father. We can ask him. You go take a shower and go back to bed."

Timothy did as he was told, and the warm shower relaxed him enough so that he was able to drop off to sleep.

⁖

It had become part of Dr. Beeman's routine to drop by on Sunday morning after church to look in on Timothy's father. Afterward he would join Millie Schmitt for a cup of coffee.

After the doctor had done his best to cheer Millie up, she mentioned her son Timothy's sudden appearance at their bedroom door the night before.

Dr. Beeman tried to hide his reaction by asking for another cup, just as the screen door to the kitchen slammed shut.

Timothy charged in breathlessly asking for "an apple or an orange or something like that."

"Whoa whoa, young man," the doctor said, pushing his chair back from the table. "Come here and tell me what's new with you. You're sure getting big. Your mother tells me you had a rough night last night. Want to tell me about it?"

Timothy grabbed an orange from the bowl on the table and spun around. "Randy and I went to the show yesterday and we saw a really scary movie."

"You did? What was it all about?"

"Mummy's trying to get people and eat them or something. I don't know what the mummy wanted with them. It was scary. Randy kept his eyes covered but I watched the whole thing. I scooted way down in my seat. I think I hurt my bottom."

"Why do you say that?" the doctor asked, stirring his coffee and searching Timothy's face.

"I'm really sore and last night I was all sticky and dirty."

"You think sitting way down in your seat during the movie made you sore and dirty?"

"I don't know. What else could it be?" Timothy asked, peeling the orange.

"I'll bet your right. You're really growing, young man," the doctor said getting up from the table. "Can I take a quick look to make sure your o.k.? It won't take minute."

23

"Why? What's the matter?"

"Why, there's nothing the matter with you that some ice cream won't cure. Come on, this will only take a minute. Let's go to your room."

"Yes sir," Timothy said, setting his orange on the table.

The doctor followed the boy back into his bedroom. He gave Timothy a quick examination and asked him a few questions.

"How do you feel?"

"Fine."

"Has anything unusual happened to you lately?"

"No sir."

"Have you been riding your bike a lot?"

"I ride my bike all the time."

"Do you remember going into your mother's room last night?"

"Yes, sir."

"Do you remember why?"

"No. I think I had a bad dream."

"From the movie?"

Timothy shrugged. "Maybe. I don't know."

"Okay, that's it, Timothy. Let's you and I see if we can talk your mother into some ice cream."

Back at the kitchen table Doctor Beeman told Timothy's mother, "It was probably just a nocturnal emission."

Mom looked away, embarrassed. "Isn't he a little young for that? He's only eleven."

"It can happen. There are signs of irritation around his rectum. Perhaps he fell and landed wrong, or it's from riding his bicycle. In any event it doesn't look like there's been any serious damage."

On the way to his car the doctor saw Timothy on the sidewalk in front of the house oiling his bicycle. He bent and tousled Timothy's hair. "No speeding now, young man. Take good care of your mom."

As he got into his big black Packard to leave, he heard Timothy call cheerfully, "Bye, Dr. Beeman."

Pulling away from the curb he glanced in the rear-view mirror.

Timothy was sitting cross legged on the sidewalk, his attention only on his bike.

⁂

Officer Tom Larson was at his usual spot, parked in the gas station across from the supermarket. He often used this location to watch for speeders or someone running the traffic light.

He was just starting his bike to go after some old guy that almost ran over a woman in the cross walk when Dr. Beeman pull his big black Packard up to the pumps.

Larson smiled, got off the bike to walk over and say hello.

The two had known each other since before the war. Doctor Beeman was Larson's family doctor and had tended to Larson's wife before she died.

The doctor was getting out of his car as Larson walked up. Before he could say anything, the doctor said, "I just left poor old Richard Schmitt's house."

Larson's smile faded. "How's he doing?"

"I honestly don't know how he's hanging on. But the damnedest thing happened," the doctor continued. "Their kid, their youngest son Timothy had all the signs of having been raped."

"Are you sure? When?"

"Pretty sure. Millie told me the boy came into their bedroom late last night all upset. Told her he woke up on the floor near his window. Said he hurt. He described some other symptoms that in an older, more mature boy might be attributable to a nocturnal emission." He turned to look across the boulevard, look absently toward the supermarket across the way. "I really can't reconcile that diagnosis in my own mind, though, I'm afraid," he continued, turning back toward Larson. "Like I said, I think he might have been raped." His eyes searched Larson's face. "I didn't want to say anything like that to Millie, especially with what she's going through."

"Did the boy tell you what happened?"

Beeman shook his head. "He doesn't remember anything. I think he's blocked it out of his mind completely."

25

Larson removed his helmet and rubbed his close-cropped hair. "Alarming the family with something like this right now would be all they'd need, wouldn't it? I'd go by and take a look around, but it would be a tip off that something must be wrong. I wish you were more certain."

Doctor Beeman watched the dial on the gas pump for a moment, then turned back to Larson. "I'm certain."

"If I have to make out a report," Larson said, taking a deep breath, "they'd all be dragged down to the station for questioning, and I don't know what all. If the boy really has blocked all this out of his mind, putting him through that would probably bring it all back."

"I agree. But at the same time, I don't want to put other children at risk by ignoring this. I hate to burden you, but I felt I needed to tell someone. I knew I could trust your judgment."

"Well, let's take it one step at a time. I'll come up with some reason to go by and visit Tony Giuliani. He lives next door to the Schmitt's. While I'm there I'll take a quick look around. I'll let you know if I turn anything up."

"Thanks. Please let me know if you find anything, anything at all."

The following Monday morning Larson knocked on Tony Giuliani's front door.

"Hi. I hope I'm not interrupting anything. I checked the schedule and saw you were off duty today. I hoped I could drop by on my break."

He looked up and down the street, then continued, "I'm thinking of buying a home near here and wondered what you could tell me about the neighborhood."

"It's a great neighborhood," Tony replied, obviously surprised to see Larson. Sarge had a reputation as a loner and didn't socialize much, if at all with the guys.

Stepping aside, Tony invited him in. "Nice homes. Good families. Come on in."

Tony and his wife proudly showed him around their small brick house. Warming to Larson's interest in the area, they told him about the neighborhood and the neighbors.

"This really is a nice place. I sure like the way those big windows look out on the yard."

"Come on out and see the back. Gina's quite the gardener."

Tony showed him their patio, his wife's prize rose bushes, the big Pacific dogwood and the Manzanita growing along the north side of the house.

"And what do you have on the other side? That's the Schmitt's home, isn't it?"

"Yes. Poor Schmitt," Tony said thoughtfully. "There's nothing much on that side of the house, just a narrow strip of grass and the fence. The garages in all the neighborhoods here on the west side open into alleys."

"May I take a look?"

Tony looked at him curiously but led the way to the other side of the house and showed him the fence and the alley behind the garage.

Later, Officer Larson showed up at Dr. Beeman's office. The full waiting room was suddenly quiet when he came in.

He took off his helmet and nodded to the waiting patients.

Old Mrs. Kirk, the doctor's receptionist knew that Larson and the doctor were friends, so she led Larson directly to the doctor's private office.

Beeman came in almost immediately. He shut the door, walked around his desk, and sat down with a sigh. He leaned forward with his elbows on the desktop, rested his chin on his interlocked fingers and looked at Larson expectantly.

"Well?" he said. "You must have something, or you wouldn't be here."

Larson sat his helmet on the desk. "All I can tell you is that the screen on the little boy's window was bent as if it had been removed and replaced. There were footprints in the dirt next to the house, outside both the boy's and the daughter's windows. Medium-size shoes, leather soles, not sneakers. And definitely not a little kid's," he added.

"And" Larson went on, "over the past two months we've had almost a dozen calls about a prowler or peeping tom in that general area, there on the west side of town. I have a hunch that the peeping tom we've been hearing about may well be the same person that might have raped Timothy."

"Well, what next?"

"We're both supposed to report this. It could be very helpful to the detectives working the peeping tom case to know what we think happened last night."

Larson paused for a moment chewing his lip. "I know what this kind of interrogation can be like, even for an adult. Dragging a young boy through a police investigation, trying to make a little kid recall all the details of an experience like that. It would be very bad for him. I know they're going through enough as it is right now."

Beeman rubbed his tired eyes. "Yes, they really are. To be blunt, poor Schmidt isn't going to make it. It's a tough decision. But if it makes you feel any better, I agree with you. Maybe if you and Guliani keep your eyes open this guy could be caught without making it any worse on the Schmitt's."

Larson nodded and stood up. "I'll let Giuliani know what's going on. He knew something was up when I dropped in on him like that." He rubbed his chin. "Pretty out of character for me to go visiting. Also, he'll want to watch out for his wife, especially when he's pulling a night shift."

"From what I saw, the incident didn't seem to have any lasting effect on the boy—not physically anyway. I'm inclined to think it would be best if this could remain buried in his mind, forgotten."

"I hope so," Larson said. He got to his feet and picked up his helmet. He paused as he turned to leave and looked back at the doctor. Doctor Beeman looked up at him and returned his gaze, then wordlessly picked up another patient's file.

Larson shook his head and left the office.

# Chapter Six

## Marcia Schmitt

## September 1954

Again, Marcia lied to her mom, this time telling her she was meeting friends to study at the library. After dinner she slipped out the back door and headed for the alley in order to avoid Timothy and his friends. It was twilight, the evening was warm, the boys were running through the front yard playing cops and robbers or cowboys and Indians. Ever since Timothy saw Gavin drop her off after school, he teased her at every opportunity. "Marcia's got a boy friend," Timothy chanted, but her mother was too busy with her dad to pay attention and Dick just didn't care.

This was only their fourth nighttime date. But they'd seen a lot of each other during the day, sneaking off to the park or taking his folks car for a ride to the beach or around the hills. Every day she spent with Gavin had been a beautiful day. Every afternoon and every evening that she'd been with him had been a day right out of a movie.

And, since they walked to and from school together every day it seemed as if they had known each other much longer.

She just knew in her heart they definitely had a thing going.

There he was, in front of Probert's Drug Store like a god in blue jeans and white t-shirt, standing next to his parent's big brown Hudson. Her pulse beat faster just seeing him. She felt a kind of warm feeling that made her a little ashamed. At the same time though, she was terribly excited.

She forced herself to look cool, stroll slowly up to the Hudson. Gavin, with a little smile, watched her. When she got close, he took a step forward, grabbed her hand and pulled her to him. He gave her a quick kiss on the forehead, and then gallantly opened the car door. "How about catching a movie at the drive-in tonight?"

She caught her breath. The drive-in? She'd never before been to the drive-in theater. She and her friends referred to it as the "passion pit." They gossiped about kids they knew that went there and "made out" and even "went all the way."

She swallowed hard and tried to cover her excitement. "Sure. What's playing?" she asked, trying to sound as casual as she could. She really didn't care what the hell was playing, and if Gavin answered her question, she didn't even hear. She was anxious, impatient really, to see what was going to be next with Gavin, her love.

Once inside the car she slid across the seat close to him. For days now she'd wondered if it was it up to her to make the next move. Was she supposed to show him she was ready to take the next step, whatever it was? Very cautiously she put her hand on his leg. He didn't flinch or anything. Instead, he just started the car. Once they were out of the supermarket parking lot, he put his arm around her shoulder and pulled her closer.

She gave a little shake of her head, tossing her hair gently in an effort to at least appear calm, even if she wasn't. She knew she was embarking on an adventure with a boy—no, a man—that would take her into territory unknown.

When they got to the drive-in Gavin parked the car in the back row. He opened the window and got the little speaker from the stand outside, hung it on the window and closed it as much as he could. Before he was completely settled in the driver's seat, Marcia answered her own question. Impulsively she put her arms around his neck and kissed him. He immediately responded, pulling her closer and kissing her long and hard.

He slipped both hands up under her blouse.

She pulled back, but only for a moment. She had never done anything even remotely like this before. She was so excited she wished she did not have a blouse on at all. She leaned into his hands and kissed him deeply.

His fingers were on her bra clasp trying to unfasten it. The bra loosened. Freed of it she could feel the soft fabric of the blouse against her bare nipples.

It felt, well, wonderful.

She remembered what she and her girlfriends had secretly giggled about when they met in her bedroom.

She moved her hand to his lap.

He was hard. She could feel his warmth through his jeans.

She could not stop herself. She unzipped his pants and worked her hand inside.

He lifted her blouse and then her bra.

She felt his breath on her breasts.

His mouth found her nipple. She was lost, instantly became wet, almost delirious.

She moved her hand inside his pants and found his manhood.

It was the first one she had ever touched.

It was hard and hot and filled her hand. She truly wished she could see it.

But in the dark car, feeling it was the best she could do. For now, anyway.

She was holding his head against her neck.

He groaned.

She wondered who, if anyone was in control here?

But it didn't matter. His hand slid down the back of her dress, between her panties and her bare skin. It was the first time in her whole life that anyone had touched her like this.

These new sensations drove her on, swept her forward, hot and wild and out of control. She would not, could not stop.

She leaned back in the seat and pulled him to her. When he was between her legs, leaning over her, she unbuckled his pants. She worked them down.

Now he entered her.

With her hands on his ass, she pulled him in deep. She felt herself tighten around him. She began the natural, rhythmic movement, slowly at first, then quick and hard.

It was she that finished first, but Gavin was not far behind.

She never knew what movie was playing and didn't care.

# Chapter Seven

## Dick Schmitt

## September 1954

Dick lay with his hands clasped behind his head, lay on his bed staring at the ceiling.

He felt bored, trapped in the little house.

"Cute" Marcia was in her bedroom singing that dumb song. What the hell was it? "How Much Is That Doggy in the Window?" or some damn thing? She sure sounds happy about something.

Back when he'd been the only child, the apple of Dad's eye, Dick ruled the roost.

Then Marcia came along.

Cute little Marcia.

Beautiful young lady Marcia.

"Marcia this, Marcia that."

Then came Timothy.

Sweet little Timothy.

Cute little Timothy.

Dick didn't even have a room of his own anymore.

"Well," he thought, grinding his teeth, "for their information, my friend and I are going to the car show. Yeah, that's right. I have a friend. I have a life, too, by God. But I'll be damned if I'm going to tell you people about it. You can all have your cute little Marcia and your darling little Timothy, the little brats! My friend and I went looking at really great cars last weekend and today we're going to the car show and we're going to see all of next year's models. All of them."

Dick flopped over onto his stomach. He kicked the covers and checked his watch. He jumped up remembering that he had promised himself he'd go downtown and get some new clothes. Now it was too late. He brushed past his sister in the hallway and muttered; "Stop humming that stupid song."

"What's your problem?"

"Nothing that getting away from you won't cure," he growled.

He yanked the door open and stormed out, slammed it behind him.

To him, slamming the door was slamming the lid on the whole unappreciative bunch. He'd gotten good grades, damn it. He'd never gotten in any trouble damn it! Damn it, he hated them all.

Timothy and his weird little friends were playing marbles in the back yard. Timothy turned, saw him and called out, "Hey, Dick, wanna play? I just won a cat's eye."

Dick just ignored him. He opened the gate to the alley where his car was parked, thinking "Bet you wish you were cool like me, you little jerk."

His little black eight-year-old Ford gleamed in the morning sun. Dick thought it looked pretty good and he thought again about meeting Gavin. Gavin seemed so cool. Everything he said seemed so clever, so right, and so smart.

He slid behind the wheel, wondering what today was going to be like.

Damn good, he thought. Cool new friend, a pal, talking and kidding around looking at the new cars and joking about the people in the crowd.

Dick had never been to a car show before. He could only guess what it would be like, the crowds, the new cars.

He was apprehensive about being in a crowd. He always felt conspicuous, felt like everyone was looking at him, so he generally avoided people, especially large groups.

But this time he won't be alone. He'd be with his friend, his pal Gavin.

He drove down the alley, turned the corner and pulled up in front of Gavin's house. As soon as he stopped the car Gavin came out and started down the walk. Nice corduroy trousers and matching plain tan pullover. Before now, it would have never occurred to Dick to wear clothes like that. There was no denying Gavin looked sharp. The clothes he wore weren't necessarily expensive, but he looked so good wearing them. Maybe it was because Gavin's clothes weren't the same stupid things all the guys wore. Old jeans and some wash-and-wear print shirt obviously bought in the boys' department at Newberry's.

No, Gavin's clothes were different, as if he'd chosen them deliberately, like he meant to dress well.

Until now Dick never gave any thought to his appearance. Looking at Gavin, Dick realized it wouldn't be much more trouble to pick nice clothes, clothes that matched. It was certainly worth it for the difference it made.

He wished he hadn't forgotten to go downtown this morning.

The car show was much more than Dick had imagined it would be. And, instead of feeling intimidated as he would have if he had been alone, he was excited. Being with Gavin made Dick feel like he belonged, like he was part of the crowd, not apart from it.

He was thrown off guard when, wandering past the exhibitions of antique roadsters and next year's models of convertibles, Dick thought he caught one of the girls in the crowd trying to sneak a look at him.

Could that be?

Maybe she was looking at someone behind him.

She winked and gave a little wave. Should he wave back?

He looked around to see if she could be gesturing to someone else, but there was no one.

When he looked back, she was gone.

Somehow Dick thought Gavin wouldn't have any trouble talking to girls.

On the way home, Gavin asked if Dick would like to go to the drag races at the Lion's strip in Wilmington.

"Sure."

"Give me your phone number. I'll call you next Saturday morning and we'll set something up."

Gavin paused. "I may be tied up Saturday. Sunday afternoon would be better."

There were only two stores exclusively for men in town and Dick Schmitt had never been in either of them. But the next day, Monday morning at 10 a.m. he was standing in front of Torrance Men's Shop when it opened.

With a man's job and paycheck, but still living at home, Dick was that rare combination in Torrance, a young man with plenty of money.

34

He noticed the store's proprietor sigh, as if the man thought this was a hopeless case, a waste of his time.

"Good morning. My name is Lou. What can I do for you?"

"I want several outfits, pants and shirts or whatever for casual wear," Dick said eyeing a stack of sweaters. "I hope he doesn't start trying to sell me sweaters," Dick thought. "Only queers wear sweaters."

"Well, first we start with trousers," Lou said, handing him a pair of grey slacks. He pointed to a door in the back of the store. "Go into the dressing room and try these on."

Dick tried on the slacks and came back into the store still wearing his short sleeve shirt.

"Now let's try this sweater," Lou suggested, handing Dick a matching grey sweater.

Dick looked suspiciously at the sweater. Damn it! Is this what it's come to? He looked around, but no one else was shopping this early, not even passing by on the sidewalk outside. What the hell. I'll take a chance and see what this looks like.

Returning from the dressing room, he glanced in the mirror and was surprised.

"Christ! I'm as good looking as Gavin."

Then he realized what he'd been thinking. That Gavin was good looking, and he wanted to be good looking, too.

He wanted Gavin to think he was good looking.

He bought the grey slacks and grey sweater. He also bought a pair of light tan slacks and tan sweater, a brown sweater, three dress shirts, a pair of brown shoes and a pair of black dress shoes, and a suit he'd have to come back to pick up because it had to be fitted.

# Chapter Eight

## Tom Larson

## September 1954

The Torrance Police Department continued to receive calls about the peeping tom. Each one brought to Larson's mind what Doctor Beeman had told him. Should he have reported the attack on Timothy at the time? A week had gone by. He'd not had a chance to talk to Giuliani, but every day that passed further damned Larson for not immediately reporting what he knew.

Finally, as the morning shift came on duty he bumped into the detective in the hallway.

"Now is as good a time as any," he decided.

He paused next to the payphone and nodded to Giuliani "You and your wife must be very proud of your lovely home." Giuliani's odd look and the way he cocked his head were enough to tell Larson that this was the time to come clean.

"Screw it. Trying to be subtle isn't my strong suit," Larson said abruptly. "Have you got a minute?"

"Sure."

Since there were no female officers on the Torrance Police Force, Larson, hoping for a little privacy, led Giuliani into the alcove off the hallway that led to the women's restrooms.

"It may have to do with the peeping tom," Larson said. He looked around to see if anyone was nearby. "Doctor Beeman mentioned to me that he thought your neighbor's boy, little Timothy Schmitt might have been raped."

"What? What are you saying?"

Larson reached out and held Giuliani's arm. "Please hear me out," Larson said quietly, again glancing around to see if anyone was nearby.

"Of course."

"After looking in on poor Schmitt last Sunday, Millie mentioned her youngest boy Timothy. From what she said and after looking at the boy, it occurred to Beeman that Timothy might have been raped the night before. He didn't want to say anything at the time, what with all the family is going through already. And he had no real proof."

36

Larson paused and shook his head. "But I doubt he's wrong. I'm inclined to tie this in with the peeping tom."

Larson was afraid the officers passing by in the hallway would notice the stunned look on Giuliani's face.

"When did you hear this? Yesterday?"

"A week ago, yesterday. I'm afraid it's been a week now since the doctor mentioned it to me."

Giuliani reached for his breast pocket, the pocket where he kept his notebook and pencil. He looked grim. "You know that according to procedure this must be reported."

"I know. But with what the family is going through already, Beeman and I really hated the thought of bringing them down here and putting them through an investigation and all that goes with it. From what Beeman said, by the next morning the boy seemed to have forgotten the whole experience, blocked it out of his mind."

Giuliani paused while two officers passed by. "Maybe you're right," he said hesitantly. He slipped the notebook back in his pocket. "When it's just some victim you don't know, you can avoid becoming involved, strictly follow regulations and all that. But when it's someone you know well, like a neighbor, it's different. Those interrogations are hard on everyone."

Larson nodded. "When my son was Timothy's age, I wouldn't have wanted him to have to sit at a table with strangers asking about…well, about something like that. God knows what that kind of interrogation would be like for a kid. It could be as traumatic as the attack itself."

As an afterthought he added, "If there was an attack."

"Well for my part I don't see how I could interrogate little Timothy or his mother. They're my neighbors, so I guess I see what you mean. In spite of regulations, I can see now there's always the possibility that the investigation could actually harm the victim."

In an uncharacteristic gesture, Larson reached out and put his hand on Giuliani's shoulder. "I'm glad you agree. If you're willing, maybe you and I could get together from time to time and compare notes. We might just come up with some evidence on our own."

"I agree. And I'll keep an eye open around my neighborhood. This guy may have a pattern. He may well return".

It was only a few days after Larson's conversation with Giuliani that Larson and Millie Schmitt met formally for the first time. He was sitting on his motorcycle in the service station when she drove in for gas.

Seeing that she was alone, he got off his bike, removed his helmet to set it on the gas tank and walked over to her car.

She was sitting motionless behind the steering wheel, staring blankly ahead while the attendant filled the tank.

He took off his sunglasses and introduced himself.

"Hi. I hope I didn't startle you. I'm Tom Larson," he said through the open window. "We have several mutual friends, your neighbor Tony and Doctor Ralph Beeman. I just wanted to introduce myself and ask how your husband was doing."

Surprised, she looked up. Her eyes were red-rimmed. "Oh, he's still hanging on."

Without warning she broke down and began to sob.

Taken aback, Larson reached his hand inside the window and touched her shoulder.

"I'm so afraid," Millie leaned forward and pressed her head against the steering wheel. Now she was shaking, weeping uncontrollably. "He isn't going to get better. He isn't going to recover. I'm watching him fade right in front of me. I almost wish we could get it over with. That he could just go on and die."

Jesus Christ, Larson thought. What have I started here? He withdrew his hand and stepped back. Even though it had only been a gesture to try to comfort her, it was the first time he'd touched another woman since his wife died years before. "I'm so sorry. I didn't mean to upset you."

"No, no," she protested between sobs. "This has been building up inside me for a long time now, a very long time. You just happened to be here."

The attendant finished filling the tank.

"Why don't you drive your car over by my bike?" Larson suggested. "Let me get you a cup of coffee."

She nodded her head and dabbed at her eyes with a Kleenex. Then she started the car and drove to the corner of the station next to his parked motorcycle while Larson walked into the repair bay where a coffee pot was always brewing.

He filled two cardboard cups, walked to her car and handed her one through the window.

The coffee was hot, and she sipped carefully.

Neither of them spoke at first. Around them were the sounds of the traffic passing by on Torrance Boulevard and Crenshaw and the noises coming from the service station's repair bay.

Finally, she began, so softly he could barely hear her. "I suppose a lot of people go through this, watching a husband or wife take sick and begin to die. With the kids at the ages mine are, I can't talk to them about it or ask them for any help. All the neighbors have problems of their own. When something like this is happening, they stay away as if it's catching and if they get too close, they'll get it too."

"Maybe you're right. But most people just don't know what to do or how they can help," Larson replied softly. He looked away, remembering his wife's quick decline. Turning back to her he continued, "I think they stay away because they're embarrassed that there's really nothing they can do."

"At times Richard seems to almost be his old self," she continued quietly. "Less and less often now, but sometimes his eyes will come to life. He tries to kid me about something, some old memory or something about the kids." She dabbed her eyes. "But most of the time he just lays there. I never know if he's asleep or awake. And having to clean him, seeing him helpless like that and knowing what he must be going through…" She began to cry again.

Larson bent to crouched next to the car door. He was so big that even in this position his head was still above the level of the window.

"I can understand what you're going through. I lost my wife to cancer some years ago. Is there anything I can do? Maybe look in on you from time to time, give you a shoulder to cry on?"

In part he was hoping this would give him an excuse to keep an eye on the neighborhood.

There was more, though. He was drawn to her somehow. She wasn't physically attractive, but she was around his age, and—maybe he'd avoided facing it—he had been lonely since his wife died. Maybe it was his need to be needed. Not having anyone to care for all these years had left him feeling empty and useless.

So it began with Officer Larson and Mrs. Schmitt.

On his day off two days later, he dropped by the house. She was clearly overjoyed to see him. She hurried around the living room opening the drawn shades, flooding the room with sunlight, and letting in some air through an open window.

He appreciated the sunlight and breeze. The smell of the house was familiar to him. It took him back to his wife's last days.

"I'm afraid I've let the house and yard go," she said. "Other than the day I saw you when I went out for gas, I hadn't been outside for weeks. My daughter Marcia has been doing our grocery shopping for us. Can I get you some coffee?"

"Absolutely. How's the patient?"

"About the same. He sleeps almost all the time now."

"How are the kids handling all this?"

"They don't seem to be aware of what is actually happening. And each of them is caught up in their own lives. My oldest son Dick is almost twenty. He works full time on the night shift at the mill." She smiled a questioning almost uncertain smile. "I think Marcia has her first boyfriend."

My youngest, my little Timothy hasn't been himself lately and isn't doing well in school. He has a lot of friends in the neighborhood, though." She glanced toward the front window, the window looking out on the yard. "I suppose he's like any boy his age."

"It certainly wouldn't hurt for you to get out from time to time," Larson said. "Why don't you show me around your yard? Maybe I can help." He wanted to sneak a look at the flower beds outside the kid's bedrooms to see if there were any more signs of the soil having been disturbed.

She set her coffee cup on the table. "Well, Dick mows the lawn if I give him a little money, but a teenage boy isn't much help when it comes to the flowers." Getting up from the couch she smiled and said, "Come on, we'll go out back through the kitchen.".

"I'd like that, Mrs. Schmitt." He rose from the chair and followed her through the house to the little kitchen and out the back door.

"Please, call me Millie," she said over her shoulder.

"And you can call me Tom."

The Giuliani's home and the flowerbed he wanted to take a look at were on the side of the house opposite the Schmitt's kitchen.

The Schmitt's and almost everyone else on the block were German or of German descent. That included the neighbors on this side of the house, an elderly couple that kept their shades tightly shut all the time. Nodding to the house next door Millie whispered, "These old folks are as nice as they can be, but they keep to themselves. They're kind of eccentric. They water their lawn and flower beds with their dishwater and the water from their washing machine. That's why all their plants look so grey and stunted."

She turned, looked to him and continued, "Every time an airplane flies over, both of them come out of their house and wave at it and bow down. None of us in the neighborhood have any idea what that's all about," she said with a little smile.

Tom nodded, thinking Millie has a nice smile when she can get her mind off her troubles.

Their tour took them to the side of the house in which he was most interested. Yes, the dirt outside one of the bedroom windows next to a big chrysanthemum was freshly disturbed. He didn't draw her attention to it, and he hoped she hadn't noticed. Crap, he thought. It looks like we do have a reoccurring visitor.

"Why don't I go home, put on some old clothes and come back? I'll help you do some weeding. It might be fun, do you good to get out in the sunshine." Patting his stomach, he added, "And it wouldn't hurt for me to get a little exercise."

He was thinking it would give him a chance to smooth out the dirt below the window. Then he or Giuliani could look over the fence and see if the uninvited visitor had returned.

A sudden smile lit Millie's face. "That would be lovely."

While Larson went home and changed, Milly had made a pitcher of iced tea. When he returned, they spent the afternoon clearing the weeds out of the flowerbeds and getting to know each other. They chatted about Torrance, the local high school they'd both attended and, it seemed to Larson, everything else under the sun.

As he was leaving, Larson popped next door to say hello to Tony. He wanted to explain what he'd found and about smoothing the dirt in the flowerbed.

"Well," Tony said. "That is creepy. To think someone is prowling around right next to the house! Damn it, if I catch the son of a bitch, I'll kill him!"

"I'm going to be coming back from time to time. Maybe between the two of us we can find out who the peeper is. You'll spot any strangers in the neighborhood, and as an outsider I might see something suspicious that you might not notice."

But in his heart Tom wanted to see more of Millie Schmitt. He found her intelligent, and at least when he was around, she could be lively and fresh. He knew that if there was anyone that really needed him it was Millie Schmitt.

Thinking he might be needed by someone made Tom Larson feel real good.

# Chapter Nine

## Marcia Schmitt

## October 1954

Before setting it on her dresser, Marcia pondered the handbill for the upcoming school play. Her attention lingered on the drawing of the three people shown adrift in the lifeboat. The play was something about World War II, downed pilots in the Pacific.

She got a kick out of going to these performances, but suspected she enjoyed them in a way different from the way her friends did. When she watched the actors in the high school's drama class stumble through their lines, she pictured herself on the stage in their place.

Instead of smirking at the screw-ups, Marcia Schmitt always imagined how she would have portrayed the parts.

Her last date with Gavin came to mind. She'd felt no guilt or regret about her behavior, her actions and that bothered her. She searched her reflection in the fogged old mirror on top of her dresser for any sign that her virginity was gone, given up in fact with such enthusiasm, such abandon.

Would anyone be able to tell?

Mother for instance?

Would mom take a close look at her and somehow know?

She remembered a very pretty little blond girl the seniors all called "Sharon the Slut." The seniors all said Sharon the Slut put out, "went all the way" with the boys. She always wore lots of makeup and she dressed *sexy*. Marcia didn't really know Sharon very well. Sharon was a couple of years older than Marcia and her crowd.

After their date at the drive in, Marcia was apprehensive about seeing Gavin. She was afraid it might be awkward, that things might be different. What would he think of her? That she was cheap? Easy? That she did *it* all the time? Maybe he wouldn't want to see her again. Then again, maybe he would think less of her and only want to see her to make out and have sex.

Maybe her loss of virginity showed somehow, and she had become "Marcia the Slut." Maybe Gavin would tell everyone at school, and they would all talk about her behind her back like they did poor Sharon the Slut. What ever happened to Sharon anyway? Did she hear that Sharon got pregnant and moved away?

Monday, when Gavin caught up with her walking to school, he seemed perfectly natural. If anything, the two of them seemed more at ease together than ever before. He asked if she wanted to drive down to the beach after school. She relaxed a little, assured that their relationship wasn't going to become just about having sex.

She was sure he loved her as much as she loved him.

# Chapter Ten

## Dick Schmitt

## October 1954

Dick called Gavin Saturday morning. "The guys at work have been talking about the Sunday drag races at the Lion's Drag Strip in Wilmington. Do you want to go?"

"Sounds great!" Gavin answered. "I've never been to the drag races!"

"Neither have I," he replied eagerly. "Why don't I pick you up tomorrow afternoon around four o'clock?"

Dick was even more excited about the races than he'd been about going to the car show. He had to stop himself from whistling while he washed his car in the alley behind the garage. Wouldn't want the family to know he was happy.

The next day, when it came time for Dick to pick Gavin up he again drove down the alley, turned the corner and stopped in front of Gavin's house. Out of the corner of his eye he watched Gavin get in the car. Gavin checked out Dick's new clothes, the new leather jacket, sharp tan sweater, matching slacks, and new brown shoes. Dick started to feel better about himself than he'd ever felt before. He became positively chatty, telling Gavin all about work, the guys at the mill, the horseplay and joking around. He boasted as if he were a part of all that rather than an outsider.

"We're not supposed to leave the plant during the shift, but some of the guys sneak out and buy liquor. They bring it back and drink on the job," he confided as if he too, were "one of the guys." He was pretty sure Gavin was impressed.

It was almost five p.m.; the sun had gone down and it was getting chilly by the time they got to the drag strip. Judging by the full parking lot and the line at the entrance, it looked like this was going to be a big night. The bleachers were filled and crowds of guys, some of them drinking, lined the track almost halfway down to the finish line.

Dick and Gavin scouted around looking for a place to settle. The bleachers didn't seem right. Dick had this feeling that they might be dirty, and he didn't want to sit on them in his new pants. The mob lining the track away from the bleachers was drinking beer and getting rowdy, so he certainly wanted to stay clear of them.

"Let's go over there," Gavin suggested, pointing to the crowd pressed against the low fence at the foot of the bleachers near the starting line. These were mostly guys, loud, scruffy and dressed in jeans and raggedy shirts. Many of them looked greasy, like they'd just finished working on their cars.

Dick noticed three girls pushing their way through the mob amid catcalls and smart ass remarks.

The girls spotted him and Gavin. Dick hoped they would keep going, but they boldly walked right up and started talking.

"I don't think I've seen you here before," the blonde said with a big smile.

"This is a brand-new experience for me," Gavin replied, returning her smile.

Dick's mind was in turmoil. All he could think was that maybe if he seemed really interested in what's happening on the track they'd go away. He tried to ignore this intrusion by staring straight ahead at the crews and drivers on the drag strip as if something totally engrossing was going on.

But as luck would have it, at the moment there was nothing happening. The race crews were just setting up for another race.

Dick had no choice but to turn and join the conversation or look like an idiot. There was no denying the three were really attractive. What was he going to do?

"Are you up to any other "brand new experiences" tonight?" the tallest girl asked. "My name is Connie and red here is Sandi," she said motioning to the cute red head with the long legs. "The brunette is Michelle and I have a bottle of whiskey in my car."

Dick felt Sandi press her body against him. He tried to tell himself it was because of the crush of the crowd and not that she was coming on to him.

"I'm Gavin and this is Dick, and I think this is just the night for new experiences," Gavin said, grasping Connie's hand in his. "Why don't I stop by the snack bar and get some cokes so we'll have some ice?"

"Oh, you are a man after my own heart," Connie replied.

Christ, Dick thought. We're into it now. Try to act cool, relaxed. He wondered if he could. As awkward and embarrassed as he felt, he didn't see any way to head off what seemed to be happening, what seemed to be going to happen without looking like an inexperienced, awkward kid. He was trapped.

He had to go along with Gavin and the girls.

He tried to think of something clever but couldn't come up with anything, so he just kept quiet.

Connie sidled up to him and slipped her arm through his. "I like the strong, silent type."

Sandi and Michelle moved to Gavin, one on each side and slipped their arms through his.

Girls had never come on to Dick before. All this seemed to be happening too fast, faster than he could gather his thoughts.

Connie grabbed his hand. She led him through the crowd out to the parking area behind the grandstands with Gavin and the other two following behind.

It was dark in the parking lot. No one else was around. Behind them, on the other side of the grandstands came the cheering of the crowd, the cars roaring down the drag strip. Back here though, the sounds were muted, even though they were only a few yards away.

They wound their way through the parked cars and approached a big old black 1948 Cadillac four-door sedan.

"It's Daddy's car," explained Connie.

They paused next to a trashcan. Gavin emptied the cola out of the cups, being careful not to lose the ice. Connie opened the door and slid in behind the steering wheel.

By the car's dome light, Dick saw again that she was really very, very pretty. Still gripping his hand, she slid across the seat to the passenger side, pulling him in after her so that he was behind the wheel.

Gavin and the other two girls opened the rear door and climbed into the back. Connie reached for the glove compartment and got a pint of Seagram's. She handed the bottle to Dick.

"Here, open this will you?" He loosened the top and handed the bottle back to her. Connie poured a splash into her paper cup. Then she got up on her knees on the seat, leaned over the seatback and handed the bottle to Gavin and the girls.

It was almost pitch black inside the cavernous old Caddy. There was, however, enough light for Dick to see in the rear-view mirror that Sandi and Michelle were all over Gavin. They were giggling and pawing him while he tried to pour some bourbon into their paper cups.

47

Gavin seemed very happy and very excited.

Dick poured himself some whiskey. He thought maybe if he took a swig, it might help him see this through. He choked, suppressed the urge to cough it up and forced himself to swallow.

It burned all the way down to his stomach, but the effect seemed almost immediate.

Connie leaned against him, wrapped her arms around his neck and with her tongue caressing his ear whispered "Wanna make out?"

"Okay," he answered stupidly, hoping that in the dark car she didn't see his nervousness. But the whiskey had gone straight to his head. He was bold, confident of himself.

Connie moved back to the passenger side of the car, her hand still on his thigh. She tugged at his belt, urging him to slide away from behind the wheel and across the seat toward her. When he was next to her, she put her arm around his neck and drew him close.

Vaguely he heard Gavin in the back seat with the two girls.

They had all taken a drink of the whiskey and seemed to be getting to know each other very quickly. It sounded to Dick as if Gavin were giving the two girls some kind of instructions, or at least suggestions.

But Connie was all over him, French kissing him, tonguing his ear, and really getting him hot. Deftly she swung herself above him, straddling him so that she faced him in the roomy front seat of the big old Cadillac.

In one smooth motion she lifted her blouse up and over her head, leaned forward and whispered, "Undo my bra."

He did the best he could and finally he got the damn thing undone. Now her breasts were right there in his face.

He put his mouth on one. It seemed like such a natural thing to do.

She tilted her head back, moaned and then leaned forward, lifting herself up on her knees. He felt her hand struggling to undo his belt buckle and unzip his pants. Should he help, he wondered? But before he could decide what to do, she managed on her own.

He was instantly erect.

She lowered herself onto him. This was his first time, and the warm wet sensation was so much, much more than he'd ever hoped it would be. She began to ride him, lifting herself up slowly till

48

he could feel the cool night air, and then slamming herself down hard as if trying to punish herself or him for what they were doing.

She was so slender that he could, with both hands, reach almost all the way around her waist. He held her, joining her rhythm, lifting and then pressing her down on him.

From her position astride and facing him he realized she was watching the threesome in the rear seat. Watching whatever it was they were doing back there was driving her even wilder.

She climaxed very quickly, frozen in motion, gripping him tightly with her legs, her arms around his head holding him, almost smothering him between her breasts. Only one part of her was moving. That one part brought Dick to a throbbing conclusion.

She was breathing hard and held him like that for a long time, still watching the action in the back seat. She began to move again, slower this time, undulating.

He rose to the occasion. This time he took longer, and she was even wilder, completely losing control, grabbing his head and riding him hard.

The commotion from the back of the big old car reached a fever pitch.

Then there was only the sound of heavy breathing.

Connie finally spoke. "Well, that was certainly something!"

The windows of the car had clouded. Dick again became aware of the sounds of the drag races.

Gavin laughed; "Do you come here often? And I mean that in the nicest possible way."

One of the girls in the back seat giggled and said, "No, but if you'll be joining us, I'm pretty sure we will."

Connie lifted herself from Dick. "There's still half a bottle left," she said, holding his face in her hands. "I guess this proves you don't have to get drunk to have a good time."

# Chapter Eleven

## Timothy Schmitt

## October 1954

Timothy was down the street playing in Randy's back yard with Randy and Jimmy. They were trying to figure out what to do with two cardboard boxes of shiny chrome car door handles. The handles were all so pretty, with a spring-loaded button that snapped right back when it was pushed. But try as they might, the boys could not for the life of them come up with any earthly use for these things.

Timothy was sitting on the grass in the shade, leaning against the trunk of an avocado tree. He was holding two of the door handles together, studying them intently. The other two boys were rummaging through the boxes to see if there was anything else or some clue as to what they could do with these darn things.

Jimmy said, "I hope the next train wreck has something else besides car door handles."

But to Timothy, it seemed as if his friend's voice was coming from a long way off. Timothy didn't feel very good. He felt dizzy and nauseous, like he was going to throw up. He had the sensation that he was starting to slide sideways on the tree trunk. He braced himself and stole a quick look at the other boys to see if they noticed. They were busy with door handles and hadn't even looked up.

His head ached. Everything was blurry. The late November sunlight seemed too bright, even sitting in the shade of the tree. He wanted to get up, get to his feet and go home. But he was afraid that if he tried, he would be unsteady, unable to stand. He couldn't stay here where he was. He was sure he was going to be sick.

Finally, by using the tree to steady himself he managed to get to his feet. Without speaking he ran out of the yard, not even telling his friends that he was leaving, going home. He ran as hard as he could down the street. He stumbled and fell on the sidewalk, skinned his knee.

By the time he came crashing through the front door of his house he was crying hard. Mom came out of the kitchen and found him sobbing, rocking back and forth on the hassock in the living room. He was holding his head in both hands, his bloody knee showing through the tear in his pants leg.

"Timothy, what happened?"

"I fell down," Timothy sobbed. "I don't feel so good."

"Let's get you cleaned up," she suggested, feeling his forehead. "How about a nice hot bath?"

Although Timothy had never before taken a bath in the middle of the day that sounded like a real good idea.

# Chapter Twelve

## Marcia Schmitt

## November 1954

Marcia and Gavin were together as much as possible during the week and pretty much had a standing date for Friday nights.

She could not wait for Friday nights. Gavin suggested a variety of other things they could do, but all Marcia wanted was go to the drive-in and make love. He was great at it. She wondered where he'd learned so much about where things were on a girl's body and what to do with them. He seemed to know more about her places than she did, and he brought her to new heights each time.

It crossed her mind that maybe she was a nymphomaniac.

God, she loved Gavin.

If she was a nymphomaniac, well so be it.

# Chapter Thirteen

## Dick Schmitt

## November 1954

Dick and Gavin returned to the drag strip every Saturday night and either sought out Connie, Sandi and Michelle or the girls found them. After the second or third time, they stopped going to the bleacher area of the drag strip. They just met in the back of the parking lot, climbed into the old Caddy, had a drink or two of whisky and had sex. On the way to the drag strip Dick would stop at a liquor store so Gavin could pick up a bag of ice and some cups. Connie seemed to have a ready source for the liquor.

They were startled one evening by the sound of the car parked next to them suddenly starting up and driving off. They all had been so caught up in what they were doing they hadn't even heard anyone approach.

Dick wondered if the people saw what was going on in the old Caddy.

The five of them were silent for a few moments.

"You know," Gavin pointed out, "pretty soon the drag strip is going to close for the winter."

Dick's heart skipped a beat. He'd become hooked on these orgies. The very thought of having them interrupted was horrifying.

Gavin rattled the ice around in his paper cup. After a pause he added, "Maybe we could rent a motel room. It'd be nice to be in a bed instead of wrestling around in the car."

"Oh, that would be too much!" Connie agreed enthusiastically.

"That way," Gavin went on, "we could even switch partners if we wanted to."

At that, Dick went cold. He couldn't face the thought of someone else, Gavin even, being with Connie. He was pretty sure that he was in love with her. He was thinking about asking her to marry him.

But the others thought the motel idea was terrific, so Dick couldn't object. What would be his reason not to move these meetings inside? That he was jealous? That he didn't want anyone else to be with Connie? They wouldn't think that was very cool.

53

Gavin described a motor court in Lomita that wasn't too strict. It was in a quiet residential neighborhood, not on a main thoroughfare. They could meet along Pacific Coast Highway at eight o'clock on Saturday night, leave Dick's car and all drive to the motel in the Caddy. Gavin and the girls would hide in the back seat. Since he was the oldest, Dick, with Connie pretending to be his wife, would rent the room. Once that business was taken care of, they would drive the car over to the cabin assigned to them. Gavin and the two girls could sneak in unobserved.

The motor court turned out to be a left over from the 1930s. It had little individual detached cabins rather than a lot of units with common walls in a single building.

The manager's office was a separate little hut off to the side.

Dick was very nervous the first time he and Connie pretended they were married, but Connie carried the ball.

She told the fat, hairy little manager they were in town visiting her parents and that her folks lived in a trailer. Connie leaned over the sign-in desk, smiled at him and said, "My parents don't have room to put us up. They begged us and begged us to visit." She brushed her long blond hair back from her forehead and concluded with a pout, "Then when we get here, they have no place for us to stay."

Dick nodded his head in agreement.

"But Dad's not well," continued Connie with a sigh, "So we'll have to come down from L.A. practically every week to tend to them."

Dick thought it was clever the way she was setting it up for them to return again and again.

# Chapter Fourteen

## December 1, 1954

Timothy's dad, Richard P. Schmitt Sr. died Monday December 1, 1954, at 4:45 p.m.

At the time, Timothy was down the street at Randy's house. He and Randy were stretched out on their backs on the front lawn. They were looking up through the branches of the big beech tree, watching clouds drift overhead. The two were going back and forth, speculating about what they would do if they were rich.

"I would buy the planet Venus," Timothy declared.

"What makes you think I'd sell it to you?" Randy replied.

"Then I'd buy the beach instead."

Timothy idly turned his head to look down the street toward his own house. Doctor Beeman's big black car was parked in front.

Someone was on the porch.

"Isn't that your sister Marcia waving at us?"

"Yup. Guess I better go see what's up." Timothy jumped to his feet and ran down the street to where Marcia stood waiting.

He was startled when she grabbed and hugged him.

"Marcia don't do that. Randy's watching us."

When she released him and stepped back, he saw she was crying.

She pressed her palms against her teary eyes. "Oh Timothy, Daddy died."

"What do you mean?"

She sobbed, unable to respond.

"I gotta go see Mom," he said, and ran into the house, down the hall and to his parent's bedroom.

The shades were drawn, the room dark except for the light from the little cut crystal lamp on the bedside table.

His mother was sitting in the chair next to the bed and Dr. Beeman was standing beside her.

Timothy ran in through the open door and before his mother or the doctor could stop him, he was next to the bed.

He saw his father, face, grey and shrunken, head tilted back, mouth open, eyes staring dully toward the ceiling.

His mother stood and tried to put her arms around Timothy, tried to gently move him toward the door and out of the room.

He began hitting at her and screaming. "What happened to Daddy? What did you do to him?"

Doctor Beeman turned and put his hand on Timothy's shoulder.

"Timothy, listen carefully." The doctor's tone was deep, quiet, calming.

"Your dad is gone," Beeman said with a finality that left no room for question. "We need your help. It's important for you to go find your sister, see if you can help her through this. She needs you very much."

Timothy looked around the room, then back at the bed and his father.

His father hadn't moved.

Timothy knew his father would never move.

He swallowed, tears still running down his cheeks.

The doctor asked his mom, "Is there was anyone you could call?"

His mom just stood there silently looking down at the bed, her face pale. After a few moments she looked up and turned to the doctor.

"I should contact Dick. He's at work."

"I'll call the mill and see if I can get word to him. Is there anyone else?"

His mom replied so softly Timothy could barely hear her. "I suppose I should get word to Tom Larson," she said. "He's been a good friend."

The doctor turned to the door, then paused and put his hand on Timothy's shoulder. "Come on, young man. Let's see if we can find Marcia."

⁂

Funeral services were held the following Wednesday at the new cemetery in the hills overlooking the harbor.

Marcia wore a navy-blue suit. The day was cold, drizzly. She held her arms tight across her chest for warmth. The small group of mourners, the ugly hole in the ground and the casket, it was as if this were all a performance in a play, a play in which she was more an onlooker than a member of the cast.

The widow was composed, dressed in black, her children at her side. Standing nearby were Dr. Beeman, Officer Larson and a handful of neighbors.

Dick looked sharp in a new black suit. It was hard to tell if his expression registered grief or annoyance.

Timothy was dressed in corduroy trousers and white shirt with a little tie tied too short. He fidgeted as if the tie were strangling him. He was looking down at his shoes when his father's casket was lowered into the wet ground.

# Chapter Fifteen

## Marcia Schmitt

## December 7, 1954

It was still raining the following Monday. Marcia and Gavin always talked and laughed on their way to school, but today she was quiet.

Her breasts were sore, and she'd thrown up that morning. Since she hadn't been with Gavin for several days, she was pretty sure her sore breasts weren't as a result of making love. She hoped it was just hormones or emotions from her father's death.

But she wasn't stupid. Deep inside she was afraid she was pregnant.

She barely heard Gavin suggest they go bowling. Even thinking about bowling almost made her throw up.

What she really wanted was for someone to hold her, to tell her everything was all right, that she wasn't pregnant, and she could go right on doing what she'd been doing with Gavin.

But she was pretty sure that wasn't going to happen.

Instead of going to the cafeteria during the lunch hour, she went alone to the school library. On the way she stumbled in a puddle and soaked both feet. The librarian made her take her shoes off and leave them near the heater to dry, then noticed the girl's drawn face.

"Can I help you find a book, dear?"

"No no, I can find it, thank you," Marcia replied. She padded in her bare feet across the library's cool hardwood floor, headed in the direction opposite where she knew the book she wanted was kept. When the librarian wasn't looking, she quietly made her way to the section on biology. She found a book dealing with human reproduction. The old book was worn from use. It almost opened itself to the chapter she was interested in, suggesting that she wasn't the first Torrance High student to seek information on the subject from this source.

There in the book, described in painful detail were all the symptoms she was having. At age fifteen, monthly periods were fairly new for her and hadn't settled into a regular pattern.

According to the book though, Marcia thought she was about a week or ten days overdue.

The cold December rain drummed against the library windows. The room was heated against the chill outside, but her feet were still cold and wet from stepping in the puddle.

Marcia wiped beads of sweat from her forehead.

# Chapter Sixteen

## Marcia and Gavin

## December 10 1954

It was misty and rainy, but Marcia wanted to go to the drive-in anyway. She needed to tell Gavin of her fears about her condition. The drive-in and the privacy of the car would be as good a place as any.

Gavin parked in the back as usual and got out to go to the snack bar. Marcia watched him return, weaving between the cars and trying to duck the drizzle.

As soon he got back in and shut the door she blurted out, "I think I might be pregnant."

There was a long pause. She wondered if he heard her. "Gavin, I said I think I might be pregnant."

"What do you want to do?" he asked quietly.

"I don't know. I love you and I would marry you but we're both so young," she replied, trying to control her voice.

Another long pause.

"I love you, too. And I would love to be married to you, but I would want to hold off on starting a family—if I had a choice."

"What is that supposed to mean?"

"Just that having a baby changes everything. We're not in it for the fun anymore. It's all serious stuff. Working. Being a father *and* a husband. Being a daddy. We aren't even twenty, for crissakes."

She watched his tense face.

"Isn't there something you can do?" he asked.

"Something I can do? Like what?"

"I don't know. Isn't there someone you can go to?"

"Like who? My mother?" Marcia replied, her heart sinking. "After what she just went through?"

"Well, we'll think of something. I love you and we'll see this through." Gavin patted her hand.

"What do you mean by that?"

"We'll get married—if we have to."

"If we have to?"

"No, no, I didn't mean it like that. Let's plan on getting married. That would be great."

"Well, we're going to have to plan on it pretty quickly. I think I'm about six weeks along."

They sipped their cokes in silence and for once actually watched the movie.

⌢⌢⌢

Gavin dropped Marcia off at her house. He needed to think. Little Marcia had dropped a bombshell on him just as he was about to tell her his big news. He liked this girl. She was certainly beautiful, built like a brick shithouse, and a real sex machine.

But marry? That was out of the question. He was way too young for that. He had much, much bigger plans than to end up married with a job at the mill or the refinery, barely getting by, living in a little house with a two-year-old car and two or three kids.

No, Gavin Keller had bigger plans than that.

His parents both worked steady, both made good money. Gavin knew that they assumed he would go places.

Gavin felt a little stupid about what was happening with Marcia. Why didn't he see the possibility of her getting pregnant, what with all the screwing they were doing?

Well, this was Marcia's problem, but he resolved never to let it happen again.

Gavin knew what he wanted: to make big money and live like Cary Grant in that movie where Grant played a big shot in New York City. Gavin Keller intended to be just like Cary Grant, wearing beautiful expensive suits, surrounded and admired by beautiful expensive women. Busy. Barking orders. Important.

Gavin knew the way to that life involved a college education. Unfortunately, his folks weren't quite well off enough to provide him with a college education at an eastern school, a school prestigious enough to introduce Gavin to the contacts he knew he had to make.

He knew that would be entirely up to him. He was already working on it.

61

# Chapter Seventen

## Dick Schmitt

## December 12 1954

After the dash across the dark, rain-swept parking lot, the heat and damp of the motel manager's office engulfed Dick like the smell of a wet dog.

The gooseneck lamp directed at the guest register book on the countertop left the rest of the little office in shadow. Smoke curling up from a lit cigarette in the overflowing ashtray did not hide the acrid perspiration smell of the short, fat, hairy little man behind the counter.

He must live here in this little cabin, Dick thought. Probably has a little bed in back. It was always the same guy, and he was always alone. Dick couldn't recall ever having seen any other guests or even cars in the parking lot.

Tonight, as usual, the lot was empty except for Connie's big old Caddy.

He and Connie registered and were given the key to cabin four, the same one they always got. After Gavin, Sandi and Michelle joined them Gavin said mysteriously "I brought something that might interest you all. It's better than booze. And it won't give you bad breath or a headache."

"I'm interested," Connie said with an eager, mischievous smile. She set the unopened bottle on the table by the bed.

Throughout all these dates Dick kept his mouth shut and went along with whatever the others suggested.

Gavin produced two hand-rolled cigarettes.

Connie took one of the cigarettes. "Let's try this out." She looked at the other two girls. "Any objections?"

Sandi and Michelle giggled. Sandi nodded yes.

Dick knew what the cigarettes were. He didn't smoke and had never been anywhere near marijuana, but he was aware of it through films he'd seen in high school health class on the subject of "the devil weed." Guys at the mill sometimes slipped out behind the building and came back smelling like an unusually sweet smoke. What the hell he thought. I haven't gone wrong following this crowd yet. I won't inhale; I'll just pretend to smoke it.

The others began taking off their clothes.

Sandi, her small firm breast and long legs. She squirmed and wriggled out of her red panties. Gavin took them and draped them over the lamp in the corner. Now the lighting in the room was dim, diffused.

Gavin moved to the bed and sat cross-legged on the pillows, leaning against the wall. Sandi and Michelle moved to either side of him. It struck Dick that Gavin looked like an oriental potentate with his harem.

Dick sat at the foot of the bed with Connie behind him, her arms around his waist, her bare breasts pressed against his back. He watched Gavin light the cigarette and hand it to Sandi. Sandi took a drag, coughed, took another drag and handed it back to Gavin.

As he took the cigarette from Connie, she put her arms back around his waist and slipped her hand down his stomach. Startled, he forgot he was only going to fake taking a drag and instead inhaled deep.

As the smoke hit him, Dick heard Gavin say, "I have another idea." Gavin got off the bed and pulled the big dresser around, angling the big mirror on it so that it reflected the action on the bed.

Dick took a second drag. Connie moved around on the bed. Now she faced him. She leaned forward, bowing to his lap.

He wasn't exactly sure what happened after that, but he knew it was wild.

# Chapter Eighteen

## Marcia Schmitt

## December 13 1954

It was raining hard when she left for school. She'd waited inside the house, waited for Gavin for as long as she could. She finally had to leave or be late for class. She didn't see him walking on the wet streets in front of her the whole way to school. She looked back behind several times—but no Gavin.

All through the gray day she looked for him on campus. She didn't see him, not even once. At first, she thought that was just as well, that she didn't want to see him, that she wanted some time to herself to think.

But as the day wore on it occurred to her that something might be wrong.

Since she'd been spending all her time with Gavin, she'd drifted away from her friends. Now, without him she was alone. She stood by herself next to the Senior Patio, huddled under the stairway that led up to the school library. Students were hurrying to their classes, vainly trying to shield themselves from the wind and rain.

Tuesday was rainy, gray, and cold, a repeat of Monday. No Gavin on the way to school, and no Gavin to be found anywhere on the campus.

After school, she walked to the supermarket.

No Gavin.

Wednesday and Thursday still no sign of him.

The rain continued all week.

When she got home from school on Friday, she worked up the courage to walk down the street toward Gavin's house. The Keller's lived next door to Timothy's best friend Randy's and the two boys were on the front porch, playing in a tent that they'd rigged up to shield themselves from the weather.

A look of panic crossed Timothy's face when he spotted Marcia on the sidewalk. She knew he must have thought she was bringing more bad news about the family.

"What's the matter?" he asked.

"Nothing," she said, trying to act casual, as if she were just out for a stroll in the rain. "Just taking a walk." Trying to keep her voice steady she swallowed and asked, "What's new in the neighborhood?"

"Nothin," Timothy answered cautiously.

Randy piped up. "The people next door moved out."

"What people?"

"Those people," the boy said, pointing at Gavin's house. "They said this town wasn't a good enough place to raise their kids, so they moved up to Inglewood."

"When did this happen?"

"They moved out last Saturday. They'd been talking about it for months. They sold the house about a month ago. The new neighbors are from Wisconsin and they're moving in tomorrow," he concluded smugly, pleased for having information that seemed to mean so much to her.

Marcia was stunned. It must have shown in her face because Timothy asked again, "What's wrong?" in his curious little boy voice.

He sounded so sweet and concerned that she almost burst into tears. "Nothing," she said. She turned and almost ran home.

She got to the house just as Dick was walking to his car to go to work. She couldn't help herself and had finally started to cry.

Grabbing his arm, she pleaded with him "Dick, I have to talk to someone—you. I'm…I'm pregnant. Is there any way you can help me somehow?"

He yanked his arm from her grip. Her heart sank when he sneered and said, "Get lost. You wanna play, you gotta pay."

"But what am I going to do? I can't tell Ma," she whimpered.

Wordlessly Dick turned, got in his car and started it. She could see her pale tear-stained face reflected in the car's closed window and through the glass, her brother's cold unfeeling expression. He looked up at her and shook his head. He put the car in gear and drove away.

She was left crying alone at the curb.

The wind stirred the wet leaves on the street, blew them along the gutter. The familiar house behind her, the house she'd lived all her life, the whole neighborhood seemed strange, remote and unmoved.

# Chapter Twenty

## Millie Schmitt

## December 14 1954

After Timothy dropped off to sleep, Millie went to her own room.

She sat in the chair next to the table and turned on the little cut-glass lamp.

Looking at the empty bed Millie, didn't feel grief over Richard's death. He'd been sick for so long and suffered so much she was already used to his no longer being there.

But she worried about her family. Despite the rain and the chill of winter in the air, earlier that day she'd opened all the windows to try to rid the house of the smell they'd lived with these last months.

She picked up the framed black and white photograph on the table next to the open book she'd been reading to Richard.

The photograph was of Marcia at age six sitting on the steps to the front porch, beaming at the camera.

She was holding little baby Timothy.

Millie set it back on the table and picked up the book. It was titled *California Wildflowers* and was opened to the picture of the California poppy, Eschscholzia Californica. While reading the book Richard was able to forget his sickness. When he became too weak, she read it to him, would hold it up to the light of the little lamp so he could see the pictures of the flowers.

She closed the book for the last time and rose from the chair to go to the closet. She put the book in the cardboard box with his clothes and other belongings, and then turned to face the empty bed and the chair where she'd spent so many hours.

Again, her gaze settled on the photo of Marcia holding little Timothy.

Recently she'd sensed a change in her younger children, Marcia and Timothy.

Usually Timothy was as always: happy, noisy, playing hard with his friends.

But lately he wasn't the same. She'd noticed the change even before his dad's death. Now there were times when Timothy would become irritable. He was often moody and sometimes downright mean. He would talk back to her, lose his temper and almost have a tantrum like a four-year-old.

And Marcia certainly wasn't her usual vivacious self either. She seemed distant, as if something was troubling her. Millie didn't know if it was because of her father's illness or not. She knew Marcia was doing well in school, but she missed Marcia's friends giggling and talking in her bedroom or coming by to pick her up on the way to some place or other.

For once Dick seemed to have a life of his own. When he wasn't at work, he was out on dates. Besides, her oldest hadn't participated in the family for a long time.

For years he'd just lived here.

Millie knew it was up to her to re-energize her family and bring them back into the land of the living.

The holidays were upon them, and a warm Christmas could be an opportunity to try to redefine her now smaller family.

The next morning, Millie put on her best dress, carefully made herself up and headed for town to do some Christmas shopping.

Although it wasn't exactly on the way, she drove past the gas station where she knew Tom Larson liked to "lurk for miscreants" as he called it.

Sure enough, there he was in the gas station, sitting on his motorcycle. Although her car had half a tank of gas, she pulled into the station hoping Larson would see her and would walk over to say hello.

She told the attendant to put in a dollar's worth of regular.

Then she watched in the rearview mirror.

Larson got off the bike and walked toward her car.

"How are you doing, Millie?" he asked smiling.

She returned the smile. "Pretty well in fact. I thought I'd try to restart our lives and actually make a nice Christmas for my family."

Millie paused and looked down at her lap. "Could you join us?"

"I would love to."

Millie breathed a sigh of relief. "Well, I plan turkey and all that goes with it, lots of presents, a tree, and everything. I think it's just what the kids and I need."

Beaming, Larson replied, "I would love to be a part of that. My son has moved up to his college campus and I was afraid I'd be spending Christmas alone, sitting at Howdy's eating a turkey sandwich with the other old-timers. Just tell me what to bring."

"I'll take care of everything."

With a wave, Millie drove away from the gas station, her heart lighter than it'd been in years.

‿‿‿

Christmas Day 1954

Although money was tight, Millie bought Timothy a new Monarch Silver King bicycle with a battery-operated horn and for Marcia a new-fangled Hi-Fi radio and record player along with a half dozen records.

She even got Dick a present for his car, a set of new hubcaps, "moons" they were called by the kid at the auto parts store.

Timothy and Marcia were cheerful and even Dick was pleasant enough. All in all, the day went very well.

She had told the kids that her friend Tom Larson was going to join them for dinner.

When he arrived, he had presents for everyone. He was a likeable guy and the kids seemed to accept him. Even Dick was civil enough, although he excused himself after dinner muttering that he was going out.

Marcia took her new radio/record player to her room and Timothy went with her, more excited with this new device than she was. Soon, from the back of the house came the voice of Bing Crosby singing "White Christmas."

Larson handed Millie two gifts. She blushed and opened the first, protesting that she hadn't gotten him anything.

"You gave me a fantastic meal and good company."

Millie opened a colorful scarf and draped it around her neck. "Look, Tom, it matches my dress!" Then she unwrapped the current bestselling novel, *Not as a Stranger*. She ran her hand gently over the book cover. "Having you here with us is the best thing that's happened to me in a long time".

69

"Since my wife died, Christmas has been hard for me, too. You and your family have made this the best Christmas I've had in a long time."

Larson reached across the coffee table and put his hand on top of hers and said "I'm hoping I can drop by often."

"I'm hoping you will".

"Not wishing to be nosey, but have you any plans?"

Millie shrugged. "No, not really. Just to continue as we have been. Things will be a little tight, but the house is paid for. There's a little life insurance so we should be all right for a while. If I have to work, I'll cross that bridge when I come to it."

Tom smiled. "And I'll watch out and make sure you're o.k."

They settled back into the sofa, shoulders touching, sipping their coffee.

Outside the winter wind was blowing and tree branches rustled against the house. The sounds made the warm living room with the opened presents and scattered wrapping paper seem even cozier.

# Chapter Twenty one

## December 28, 1954

A developer was building a group of houses and creating a whole new neighborhood on the other side of the railroad tracks. The big vacant field had been graded, foundations poured, and framing had begun.

It was cool, almost chilly, but the rain had held off for another day. Two twelve-year-old boys, Timothy Schmitt and Randy White clambered down the bank, crossed the railroad tracks and climbed up the bank on the other side and into the site.

It was Sunday, so no workmen were about, and the project was empty.

The boys explored the deserted ghost town of partially finished houses, picking their way through the lumber and scraps of construction material.

"I love the smell of sawdust," Randy said, kicking at a pile that had remained dry, protected from the recent rain by a workman's table. A gust of wind picked the sawdust up and swirled it across the damp dirt next to a foundation form.

Timothy stepped between the bare two by four studs of an unfinished house and stomped across the wooden sub floor. "Listen! You can hear our footsteps echo."

"I bet that's the bathroom," Randy said, pointing to big pipes breaking through the floorboards.

"And I think this is another bedroom," Timothy added.

"There are so many rooms. I wonder when they'll put up the walls."

"I like it all bright and open," Timothy said, jumping from the floor decking.

He ran across the dirt to the next building site. No framing had begun for this structure, but the shape was outlined by the forms for the foundations held in place by three-foot long steel stakes the builder had driven deep into the ground.

Timothy tried to pull one of the metal stakes out of the ground, but it was solidly embedded. The top of the stake was jagged, smashed flat by sledgehammer blows, but the sides were smooth steel.

Timothy gripped the metal stake and yanked with all his might. Hard as he tried, it resisted his efforts.

Randy watched from between the framing and laughed.

Timothy turned and glared at Randy. He frowned and tried pulling again. His hand slipped and caught on the jagged metal of the flattened top.

It hurt, and now he was angry and embarrassed that his friend had seen him fail to pull the stake out of the ground.

Randy walked toward the forms. "You better not do that," he cautioned.

"Maybe you better not tell me what not to do," yelled Timothy, giving his friend an angry shove.

Randy half laughed, surprised at Timothy's outburst.

Timothy started toward him and gave him another push, this time harder. Randy stumbled backwards almost falling. "Hey, Timothy, cut it out."

But Timothy pushed him again. "Make me."

"I'm gonna go home now," Randy said, turning to walk away.

Timothy ran and pushed him roughly from behind. Randy, caught off guard, stumbled over a foundation and fell forward onto one of the steel stakes. His weight and momentum rammed the rough hammered top through his stomach, completely through his body and out his back.

His short scream was quickly lost in a gurgle.

He twitched for a moment and then was silent.

Timothy stood and watched the blood spread from under his friend's body.

It quickly soaked into the fresh dirt.

Randy's head was turned, the right side of his face resting on the damp dirt, his eyes open and staring.

Timothy knelt next to his friend.

"Randy?"

Randy's eyes had already become dull, his face slack, vacant.

Just like Dad's face had looked, Timothy thought, like there was nobody in there anymore.

Timothy stood and looked around.

The whole place was empty.

He was completely alone.

He felt chilled. He put his hands in his pockets and started walking toward home, past the gaunt shadows cast by the skeletal frameworks of the partially completed houses.

# Chapter Twenty Two

## Tom Larson

## December 29 1954

It wasn't until the next day when the construction crew returned to the site that Randy's body was discovered impaled on the stake.

The neighborhood had been looking for the boy from the time he failed to come home on Sunday, but no one had thought to look in the new development on the other side of the railroad tracks.

Randy's family and the police had asked Timothy if he knew anything.

Timothy said he hadn't seen his friend.

The police searched the site as best they could but there were too many footprints in the dirt and there were no particular signs of a scuffle or any clue that something suspicious might have caused the tragedy.

They concluded it was probably just an accident. Perhaps the boy had been alone and running through the site when he tripped and fell on the stake.

Sergeant Larson heard about the incident mid morning and dropped by to take a look around.

The body had been removed, the site was once again busy with workers hammering, sawing, and pouring concrete. A foreman showed Officer Larson where they'd discovered the body. Larson scanned the place, his attention settling on the far side, the side that bordered the ravine for the railroad tracks.

After only a two-day break the wind and rain had returned. Even wearing his leather jacket Larson felt the cold. He walked between the partially completed houses to the edge of the ravine and looked across to the homes in the neighborhood on the other side.

It was a short walk—only a block or so across the tracks to and from the victim's house.

From the Schmitt's' house, too.

He wondered if there was a connection between this incident and the peeping tom.

Larson shook his head. Maybe he'd just become obsessed with the peeping tom case and the attack on Timothy.

Only Detective Giuliani, Dr. Beeman and he knew about the attack. No report had been made, so there was no reason for the police or anybody else to link it to the dead boy.

But Larson thought otherwise. When a god-awful thing like this happened in a small town there was almost always something behind it that connected it to something else.

That afternoon, after his shift he dropped by to see Millie.

She greeted him at the door and offered him a hot cup of coffee.

"Winter has come," he declared in a mock stentorian tone as he entered the house.

"Welcome to me hearth and home," answered Millie with a curtsey. "Timothy's playing alone in the garage, all bundled up like an Eskimo, and Marcia's taking a hot bath. I suppose you heard about the accident."

"Well, yes. I dropped by there earlier today. There wasn't much to see."

"The family lives just down the street. They're in a state of shock, I can tell you."

"How is Timothy taking it?"

"Maybe it hasn't sunk in yet, but he doesn't seem bothered at all."

"Randy was his best friend, wasn't he?"

"Yes, he was. I don't know what to think. Maybe Timothy just hasn't begun to miss him, or he doesn't understand Randy's really gone."

Larson wrapped his hands around his cup of coffee and leaned forward across the table.

"Millie, I've been thinking. With Dick working nights and just you and the kids alone here in the house, maybe you could use a little protection."

Millie looked surprised. "This is a quiet neighborhood and we have never had any trouble here."

"Times are changing. Even in sleepy Torrance there's more crime now. With your husband gone and Dick away at night, I worry about you and your young ones here all alone. Would you be terribly uncomfortable with a gun in the house? For protection? It would make me feel better knowing you could defend yourself."

"Where am I supposed to get a gun?"

"I happen to have one for you. It's a .38-caliber revolver, a Police Special. I'll bring it by Saturday. I'll take you to the shooting range and show you how to use it."

# Chapter Twenty Three

## Timothy Schmitt

## December 29, 1954

Timothy wasn't alone in the garage.

Timothy was in the alley behind the garage, crouched down beside the Robinson's old Plymouth.

He had his jacket hood pulled over his head to shield him from the rain and wind.

He was letting the air out of the old car's tires, one by one.

As each tire deflated and the car settled, Timothy thought of how Randy had looked when he fell on the stake and died. Randy had kind of deflated, gone limp; his blood, his breath and his life seemed to go out of him like the air out of these tires.

When he'd let the air out of the last of the old Plymouth's tires, Timothy squatted on his haunches for several long moments, staring.

Finally, he got to his feet and walked down the alley looking for another car.

But there weren't any.

He left the alley, crossed the busy boulevard, and walked to the supermarket.

There were always plenty of cars in the supermarket parking lot.

# Chapter Twenty Four

## Marcia Schmitt

## December 29, 1954

Marcia stood beside the bathtub and stuck her toe in the water to test it.

She'd filled the tub with hot water using no cold water at all.

She was cold all over.

The day was cold.

Gavin was gone.

Dick had rejected her plea for help, a rejection she should have expected.

Marcia felt utterly alone.

She was hurt, hurt on a scale she would never be able to describe.

Gavin had lied to her.

Gavin had been lying to her the whole time.

He not only didn't love her, he never had. The obvious proof was he never even told her his family was moving. He must have figured on leaving her flat all along.

The hot water had steamed up the mirror on the medicine cabinet above the sink. She took a washcloth and tried to clear its surface enough to see her reflection.

"Christ, my breasts are huge! I look terrific!" She felt them, lifted them. They felt heavier, but that could just be her imagination.

She started to climb into the tub.

Her mood, her frame of mind was changing. That Gavin had so callously betrayed her stunned her at first. But when she began to assess the extent of his betrayal, her anger began to rise like the steam from the water in the tub.

She watched her body settle into the scalding water.

Was it her imagination? Were her breasts larger? Were they getting bigger because of her condition? Maybe she was just maturing, becoming a woman. Her stomach was still schoolgirl flat and there were no other outward changes in her body, at least not yet.

God, the water was really hot. She was torn between running cold water to cool the bath or punishing herself by scalding.

She could hear her mother and Officer Larson talking in the living room. He sure was a nice man. Were most men like Officer Larson or were they mostly like Gavin, like Dick? Officer Larson had come into their lives at just the right time. Or had he been there all along, or at least for some time before she became aware of him?

Suddenly Marcia didn't feel so good. She leaned her head back against the bathroom's cool tile and closed her eyes.

She felt dizzy, nauseous. Maybe it was because the water was so hot.

Just as she leaned forward to turn on the cold water, she felt a wrenching cramp in her stomach, then blood stained the water between her legs.

"What the hell is happening to me now?" The pain was so intense she almost cried out.

She bit her lip. She didn't want her mother and Officer Larson to wonder what was happening and come running.

It really hurt and she was really scared, but she was pretty sure that if she could get through this, she wouldn't be pregnant anymore.

And if she wasn't pregnant, that changed everything. She could make plans for her life again and turn her attention to Gavin—and getting even.

The intense love she had thought she had for him had turned into a hate just as intense.

With her toe, she pulled the little chain that held the tub's stopper to let the water out.

Her pain seemed to swirl away down the drain with the red water.

She stayed in the empty tub, her bare skin against cooling porcelain. Utterly relaxed, she drifted detached, just thinking.

Finally, she got out of the tub. Slowly drying herself, her thoughts cleared, became focused. It was as if a fog was lifting along with the weight of her worry about being pregnant.

# Chapter Twenty Five

## Millie Schmitt

## January 1955

Millie had been trying to pretend everything was all right, however she finally had to face the fact that something was wrong with Timothy. He just did not seem to be growing up, maturing at the same pace as his friends.

And he clearly wasn't keeping up in school. His grades were never particularly good, but now he was failing.

He was lying on the floor in front of the T.V after dinner and as she gathered the dishes from the dining room table, she asked him if he missed Randy.

Timothy turned to her with a blank look and asked, "Who?"

Millie had to fight her alarm. Randy had been his best friend, the boy he'd played with all his life. Timothy's reaction was as if he had no idea who she was talking about. She tried to let it go, thinking poor little Timothy's losing both his father and his best friend at almost the same time must have been too much for him.

But she felt a cold knot in her chest and a terrible sense of foreboding.

# Chapter Twenty Six

## Marcia Schmitt

## May 1955

A drama major. Well, who would have thunk it?

Here she was, Marcia Schmitt standing in the wings of the school auditorium waiting to go on stage for the Torrance High School Junior Class production of "Christmas with Little Women."

What was it Tom Larson had said when she told mom and him that she had the role of Meg? Break a leg? Well, I'm not going to break a leg. I'm going to leave them begging for more.

She stole a peek through the curtains, checking the audience before they turned down the house lights. All the seats were filled. She and the rest of the cast knew those students were there not only to get out of classes, but also hoping that someone on stage would screw up royally, right in front of everybody.

"But I've studied my lines and my part," she told herself confidently, "and I'm not going to screw up!"

After what she went through, her hard introduction to adulthood and Gavin's betrayal, she'd made an effort to reconnect as best she could with her friends.

But to her they somehow seemed to have become childish, shallow.

It wasn't that she didn't still like them. She did, but now there was a distance. She tried to hide it, but to her they seemed like children, or pets.

Marcia Schmitt was no longer one of them.

She'd abruptly changed her major to drama and took every class even vaguely related to the subject.

Only once did one of her friends ask what had happened to her boyfriend. She just told her that he'd moved away. Other than that, she never mentioned Gavin to anyone, and she certainly hid any sign of what she'd been through.

It required a bit of acting on her part to pretend she was still an inexperienced little schoolgirl and not an almost mother. She gossiped, pretended to speculate with the rest of her friends as to what boys and sex were all about.

But Marcia Schmitt knew.

She knew very well.

And she vowed never to forget Gavin son-of-a-bitch Keller.

She had not and would not forget a single moment they'd had together, nor would she forget a single thing he'd ever said to her. The times he told her he loved her, the promises he made. Every gesture that she'd thought was beautiful at the time she now saw as a deceitful part of his treacherous plan to ensnare her. She intended to keep alive the memory of what he did to her as if she were stirring embers in a fire, just enough to keep it from going out, but not enough for it to come to a full blaze—at least not yet.

No, not until she could make him pay, really pay.

A woman scorned? You bet.

She didn't have a clear idea of what she was going to do, but she knew that whatever her revenge was going to be, it was going to be thorough, complete and as full of irony as she could possibly make it.

Sometimes when her hatred seemed to dim or waver, she deliberately dredged up those things he'd said, things they'd done together and the trust he'd built.

It was only when she was studying lines or concentrating on a part that she put Gavin and that part of her life out of her mind. When she was on stage she drew on that passion or anger or hurt, whatever emotion the part called for and used it.

Obsessed? Yes, but it was an obsession that drove her to study more, to try harder to become an actor, a professional.

Was she trying for an acting career on the stage? In the movies?

It doesn't matter at this point as long as she could lose herself in the script's imaginary world and escape her own life.

# Chapter Twenty Seven

## Dick Schmitt

## September 1956

Dick was half asleep, his mind wandering.

He had worked at the mill now for, what was it, three, four years? He couldn't remember. It was just putting in time.

He got up midmorning every weekday, screwed around the house, had breakfast, lunch, went to the mill.

He had no friends at work, but he didn't give a shit. Thanks to the union he got periodic raises along with everyone else. Because he was living at home, he had no real expenses, so he was able to accumulate a nice little nest egg.

Dick lived for that one night a week, Saturday night. Even after his family had moved Gavin still came down to meet up with Dick and the girls to party at the motel.

That night was more than enough.

This routine had been going on for two years now. It seemed to him that Gavin or Connie had a new idea almost every Saturday night, and none of the four complained about any of them. With the assistance of the marijuana, the world within the walls of the motel room became a soft, slow motion, totally erotic dream.

Dick let himself float back to full consciousness. Lazily he looked around, trying not too hard to get his bearings.

The motel room looked like a war zone.

Did he smoke a whole joint? He remembered Gavin kept handing them out and Connie kept lighting them and passing them around. He thought Gavin rolled four before he lost count.

Did he fold his clothes and put them in the top dresser drawer?

Yeah. Now he remembered. That's what he did because he looked at himself in the mirror afterwards.

Did they pull the bed over there? They must have, but it would have taken at least two of them to do it.

What the hell time is it? 11:30? Midnight?

He saw Gavin on the bed with Connie and one of the other girls. It looked like the other girl was Michelle, but he couldn't tell. Yeah, that must be Michelle under Connie. Sandi is still lying on her stomach on the overturned chair where he left her.

And as usual, somebody's panties were hanging on that lamp.

What a royal mess.

Through the smoky haze he watched Gavin, Connie, and Michelle finish with a noisy thrashing of bodies.

Connie stretched, reached down, and grabbed the corner of the bedspread that had fallen on the floor and dragged it up on the bed to cover her body. God, she is beautiful. So is Michelle. So is Sandi, even lying there on that old, overstuffed chair with her ass up in the air.

In fact, especially lying there with her ass up in the air. Christ, he thought he could do her again.

Gavin is saying something. What the hell is it?

"My family's moving to Utah, and I'm going with them to go to the university there."

Although exhausted and in a marijuana-induced haze, each member of the group slowly sat up looking stunned.

"Oh no, Gavin," Connie began. "You're the architect here, the conductor of the orchestra. And it's so good."

But Gavin made it clear that commitments had been made and he'd already enrolled in classes. There was no way he could change those plans, much as he regretted the end of his participation in the Saturday night parties.

This night would be his last.

Dick didn't know what to think, what to say. He wouldn't have any idea how to continue without Gavin. What was he supposed to do? Try to go on alone with the three girls? Could he do that? He wasn't certain that he could. But if the girls were willing, he knew he had to try.

He could not face giving up these Saturday nights. They were all he had to live for.

It turned out the girls were willing. They wanted to go for it again the very next Saturday.

Dick was nervous all week, half dreading, half anticipating what would happen, how it would work without Gavin.

At last Saturday night arrived and it was time to find out.

The motel parking lot was dark and empty as usual, only the glow of the light in the window of manager's office.

Sandi and Michelle waited in the back of the car, this time without Gavin, while Dick and Connie walked up the steps and into the smelly little office.

The manager, wearing what must have at one time been a white t-shirt, was bent over the counter reading a girlie magazine. He didn't bother looking up at first, even when the screen door slammed with a bang behind them.

Finally, he looked up and said with a smirk, "Welcome back. Will you want your usual room?"

Having played the role of husband so many times, Dick was no longer nervous to the point of speechlessness.

"That would be fine."

The manager's gaze went from Connie back to Dick. "Oh, and by the way," he coughed and said, "I have some films you might be interested in."

"I doubt it," Dick replied.

The manager put his cigarette out in the overflowing ashtray. "Oh, I think you will. Take a look. Here are some prints."

The little guy stooped to take a manila envelope from under the counter. "They're a little grainy. I took them off a 16-millimeter motion picture film." He leaned close to Connie. "Notice they're in color." Without taking his eyes from her he spun the envelope across the counter toward Dick.

Dick felt Connie at his side as he opened the envelope.

He pulled out several pictures.

Dumbly, he wondered what the hell this was all about?

Then he saw. There he was, in full color. He and Gavin, Connie, Sandi, and Michelle.

Naked.

In the motel room.

On the bed.

On the floor.

On the overturned chair.

Even standing up. In a whole variety of positions, some reflected again in the big mirror on the dresser.

He felt Connie's fingernails dig into his arm.

Stunned, Dick thumbed through the prints.

They were explicit.

Some of the scenes he remembered clearly and others he didn't remember at all.

But he knew they definitely took place.

The pictures in his hands proved it.

The motel manager broke the silence, choking back a laugh that evolved into a coughing fit.

He cleared his throat, spit into the wastebasket next to the old filing cabinet and lit another cigarette.

Resting both elbows on the counter, he leaned toward them.

"Now here's the deal, kids" he said, looking Connie up and down.

"I want the small sum of $100 each month in cash and I want to join in the fun, now that you're one player short."

This turn of events was so unexpected and was unfolding so quickly that Dick still didn't understand what was going on.

Connie grabbed his arm. "We'll get back to you," she said quietly. "We need time to think."

Dick handed the prints back to the manager as Connie pulled him toward the door.

"I'll tell you what," Dick heard the little man say as they stumbled outside. "I'll give you till next Saturday. Otherwise, I take these public. I'll expect you here around seven. And from now on I'll be joining in the fun."

Dick and Connie walked across the dark parking lot and got in the old Cadillac. He turned on the headlights and backed slowly out to the street.

"We need to talk," Connie said. "Pull around the corner and park and turn off the lights."

Dick drove around the corner and did as he was told.

"What's up?" Michelle asked from the back seat.

"Yeah, what's up?" Sandi echoed.

"We're screwed!" Connie rasped angrily. She went on to explain what had just transpired in the manager's office and about the film.

Dick heard Sandi say in a panicky voice; "Christ, now my husband will find out what I do while he's at work! He'll kill me!"

"I'm supposed to come up with $100 a month to pay him off," Dick said. "I'm going to have to think about that."

Connie, glowering at the windshield, spoke through clenched teeth; "That fat ugly creep thinks he's going to join in. I'm certainly not going to fuck him!"

"We're going to have to come back here next Saturday night with our answer," Dick pointed out, vaguely aware that Connie was getting something from the glove compartment.

In a voice so soft he barely heard her she said, "I've got his answer right now. Come with me," she commanded, opening her car door.

He got out to follow her. She walked purposefully back to the corner and up the dark street to the motel, their footsteps on the sidewalk the only sound in the quiet neighborhood.

Ahead of them, across the empty parking lot, the glow in the office window was the only light in the dark motel.

Connie walked up the steps to the door, pulled it open and walked in, Dick right behind her.

"I guess you've made your decision," the manager said, looking up from the girlie magazine. "Your films are right here, and they are professional quality, if I do say so myself."

He lifted a paper bag onto the counter and dumped out six reels of film and the half-dozen prints. "I'm glad you see the value of my offer, honey."

Connie said, "Here's your answer, asshole."

She lifted a revolver out of her purse and shot him square in the middle of his face.

The force of the gunshot at such close range almost lifted the fat little man off his feet, propelling him backward against the old file cabinet and knocking it over along with an ashtray full of stale cigarette butts and an old fan sitting on top of some newspapers.

He was dead before he hit the floor.

Dick stood open mouthed. The roar of the gun in the confines of the little office had been deafening.

Connie put the gun back in her purse and grabbed the film canisters off the countertop.

"Grab the prints. Let's get the hell out of here." She was out the door while Dick still stood stunned at what had just happened.

In a daze he picked up the envelope, tucked it under his jacket and into his waistband. He stumbled after her, the door banging shut behind him.

They walked quickly across the parking lot to the dark street and around the corner toward the parked car.

There was still no one out and about.

A dog barked once, but otherwise all was quiet.

No cars passed, no one came outside.

Dick's mind was in turmoil.

What have we done?

Didn't anyone hear?

Is anyone watching?

Would anyone look out the window and see the car?

Is it possible that as loud as the gunshot seemed to him, it wasn't heard outside the little office or as far away as the nearest house?

With measured steps Connie walked relaxed at his side as if they were out for an evening stroll.

But Dick could not calm down, could not bring himself under control. He was scared to the point of panic. His knees felt weak, watery. It was as if he couldn't depend on them and that with the next step, they might betray him and let him fall.

He watched the houses as they passed.

People were inside their homes watching television and going about their lives.

Were all these people indeed oblivious to what had just happened in their dark, quiet, and secure little neighborhood?

When they reached the car and opened the door Sandi in the back seat asked what happened.

Connie slide in the front and replied calmly; "Nothing much, except we won't be coming back."

Dick got in behind the wheel. He was shaking so hard he couldn't get the key in the car's ignition.

"What's the matter with him?" Michelle asked.

"I think he needs a drink," Connie answered. "I know I do."

Out of the corner of his eye he saw the little light come on when she opened the glove compartment.

Shielding her actions as she was, the girls in back couldn't see her put the pistol back.

To Dick the gun looked immense, black and deadly.

She got out the half pint of Seagram's and opened it. She took a swallow and offered it around.

Dick, shaking his head silently, declined.

He started the old Cadillac and drove slowly down the street, not thinking to turn the headlights on until they reached the corner.

He was shaking but found if he gripped the steering wheel so tightly his knuckles were white, he was able to control himself and drive.

Michelle and Sandi were chattering away in the back seat as if nothing had happened. Of course, they didn't know that anything had happened, much less that their good friend and sex partner Connie had killed the motel manager.

Dick drove back to Pacific Coast Highway where he'd parked his old Ford.

He was numbly aware that life still went on around them.

There were no sirens, no parting of the heavens and no hand of God reaching down to smite them.

Heavy traffic, as usual, passed in both directions.

In the momentary illumination from the headlights of the passing cars, he saw his face in the rear-view mirror.

He was white as a sheet.

He parked the Cadillac behind his own car and got out, still in a daze.

From the back-seat Sandi asked; "What about next Saturday night?"

Connie answered, "There aren't going to be any more Saturday nights."

Dick stumbled back to his car.

He unlocked the door and got in.

Turning the key in the ignition he glanced over his shoulder. Connie had slid across the front seat of the old Caddy and was behind the wheel, her face empty of emotion.

Dick pulled away from the curb and merged with the traffic on busy Pacific Coast Highway.

In his rearview mirror he watched Connie following.

After they'd driven for several blocks, she turned left down a side street and was gone.

It was still early on a Saturday night, and he just could not go home, couldn't face going in the house and couldn't face the family.

They'd all still be up when he walked in.

But where could he go?

His mind was in turmoil.

What the hell had happened?

What had happened to his orderly, methodical life?

Work all week, party on Saturday night.

He could not even picture going back to the mill Monday morning, could not imagine even staying here in this town, this familiar town that had been his home, the place where he grew up and spent his whole life.

He had to get away.

Vaguely he realized he'd left Lomita and was back in Torrance, driving down Torrance Boulevard past the Lincoln Mercury dealership.

Like an island of hope in the midst of the blackness of his despair, the hundreds of bright lights illuminating the car lot caught his attention.

There, glittering like a magic chariot promising to fly him away from this hell was a baby blue 1957 Thunderbird, the car of his dreams. It was proudly displayed on a platform under a fluttering canvas banner that said OPEN TILL 9 ON WEEKENDS.

Dick quickly checked his watch. It was only 8:30.

It was after eleven by the time he finished buying his dream car, driving it home and parking it in the alley behind the house.

The house was dark and silent, the family asleep.

He tiptoed to his room, exhausted by the horror of the evening's events.

Should he go to the police and confess? Confess he'd had been a party to a murder? Confess he'd smoked dope and was in he didn't know how many pornographic films?

His decision to buy the car, his doubts and uncertainty about such a major decision.

He had to keep asking himself; was there any alternative? Did he have any choice?

No, he had no choice.

He had to get away from here.

He stripped down to his underpants and fell into bed.

In the dark bedroom just a few feet away, separated by the dresser and the blanket suspended from the ceiling, Timothy snored noisily.

Dick was tense as a coiled spring.

The roar of the gunshot in the little office.

The small hole the bullet made when it slammed into the manager's fat face.

The mess it made when it came out of the back of the man's head.

All this replayed itself over and over in Dick's mind.

On his bureau, like evidence tagged exhibit "A" for the trial of Richard Schmitt II, accessory to murder, dope fiend, pornographer, loomed the envelope.

He stared at the clock on the dresser for what seemed like an eternity.

By 4:30 he could take it no longer.

He got up, dressed, grabbed the envelope and quietly left the house.

He made his way along the short concrete walk from the house to the garage and the gate to the alley and his beautiful new car.

It waited for him in there in the shadows, waited patiently just for him, for his escape.

The car started quietly, easily. He slipped the floor shift into drive. It moved smoothly away from the old garage and down the alley toward the street.

He drove to Torrance Boulevard and turned right, heading for the beach and the pier in Redondo.

It was not yet daylight when he parked on the street above the pier.

Under bright floodlights, fishing boats were tied up alongside the pier, rising and falling on the swells. Four or five fishermen were unloading their catch as he walked past.

Beyond, the pier was dark and empty.

He knew there was an underwater canyon next to the pier. It was here, here at the pier's end, above that black bottomless abyss that he flung the envelope with the films, threw them as far as he could.

He returned to the car and tried to think.

In spite of his fatigue, a plan began to take shape, one he was just exhausted enough to believe he could pull off.

Of course, he was going to get the hell out of Torrance.

It was only 7:30 in the morning when he returned home. The family was just getting up. Without a word he went to his room, got as many clothes as he could carry and took them out to the car.

He returned to the house and gathered up another armload. He paused at the door.

"I'm moving out." His voice was hard, abrupt, and left no room for discussion.

Millie stood in silence for a minute, fingering her housedress. She sighed and said "Well, you're twenty-one years old. All grown up. Where are you going?"

"I'll let you know."

Timothy ran into the room; "You should see the cool T-Bird parked in the alley. Its blue…Hey, what're you doing, Dick?"

Dick pushed past him without replying. As he left, he heard his mother tell Timothy, "Your brothers moving out, dear. He's going to get a place of his own. Now you can have a bedroom all to yourself."

Dick didn't look back.

He put the last of his clothes in the trunk of the baby blue Thunderbird and closed the lid. Then he opened the door, got in behind the wheel and drove out of the alley for the last time.

# Chapter Twenty Eight

## Gavin Keller

### September, 1956

Gavin was surprised when he called the motel and someone else answered. "Sorry. The guy got hisself murdered last Saturday" said the voice on the phone. "Who's calling?'

"Never mind," Gavin replied and hung up.

He sat next to the phone in his parents' new house thinking about this unexpected turn of events. The fat little shit murdered? Gavin wondered how, but figured it was creepy Dick who did it when he found out about the films.

Doesn't matter. Stay clear, cut losses and move on.

The whole project wasn't a loss by any means. Other than the sample he'd left with the guy to use as blackmail, Gavin had kept the rest, a whole lot of really good, if not great, films. They were stored in two 55-gallon drums buried in the backyard of his parent's new home in Inglewood.

Gavin had enrolled in photography and film courses at his new high school. He had access to the equipment needed to edit any scenes that could identify him as one of the participants. With this equipment he could reproduce all the 8- and 16-millimeter color copies he wanted. He was confident that these were films high school boys would really be interested in renting.

Not buying.

Renting.

He wasn't just about to sell these films.

Meeting the girls at the drag strip and the parties in the car had given him the idea. It all fell into place when he got the group to move the orgies to the motel. Enlisting that fat little pervert motel manager and getting him to make three holes in the wall in just the right places was easy.

Now, with him gone Gavin had all these films for himself. The next thing on his list of things to do was to set up a distributor here at his new school. Some dupe to act as the front man in generating business for his little enterprise. Gavin didn't want to be known as a pornographer. He needed someone else to go around the school whispering in horny teenager's ears: "You want to see some dirty movies?"

This person could not be in a position to double-cross him. It had to be someone he could control, preferably through fear of exposure.

High school boys, awkward and unsure of themselves, almost always had secrets, something to hide, and something they thought important enough to keep from their parents or friends. It almost always had something to do with sex. Most teenage boys were hugely self-conscious about their sexual inexperience, clumsy and unsure of themselves, scared to death of rejection or of looking foolish.

Gavin never suffered from this affliction.

One night shortly after he'd learned of the motel manager's murder, a night he was out just cruising around, he found himself driving down Beverly Boulevard in Hollywood.

Young men, some alone and some in twos and threes were loitering or walking along the sidewalk.

Standing on a corner under a streetlight with another boy was a kid that looked familiar. Gavin turned his folk's big Hudson up a side street at the next corner, and then turned right two more times till he was coming back toward Beverly. Approaching the corner for the second time he recognized that the boy standing under the streetlight was a classmate at his new high school. He was a football player, not varsity but on the B team, good looking and popular, average height, blond hair.

Gavin hadn't met him, but he remembered the boy's name was Tom or Tommy.

Gavin drove by a second time and then pulled the car into the parking lot of a liquor store across Beverly Boulevard. He watched the pair in the rear-view mirror.

Every so often a car would pull over to the curb. After short conversation with the driver, either Tommy or the other boy would get into the passenger seat and ride off, returning a half hour or so later.

Gavin waited until Tommy's companion got a ride, then started the Hudson, drove around the block, and pulled up to the curb next to the boy.

"Going my way?" he asked from the dark interior of the Hudson.

"For five dollars I am."

"You're on," Gavin said. "Hop in."

Gavin drove to the big parking lot of the Farmers Market on Fairfax and parked as far away from the lights of the busy market as he could. Cars were constantly coming and going so he was fairly sure they wouldn't be interrupted.

Afterward he returned the boy to Beverly Boulevard and headed for home. Now he had an ally, willing or not.

The next day was Monday. During the lunch break at school Gavin saw the boy in the hall talking to two other B team football players.

Gavin walked over and stood next to them for a few minutes.

Finally, the boy looked over at Gavin and said, "Is there something you want?"

"No," Gavin said. "I just thought I would stop and say hello. We met last night in Hollywood."

After a pause he added, "On Beverly Boulevard."

For a moment Tommy's face was blank, then his jaw dropped, and he went white.

Gavin smiled. "How about joining me for a walk around the campus?"

Tommy cut short his conversation with the other boys, turned to Gavin and said, "Let's go."

They fell in step together and strolled across the campus looking just like any other pair of students taking a walk between classes.

"Well, what do you want?" asked Tommy, looking straight ahead.

"Look," Gavin said, pausing at the tennis courts and leaning against the chain link fence. "I don't intend to cost you anything or do you any harm. I have a business proposition, strictly business. It would be profitable for us both."

"Oh?"

"I'll get right to the point. I have several dozen really top-quality pornographic films, dirty movies. I want to go into the business of renting them for stag parties or whatever." He looked around, and then turned back to Tommy. "I'm new here and I don't know anyone. I'm not out for any sports or anything, so I have no connections. If you can act as the distributor, you and I could split the profits fifty-fifty."

96

Tommy didn't respond right away and seemed deep in thought, gazing at the students playing tennis on the courts behind Gavin.

Finally, he turned to face Gavin. "I'd like to hear more about this idea."

"Good. I think the first step is for you to see what I have."

"Agreed. Where and when?"

"I'm in the Audio-Visual class. After everyone leaves today, I'll set up a projector in the storage room. You meet me there at 3:30 and I'll show you one of the films."

That afternoon after everyone else left for the day, Gavin waited for Tommy in the storeroom. Tommy showed up at three thirty, right on time.

Gavin locked the door and led Tommy between the shelves and clutter to a clear spot at the far end of the storeroom.

A projector was positioned on a table facing a screen.

He turned off the lights. Now the room was almost dark, the only illumination in the storeroom was from a lamp on the work bench used for splicing film.

He returned to the projector and turned it on.

The screen lit up.

In vivid, glorious color five attractive young people, three gorgeous young girls and two nice looking young men came to life, romping around on a bed and fucking their brains out. A big mirror even displayed the action from another angle making the scene even more erotic.

Tommy gasped. Without taking his eyes off the screen, he said so softly that Gavin almost couldn't hear him over the clatter of the projector, "I haven't seen very many dirty movies, but the ones I have seen were shitty—grainy, black and white, with ugly people. This is a whole different thing!"

"Christ," Tommy continued, "this is really something." Then he added excitedly, "Jesus! Once I get the word got out, renting these would be no problem! How much would you charge people to see these?"

"I figure we could rent them to groups or individuals or just show them somewhere, a rented hall maybe, and charge admission."

"I live out toward Gardena," Tommy said. "The neighborhood is semi-rural. In fact, a lot of the people around there still keep chickens and horses and goats and stuff. We got a good size yard, almost a ranch, with a barn and all. Dad's a drunk. Been out of work for months. Just sits in the living room drinking and watching TV till he passes out. Mom works nights in a bar near the airport. I stay as far away from them as I can. I could just wait till dad passes out and then show dirty movies in the barn. It's big enough and far enough from the house."

Gavin turned off the projector and turned the storeroom light on. He put the film back in the canister and hoisted himself up on the workbench next to the editing equipment. "My mom's a nurse and I can get certain prescription drugs that will all but guarantee that your dad will stay passed out through the night."

The next day Tommy began circulating the word among his friends that he was going to host a party showing a dirty movie in his barn and the charge was only $5 each. Gavin and he agreed that they would parcel out showing and distributing the films, showing them only one at a time so the supply would last longer.

Friday and the night of the premier arrived.

Gavin had no intention of attending the showing, so he met Tommy after school.

"Here," he said "Take this pill and slip it into your dad's drink. It's Valium. With the booze, it should put him out for the evening."

Tommy reported the next day that the Valium, along with a half pint of Early Times worked very effectively. "It's fortunate it did," he told Gavin, counting his share of the money, "because 104 of the horniest sons of bitches you ever saw showed up at the barn. Hard as I tried to keep them quiet, once the film started all hell broke loose."

Word spread very quickly. Another showing was planned for the following Friday night and again for Saturday night.

By the end of the first month, showing the films only in Tommy's barn, they each made $2,000.

"That's almost five times as much as Dad used to make when he worked at the aircraft plant," Tommy told him.

The partners branched out, and subject to a substantial deposit began renting the films plus continuing to show them in Tommy's barn. Tommy was sure his dad sank into a drunken stupor minutes after he set him up.

He assured Gavin that his dad was totally unaware of what was happening.

"For the first time since I was a kid, he's actually nice to me," Tommy told him. "I almost don't hate the drunken slob, at least not as much as I used to. The old bastard appreciates my thoughtfulness. Every night when he settles himself in his dirty old easy chair in front of the damn TV set, I bring him a glass of ice and a bottle of Early Times. He's good for the rest of the night."

Better safe than sorry, thought Gavin. Going through his mother's medicine supply he found a full, unopened bottle of valium and another half empty bottle. He took three pills out of the half empty bottle. Then he opened the other bottle, carefully so it wouldn't look like it had been tampered with and took five pills out. Now he was able to furnish Tommy with a short supply in case they didn't see each other during the day before a party in the barn.

Don't want that old fool stumbling in on our little scheme, he thought.

Weeks passed and the venture continued successfully. They showed the films in the barn and rented them out to students.

As the word spread, they included lodges and men's clubs. Some students moved to other towns and enrolled in other schools, so the word spread further, and the business grew.

One Friday night Tommy was in the kitchen opening a half pint of Early Times. His dad, wearing only soiled underpants, t-shirt, and a pair of dirty white socks had already settled in his easy chair with his cigarettes.

The TV was, as usual, blaring.

*The Adventures of Rin Tin Tin* or something.

The phone rang and Tommy answered it. Wrong number.

"Who was that?" his dad yelled.

"Just a wrong number," Tommy answered.

"Can you bring me a bottle?"

"I'm just bringing it now."

Tommy wondered, did he put that pill in yet? Damn! He couldn't remember. Well, why take the chance. Better drop one in, just in case.

After setting his dad up with the bottle, he went out the back door and across the dirt yard, past the corral to the barn to get it ready for another showing.

He and Gavin had decided to limit the size of the audience so things wouldn't get out of hand and to make certain that parking wouldn't be a problem.

Tonight, there were only fifty guys in the barn. They'd be sitting on bales of hay or on folding chairs, paint cans and anything else that could be scrounged up.

Later, about eleven thirty that night after all the guys had left, he straightened up the barn and went into the house to go to bed. His dad was still sitting in the chair in his underwear, his eyes closed and his chin resting on his chest, the television set blaring away.

Tommy turned the volume down and stood for a moment looking down at him.

At one time he'd worshiped his dad. Tall and handsome, he taught Tommy how to play football, baseball, even how to swim. When Tommy was a boy, dad would take him to the beach. Dad looked so good in a swimsuit that the young girls would steal looks at him.

Tommy had been so proud of his dad back then.

But look at him now, Tommy thought in disgust.

And his mother, Claire.

She'd been so beautiful. The two of them looked so great together that their friends nicknamed them Fred and Ginger.

But when his dad lost his job and started drinking, his parents began to argue and fight all the time. Tommy could not stand to be anywhere near them.

After his dad hit his mom a few times, she stayed away from him too.

Tommy sensed she was building her own life and it didn't include her drunken husband.

It didn't include Tommy anymore, either.

He turned off all the lights but left the TV on and went to bed.

His mom got off work at two in the morning, but usually didn't get home till five or six.

Tommy woke to the sound of her screaming.

100

He jumped out of bed, and in his pajama bottoms ran into the living room. His mother, the lace trim on her waitress uniform's short black skirt stuffed into the top of her pantyhose in back, was standing next to his dad's chair.

Her lipstick was smeared.

Her peroxide blond beehive hairdo was leaning to the left and looked like it might collapse forward over her face at any moment.

Her eyes were as big as saucers.

Tommy's dad was still sitting in the easy chair.

"He's dead!" she screamed, pointing.

James Huber didn't really look any different than he usually did in the morning. Kind of slumped down in the chair, feet in dirty white socks propped up on the hassock in front of the television set. He looked like he might be dozing or sleeping, his whiskered chin resting on his chest.

His t-shirt had ridden up, exposing his hairy little pot belly.

The television set was still on, the volume just as Tommy had left it the night before. On the table next to the chair were the empty bottle of Early Times and the smudged drinking glass, still holding a little water from the melted ice. His dad's left arm hung loose over the arm of the chair, fingers limp. On the floor below was a hole burnt in the carpet where he'd dropped the cigarette he'd been smoking.

Tommy bent and looked a little closer.

Yes, his dad was dead all right.

His mother had finally shut up.

Now she just stood shaking.

In the harsh morning light, the makeup on her pale face and her eyes, heavy with mascara made her look almost scary. Tommy thought she resembled some pallid creature of the night suddenly caught out during the day and that, like a vampire, might melt in the unaccustomed light of the sun.

Was it real remorse or just the sight of a dead body that was so unnerving her?

"Better call the cops," Tommy suggested.

His mother nodded her head dumbly in agreement.

The police arrived an hour later and only made a cursory report.

Just another alcoholic that drank himself to death.

The coroner did a quick check on the deceased's urine and found the alcohol and the valium.

He also found considerable traces of Contact, an over-the counter cold remedy. The coroner stated that the combination was enough to fell a horse.

The death of his father paved the way for more elaborate parties at Tommy's house.

Since there was no life insurance, his mother had to continue working. But with one less mouth to feed the two of them were better off financially.

Not including, of course, Tommy's substantial but secret income from the stag parties.

Tommy had a knack for distributing these films, and as word of their quality continued to spread to other schools, Gavin made more copies to fill the demand.

By the third month of operation, Gavin and Tommy were each making $3,000 a week, far more than any of the teachers or the principal at the high school.

∴

Gavin quietly opened a savings account. When his balance reached $20,000, he dropped into a new stock brokerage firm on Crenshaw Boulevard.

"My father asked me to stop by and pick up any papers necessary to open an account," he told a young man sitting at a desk in the little office.

"Here you go," said the broker. "All we will need is his signature, his driver's license number, and social security number."

Gavin took the papers home and filled them out in his own name using his own driver's license and social security numbers. He returned to the office the next day with a check drawn on his own account for $10,000.

By the time he graduated from Inglewood High School, Gavin had $62,200 in the bank and stocks worth $80,000.

Practically everyone he knew—his dad, his friends, and his friends' parents—all worked in factories or refineries.

But Gavin Keller was determined to escape that life. Coming from a small blue-collar town in the South Bay, it was going to be a long hard pull.

He'd be sailing in unknown waters with no guide, no mentor to give him any advice or help.

No one to guide or mentor him that is, until he graduated from Inglewood High and enrolled in pre-law at El Camino Junior College.

That's where he met Professor Horatio Blusk.

Blusk, a large flamboyant man in his middle years, always wore a cloak or judge's robes. Every day he swept into the classroom just a little late in order to make an entrance. One of the second-year students would stand and say, "All rise," as if court were coming to order.

There were only seven other students in the class, all male. Gavin found out Blusk had slept with three of them.

Seeing a way to expedite getting through junior college and begin his career, Gavin too, agreed to "extra tutoring."

His grades continued to be excellent and with Blusk's help, after two years he was offered a partial scholarship to Harvard. He told his parents it was a full scholarship and all he would need was a small allowance. He didn't want them to become suspicious about how the rest of the costs would be covered.

Gavin had only been out of California once when he was five years old. His parents had loaded him and his sister Val into the family car, an old Plymouth. They had driven back to see his grandparents in Detroit, and that damned old Plymouth broke down nearly every day of that endless, miserable nightmare of heat and bad roads.

But by god it turned out to be no worse than flying from Los Angeles to New York with stops in Denver and Chicago in a damn DC 7.

Gavin suffered through the experience, a nightmare he was determined not to repeat any time soon.

At last he arrived in Cambridge, Massachusetts.

# Chapter Twenty Nine

## Millie Schmitt

## 1956

Midway through his sophomore year the school called Millie and told her that Timothy had stuffed wet clay into the gas pipe of the pottery kiln in the shop class. This caused an explosion that blew out all the windows.

She met in the principal's office with the shop teacher.

"Fortunately, no one was hurt," the shop teacher said standing next to the principal. "But from the sound of the explosion and the flying debris, I thought it was the end of the world. Someone could have been seriously injured or worse."

The principal sat facing her, his back to the window looking out on the campus.

Millie held her hands tightly on her lap and looked from the worried principal to the bedraggled shop teacher. Outside she could hear the sound of the students going to class, laughing and talking.

"Timothy is really a good boy," she tried to explain, "but he's having a tough adolescence, what with his dad's death and all."

"I don't doubt he's a good boy, but his careless, impulsive behavior makes him a danger to himself and others. He just doesn't think, doesn't pay attention. This isn't the first time he's done something that could have hurt someone."

The shop teacher leaned forward and rested his hands on the desk. "Please believe me, I'd overlook this if I could, but I'm really convinced it is a very serious matter."

"I'm afraid I agree, Mrs. Schmitt," The principal interjected. "The school doesn't take this action lightly. In addition, I've reviewed his grades and its clear Timothy isn't keeping up."

"Look, Mrs. Schmitt. This is just the latest incident." The shop teacher shook his head. "He's going to end up hurting himself or someone else."

There was an awkward pause. The principal cleared his throat. "We're considering putting him in a special class."

Millie froze. She'd been afraid that something like this was coming. Still, she'd hoped that Timothy at almost sixteen would have a spurt of maturity and catch up with the other boys his age.

"I understand what you're saying," she said quietly, "but I'm concerned that will make him think he isn't normal, that he's different from everyone else. His best friend, his playmate since childhood, was taken from him just days after his dad died. If he's set apart from his friends at this age he could be doomed to being an outsider for the rest of his life."

The principal leaned forward in his chair and looked through the manila file folder labeled TIMOTHY SCHMITT.

"The only other choice is for Timothy to take some time away from school, perhaps the rest of this year. We can revaluate his behavior next fall and see if he's improved."

She knew the principal and the shop teacher's minds were made up, that they were not going to let Timothy continue in school.

She sighed. "If that's the best we can do I'll try to make that work somehow."

The principal agreed and Millie got to her feet to leave the office.

She looked one last time into the faces of the two men.

The principal quickly picked up the file on his desk as if to study it. The shop teacher folded his arms across his chest and looked down at his scuffed brown shoes.

Millie left the office, quietly shutting the door behind her. She turned to Timothy. He'd been waiting outside, slumped in a chair by the secretary's desk.

"Come along, Timothy. We're going home."

Timothy looked up relieved. "Yeah!" With a big grin he followed her out of the administration building and down the steps to the car.

"Can I drive? I have my learner's permit with me."

For the next few weeks, he seemed relaxed and cheerful enough, treating the break from the daily grind of going to school as if he were on summer vacation.

At first Millie tried to make him spend a few hours a day on the books the school had sent along.

But without the school's structure it was hopeless.

It wasn't long before he was just drifting, killing time spending his days playing the same games he'd played as a little boy.

Only now he was alone in the yard and around the neighborhood. Even when school let out for the day and on the weekends, he was still alone.

The other kids, the boys he'd always run around with had school as their connection. They were facing their teen years together, maturing and moving on.

Since Timothy didn't go to school, he just wasn't one of the guys anymore.

Millie thought that most of the time he was as sweet and likeable as he had been as a child.

But it wasn't long before he was spending more and more time just watching T.V.

And more and more often he just blew up, lost his temper for little or no reason.

She tried to keep Timothy's troubles to herself, but one evening she and Tom Larson were sitting on her old couch in the living room watching television and she abruptly burst into tears.

Startled, Tom put his arm around her shoulder. "Tell me what's wrong, Millie."

Sobbing, it all began to spill out. Timothy's troubles at school, forgetting all about his best friend, his mood swings, and tantrums and all the rest.

"I'm so afraid something is really, really wrong and I don't know what to do. I have this terrible feeling, this terrible premonition."

She hoped Larson would reassure her that it was all part of growing up. As a police officer he must have seen young boys go through stages like this. Maybe he'd say Timothy was just being an adolescent and would catch up.

But Larson just hugged her a little tighter and said nothing.

# Chapter Thirty

## Tom Larson

## 1956

Larson dropped in to see Doctor Beeman the day after Millie broke down and told him about Timothy.

The receptionist showed him into the doctor's private office. Larson was standing facing the bookshelves, his helmet under his arm when Beeman came in.

He turned. "You may already know this, small town gossip being what it is, but Millie Schmitt and I spend quite a lot of time together."

Beeman smiled and gestured for the big policeman to take a seat in one of the chairs facing the desk.

"So I've heard, Tom. I'm happy for you both."

Larson set his helmet on the desk and leaned forward in the chair. "It started at the time you told me of your suspicions about her son Timothy having been raped, about the time we were getting those reports about a peeping tom."

He leaned back in the chair and took a deep breath. "I kept going over there even when the signs of a trespasser stopped."

"That was a tough time for them. The family suffered a lot."

"Well, I'm afraid it isn't all over." Restless, Larson left the chair and began pacing. "Timothy's been in and out of trouble, mostly typical teenage mischief. He was finally kicked out of school. Millie broke down last night and told me she thinks there's been a change in Timothy, a change in his behavior."

"A change in his behavior? How do you mean?"

"Well, he isn't contrite or apologetic about the screwy things he does." Larson went on to describe the episode in the school shop class and Timothy's lack of emotion about Randy's death. "He just seems not to care. It's as if these things have nothing to do with him."

The doctor leaned back in his chair, lost in thought.

Larson stood in front of the desk and studied the doctor's face. "Should I have reported this back then? Even now, I'm still not convinced."

He rubbed is close-cropped hair. "I'm truly trapped with this secret."

The doctor turned sideways, his arm resting arm on the desktop.

Larson followed the doctor's gaze.

A bookcase, the bookcase that Larson had been staring at when the doctor came in the room, filled the wall. One shelf had old copies of Reader's Digests. Larson wondered if the doctor used the articles in them, articles like, "I Am Joe's Brain" or "Living with Heart Disease," as reference material to diagnose his patients.

On the shelf below was a dusty, partially transparent plastic model that Larson was afraid represented a uterus.

Finally, Beeman turned in his chair and looked up at Larson.

"You may be right about the cause of his behavior. I've thought about that whole episode and what might have happened. Even though I'd hoped it would be suppressed, buried and forgotten for good, it's possible that what was done to him that night did injure him physically or mentally or both."

"How?" asked Larson.

"Well, I remember when I looked him over, I thought I detected a slight odor in his hair that reminded me of my office. An odor like chloroform. Perhaps the attacker used chloroform and put Timothy out. It's difficult to predict what could have happened if the attacker held it over Timothy's nose and mouth for too long."

"Christ! If something like that happened, it could have destroyed Timothy's whole life. Who the hell would have access to chloroform?"

"It would have to be someone who worked in a doctor or dentist's office or someone who knew somebody that did. Oxygen deprivation to the brain or an overdose could explain the behaviors you describe, problems like concentrating and tantrums. That or the suppressed memory of what we think happened that night might account for his failing to mature and his suppression or indifference to things he doesn't want to remember or to address."

Angry and frustrated, Larson clenched his fists and paced the small room. "I can't stand by helpless, doing nothing about this. I can't tell Millie that her son Timothy might have brain damage. I would have to go back to what happened that night and the fact that we kept it from her for all these years."

The doctor sighed. "Don't blame yourself, Tom. There was nothing anyone could have done about it at the time anyway. And at this point we don't have any choice. All we can do is watch and wait and hope for the best."

# Chapter Thirty One

## Marcia Schmitt

## 1956

Over the hubbub of students excited about the graduation she heard someone calling "Marcia! Marcia!"

She turned.

Her childhood friend Jill came running across the Senior Patio, clutching her graduation cap in one hand and her yearbook in the other, her open gown flapping behind her.

Marcia smiled. In that in that black graduation gown, Marcia thought Jill looked like a giant crow trying to gather enough speed to take flight.

"Sign my yearbook," she said breathlessly. "There, next to your homecoming queen picture. And say something funny."

"Sure," Marcia replied, taking the yearbook. Jill had left the page open to the picture of Marcia wearing a tiara and formal gown.

I suppose I'm expected to remember that moment for the rest of my life, Marcia thought to herself, but I've pretty much forgotten it already. At the time mom sure was proud though, fussing over the fitting and all. But then there was that Miss Beer thing—Miss Finegold or something—and I had to ride perched on that float in the Rose Parade. Cold? My nipples hadn't been that hard since Gavin.

Marcia kind of chuckled, thinking she really did have a lot to be thankful for. What is it they say? Something about, "Anything that doesn't kill you makes you stronger." Well, being pregnant, Gavin walking out on her and all just as Dad died didn't kill her.

Instead, it made her tough, determined.

"How does this sound? 'To Jill. Roses are red, Violets are blue, like library paste, I'll stick by you."

Jill shook her head up and down like an excited puppy. Marcia wrote the message in Jill's book and watched her hurry off, darting from classmate to classmate.

Students and their parents were scattered in little groups taking pictures and talking and laughing and crying.

Marcia, like the others, still wore her cap and gown.

She stood off by herself at the edge of the patio, waiting for her mom and Tom Larson. Fellow classmates from the graduating class of 1956 came to her one by one, approaching with what seemed to be an air of diffidence, asking for her autograph or to write a message in their yearbooks.

She never intended for it to be this way, but somehow Marcia Schmitt had become a person apart from the others, her former friends and classmates.

After winning the beauty contests, becoming the homecoming queen and Miss Finegold, appearing in all the school plays and all the rest, she was no longer considered "one of the gang."

None of that mattered to her anyway. Being an outsider allowed her to watch and assess people more objectively. To her, observing others was truly fascinating. Attempting to categorize them led her to guess how they would behave, how they would react to the different situations in which they found themselves. Marcia was usually able to predict what they would do, how they would react.

She was seldom surprised.

She especially loved to study faces and listen carefully to their voices.

She must have been doing it unconsciously for a long time. She only became conscious of it one day in Social Studies. Principal Lipton had come in and interrupted the class to announce that she, Marcia Schmitt, had been elected Homecoming Queen. In the same class was the other contender for the title, the captain of the football team's girlfriend.

The girl was certainly beautiful enough. Watching her trying to hide her disappointment when she wasn't chosen didn't make Marcia feel any better.

Marcia hadn't cared if she won or not. But it was a learning experience, watching the play of emotions behind the girl's attempted mask of indifference.

To Marcia, that was the real prize and she filed it away for use in some future performance.

Then, in an effort to cover the awkward silence that followed after Principal Lipton left the classroom, she stood and did a mock acceptance speech as if it were the Academy Awards. She thanked all the 'little people' and her mom and dad and the postman and everyone she could think of, but in the principals voice, imitating his lilting, nasal tone and all.

The whole class laughed, including the girl who lost.

Marcia also analyzed her own behavior, in particular that pivotal moment in her own life.

Why had she fallen for Gavin the way she had? Was he really that fascinating or had it been a combination of her being young, infatuated?

She'd learned a lot from being so wrong about Gavin. For his part, she knew Gavin's whole relationship with her had been a sham.

At the end of the day though, Marcia had been saved from the disastrous fate of becoming an unwed mother at 15 years of age. Her dreams, in fact, any sort of a future for her would have been over.

Dick's cold rejection of her plea for help when she needed it the most was truly a lesson in how shallow and heartless someone could really be. Marcia suspected her mom and Timothy were as glad as she was when Dick moved out. It was only after he left that everyone realized how strained and oppressed the household had been.

Her run in with Gavin had taught her about passion though, and what it was like when a person cast caution aside, lost themselves in the heat of the moment, mistaking it for love. It also taught her understanding and compassion for mom—her confidant, her closest friend—and sympathy for her little brother, who lately seemed terribly, terribly lost.

All that happened two years ago. Since then, the remainder of her time in high school had been spent as an adult acting the part of a teenager. She was fairly sure she succeeded in that role, gossiping with friends and following styles in clothes and boys.

She'd heard that the others had nicknamed her The Ice Queen. Today, standing here alone in the senior patio while all the others gathered in groups laughing and talking was proof of that. They thought of her as remote, an outsider always watching, studying and copying their behavior, then presenting it back to them as caricature in her performance in the school's plays.

Without her knowing it, someone in the school administration, Principal Lipton probably, put her name in as a candidate for a dramatic arts scholarship to the University of Southern California. When the envelope with the university's return address arrived mom read it aloud, then started jumping up and down. "No one in this family has ever gone to college, much less on a scholarship. I am so proud of you."

# Chapter Thirty Two

## Timothy Schmitt

## 1957

When he turned sixteen, Timothy, by mowing lawns and doing odd jobs scraped together enough money to buy a car. It was an old Ford, older than his brother Dick's first car. Millie wasn't happy about this, but since all of Timothy's friends had cars, she couldn't deny him getting one without making it appear he wasn't their equal.

Sure enough, not long after he got it Timothy came home with a bump on his forehead.

"Ma, I flipped my car."

"What do you mean, you 'flipped your car?"

"You know, like that," he said, motioning with his hands. "Come see."

Millie followed him out to the alley. There was his old Ford, looking sad and dejected. The whole top of the car was slightly askew, the windshield was cracked, and there was a big dent on the roof above the driver's side. The hood ornament was gone, and the scratched hood no longer fit.

"Oh no! It looks awful. Were you hurt anywhere else?"

"Nah, just got this big bump on my head."

"Was anyone with you? Did you hit anything?"

"No, Ma, I was alone, and the street was all wet and muddy and the car skidded and hit the curb and flipped. Some people helped me push it back over on its wheels so I could drive it home."

"There's no insurance, Timothy," Millie reminded him. "You won't be able to get it repaired, at least not right away. I simply don't have enough money and you don't either."

Millie later overheard Timothy tell his friends the story of the crash as if it were something to be proud of. The way he told it, he'd been racing a Thunderbird like his brother's or a Corvette, or a hot rod with a souped-up engine. He'd tell them he was winning but he had to swerve to avoid hitting a child, or a dog, or an old lady carrying groceries.

Millie could tell he was beginning to believe his own tall tales. Soon he interpreted the whole mishap as a tribute to his skill as a driver and to the sturdy construction of the car.

"After all," she heard him boast, "At 100 miles an hour I could have been killed if I hadn't known what I was doing, and the car wasn't so good."

Millie finally asked Larson about it, and he told her the real story.

Timothy had been driving only about twenty miles an hour on a residential street near the new high school in North Torrance. The street was being prepared for paving and the surface had been graded smooth by bulldozers. An unexpected rain had delayed paving the surface, and it was very slippery. Timothy lost control of the car. It skidded sideways, hit the curb and flipped over on its top before settling back down on the driver's side.

Timothy got the bump on his head when the old lady whose picket fence he damaged hit him with her umbrella.

# Chapter Thirty Three

## Timothy Schmitt

## 1963

"What's the matter with you, young man? Pull yourself together!" the old doctor demanded angrily.

But Timothy couldn't stop shaking, couldn't pull himself together. All these naked guys, all the noise and confusion, the smells of hundreds, maybe thousands of others his age, all in their underpants, all standing in lines being poked and prodded, all being herded through their physicals for the draft.

Timothy could not help himself. Except for his underpants, he too, was naked and scared to death. Almost every one of these guys were strangers, and many were bigger than he was.

Some were from Torrance, guys he knew but hadn't seen since he dropped out of high school six years ago.

"Why didn't you urinate in the cup like you were told?" the old doctor yelled at him impatiently.

The other guys standing around him in the cavernous old building that housed the army's draftee processing center looked his way. They'd bumped against him in line, their bare skin touching his.

The line he'd stood in for the eye test.

The line he'd stood in for the chest x ray.

The naked boys he'd stood in line with all day in this old building, all undergoing their physicals to go into the Army.

"I...I couldn't, sir. I'm sorry, sir," Timothy answered. He had to pee so bad it hurt. But he could not, he was so nervous.

The doctor pointed toward the big cold bathroom. "You go back in there and you urinate in this cup!" he commanded angrily.

Panicked, holding the little paper cup gingerly as if it were dirty, Timothy searched the faces of the guys around him, guys standing in line nearby. They looked down at the floor, pretending they were unaware of his humiliation. One of them smirked and leaned to say something to the guy in front of him. The guy looked toward Timothy and grinned.

"Go on, now. What are you waiting for?" the doctor said, giving him a shove. "Go on in there and urinate in the cup like I told you to!" He glanced at his watch. "Hurry up!"

In his bare feet and carrying his jeans, tee shirt and shoes, Timothy padded past the line toward the bathroom. Some of the guys looked at him and some looked away, embarrassed.

Back in the bathroom again, the cold tile on his bare feet and the racket the guys were making, kidding, and yelling, made it impossible for him to pee in the cup. Bad as he had to go, he just could not do it. The longer he stayed in that noisy room, with its stained and stinking toilets, its filthy urinals and chipped sinks, the more impossible it was for him to pee. Dozens, hundreds of others came in, peed in their cups, looked curiously at Timothy, and left.

Still he could not do it.

Finally, a soldier in uniform, a guy shorter than Timothy came in.

"What the hell you doin' in here?" he asked. "The doc sent me in here to find out where the hell you went. What the hell's the matter with you?"

"Nothin, sir. I just can't seem to pee."

"Don't give me that shit. Pee in the goddamn cup and get the hell back out here. We've run almost 10,000 jerks through this old building today and you're the only one giving us any shit. You queer or something? You like hanging around in here looking at naked guys?"

Timothy had always hated being around naked people. During his short time in high school, he dreaded showering in gym class. Right now, he was so scared he was shaking. He could feel himself start to tear up, like he was going to cry.

"Come on, ya little shit," the soldier ordered. "Follow me." He led Timothy back into the big room.

The doctor was putting his jacket on to go home.

"This guy won't pee in the cup!" the soldier told him.

It was almost five o'clock. The place was emptying, this old building in downtown Los Angeles that served as a fort for inductees. It had seen an army of young men again this day, and all of them, no matter how bad off, had been accepted for the draft.

117

The doctor looked at Timothy wearily. Did a quick expression of pity, of compassion flitter across his bitter old face? He took the chart, looked at it, and then looked back at Timothy.

Timothy knew he was drafted, knew he faced countless shots, inoculations, and injections. He hated needles. He could not face going in the army. Living in barracks with other guys, other guys being naked around him, him being naked in front of them. He could not do it.

"I'm classifying you as 1Y," the doctor said.

"1Y"? Timothy knew the classification that got you drafted was IA. What was 1Y?

"You will be deferred for now. You will be recalled in twelve months to return here to take your physical again."

Timothy wasn't sure he understood what the doctor said, what this meant. Was he not drafted? All the other guys had been accepted. Why didn't they take him? Was it because he was too nervous to pee? Was that it? Christ, some of the others he saw today were practically decrepit, although no older than he was. The four or five short years since high school had from all appearances taken a heavy toll on some of them.

They all got drafted anyway.

Was there something wrong with him? Something so bad they wouldn't even take him in the army?

He found his way through the old building, back down the stairs and out onto the street.

The sun had gone down.

In the dark everything in this seedy part of Los Angeles looked different, strange. He was disoriented. He should have paid more attention to his surroundings when he got here this morning. He remembered he'd parked in a parking lot two blocks away from the induction center. He worried he'd get lost and be unable to find the lot where he'd left his old Ford.

There were no businesses open. This part of L.A. had been run down for years, given over to the bums and vagrants. There were bums walking along carrying their belongings in garbage bags, bums sleeping in the doorways of old abandoned buildings.

He'd been in near panic all day and now he was exhausted. Exhausted and scared that he might not be able to find his car, that he would end up wandering around in the dark becoming increasingly confused in this strange city.

118

And he had to pee.

After all day of not being able to, now he really had to pee.

Timothy could not hold it any longer. He stopped to pee against a chain link fence surrounding a vacant lot.

His bladder just let loose. It felt like a flood, pouring out in a gushing stream he would not have been able to stop even if he wanted to.

Not even when headlights approached, illuminated his out-of-control urination.

Timothy looked over his shoulder. The headlights belonged to a Los Angeles Police Department patrol car.

"Hey you!" someone yelled. The car's door opened. "What the hell do you think you're doing, you fuckin bum?"

But Timothy could not stop the stream.

Approaching, the cop screamed. "Pay attention when I'm talking to you!"

Timothy turned. It was a young guy, a guy about his own age, dressed in the new blue uniform of the Los Angeles Police Department.

But still Timothy kept peeing. He peed all over the young cop's pants and shoes, all over the sidewalk, all over himself.

"Goddamnit!" screamed the cop. "Let's see how you like this." He hit Timothy on the back of the neck with his club, knocking him to his knees on the sidewalk wet with pee.

"Get in the back of the car," ordered the cop, grabbing Timothy by the collar and dragging him toward the curb.

Dazed, Timothy tried to get to his feet. The young cop clubbed him again.

It was a short ride from Broadway to the Central Division Station where Timothy Schmitt was booked for public indecency and vagrancy.

In the glare of the police station's bare ceiling lights, it all seemed like a nightmare happening to someone else.

He hadn't eaten all day. He was dizzy, disoriented.

They emptied his pockets and pushed a paper forward for him to sign.

119

The flash of a camera nearly blinded him.

The officer unlocked the door to the drunk tank and pushed Timothy inside. The cell was filled with the night's derelicts, all looking dark, vicious and threatening.

Timothy Schmitt spent the whole night on his feet standing at the cell door. He never loosened his grip on the bars. If he did doze off, he was abruptly awakened when his head drooped and banged on the door's cold steel bars.

At six a.m., an officer clanked his billy club along the bars of the cell door. "All right, alla ya bums," He snarled. "Get outa here and don't let me see ya in here again tonight."

Timothy's stiff fingers felt glued to the bars. He painfully pried them loose, went to the counter to collect his wallet and other belongings and then stumbled along with all the drunks and derelicts toward the door and out into the morning. He blinked in the bright sunlight and watched the others, all wandering off in different directions.

He wondered where he was, where his car was. Was it miles from here?

It was still so early that there was no traffic, and no businesses were open. He shook his head to wake himself.

Which way should he walk? The last place he remembered was the old ten-story building where draftees were processed.

What was the address? 1010 North Broadway?

Where was that?

Where was he now?

Would he be able to find his way back to the parking lot?

He had to move on. He followed the largest group of men, now about a block ahead of him. Soon Timothy began to recognize a few of the cross streets. He hoped he was headed in the right direction.

He hadn't eaten anything since the day before yesterday and he was starving. But now he worried that he might not have enough money to pay for parking his car.

He checked his pockets.

He only had two crumpled dollar bills.

# Chapter Thirty Four

## Millie Schmitt

## 1964

It was dark by the time Millie got home from the store.

She juggled one bag of groceries atop the other, almost spilling the canned goods and a carton of eggs as she struggled to find the key in her purse and unlock the door.

Once inside, the little trailer seemed emptier than ever. A wave of loneliness and depression swept over her. She crossed through the dark living area to the kitchenette and sat the two bags of groceries on the counter. Then she returned to the door and turned on the little cut-glass lamp.

She hoped that some light would chase away the chill.

But the glow from the lamp was no match for the trailer's shadows and what light it did cast failed to lift her mood.

She turned up the thermostat and walked back to the kitchenette to put the groceries away, then paused and gazed at the two bags on the counter.

Millie had run into Marge Moore at Jim Dandy Supermarket. Marge had bragged about her son Jerry, a boyhood friend and classmate of Timothy's.

Jerry had a good job at the lumberyard and was making a man's wages.

Millie's mood sank even further at the thought of how unlikely it was that Timothy would ever get a job.

Trying to shake her depression she busied herself putting the groceries away.

Meat and cheese for her and Tom Larson.

Canned soup and vegetables.

For dinner tonight she would prepare a stew. She would make more than enough for her and Tom in case Timothy came by.

Tom joined her for supper every night. Afterwards they sat quietly on the couch watching television. They had settled into a comfortable routine that didn't require either of them to entertain the other.

She turned on two burners to heat a skillet and to boil water, then began cutting up the meat and potatoes.

Her thoughts drifted to the conversations she and Tom had about the kids.

Certainly, talking about Marcia and her career was always fun and interesting.

But Millie had begun to feel it necessary to explain to Tom what Timothy was up to, why he had no job.

The water had come to a boil. She dropped the potatoes in and put the meat in the skillet.

Within six months of her moving into the trailer park the owners had sent around a mimeographed notice announcing that they were converting the park to a seniors-only facility. Thereafter the minimum age for any resident was going to be fifty. Millie couldn't help but wonder if Timothy, coming home roaring drunk at 1 a.m. in his beat-up old Ford had anything to do with this change in policy. However, there was no one else in the place anywhere near Timothy's age so he didn't like it here anyway.

Still, Timothy had never formally moved out.

No, at first it was only an occasional sleep-over, spending the night at his friends' place. But that turned into two days at a time, then three, and now it was to the point where he truly no longer did live with her.

He only dropped by to borrow money.

She knew he smoked cigarettes and drank.

She was certain it was smoking that took his father. She tried not to think about that too much, hoping Timothy was just going through a stage, showing off to be one of the gang. She hoped that he would stop on his own.

Timothy was adrift and she could not see where this would end, but what could she do? She was coming to the conclusion that continuing to loan him money, more like giving it to him, was not the answer.

Doing that was only allowing him to continue coasting along.

A car came up the drive, its headlights casting shadows that moved quickly along the walls in the living room.

It was too early to be Tom.

122

Maybe it was Timothy, coming by to see her, to tell her he had a job and had been at work all day.

Maybe he would talk to her, ask her how she was, how she was doing, instead of just asking for money.

Maybe he would stay and have dinner with her and Tom.

But the car passed on by, its driver going to see someone else in the trailer park.

Worrying about Timothy did nothing to lift Millie's mood and her sense of foreboding.

She pressed her fingers to her temples and shifted her thoughts to Marcia.

Thinking about Marcia always cheered her. She glanced at her reflection in the dark glass of the window above the sink.

At first Marcia's full scholarship had allowed her to live in a dorm near the campus. Leaving home didn't seem to bother her nearly as much as it did Millie.

Marcia had quickly become engrossed in college life and pursuing her dream of a career in the theater. In a way it kind of hurt Millie that her daughter, with whom she had always been so close, was so easily able to spread her wings and take off on her own.

She turned back to the stove to stir the meat in the skillet.

She looked toward the living area and some of the furniture she had brought with her from the house on Beach Street. The couch and that overstuffed chair with the dark spot on the back from the boys' hair pomade, the little end table and on it the little cut-glass lamp.

These things helped to make the trailer a home.

Marcia had never lived with her here. Millie had sold the house and moved here after Marcia moved to the dorm.

It crossed her mind that since she'd moved away from her old home and her children were gone, she would have been almost completely cut off from her friends in her old neighborhood, her old life, if it weren't for Tom Larson.

She added milk and flour to the meat in the skillet. She covered the simmering stew, wiped the flour from her hands on her apron and turned again to the living room.

In its special place on top of the television set was an old black and white photograph of Timothy. He stood on the porch of the house on Beach Street wearing a western gun belt and cowboy hat. He must have been around ten years old when that picture was taken. He looked gleefully tough, one hand on his hip, a little smile playing on his freckled face.

Hanging on the wall above was a gift from the studio, a portrait of Marcia in full makeup and costume for her starring role in *Eleanor of Aquitaine.*

Millie did not care that the portrait was big, almost life-size and way too big for the trailer's little living room.

How quickly life had changed for Marcia. It seemed like only a short time ago, no time at all after she enrolled in college that a talent scout attending the school's production of *Cat on a Hot Tin Roof* took notice of Marcia's performance.

He met Marcia backstage after the play. He told her he was so impressed with her talent that he would put her in touch with an agent, guide her through the process of joining Screen Actors Guild and help her get work.

At first Marcia appeared in television commercials, followed quickly by roles in regular programs.

In the early days of her career, when one of her commercials or parts in a TV program was scheduled to air, Millie, Marcia, and Tom Larson made an occasion of it. Larson would pick Marcia up at her dorm and bring her down to Millie's where they would fix popcorn. The three of them would sometimes sit talking and laughing till two in the morning waiting for one of her commercials.

It seemed like only weeks, certainly no more than a few months before she began to get dramatic parts and her work was shown in prime time.

Then the big break came.

Millie had been vacuuming and almost didn't hear the knock on the door that day. She only happened to glance up. Standing on the porch was a wizened little man in an expensive suit and wearing a fedora.

She couldn't remember the last time she had seen a man with a fedora; they had gone out of style so long ago.

124

He was cool as a cucumber and very gentlemanly, sweeping his hat off and introducing himself.

"I'm Tevye Greenberg, Marcia Schmitt's agent. You can call me Turnip Green. That's my name in the business," he said, reaching in his coat for his business card. "I'm trying to locate Marcia. The girls in her dorm thought she might be here."

"I'm sorry" Millie said from the doorway, "but she's not here right now."

He pursed his lips. "I have important news for her. I tried to locate her at the school. I have to get back to L.A. Please try to track her down and ask her to call me."

He got his business card from the inside pocket of his suit coat and handed it to Millie. "She's being considered for a leading role in a feature-length action-adventure film," he explained. He tugged at his cuffs and puffed out his chest. "She's a shoo-in for the part."

"I'll be sure to tell her."

"I don't mean to be pushy, madam, but this is a big opportunity. She's got to show up in person tomorrow afternoon."

"Okay, okay. I'll make sure she gets the message."

In less than a year, Marcia was caught up in a success and fame none of them could have imagined.

Marcia and Millie had to make some big decisions. Marcia was now so busy she could no longer attend USC. She moved out of the dorm and into a nice apartment at the Chateau Marmont in Hollywood.

Tom Larson took Millie to see the place, and both thought it was great.

But after only a few months Marcia told Millie the Chateau Marmont was too busy, too full of other ambitious young girls. Frankly, she could easily afford something much nicer. She said she wanted to try living in San Francisco, in a hotel. She said that would give her just enough distance to avoid falling in with the Hollywood crowd, but close enough to get back for work and to see Millie.

Millie had a little trouble understanding this reasoning and could not comprehend the amount of money Marcia was making, but Tom pointed out that her daughter wasn't letting success go to her head.

Old-fashioned elegance, Tom called it.

Then there was Dick.

Dick, her firstborn.

After his abrupt departure, she never heard from him again, not even once.

She got his address when a little man in a cheap rumpled suit came around to interview her and some of the neighbors as part of the process for Dick to get a government job, a job with Customs and Immigration.

She wrote Dick every two weeks. This became a ritual for her, like keeping a diary.

But he never wrote back.

Probably he was just too busy to respond. Anyway, she didn't miss him very much. She just wondered about him.

By the time she heard Tom walk up the steps to the door, Millie's mood had lifted.

She wasn't worried about Marcia, or even Dick.

Timothy was her only concern.

# Chapter Thirty Five

## Marcia Schmitt

## 1965

The change in the pitch of the engines woke Marcia as American Airlines Flight 116, arriving from Argentina by way Mexico City began its descent into San Francisco International Airport.

She never had trouble sleeping on a plane. She never had trouble sleeping in any noisy environment and had always attributed that ability to growing up near the railroad tracks during the war. Just about everyone in her old neighborhood had adapted to the noise of the troop and supply trains.

They were only disturbed if there was a change or interruption in those sounds.

Since Marcia was returning from South America, she'd have to clear Customs.

Customs and Immigration at San Francisco International had a special section for celebrities. Marcia had been through this many times. Although she felt a little guilty about the special treatment, there was no denying it really did make life a lot easier.

As soon as she deplaned a smiling steward picked up her bag and escorted her into the building and to the corridor leading to Customs and Immigration.

The special section was a comfortable room painted an unfortunate institutional green. On the wall to the right, a one-way glass looked into the big hangar that housed the main floor.

The young inspector began flipping through her passport and opening her bags. Marcia turned to the glass.

Outside was a chaos of tired, disheveled passengers, struggling their way through the process.

Across the big space, on the far side of the hangar an older man in a uniform stood watching the milling arrivals and the inspectors bent over the tables.

She guessed he must be a supervisor.

The man was glaring across the crowded room at one table in particular, a table strewn with clothing. A tiny Asian woman holding a crying baby stood on one side of the table. Facing the woman, his back to Marcia, was a clearly unsympathetic customs inspector.

It was distressing to see the woman so obviously very tired and on the verge of tears. Marcia wished she could help, maybe hold the baby or help the woman put her clothes back in her luggage.

But something other than her being an inveterate people-watcher drew Marcia to this little drama.

The inspector.

The scene was fifty or sixty feet away and the inspector had his back to her, but his manner gave her a chill.

She looked back at the gentleman she took to be the supervisor. Even from this distance she could see that he was angry and probably about to intercede.

Marcia's attention returned to the inspector and the Asian woman.

The back of the inspector's neck seemed to tense, as if he sensed he was being watched, He looked furtively toward the entrance to the immigration section.

Then he looked in the direction of the supervisor.

And as he turned Marcia saw his profile.

The customs inspector was her goddamn brother Dick.

# Chapter Thirty Six

## Timothy Schmitt

## August 16, 1965

Shielding his eyes from the glare of the sun, Timothy rubbed his forehead with his thumb and forefinger. He hoped this would ease the dull headache before it got worse.

"Timothy Schmitt, you be careful and look both ways before you cross the street," his mother's voice warned him. Her voice seemed to come from somewhere behind him. But when he turned to look, there was no one there.

He was alone on the empty sidewalk, just at the corner of Cabrillo and the street that bordered Torrance Park.

Heeding her warning he paused and looked up the street to check for traffic before stepping off the curb.

Almost at the other end of the block, sitting in the shade of the tall eucalyptus trees that bordered the park was a black and white police car.

"They saw me looking at them," he thought. 'They'll think I'm nervous, that I have something to hide. They're going to come after me. They'll ask me what I'm up to, where I'm going, where I've been."

When the squad car didn't move, he started across the intersection.

He quickly put it out of his mind and returned his attention to avoiding the cracks on the dusty sidewalk.

Step on a crack.

Break your mother's back.

He'd been muttering this hateful little verse over and over, monotonously in a mindless cadence with his footsteps ever since he'd begun this long walk to his mothers to borrow money.

All he needed was a lousy five dollars.

Step on a crack.

Break your mother's back.

He hated this rhyme. When he became conscious of what it was about, that if he stepped on a crack in the sidewalk his mother would come to harm it made him feel bad.

Step on a crack.

Break your mother's back.

The distance between the cracks in the sidewalk didn't match his stride. After a quick nervous look to see that no one was watching, he did a little hop to be certain his next step would land him in the very middle of the next concrete square.

Without thinking, he reached for his shirt pocket. Then he remembered he was out of cigarettes.

Block after block, mile after mile, he walked in the dusty dry heat, a lone figure trudging along the empty sidewalk beside the roaring traffic.

Breathing the hot air was like inhaling air coming from the open door of an oven.

His dirty clothes felt gritty and tight and because he was wearing everything he owned he was really sweating. His t-shirt's soiled collar had already rubbed his neck raw. His feet, trapped in sweat-damp socks, felt like they were cooking in his shoes.

But he had to keep walking. He had no money, not a dime. If he could just get his hands on five dollars, he was convinced it would be enough for a fresh start, enough to turn his life around.

Step on a crack.

Break your mother's back.

He'd already bummed all he could from his friends, and there were no more odd jobs to do for a few bucks to keep him going.

He was desperate to get a real grownup job somehow. The only hope was his mother.

"I gave her money a couple of weeks ago. She can loan me at least five dollars," he reasoned. "Hell, I don't even have enough gas to drive my car. Nobody could expect me to go looking for a job on foot," he muttered self-righteously.

He coughed and stopped to spit, catch his breath, and wipe the sweat off his forehead with the dirty sleeve of his worn leather jacket. The three- or four-mile drive to the trailer park where his mother lived never seemed far, but on foot the trip was endless.

A hole in his shoe had rubbed a blister on his heel. Using a bus stop sign to steady himself he paused and tried to adjust it, so the sore touched a different part of the worn soles. The sun beating on the metal sign had made it so hot it burned his hand. He jerked away and looked around sheepishly to see if anyone noticed.

A lull in the passing traffic left a sudden silence, the only movement a piece of newspaper fluttering along in the gutter.

The moment passed and the flow of traffic returned.

Once again cars and trucks were rushing past, all stirring up dust and making a reality of the headache that until now had only been hinted at.

He tried massaging his temples again hoping if he pressed hard enough the throbbing would ease.

There was no shade anywhere.

Step on a crack.

Break your mother's back.

Carefully he picked his way over the railroad tracks that crossed the road. He paused for a moment and looked down at the rails, thinking they were supposed to remind him of something. He could not quite think what it was, so he shook his head and kept going.

His last job, if it could be called a job, was a one-night stint months ago, tending bar at his friend Rueben's place.

Former friend, he should say.

The Owen twins, John and Joe, and all his other pals had been in the bar laughing and drinking that night. He dimly remembered one of the guys saying something like "Timothy, why don't you have a drink? We'll buy."

The next thing Timothy remembered was waking up face down on the filthy floor behind the bar, Rueben standing over him screaming and kicking him. Timothy's pals were gone. They had helped themselves to all the booze they wanted, trashed the bar and left the door wide open.

For the last several days he had been staying in Howard's little apartment above the laundry. As Timothy left this morning, he drank the last beer from Howard's refrigerator.

Now it was wearing off, leaving a bitter, acrid taste in his mouth.

131

He knew when Howard got home from work this afternoon there'd be a row and that would be the end of crashing there. That's why he'd put on his t-shirt, a sweater and his leather jacket, all the clothes he owned. He was pretty sure that when Howard saw the last of the beer was gone, he'd throw Timothy and all his stuff out in the street.

Now he was just plain frying, wearing all these clothes in this heat.

If he could have just one more cold beer, he knew his throat would no longer feel raw and dry, his headache would go away, and he'd feel all better.

It was still a mile or more to his mother's when he finally turned onto Western Avenue.

Now he was walking directly into the glare of the afternoon sun. Hitting him full in the face, it seemed to fill the whole sky. He was dizzy with the heat and his hangover, almost faint.

He stumbled on an uneven place on the sidewalk and again almost fell.

He just knew they're looking at him, the people driving past, talking about him and laughing.

A driver in a passing car caught his eye and he imagined the driver thinking, "Look at that fool, walking in this heat. Almost fell on his face. Why it's Timothy Schmitt. Bet he's drunk. Looks like his fly's unzipped, too."

Furtively Timothy checked his zipper.

At last, ahead in the shimmering heat, was the entrance to the trailer park.

Mom moved here several years ago after dad died, saying it was cheap. She could live on the money from the sale of the family's home, the house on Beach Street where Timothy, his big brother Dick, and his sister Marcia had grown up.

His big brother Dick.

If only his big brother Dick had been nicer, taken him under his wing and helped him along. Maybe then things would have turned out differently.

But Dick really was a dick.

All his life Timothy had idolized his big brother. He'd desperately wanted Dick to like him, be nice to him. But Dick had always been mean and nasty to Timothy, made him feel like he was stupid and ugly.

Dick was tall and reasonably good looking.

132

Timothy thought that with his own brownish hair and average height he could only be considered plain at best. He didn't like looking in the mirror. He didn't like what he saw. He had freckles that someone had told him he could get rid of by rubbing his face with lemon slices.

That didn't work.

A childhood mishap lighting a gas stove had burnt off his eyebrows.

They never really grew back.

He really missed his father. Dad had been a great guy, always laughing and kidding around, and so tall Timothy had to look way up high to see his face. When Timothy was a little boy, dad always found time for him and his friends. Every day when dad came walking up the street after work Timothy and all the kids in the neighborhood would be waiting for him. They'd all run to him yelling and laughing. Dad would stop right there on the sidewalk in front of the house, pick them all up one by one and swing them around high in the air, greeting them all by their names, as if each of them was his special friend.

But just when Timothy needed him the most, his dad faded, no longer laughed and kidded, no longer took time for Timothy and his friends.

Dad died, Mom sold the little house, their home, and moved away from all of Timothy's friends and the familiar neighborhood.

A trailer, for cripes sake! If Mom hadn't sold the house, he could live with her, find a good job and take care of them both. Maybe then he could find a girl and get married and the three of them could live in the little house in the old neighborhood where he grew up.

A girl.

In Rueben's that night, before he got drunk and passed out his friends had been bragging about sex. Timothy had kidded and laughed along with them. But one of his darkest secrets was that at twenty-two years of age Timothy was still a virgin.

Ever since their teens, all his pals had bragged about their experiences with girls, but somehow Timothy missed out. How had they learned about girls and what to do?

Finally, he reached the trailer park's entrance. The rows of trailers and the concrete block wall that surrounded the park muted the sound of the traffic passing on Western Avenue. The wall also blocked any breeze, so it was even hotter than it was out on the street.

From somewhere he could hear the sound of a television set turned up too loud.

At least he was off the busy street with all the traffic and no longer where all kinds of people driving by were looking at him.

He walked to his mother's trailer, climbed the four wooden steps to the little porch and banged on the screen door.

"Ma? Ma, are you in there?" Sometimes mom would go over to a neighbor's trailer for coffee and to talk. He could never be sure that she would be home.

"Yes, Timothy," he heard her say from the dark interior, "I'm here."

"How are you, Mom?" He said trying to smile as he entered.

The bang of the screen door slamming behind him was like a spike being driven through his aching head.

"Trying to keep from melting."

The shades were drawn to keep out the glare of the sun. Although she'd left the trailer's front and back doors open to try to capture a little breeze, the interior was airless, stuffy.

His eyes adjusted to the trailer's dark interior.

His mom was sitting slumped on the sofa, her kimono sticking to her body, little beads of sweat on her forehead. She was watching "Queen for a Day" with "your host Jack Bailey," on television. The camera was panning the applauding audience. Timothy thought his mom, a little on the heavy side, with her worn face and sad eyes looked like many of the women on the television screen.

Without thinking he blurted; "I need five dollars."

She continued to stare at the television. He wasn't sure she heard him, so he started to repeat that he needed five dollars.

She turned, looked up at him and said quietly, "Timothy, I'm sorry but I can't let you have five dollars. The mailman won't be bringing me my Social Security check till next Thursday."

"What about the money I gave you two weeks ago?" he asked. He was taken aback by her refusal. He had given her ten dollars out of the forty dollars he had made mowing lawns and doing odd jobs in the old neighborhood.

She gazed steadily into his eyes until he almost looked away embarrassed.

Finally, she said, "I'm holding on to that money…just in case."

He thought he detected a note of exasperation in her voice.

"Just in case? Just in case of what? I need money now! I need to get gas for my car so I can get me a job."

"You? Get a job?"

The sarcasm in her tone came as a complete surprise. She'd always been there for him, always encouraging him no matter what the problem.

"You? Get a job?" she said again, her voice rising. "How many times have you come to me asking for money for gas so you could go look for a job? What is the matter with you? You're twenty-two years old and you don't have a job. In fact, you have never had a real job. All of your friends are grown and you're still acting like some kid, borrowing money from your mother."

She rubbed her eyes and ran her hand through her white hair. Timothy could see the loose skin hanging from under her arm and for the first time he realized she was getting old.

He tried to shake off the fear that crawled up his spine. "It's my money to begin with," he said. "I gave you $10 two weeks ago!"

"May I remind you of the many times you borrowed a dollar here and five dollars there and never once paid me back?" she said, struggling to her feet. "I can't stand the smell of you," she snapped as she approached him. "You reek of beer and cigarettes. And your sweat! When was the last time you showered or bathed? You don't even take care of yourself."

She was coming toward him, almost shouting now. To him, her words were like blows. He backed away from her in confusion and as he did he tripped over a footstool and lost his balance.

A little cut-glass lamp stood on the small table next to the door.

He grabbed at it as if to steady himself. The lampshade came off in his hand.

The lamp fell on the floor and broke.

She froze when she saw the broken lamp.

Then her face contorted, and she began to cry.

Timothy was so sorry he did not know what to say or do. It was just a poor cheap old lamp, but he knew that before they were married his father had won the little lamp for his mom at a concession stand at the Long Beach Pike. His dad had won it by throwing baseballs at milk bottles. How many times had Timothy watched his mom look at that little lamp, touch it gently and tell the story of that night many, many years before, back when she and his dad were just dating, back before the war? How many times had she told him of that night at the Pike, the bare light bulbs of the midway shining bright against the chilly black sky, the two of them, her and his father, young and in love.

That lamp had been a part of the family for as long as he could remember. It had its special place on the table next to her bed when they all lived in the house. When she moved to this trailer, she put it where she would see it every day.

"You're drunk, aren't you?" she said more in accusation than a question. "You came over here drunk, stinking of booze and cigarettes, trying to borrow money from your poor widowed mother."

Trying desperately to recover Timothy blurted. "I need money!"

But in the closeness of the trailer the words came out much louder than he meant them to. Startled by the ferocity of his tone his mom stepped back.

Off balance she sat down hard on the couch.

He was almost blinded by his pounding headache now. "I am going to get that five dollars and I am going to get a job! Now where the hell is the money?"

"If you don't leave, I'm calling the police!" she said reaching for the phone on the table next to the couch.

In the stuffy, dark trailer, the heat, his headache, and his desperation made him think that the money might be in the drawer of the table she was reaching for, the end table next to the couch.

He walked over and yanked the drawer open.

Inside the drawer, on top of some tattered old copies of *TV Guide* was a .38-caliber revolver. He picked up the gun, thinking maybe she had stuck the money between the pages of one of the magazines underneath it.

Behind him he heard a neighbor knock on the screen door and ask in a trembling voice, "You all right in there, Millie? Do you need anything?"

Timothy turned and walked to the door. Through the screen he could see the look on the neighbor woman's face. Eyes wide, the woman put her hand to her mouth, took a step back on the porch and quickly scrambled down the steps.

Behind him he heard his mother talking to someone on the telephone. It sounded like she was giving someone directions. "Yes, he's here now and he has a gun."

She held the phone away from her and said, "There. I've called the police and they're on their way, so you better leave now."

"You must be kidding. It's me, Ma. I just want to borrow five bucks. To get gas for the car. To look for a job."

"Timothy, please leave," she said softly.

He stood motionless in the dark trailer, not knowing what to do. He was going to come away empty handed.

No money.

His long walk in the hot sun was for nothing.

And he faced a long, long walk back.

Back to where?

He had nowhere to go, no one he could turn to.

What was he going to do?

"Ma," he begged. "Ma, if you could just let me have some money, I could get some gas for my car and look for work. Get myself a job. Then I could pay you back."

She looked up at him from the couch. The look on her face hurt him more than anything else.

"Please go."

In a daze Timothy stumbled out the door, his head aching so bad he wasn't even conscious of the weight of the gun he still held in his hand. Leaving the trailer's dim interior and stepping out on the porch the glare of the sun blinded him and his foot caught on the threshold.

He pitched forward and grabbed at the railing for support.

The shrill sound of sirens coming down Western Avenue got louder and louder.

The sound reverberated in his throbbing head.

For God's sake now what? The sirens were coming right into the trailer park. They were police cars, and they were skidding to a stop two trailers up the road.

Why were they here?

Why were the cops in such a hurry to get out of their cars?

Jesus Christ, what was going on? Why are they taking cover?

He raised his left hand to shield his eyes so he could try to see what was happening.

Someone shouted, "Drop the gun!"

Who the hell were they yelling at?

It was only then that he remembered the weight in his hand hanging at his side.

He looked down, realized what it was, what he was holding.

The gun.

Just like cops and robbers. Just like we played back on Beach Street, me and the guys.

Just like cops and robbers," he thought wistfully.

He started to raise it, but the gun was heavier than the toy guns he played with as a kid.

And in the moment it took Timothy Schmitt to try to lift the heavy gun, a moment longer than lifting a toy gun would have taken, there was a very loud noise, louder than the bang-bang he and his friends used to make playing cops and robbers.

At the same time there was a thud, a thud like the sound a butcher's wooden mallet makes hitting meat, a thud he both heard and felt. The thud came from his chest. He felt himself lifted, thrown backward.

He landed on his ass on the wooden steps of his mother's trailer.

He tried to get up, but something seemed to be holding him down, a weight or something.

Whatever it was, it would not let him up.

Oh God, this is embarrassing. I can't let everyone see me like this.

All the shouting, the noise, too loud.

What the hell is going on?

What are they saying?

Are they talking to me?

138

The glare of the sun seemed to be making everything around him hazy. He just could not catch his breath. He tried to pull his legs up under him, but for some reason he couldn't get them to work. They felt heavy, leaden. His whole body—arms, legs, even his head—everything felt heavy. If he could just get up on his feet, take a deep breath and look around, maybe he could clear his head and see what was going on.

With his left arm he tried to reach for the handrail to help himself up.

But his arm was heavy, so heavy. He swiped at the air but there was nothing to grab on to. He gave up trying and sank down on the steps. He started to wipe the sweat from his eyes, but his right hand was so heavy he couldn't lift it at all.

He squinted, tried to focus.

His right hand rested on the cracked old wooden porch.

He was still holding his mother's gun.

Timothy tried to look around, to figure out what was happening. He wanted to get up, get going wherever he was going.

But he was tired. It was so much easier to just give in, to relax and just lay here. Not even the heat of the blazing sun above or sharp edges of the steps digging into his back seemed to bother him anymore.

With one last effort he tried to lift his head. Something—the heat or the glare or the noise—had drained all his energy.

Timothy let out a long breath, making a deep wheezing sound he had never heard himself make before.

Then he gave up. The back of his head hit the porch. Looking up, his eyes focused on the unpainted underside of the porch's weathered wooden railing.

Step on a crack

Break your mothers back.

# Chapter Thirty Seven

## Jim Miller

## August 16, 1965

Somehow, I got the car door open, but I still could not make out what the hell was going on. What was I supposed to do? Sergeant Larson had opened his door and practically fallen out of the car on his knees.

He was drawing his gun.

Oh my God! What the hell is this?

I was out of the car and into the intense heat.

Sergeant Larson hissed at me through clenched teeth, "Get down! Get Down!"

I crouched behind the open door, peering between it and the front fender. It was hot, so hot I could feel the heat from the trailer park's asphalt drive through the soles of my shoes. The sun beating on my dark blue uniform was cooking me.

After the wild ride my heart was beating like crazy. I had no idea what the hell was going on or what I was supposed to be doing.

Should I draw my gun or something?

My hat.

I'd left my hat on the seat in the car.

Larson had his hat on

When did Sarge put his hat on?

We had both taken our hats off when we were sitting at the park.

The LAPD guys had their hats on.

I was the only one who wasn't wearing a hat.

Should I take my eyes off the scene to get my hat out of the car?

What was I supposed to be doing?

Should I take my gun out of the holster?

If I drew my gun, what was I supposed to do with it?

The officer in the lead LAPD car was yelling at some guy coming down the steps of a trailer up ahead.

The guy looked familiar. Wasn't it the same guy I saw earlier, the guy crossing the street near the park?

The guy had a gun in his right hand.

For Christ's sake the guy was Timothy, Timothy Schmitt.

I knew Timothy.

I knew him from grade school, from high school, from the years growing up in this small town where everybody knew everyone else. I knew Timothy was a quiet, harmless, not very bright guy who never caused any trouble.

For God's sake what the hell was Timothy doing?

Why was he here?

What the hell was he doing with a gun?

What was the matter with him?

He seemed dazed or something.

I heard a "pop."

It seemed to come from a long way off.

Timothy fell backward onto the porch steps, looked down at his chest, and then reached for the porch railing to try to lift himself.

"Timothy!" I screamed, but only in my mind.

This was all happening in slow motion. A slow-motion nightmare in the hot, bright sunshine.

The sounds of the officer yelling seemed far away and indistinct.

I watched the officers cautiously approach the porch and Timothy.

I watched Timothy try to get up.

I watched Timothy stop trying.

I reached inside the car for my hat, got to my feet and grabbed the car door to steady myself. The car's metal was hot, so hot it burned my hand.

141

# Chapter Thirty Eight

## Tom Larson

## August 16, 1965

Larson was on his feet and running as fast as he could past the parked police cars toward the trailer. Christ, why couldn't he have got here sooner? Why couldn't he have been the first one on the scene? This would never have happened. He could have stopped it.

He reached the railing. Using it for leverage, he vaulted up onto the porch above Timothy's body. Out of the corner of his eye he saw an LAPD officer, a shotgun in his hand. The officer cautiously approached the trailer's steps and nudged the body with his foot.

Jostled, Timothy slid down a step, startling the officers.

They jumped back, their guns ready.

"God damn it, don't shoot him again," Larson hissed. The screen door was torn and hanging at an angle.

He pushed it aside and entered the trailer.

"Millie! Millie, are you all right?"

She stood in the middle of the living room next to the counter separating it from the little kitchenette. A broken lamp and crumpled lampshade lay on the floor near the door. From her expression, Larson wasn't sure she knew what had happened. He reached out to touch her shoulder, turn her to face him, and draw her close.

"I called the police on my own son," she said softly.

"What happened?" he asked.

"He came here asking for money. He seemed a little crazy. He got that old gun out of the drawer. I was afraid he was going to hurt himself or shoot somebody. I only called the police to scare him, to make him go away. Is he all right?"

Larson was afraid for a moment that she was refusing to recognize what had just taken place outside. But then he realized she'd been inside the dark trailer the whole time.

"Timothy's dead," Larson said softly.

One of the LAPD officers was at the door and asked, "Is everything all right in here?"

142

"Yes," Larson replied. "I'll take care of things in here. I know these people."

"We'll have to talk to everyone in order to make out our report," the officer said.

"I know, I know. Please just give us a few minutes." He led Millie back to the couch and sat down next to her, holding her hand, not saying anything.

From outside, he could hear the police car radios and murmur of conversations.

Finally, Millie said, "I'll be all right, Tom. I have to be all right."

"Can I get one of the neighbors to come and be with you?"

"I'll do it. I'll get Bernice or someone. You go and do what you have to do and come back when you can."

Larson looked up at the portrait hanging above the television set. Millie's daughter in costume and make up for her part in some movie about knights and castles.

"Can I call Marcia for you?"

"No. I'll do it."

He got to his feet, turned, and looked down at her. "All right. I'll be back as soon as I can get everything…" Larson paused.

While he'd witnessed his share of tragedies, he rarely had to deal with the aftermath. But this time, instead of just riding off into the sunset and leaving the debris for others to struggle with, he was going to have to see it all the way through.

For Millie's sake.

For ten years now, ever since her husband died, he'd looked after Millie and her daughter Marcia. They'd become his family, his responsibility.

They needed him.

Larson stepped out on the porch. The police officers and the neighbors who'd gathered to see what was happening all looked up at him expectantly. It was one of those moments when everything went eerily quiet.

Even the police car radios paused in their chattering.

He stood on the porch, scanning the silent scene spread out below, framed by the trailer next door to the left and the ones parked across the lane.

The parked police cars, their engines idling in the hot sun, the red lights flashing on their roofs pulsed with the tragedy. The three police officers hovering over Timothy's body on the steps paused and looked up at him.

They blocked Larson's view, but for just a moment he got a glimpse of Timothy's upturned face, eyes open and staring.

For the first time since Larson had known him, Timothy seemed at peace.

Another police car pulled up and the moment passed. The eight or ten neighbors from other trailers in the park went back to trading their versions of what they thought happened, the officers returned to the task of quietly taking notes.

Larson looked down the drive toward their squad car.

His partner, Jim Miller was sitting on the sill of the open door. He had his hat in his lap and it looked like he'd thrown up in it.

Still standing at the top of the stairs above Timothy's body, Larson asked if anyone had called the coroner. One of the officers said he had, and then he went back to going through Timothy's pockets looking for identification.

"I know the…I know him," Larson said, somehow not wanting to call Timothy the *victim* or the *deceased*. "I can help you with your investigation." Maybe he could somehow minimize the ordeal for Millie.

"That could be very helpful," said one of the other officers. "Let's start with names and what happened inside."

Eventually the coroner arrived and took Timothy away. It was late afternoon by the time Larson and Jim left the scene and checked in at their station to go off duty.

For once Larson said he would fill out all the forms and reports, a chore he usually delegated to his junior officer. He wanted to try to put this all in the best possible light, if there was such a thing.

Maybe he could minimize any further interviews of Millie.

When he finally left the station, he stopped to pick up some take-out.

It was after six o'clock when he finally got back to Millie's place.

As he came in the door she got to her feet. Even in the trailer's dark interior he could see she was trembling. He set the food down on the side table where the cut-glass lamp used to be. Without a word he went to her and held her.

When she'd calmed a bit, he said, "Come on now, let's sit down and get some food in you."

"I don't feel much like eating anything," she said, sitting down at the kitchen table.

The overhead light illuminated her white hair. Larson was struck by how gentle, yet resilient she looked sitting there with her folded hands resting on the tabletop in front of her.

He went to the little table by the door to get the bag of takeout, brought it back and sat down across from her.

"I got us some Chinese, just what you like. Have some of the soup while it's hot."

Like castaways, they sat silently at the table in the dark trailer, clinging to one another on the little island of light from the overhead lamp.

Larson kept quiet, waiting to see what she was going to say or do.

The soup, still hot in the cardboard container seemed to be just what Millie needed. She was able to finish it, although she didn't have an appetite for the rest of the meal.

Finally, she began softly, so quietly he could barely hear.

"From the time he was 12, 13 years old I had a bad feeling when it came to Timothy. I think there was a kind of inevitability about all this, as if sooner or later something terrible had to happen."

She stared straight ahead, past Larson at some distant point in the dark recesses of the trailer.

"When Timothy was just a little boy, six, seven, eight years old, back when we lived in the house on Beach Street, he was all right. Just like any of the other boys in the neighborhood. Maybe even a little more popular. A bright, happy boy with lots of friends. Everybody liked him. He was my pride and joy, the life of the family. Always happy, always playing. His friends, all of them running in and out of the house all the time. You could not ask for a warmer, happier family. Before he took sick, Richard, my Richard was a great husband and a wonderful father, involved with the kids and all. We were very happy." She paused, put her hand to her forehead as if shielding her eyes from the light of the lamp overhead.

145

"But something seemed to go wrong with Timothy when he was eleven or twelve, about the time his father died."

Larson sat quietly, letting her talk.

She turned and looked at him without seeing. "Timothy changed," she continued absently, as if talking to herself, "and I just didn't recognize it. Or if I did, I didn't know what to do about it. Was it because of what was happening to his father and my being occupied with him?" Millie tipped her head and pressed her fingers against her temple. "But this change in Timothy started before Richard died. I remember now, in fact it was some months before his death."

Larson got up from the table and put the leftovers away.

"He started behaving differently. With his friends. With me." she said, turning in her chair to look at Larson, look at him as if seeing him for the first time. "Now that I think about it, I can place it in time because I was a little apprehensive when I met you, when you first came by the house while my husband was still alive. I was worried about how Timothy would behave around you, a stranger. I was afraid he might say or do something odd, unexpected. And it became more and more obvious that he'd changed. But I did my best to ignore that Timothy was becoming—had become—a problem. His friends came around less, began to drift away even before he started having troubles at school."

"So, you don't connect the change in Timothy with his father's death?"

"No, I don't. I never did. I don't know what happened to him, what made him change."

146

# Chapter Thirty Nine

## Marcia Schmitt

## August 17, 1965

It was early morning and still cool when Marcia arrived.

The plain, faded trailer in the park full of plain, faded trailers gave her a pang. She was sorry she had let her mother sell the house and move away from her friends on Beach Street. These little places seemed so sad, so desperate, struggling with the help of little potted plants to achieve the appearance of being someone's home.

"Mom are you here?" she said, knocking on the screen.

Almost instantly Millie opened the door and threw her arms around her daughter.

"Oh, my God, am I glad to see you!" She stepped back and looked at Marcia. "How do you manage to look so beautiful and glamorous this early in the morning?"

"It's hereditary," Marcia answered with a little grin. She searched her mother's face. "How are you holding up?"

Millie wiped her hands on her apron. "Tom Larson or Bernice from next door has been with me the whole time," she said with a tired shrug. "I don't know what I would have done if they hadn't been here."

Marcia smiled, trying to overlook the fatigue and sadness in her mother's eyes. She dropped her purse on the sofa and went to the counter that separated the small eating area from the kitchen.

"What happened? With Timothy, I mean."

Millie slipped past her and went to the stove to make coffee. She began telling Marcia all about Timothy coming by trying to borrow money, their conversation, Timothy finding the gun—and how things went from there.

Marcia didn't know what to say. She really was not sure that she should say anything.

"I guess I never knew what to do about Timothy," she finally offered. "It always seemed like I was too busy with my own life, growing up and all. What can I do…for you?"

Millie smiled. "You're here with me. That's exactly what I need."

Marcia took her mother's hand. "I'll stay as long as you like, mom."

# Chapter Forty

## Tom Larson

## August 17, 1965

Larson got to the station early, well before he was scheduled to go on duty.

The whole injustice of Timothy Schmitt's ruined life haunted him. Larson decided to go through the police department's archives and review the records twelve, thirteen years back. Maybe it was just a hunch, but all through the years he'd been convinced that the reports of a peeping tom and the attack on little Timothy were connected.

If so, he was fairly sure that all of Timothy's problems began with that night in 1954.

He pulled the files back to September of that year, took them to an empty briefing room and spread them out on the table. Studying only the reports of a peeping tom, he saw that all the incidents took place on the west side, all within a six- or seven-block area and all had occurred before eleven thirty at night.

Holding the reports, Larson stepped to the map of the city on the briefing room wall. He began putting a red pin at the location of each incident. It immediately became clear that the neighborhood where the Schmitt's lived was right in the middle, not at the edge of the area where the pins were concentrated. He had to conclude that the peeper must have lived at or near the middle of that area and that he traveled on foot. That much should have been obvious from the start if anyone really thought about it. The area was divided by railroad tracks.

The streets dead-ended at the tracks.

There were incidents reported on both sides of those tracks.

If the peeper had been driving a car, he would have had to drive all the way to the main street where it crossed the tracks, then back to the area across from the Schmitt's neighborhood. And if he were driving, he wouldn't have restricted his activities only to that parameter.

There would have been reports of a peeping tom elsewhere in Torrance and there weren't.

Obviously, the suspect had been on foot and simply walked across the tracks.

Larson had already concluded that the suspect was a young male, probably a boy in his teens and certainly no more than twenty or so.

Larson also noted that the reports consistently occurred Monday through Thursday nights, never Friday night or weekends. And that they abruptly ended in December 1954.

Should he drop in on Millie's old neighborhood and ask around, see if anyone recalled any of the young men living in the area in the early fifties or knew anything else that could be a clue? No, Larson was a traffic cop, not a detective. He had no authority to go around asking questions.

Worse, his and Dr. Beeman's suspicions had never been reported. If it came out now that he knew or even suspected such a crime and never reported it, he and the doctor and Tony Giuliani would be up shit creek.

The noise level in the station house was picking up as the graveyard shift checked in.

Larson got up and started gathering the records just as Detective Giuliani stuck his head in the door.

"I heard about poor Timothy Schmitt," he said. "Is there anything you think I could do for the family?"

Larson turned to him. "Can you spare me a minute?"

"Sure," the detective replied, stepping into the room.

Larson moved around the detective and pulled the door shut. "Do you remember ten or twelve years ago when we had all those reports of a peeping tom and I told you of Doctor Beeman's suspicion that little Timothy had been attacked?"

"Hell, yes!"

Larson motioned toward the map on the wall and the pins indicating the locations of the incidents. "Well, I think I've come up with something interesting." He then proceeded to tell Giuliani about the pattern of the peeping tom reports and the way they abruptly stopped.

"You know," Giuliani said, peering at the map, "I can only think of three single males in that age range living on the block at that time. One was Dick Schmitt, but he worked nights. Another was Ken Simpson, and back then he would have been, oh, late thirties or so. There was one thing about Ken that stood out. Every year between Thanksgiving and Christmas he took off on a vacation by himself. He would drive his big Lincoln clear to Mexico or take some other extended long-distance trip. He didn't have to work. He and his father owned some oil wells, and they gave them a nice income. Ken would be gone for a month or more at a time."

149

"That would seem to eliminate him as a suspect," Larson said, massaging the back of his neck.

Giuliani had his coat pulled open and was slipping his belt through the bottom loop of his shoulder holster. He paused. "The only other one I can recall was a sixteen or seventeen-year-old boy named Gavin Keller. His family moved away right around Christmas in '54. I remember because theirs was the only house in the neighborhood that didn't have any decorations that year. I'm sure it must have been 1954. I got a new 1953 Ford at the end of that model year, last of the flat heads. I should have gone ahead and got the '54. That was the first year Ford had the overhead valve V8 engine." Giuliani glanced at his watch and moved toward the door. "Funny how you can place things in time by something like that. Seems to me this Gavin dated Millie Schmitt's daughter for a while."

Larson was staring at the map.

He nodded. "Keller sounds like a real possibility. Thanks. You've been a great help."

As Giuliani opened the door Larson added "By the way, you're lucky you didn't get one of Ford's first overhead valve engines. They were a pile of crap and the transmission stunk."

Millie's daughter Marcia was the apple of Larson's eye. He was as proud of her as he would have been if she were his own daughter, so he was both pleased and relieved when she greeted him at Millie's trailer late that afternoon.

"Come right in. Mom's in the bath. I was just having a cup of tea. Please sit down and let me get you a cup."

"Let me get it. I know my way around here pretty well. Your mother and I spend a lot of time together, you know."

"Yes, I do know," Marcia said, smiling. She sat down at the kitchen table.

Larson went to the cupboard to get a cup and saucer. "I'm really relieved that you're here," he said over his shoulder. "It means so much to Millie."

Marcia picked up her cup as if to take a sip, then set it down on the table and looked up at him. "We loved Timothy. He was always so playful and happy as a child. We could not understand what was going on with him when he began to change. We didn't know what to do. Mom feels

150

what happened was her fault, but neither of us can see how, or what we could have done to make things any different."

Larson brought a cup and saucer to the table, set them down across from Marcia and paused, thinking. He glanced down the short hall toward the back of the trailer, and then turned to her.

"If we can have a quick moment before your mother comes in," he said quietly, "I'd like to ask you something."

"Sure," Marcia replied, puzzled.

"Going back to 1953 or 1954," he said, pulling up a chair and sitting across from her, "do you remember a boy named Gavin Keller?"

The shades in the trailer were drawn in a vain effort to keep out the late afternoon heat. But even in the shadowy interior he saw a startled look flicker across her face.

"I suppose I do. Why?"

"There was a rash of reports about a peeping tom around that time. Judging from their pattern, your old neighborhood was right in the midst's of them." Larson poured himself a cup of tea, took a sip and then continued. "Gavin Keller was about the only person that seems to fit the profile as a suspect. Right age, single, and the reports stopped when his family moved."

Before Marcia could reply, they heard Millie Schmitt finishing in the bathroom. Larson put his finger to his lip and whispered, "Can we talk about this later, sometime when we're alone?"

"Certainly," Marcia replied, and quickly changed the subject. "And my latest movie was filmed in Mexico. The next one is in Montana."

"Marcia was telling me all about being a movie actress," Larson explained as Millie came in.

Animated and vivacious, Marcia entertained them with celebrity gossip and what was happening in her glamorous life until eleven o'clock that night. By the time Larson got up to leave, Millie's spirits seemed to have improved.

As her mother gathered up the teacups, Marcia rose from her chair and said, "Let me walk you out to your car."

"Don't pass up a chance for a short walk with this beautiful woman," Millie said as Larson was putting on his leather jacket. She hugged him and added, "See you tomorrow, dear."

Hot as it had been all day, by almost midnight it had turned a little chilly. Marcia put on a coat and the two walked down the steps to Larson's car.

"There's more to it, isn't there? About Gavin, I mean," Marcia asked when they were out of earshot of the trailer.

"Yes, there is. And I get the feeling you have more to tell, too," he said, turning to look at her.

They studied each other for a moment, each searching the other's face in the dark.

"I think we might as well both come clean," Marcia said, stuffing her hands deep into her coat pockets. "We can play games with each other all night and not get anywhere. What's up?"

He smiled. "I could say, you first."

"Okay," she said. "I dated Gavin. For several months. I remember it was during the time Dad was sick. Dying, as it turned out. Gavin and I must have started dating during the summer and it lasted through December or the end of the year."

"What do you know about him?"

"Not much really. He had an older sister, both parents worked." She paused for a moment and looked up at the dark sky. Then she turned to Larson and continued. "I don't know if I ever knew where his dad worked. I remember his mother was a nurse, but I don't know if she worked at the hospital or in a doctor's office somewhere. Now it's your turn."

He hesitated, stared into her eyes, and then plunged ahead. "I'm going to have to trust you. I'm going to tell you something I never told your mother in all these years, so before I do, you have to tell me everything. Was there any more to your relationship with Gavin Keller?"

"No," Marcia replied perhaps just a little too quickly. "No, we just dated for a while and then he and his family moved, and I never heard from him again."

Larson sensed that she was lying, that there might be more to it, but he couldn't be sure, and he had no right to press her.

"Now you," she said, leaning against the car's fender.

Trapped, he had to plunge ahead. "We…"

"Who's 'we'?"

"Dr. Beeman and I. Dr. Beeman suspected that Timothy was attacked and raped one night that September. Beeman concluded that the trauma caused Timothy to suppress any recollection of the event. I've known Ralph Beeman for many years and trust his judgment completely. I do not doubt his conclusion. Between us we theorized that the attacker used an anesthetic that may have caused an injury to Timothy's brain. We believe this may have resulted in the change in Timothy's behavior and handicapped his development."

Even in the dark Larson could see that, actress or no actress Marcia was stunned. "How could such a thing happen? Where could it have happened? Who on earth could have done such a thing to a little boy?"

Larson took a deep breath, glanced toward the trailer, then looked back at Marcia. "To me, Gavin Keller would seem to be the chief suspect. There was a rash of complaints about a peeping tom and your old neighborhood was right in the center of the area where the complaints were concentrated. And they stopped at exactly the time the Keller family moved. Torrance was a small town in those days. Other than your older brother Dick, Gavin Keller was the only teenage male living in that area."

He paused, then continued; "You mentioned you recall Gavin's mother was a nurse. That could have given Gavin access to anesthetics." Larson then went on to tell her of his conversations with the doctor and Giuliani. Finally, he explained their reasoning for not filing a report and not telling Millie.

Marcia stared at him, speechless.

He looked at the ground, then back to Marcia, trying to read her expression.

"It's hard to know what we should have done," he said almost in a whisper. "It was a hard decision to make at the time, especially knowing what an investigation and interrogation of Timothy would have been like. And with what you were all going through with your dad's illness, we made the decision to spare your family of all that." He reached out and touched her shoulder. "Even now I don't know if I would have done anything differently."

They heard the trailer door open. "Are you two going to spend all night out there?"

153

Turning toward the trailer, Marcia answered, "Coming, Mom." She turned back to face Larson. "We've all had to make some tough decisions in life, Tom. I guess I understand why you did what you did."

She touched his sleeve. "And, it might not have been Gavin Keller."

# Chapter Forty One

## Dick Schmitt

## August 1965

The roar of the gun in the tiny office.

The fat, disgusting little man hurtled backward by the blast.

The sound of that gunshot and the memory of that scene replayed itself endlessly, day and night in Dick Schmitt's mind, haunting him at work, in his apartment, even driving his car.

It was always with him.

He never thought of the other nights with Connie and the girls and Gavin.

Just that one moment, that one moment that night seven years ago in the smelly little motel manager's office.

In the dining room of his apartment in Pacific Heights, the old schoolhouse clock chimed three times.

Dick Schmitt sat alone in the dark living room, sat alone rocking back and forth in the chair as he did every night, looking out the bay window at the empty street below.

He was tired.

He could get up from the rocking chair and walk down the hall to his bedroom. All he had to do was lift himself up, turn to his left, and walk through the dark apartment. He knew where everything was—every piece of furniture; the coffee table, the floor lamp by the door, the armchair, everything.

He would not even need to turn on a light.

Except for work and shopping for necessities, he only went out for one other reason.

To buy clothes.

He was obsessed with clothes. He had closets full of custom suits, slacks, shirts, sweaters, shoes, and even hats.

He never wore hats.

He never wore any of these things outside his apartment.

No, when he left his apartment, no matter where he was going, he always wore one of the two-dozen custom-fitted immigration inspector uniforms he'd had made up by the tailor in Oakland.

Every evening, alone in his apartment, he would try on a different suit or a different combination of slacks and sweaters and model them in front of the floor-length mirrors.

Then he'd go to the living room to sit in the rocking chair by the bay window and watch the street.

Indeed, Dick was haunted. Only by occupying himself with this obsessive attention to his clothes and to every minute detail of his apartment—an apartment no one else had ever entered—could he hope to force that night in Lomita from the forefront of his mind.

Dick dreaded the thought of sleep. Every night he'd put off going to bed as long as he could, as if somehow, he'd discover a way to avoid sleep altogether.

But sooner or later he had to give up, had to leave the rocking chair and go to his bedroom. He would take off whatever clothes he'd been modeling for himself, carefully return them to the closet and get under the covers.

He knew though, that as soon as he shut his eyes in the futile hope that he might drop off to a dreamless sleep, the horror of what happened that night in that little office would come flooding back.

Even at work, with all the noise and distractions of the customs and immigrations section it lurked in his consciousness like some dark, evil shadow.

But it was so much worse when he was alone. He rationed one night a week to thoroughly cleaning his whole apartment from top to bottom. He would strip down to his shorts so he wouldn't wrinkle any of his clothes or somehow get them dirty.

Then, he would begin to vacuum, wash walls, woodwork, and windows. He dusted all the shelves, the pictures, tables, everything. Next, he scrubbed all his dishes and pots and pans, even the ones he hadn't used.

And when he was through, at two or three in the morning, he usually started the whole process all over again.

When, in sheer exhaustion, he could avoid sleep no longer and did drop off he would immediately bolt awake drenched in sweat, the thunderous roar of the gun echoing in his head.

Over and over that nightmare replayed itself, the explosion of the gunshot so real, so loud that he was sure others in the apartment building heard it. He was afraid the neighbors would come running to see what had happened. Every night he would try to force himself to stay between his sweat soaked sheets, try to convince himself it was all in his mind, that there had not been any sound of a gunshot.

But it was so real he just could not help himself. Every night this nightmare was repeated. Every night he found himself sitting up, getting out of bed and padding in his bare feet across the cold hardwood floor to his door. He would quietly open it a crack and look out into the hallway to see if anyone else in the apartment building had been awakened, disturbed by the gunshot in his nightmare.

No, the hot, sexy nights spent in the motel room with Gavin and the girls never came to mind.

Only that scene in the motel manager's office, the sudden look of surprise, panic on the fat little man's face when Connie's hand lifted the gun from her purse.

The deafening roar filling the small space.

The little man lifted by the impact of the bullet and slammed against the filing cabinet.

As if in slow motion, the filing cabinet knocked backward, the fan on top tipping forward and falling, bouncing off the man's head and onto his fat belly. All the papers and the ashtray filled with stale cigarette butts raining down on him as he crumpled to the floor in the small space behind the counter.

Over and over, again and again that scene replayed itself in Dick's mind.

It was not regret about the man's death.

Nor was it guilt about the crime of murder committed by Connie and to which Dick was an accessory.

No, it wasn't Dick's conscience that was causing this insanity.

Dick was deathly afraid of getting caught.

Alone in his apartment he listened constantly for footsteps in the hallway, waited for the knock on the apartment door, the knock of the police come to take him away in handcuffs, arrested for murder.

There would be people watching him being led down the stairs.

157

There would be people watching him being led out onto the sidewalk in front of the apartment building.

There would be people watching him being led to a waiting police car.

He could see them in his mind, hear them whispering and pointing at him.

"Murder" he could hear them say. "They're arresting him for murder."

Worse, he feared this scene being played out at work.

He imagined men in suits appearing at the entrance to the Customs and Immigration hanger. Men walking over to one of the other immigration inspectors, or worse yet, the supervisor and asking: "Which one is Richard Schmitt?"

"That's Dick Schmitt over there," the supervisor would say, pointing toward Dick. Everyone, the other inspectors, the travelers, all of them would turn to stare at him. The men in suits would watch him warily, not taking their eyes off him as they moved cautiously through crowd. They would make their way past the tables with the opened luggage, coming to get him, coming to arrest him for murder.

Would he just stand there?

Shouldn't he run?

Run?

Run through the Customs and Immigration section of the San Francisco International Airport?

Run between the tables with the open suitcases?

Run, pushing his way through the staring travelers?

Run? Run where?

Where would he go? Out to his car, to his poor old Thunderbird?

Every minute of the day and alone in his apartment at night, his heart in his throat, he watched and listened.

All because of Gavin Keller.

Dick had really liked Gavin. Gavin was the first person Dick had ever got to know, the first person he had ever trusted enough to let become a friend.

He had first met Gavin right there in his old neighborhood.

Cars.

He was looking at some cars when Gavin walked up. Next, they went to a junkyard, they went to the auto show, they went to the drag races.

He wished to God he'd never gone to the drag races. They met the girls at the drag races and took up with them there first.

But then it evolved to the motel.

Gavin said he knew about a motel that didn't ask too many questions.

Gavin introduced marijuana to the group.

Gavin moved the dresser with the mirror to reflect what happened on the bed.

Gavin always seemed to know all kinds of interesting things for them to try.

Didn't Connie call Gavin the architect, the conductor of their orgies?

Dick got rid of those prints the next morning, but he remembered them vividly, as if only moments ago he held them in his hand.

The pictures were clear, focused.

Except now that he thought about it, none of the five or so pictures Dick had grabbed off the counter showed Gavin's face. Certainly, Dick and the three girl's faces were clear enough.

There was no mistaking any of them.

But not Gavin.

He knew the other guy was Gavin, but there was no way anyone else would recognize him from those pictures. Gavin's face just did not appear. Was it by accident that he was looking away from the camera, or could it have been deliberate? Maybe Gavin's face showed clearly in the movie, but Dick suspected it didn't.

The scenes of them on the bed, reflected again in the big mirror on the dresser captured everything. The lighting of that scene didn't seem like it could have been an accident either.

It was too good.

Gavin had draped Sandi's panties over the floor lamp in the corner, diffusing the light and giving the room an even more erotic look.

What was it the motel manager had said that last night? "Now that you're one player short." How would he know that they'd be "one player short," that Gavin had dropped out of the group? Hell, the man was not even supposed to know about Gavin and the other two girls.

After not thinking this through for all these years, Dick had to face the fact that he'd been set up.

And he must have been set up by Gavin.

The girls were caught up in it the same way as he and the motive was blackmail for a miserable $100 a month.

But then, there could be additional copies of those films, copies someone could sell. They went to the motel every Saturday for months, for over a year maybe. The manager only intended to give him and Connie half dozen copies of those films.

The manager and Gavin.

Were there other copies of those films? How many films? There could be several dozen. Hell, movies of him smoking marijuana and having sex in every conceivable way and every conceivable position. Movies that could be in circulation all over the country. That motel manager had probably been selling copies before Connie killed him.

Maybe Gavin sold some.

Come to think of it, who else knew what happened at the motel that night? Dick was sure Connie wasn't going to tell anyone, but what about Gavin?

Had he really moved to Utah?

Why the hell should Dick believe that? Gavin would have intended to stay in touch with his partner the motel manager. And when Gavin didn't hear from his partner, Gavin would have checked to find out what happened to him.

It would not have been difficult for Gavin to guess who killed the man. The murder had taken place on a Saturday night at the time the group usually checked in to this always vacant motel.

"So," Dick concluded, "Gavin knows the little man was murdered and he probably thinks I did it."

And Gavin is out there somewhere.

# Chapter Forty Two

## Gavin Keller

## August 1960

## Cambridge, Massachusetts

Gavin arrived in Cambridge and settled in his second-floor dorm room two weeks before the semester was to begin.

Just two beds, a desk with a chair and an easy chair near the window looking out on the street.

His roommate, whoever that was going to be, had not shown up yet.

Gavin, although he didn't need the money, had already found himself a job.

He'd been exploring the Harvard campus. In the hallway of the Law Building was a bulletin board posted with notes advertising used books, used cars, apartments to share and jobs.

One carefully typed three by five card sought applications for a junior law clerk or paralegal for an insurance company in downtown Boston. He made a note of the number, cut short his explorations, and hurried back to his dorm.

First Boston Insurance and Reinsurance was located on Batterymarch in downtown Boston.

His boss was a very nice gentleman, Rob Stone, head of the legal department.

The canyon of tall buildings and narrow old streets, the crowds, the hustle and bustle, the energy and the tension that went with it were everything Gavin Keller imagined the big city would be.

Just like that Cary Grant movie.

First Boston Insurance and Reinsurance occupied the entire building and the legal department, hundreds of busy people working at a sea of desks took up the whole ninth floor.

Gavin's hours were arranged around his schedule at school. He would be reviewing cases involving possibly fraudulent claims and fraudulent practices by the insurance company's own agents.

"Independent retail agents' deal with the insurance buying public and act as a middleman between First Boston and the customer," Rob Stone had explained.

Gavin's first few days were spent reviewing files at a desk just outside Stone's office. By the second week he was feeling pretty much at home when Stone called him into his office.

On Stone's desk were several folders.

"Here's a case for you to dig into as part of your education," he said, handing Gavin three folders. "It seems one of our agents down in Haddonfield, New Jersey, Sol Jamaica of Insurance Coverage, Inc. used our name and went into the insurance company business for himself. We are pretty sure he's been issuing "binders" or evidences of coverage to his clients without reporting to us and then keeping the premiums he collects. This happens occasionally," Stone continued, "and the usual practice is for companies to just take the loss of premium and dump the agent."

"Why isn't the agent prosecuted?" asked Gavin.

"That would require reporting it as a crime and going to court. If it became known how easy it is to do this, more agents might try it." Stone paused, looked at Gavin. "You'll find after you've been here awhile that our business relies a great deal on trust," he concluded with a wry smile.

Gavin took the files back to his desk and spent the rest of the day thoroughly reviewing them. It was clear that Jamaica had been operating as Stone described for several years, placing just enough business legitimately with First Boston to keep his agency agreement active.

Gavin was already at his desk when Rob Stone arrived the next morning. He got up from his chair as Stone passed by. "I see what you mean about this Sol Jamaica thing," he said, handing the folders to Stone.

Stone nodded his head; "We believe that when one of his clients had a claim Sol just paid it out of his pocket." He gestured for Gavin to follow him into his office and continued speaking over his shoulder: "But his luck ran out when one of his policyholders had a serious auto accident and was sued for over $1,000,000. Sol tried to pay the legal costs and stall as long as he could, but we figured out what was going on when we were served by the plaintiff's attorney, and we couldn't find any record of the insured."

Stone set the files on his desk and leaned against the wall next to the window looking out on Boston Harbor. "Sol Jamaica refuses to cooperate and told us to go pound sand. He is a cagey old fraudster, and he knows we won't bring charges. If we did, the matter would certainly go to court, the newspapers would find out about it, and we would have more to lose than Sol Jamaica." He stepped to his desk and picked up the file. "Any ideas, college boy?"

"Well, yes. I'd like to take a trip down to Haddonfield and see if I can't get Mr. Jamaica to cooperate with us."

Stone sat down and looked up at him. "You seem to be a very bright young man, but I can tell you Sol Jamaica must outweigh you by 100 pounds and is meaner than a rhino with a tooth ache." Stone straightened the papers in the folder and tapped them on the desktop. "I shudder at the thought of you confronting him."

The glare from the morning sun shining through the window behind Stone made it difficult for Gavin to read the expression on his boss's face.

"We have sent several representatives, claims people and others including myself out to see Jamaica," Stone continued. "We have written threatening letters. Sol Jamaica has told us to go shit in our hats." Stone leaned back in his chair. "It's hard for me to see what you could do."

Gavin shrugged. "You have nothing to lose then."

"Christ, you've only been here a couple of weeks and you think I should send you off on a trip?"

"I didn't mean to be presumptuous, but we would both find out if I'm up to it or not. And again, what have you got to lose? As it is, this is going nowhere."

Stone laughed. "You should have been in sales."

"It's Wednesday. I could go tomorrow and be back Friday. School starts Monday so it's now or never."

Before Gavin left the office that afternoon, he pulled the personal auto and fire policies for Sol Jamaica and his wife and studied the inspection reports the company routinely obtained on all its policyholders.

The next morning Gavin, dressed in a dark blue suit, white shirt, and grey tie, rented a nondescript Ford sedan and headed for Haddonfield.

The drive took four hours and gave him plenty of time to think. Why had he volunteered for this? He didn't need to. He wasn't expected to. Stone had only given him the file for educational purposes, not as an assignment.

But Gavin knew why he did it, why he volunteered for this.

Other men, experienced men, old timers in this new world of his, men including his boss Rob Stone himself had tried and failed.

For Gavin Keller this was a test, a challenge. He wanted to see if he was up to it.

What did he have to lose?

Even if he did not get the best of the evil dragon Sol Jamaica, he'd still have his job.

And too, he was quite sure today's adventure would be a learning experience, if nothing else.

⁂

Haddonfield is a pretty little town with tree-lined streets and lovely homes on broad green lawns. Gavin got there just after lunch, grabbed a hamburger at a place on Kings Highway East, and asked for directions to the neighborhood where Jamaica lived.

The Sol Jamaica residence was much like the other homes on the quiet street, set back from the curb with a well tended lawn in front.

A new Lincoln was parked in the driveway.

There were no signs of children in the Jamaica household, although there were kids playing elsewhere on the tree-lined street.

Gavin parked in front of the house, got out of the car and walked the long walk to the front door to ring the bell.

From inside he heard a woman's voice yell for someone to "see who the hell that is."

Shortly, a fat hairy guy in a t-shirt and shorts opened the door. "What do you want?"

"I work at First Boston Insurance and I'm on my way to the IRS office over in Cherry Hill. I thought I would drop by and see you first," Gavin said smiling.

"So?" said the man.

"I understand the IRS pays a reward for information about people who don't pay their taxes. I don't make much money at First Boston Insurance. From reading their records it appears to me you have a substantial income. My guess is that you failed to report all of it to the IRS."

There was a long pause. The man holding the door took a deep breath and finally said "Why don't you come in? Maybe we can work something out."

164

"You are, I presume, Sol Jamaica?"

"Yeah," said the man leading him into a spacious and very nicely appointed living room. An attractive and very fit blond woman in her mid thirties, wearing shorts and halter top and carrying a tennis racket, was obviously on her way out.

When she saw Gavin she paused, smiled, and ran her hand over her hair to smooth it.

Sol Jamaica scowled and introduced her as his wife, Monica. Monica started to extend her hand. She stepped back and her smile faded when Jamaica added that Gavin was from the insurance company.

Gavin's friendly smile disappeared, too. He pulled a file folder from his briefcase, and in a very businesslike tone said; "I'll get right to the point. The IRS pays a reward to informers based on the amount of the unpaid tax for alerting them to tax cheats."

He flipped through the papers and started to hand them to Jamaica. Jamaica backed away as if Gavin were trying to hand him a snake.

Gavin continued; "Based on what I see from First Boston's records, it looks like you might have upwards of $1,000,000 in income that you didn't pay taxes on."

Monica Jamaica gasped and looked at her husband.

"A million dollars?" she yelled. "I thought you said it was only a couple hundred thousand!"

"No, no it wasn't anything like a million," protested Jamaica.

"My guess is that the apartment in Atlantic City cost a pretty penny and the trips to Miami weren't cheap either," Gavin said.

"WHAT apartment in Atlantic City and WHAT trips to Miami?" Monica screamed. "You said they were business trips to Newark, you asshole!"

Sol Jamaica was sweating.

Gavin sat down in an easy chair, put the file folder back in his briefcase and settled in to watch developments.

Monica picked up a heavy glass ashtray and advanced on Sol.

He retreated backward around the coffee table, toward the couch facing Gavin.

"What the hell are you talking about?" whined Sol. "What apartment? What trips to Miami?"

His foot caught on the coffee table leg, and he pitched sideways, landing on the couch.

His enraged wife towered over him holding the heavy ashtray.

Gavin started to open his briefcase as if to bring out papers. "You know, there may be a way to work this out without involving the IRS."

"To hell with the IRS!" shouted Monica Jamaica.

"Wait! Wait!" pleaded Sol. "What is it you want?"

"Well, it would do wonders for my career at First Boston if I could get a list of people you told were insured with them, along with a few bucks for myself."

Suddenly Monica Jamaica swung the ashtray as hard as she could.

She brought it down on Sol's balding head with a loud thump, leaving a bloody gash.

"What about the apartment in Atlantic City?" She screamed again. "What about the trips to Miami?"

Monica Jamaica didn't weigh more than 100 pounds, but she swung the ashtray like a tennis player serving, putting her whole body into it. Her next swing caught Sol just above his left ear. It looked to Gavin like she'd nearly knocked her husband unconscious.

Breathing hard and looking dazed, Sol Jamaica was bleeding all over the couch.

Monica placed the ashtray back on the coffee table. "I'm going to get a wet rag to sop this up. I plan to keep the couch, along with the house and everything else when I throw your ass out," she told her cowering husband.

She marched off to the kitchen.

Gavin got up from the easy chair and followed her. "Of course, part of the money went to the tennis club and the lessons with the pro," he said when they got into the kitchen.

She froze, standing motionless at the sink and holding the washrag under the running water.

Gavin could see thoughts flicker across her face.

"Just how much do you know?" she asked.

"I know more than enough."

"Crap."

"I suggest that it is in your mutual best interests to clear up matters with me first, and then deal with your personal problems."

She looked Gavin up and down and said, "I'll go get his books."

"Bring his checkbook, too."

⁂

Gavin was back at his desk when Rob Stone arrived for work the next morning.

Stone kind of smirked as he passed by, but his expression changed when he looked in his office.

In the middle of his desk was a ledger book and on top of that, a manila envelope.

Stone took off his jacket and hung it on the coat rack. Then he went to his desk and picked up the envelope.

Gavin, still seated at his desk, turned in his chair and watched.

Stone opened the envelope and a check fell out. It landed face up on his desk.

His jaw dropped.

It was a check for $225,000 drawn on the joint account of Mr. and Mrs. Sol Jamaica and it was payable to Gavin Keller.

Gavin got up from his chair and walked to Stone's office door; "If you will look at the reverse side of that check you'll see that I've endorsed it over to First Boston 'in consideration of premiums owed by Insurance Coverage, Inc.' Nodding toward the ledger he continued, "Those are the records of Insurance Coverage, Inc. Hopefully they will show that the amount will come close to what Jamaica collected from his victims.'

Gavin stepped to Stone's desk and opened the ledger book to show him the list of names, addresses and premium amounts. "Jamaica claims the total amount they collected using First Boston's name was $225,000." he said, running his finger down the columns. "They were also pulling the same scam on other insurance companies."

"I never thought we'd recover a damn thing from those crooks." Stone said shaking his head. "How'd you pull this off?"

"I reasoned with them."

From then on Rob Stone saved the more difficult and complex assignments for Gavin.

167

To Gavin, it was a crash course in skullduggery.

For the two weeks that Gavin had lived in Cambridge he only knew it to be a quiet, sleepy, almost deserted place.

But when he returned from work that afternoon the neighborhood around Harvard was coming alive. Cars and station wagons were parked along the curbs in front of the dorm buildings on Mellen and Oxford and the other streets. All were delivering students and their luggage for the new semester.

When he opened the door to his dorm room, he saw his roommate had arrived.

The guy was about the same size as Gavin, well dressed, nice looking, with a lot of thick black hair and a five o'clock shadow.

He'd pulled the easy chair over to the window and was sitting watching the students and their parents milling around on the street below, unpacking their cars and saying their goodbyes.

Hearing Gavin come in, he jumped to his feet excitedly.

"Johnny Monreale," he said, eagerly extending his hand.

This guy was very animated, first returning to the window, then crossing the room and throwing himself down on his bed, talking nonstop the whole time.

"How long have you been here? You look like you're from California. Are you? Want to go get some beer? I have an I.D. that says I'm twenty-three. My family lives in Utica, New York, and we have a flat in Manhattan. Dad says I can use it if I get good grades. I have a car. It's a '55 Chevy Bel Air. Do you smoke? I don't smoke. Tried it but it smells bad, and I coughed till I got a sore throat. Do you have a girl friend? I had a girl friend in high school, almost. Do you know any movie stars? My dad's in the insurance business. I'm really twenty years old. We went to Europe on vacation. I got kicked out of prep school for swearing. Dad says I better do good in college. Harvard costs a fortune. What's your major? Mine's business administration and I don't think I'm going to like it. Can you get any grass? I can probably score some grass if you want it."

Johnny chattered on. Gavin thought this guy might come in handy if he could just put up with him. Johnny said he had a car and knew his way around New York City.

Gavin really wanted to see New York City.

The rest of Friday evening and all-day Saturday and Sunday students for Harvard, MIT, and the other schools streamed back into Cambridge for the new semester.

Gavin, with his job and his familiarity with the town and the school had already settled in and felt like an old timer.

Once classes started, he quickly saw that Harvard was just like high school and junior college. The students were more interested in beer, girls, grass and screwing off than anything else, even though college was costing somebody really big money.

He'd already seen that there was a social order at First Boston Insurance. It too, was very much like high school, with its cliques, its rumors and its politics.

Gavin was by nature a loner. Other than his business partner, Tommy back in California, Gavin never had any interest in making close friends.

The dorm had a pay phone downstairs, but Gavin always thought the receiver felt kind of sticky. So, for convenience and privacy, he and Johnny Monreale went in together and had a telephone installed in their dorm room. This made it easier for Tommy in California to give Gavin his weekly report on the porn movie business.

Tommy was continuing to rent out the movies and still sent Gavin around $2,000 a week for his share. This income, plus what he was making at First Boston was actually way more than his expenses, even including the cost of going to Harvard.

During one of the phone calls Tommy excitedly told him about an idea of his, a business renting or leasing, as well as selling antiques.

The idea sounded o.k. to Gavin, so he put up half the money.

Tommy leased a store on Wilshire Boulevard in Beverly Hills and stocked it with antiques.

Very quickly, Tommy Huber became "Mr. Thomas" of *Mr. Thomas Antiques of Beverly Hills, Arbiter of Fine Antiques.*

Tommy described the store to Gavin as being very fancy, a first-class boutique. His idea of renting antiques of all kinds to business offices really took off.

Lawyers, motion picture people, and others who wanted to impress clients but did not know anything about antiques and didn't want to spend a lot of money buying stuff they knew nothing about were flocking to the store.

169

Gavin, happy to act as a silent partner, provided cash when needed, but left the operations entirely to Tommy. Because of the leverage he had over Tommy, Gavin trusted him, and Tommy had never let him down.

And, too, Gavin made sure everything was in writing.

Gavin's roommate, Johnny Monreale wasted no time in getting to know everyone in the dorm and in his classes. He scoped out the beer joints, where to pick up girls—or at least try to—where to get grass, and what and where the popular entertainments were.

# Chapter Forty Three

## November 1960

During one of their weekly phone conversations, on an evening his roommate was out trying to get lucky, Gavin suggested to Tommy that renting their films to the students around the schools in Cambridge should be a huge success.

"These guys are every bit as horny as our customers out there, and most of them come from ritzy families who don't know shit about porn." Gavin glanced over at Johnny's empty bed. "I don't think they would know where to get it if they knew it existed at all, at least not the good stuff."

"Oh?" Tommy replied. "The business is still going strong out here. Both the Junior College guys, and the Hollywood crowd can't seem to get enough."

"I'm thinking we could double the business if we brought it to Cambridge," Gavin said, pressing forward with his idea. "There are three major colleges and universities all within walking distance of where I'm sitting right now. My guess is there are upwards of a hundred thousand horny guys within a five-mile radius." As a clincher he added, "And by the way, there were plenty of antiques in these little New England towns. You could pick up all kinds of stuff for your store."

"You have my attention," Tommy said.

"Why don't you fly out here, say Sunday night, and spend a few days looking around? You could be back in California by Thursday. You wouldn't miss your Friday and Saturday night showing."

"I'll do it! I have some salespeople now, and a store manager. I can leave the place for a few days. I'll get my tickets and get back to you with my arrival time."

"I'll make a hotel reservation for you in Boston. It's just across the river from here. You don't want to stay in this dorm, that's for sure."

◦ ◦ ◦

On Sunday, Gavin took the bus to Logan to meet Tommy's plane. Walking through the terminal to the car rental booth Tommy asked Gavin how he liked Tommy's new moustache. "I thought with my new image as an expert on antiques I needed to look older, maybe a little British," he said, smoothing it with his finger.

Gavin complimented him, but thought really that it made Tommy, with his blond hair and slightly effeminate appearance look like a fop.

On the way to Cambridge, Gavin outlined his plan, a plan that involved his roommate Johnny Monreale as the front man for the Cambridge branch of their porn movie rental business. Gavin would introduce Tommy to Johnny and explained that Tommy was enrolled at MIT. Then he would suggest that the three of them go out for beers and in the course of the evening find an opportunity to leave the two of them alone.

Step one went as intended.

The beer joint was typical of a college town. Noisy and smelling of cigarettes and urine, crowded with young men and women all excited at being away from home. Students were playing darts and pool, yelling across the room at each other, pushing and stumbling past the tables.

Gavin, Tommy, and Johnny found a table right in the middle of the place, right where half drunk students carrying full pitchers of beer were squeezing their way through the crowd, right where Gavin was the least comfortable.

On their second beer, Gavin said that he had to go to the men's room. This was meant to give Tommy a chance to broach the subject of dirty movies to Johnny. Tommy was to pretend to take Johnny into his confidence and say something like; "Gavin doesn't know it but several of us over at MIT have a whole bunch of porn." He would lead up to asking if Johnny knew anyone who would be interested in renting some. Tommy would outline the plan he and Gavin had agreed on and explain to Johnny that the guys at MIT usually had private showings and charged ten bucks a head. Tommy was to emphasize that Gavin didn't know anything about this, Gavin being such a goody two-shoes and all.

When Gavin came back from the men's room it was Johnny's turn to go. While he was gone Tommy told Gavin that just as Gavin had expected, Johnny Monreale was wildly enthusiastic about the idea and wanted in on the action. He told Gavin that they had agreed the two of them, Tommy, and Johnny, would handle the whole thing by mail.

172

Johnny was to establish a post office box there in Cambridge. Once a week, Tommy would mail a film to Johnny. After its showing, Johnny was to return the film the following Monday to a post office box in Los Angeles along with $1,000 in cash. If Johnny could establish other places to view these films and could use more than one a week, the deal could be expanded.

Tommy assured Gavin that he had made it clear to Johnny if any of the films weren't returned, the deal was over.

Tommy saw Johnny on his way back to the table. He hurriedly finished telling Gavin that when Johnny had asked why the L.A. post office box, Tommy had explained to him that the guys at MIT rotate the films weekly with some guys at USC out on the coast.

As the night had worn on Johnny proceeded to get drunk and make a fool of himself in front of two girls from Lesley when he tried unsuccessfully to balance a full pitcher of beer on his head.

That got them thrown out.

It was nearly midnight, chilly and drizzling rain, when they found themselves out on the sidewalk in front of the bar.

The inky black of the wet streets of Cambridge reflected the streetlights and the headlights of the few passing cars.

The three of them noisily stumbled toward Tommy's rental car.

Johnny was barely able to walk when they loaded him into the back seat.

His head wobbling back and forth Johnny slobbered, "Ah, I love you guys. We gotta go to New York together. My dad's gotta great apartment."

He was passed out before Tommy could pull away from the curb.

"All is well," Tommy whispered, and Gavin knew they had a deal.

When he returned to the dorm after work the next day, Gavin found Johnny with a wet towel on his head, sprawled on his bed watching television.

"Don't slam the damn door for Christ's sake," he begged.

"Tommy said he would be checking in with us, so what do you want to do tonight?"

"I think I'll just stay in," Johnny mumbled from under his pillow.

An icy cold wind was blowing off the harbor when Tommy and Gavin left the rental car with the valet at The Copley Plaza. They hurried inside and headed for The Oak Room.

"Well, what's your analysis of the situation?" asked Gavin while they waited to be seated.

Johnny began his report as the maître d' escorted them to their table.

"If everybody back here is as big a clown as your Johnny, we should be able to clean up. On top of that," he continued as they were taking their seats, "you were right about the antiques. I drove for miles through the countryside around Cambridge, Boston, Watertown, and Waltham. Like you said, there were big stores and little shops, even people selling everything from rocking chairs to huge vanities out on their front lawns."

Tommy signaled the sommelier and ordered a bottle of wine.

"Almost all this stuff was priced far below what I could get for them on the west coast," he continued. "This place is a gold mine for antiques."

The sommelier brought the wine. Gavin suppressed a laugh when Tommy went through the ritual of smelling the cork, and then motioned to the man that his glass be filled to the brim.

Tommy really played the part of Mr. Thomas to the hilt.

The sommelier moved to fill his glass too, but Gavin waved him off.

Tommy took a sip and leaned back in his chair. "How do you like it here so far?"

Gavin picked up the menus and handed one to Tommy. "The weather is unforgivable and the people at the university are mostly like Johnny. Some are even worse. They look at school as an opportunity to party and fuck off."

He shrugged, looked around the almost empty dining room, and continued. "The guy I work for at First Boston is terrific, and I'm learning a lot there."

Tommy topped his glass off again and took a big swallow.

"Gavin, I think the films will go over huge."

Gavin signaled for the waiter so they could order, and then turned back to Tommy. "As long as my name isn't in it, and you're three thousand miles away, we should be okay."

Tommy returned to L.A. Without telling Johnny Monreale, he returned almost every week to buy antiques. The porn movie rental scheme was working smoothly. School settled into a routine for Gavin, and the days and weeks passed by.

At work, Rob Stone was giving Gavin more and more interesting challenges. This gave him the opportunity to learn about the insurance business and to see law in practice from First Boston's viewpoint.

Johnny Monreale, on the other hand, was overly eager, generous, always trying to please and be one of the guys.

And he was a miserable student. Using his income from porn so his parents wouldn't know, he bought his exam answers and paid others to do his work.

According to Tommy, there seemed to be an insatiable appetite for dirty movies in and around Cambridge. He told Gavin that if there was one thing Johnny Monreale seemed born to do, it was to make money from porn. And Johnny believed that the whole arrangement was just between him and Tommy out on the West Coast.

# Chapter Forty Four

## February 1961

Winter settled on the east coast like a blanket of misery

Gavin and Johnny were holed up in their dorm room, the howling wind and rain beating against the window.

"I hate this shit!" Johnny screamed. "I gotta get the hell out of here, go get a beer and that's that."

He grabbed his London Fog. With one arm through a sleeve he stormed out of the dorm.

Trailing behind him, the coat was caught as the door closed. He cussed a blue streak re-opening the door to free it.

Gavin didn't look up. Within minutes the door opened again, and a thoroughly soaked Johnny was back. He stomped into the bathroom, took off his London Fog and threw it in the tub.

"Goddamn, it's colder than a bat's butt," he said through the bathroom door. He came back into the room, threw himself down on his bed and stared at the ceiling.

"You know," he said absently, "we never did get down to New York." He turned to face Gavin, "Why don't we make plans?"

Gavin set his book on the desk, leaned back in the chair, and rubbed his eyes. He would really like to explore New York City, but not with Johnny and a bunch of others like him. The idea of a loud, drunken mob of students careening through Manhattan sounded like a recipe for disaster. Guardedly he asked, "What do you have in mind?"

"We take off Friday right after school." Johnny sat up excitedly. "Won't even change clothes till we get there, just wear what we have on for the trip. We just take the train to Penn Central and grab a cab to my folks' apartment, change and go out on the town. We'll come back Sunday. We can go to Club Twenty-One and all kinds of places my family goes to all the time. Everybody knows us."

"Just the two of us?"

"Unless we get lucky." Johnny said grinning.

"It's a deal. When do you want to do it?"

"How about this coming Friday?" Now Johnny was really excited. "You can take off one afternoon from work, can't you? That way we can just come back here right after our last class, pack and leave."

By Friday, the rain had stopped and was replaced by the bitter cold of the East Coast winter. The train station in Boston was busy, but nothing compared to Penn Station. Once they got to Manhattan and got a cab, the trip was more like a battle, inch by inch, foot by foot as the driver fought and sparred his way through the traffic.

Just past the museum the driver made a quick left turn off Fifth Avenue onto 78th Street and stopped in front of the second building from the corner.

The building, like the others nearby, was old but elegant. From the cab driver's reaction Gavin concluded having a place in this neighborhood must really mean something.

The driver double-parked and got out, opened the trunk and set their luggage on the pavement.

Gavin started to pick up his bag, but Johnny motioned toward the building. A uniformed doorman had unlocked the apartment building's thick glass doors and was hurrying across the sidewalk. Nodding toward the doorman Johnny said, "Charles will help us with our stuff."

The doorman addressed Johnny by name, picked up the two suitcases and led them inside. Once in the lobby, Charles set the suitcases down, turned and carefully relocked the doors.

The lobby was opulent. Floor of white marble, elegant wall covering, mirrors. Polished stainless-steel elevator doors reflected the colors of the flowers in a large vase on the doorman's counter.

Gavin started for the elevator, but Johnny motioned and said "This way."

He led them to the left, past the doorman's counter and up three marble steps to a landing off the lobby.

He unlocked the door, and they entered a huge, lavishly furnished apartment.

The place didn't really suit Gavin's tastes, but he guessed this must be the height of New York luxury living. Even after Johnny turned on the lights Gavin thought the place seemed gloomy, almost spooky, with its ten-foot ceilings, hardwood floors, Persian carpets, and overstuffed furniture.

"I'll go ahead and call for a cab. We should be ready to go by the time it gets here."

177

Johnny picked up the phone. "That's odd," he said, "the damn phone doesn't work. I can't even get a dial tone." He set the phone back down and nodded toward an open door.

"You can use that bedroom to change."

Gavin picked up his bag and headed for one of the three bedrooms. When they met back in the living room a few minutes later Johnny, his London Fog draped over his arm, was wearing a gray suit with a silver tie and white shirt.

Gavin was wearing a tan, knee length mohair overcoat over a dark blue suit, white shirt, and paisley tie.

"Wow! That is some coat you've got there!" Johnny said. "If you're going to be that dressy, I'm going to wear my dad's cashmere coat. He and I are both the same size and he'll never know the difference."

Johnny went back into the master bedroom and returned wearing a white, ankle length cashmere topcoat. He tugged the lapels and did a little turn.

"How does this look?"

Gavin thought it looked way over the top but answered, "That's very impressive."

They left the apartment, pausing on the landing while Johnny locked the door.

Charles had been leaning over his counter reading a paperback. When he heard their footsteps, he turned the book over on its face and looked up. He grinned and started around the counter to unlock the big glass doors and let them out.

Gavin was looking past the doorman toward the dark street outside. Cars were parked all along the curb bumper to bumper, so close together that he wondered how the hell anyone could get out of their parking space. On top of that, more cars were double-parked, leaving only a narrow passageway in the middle for traffic.

A car was stopped with its lights off right in front of the building.

Condensation from the car's hot exhaust rose in the cold night air.

The car's engine was running.

Johnny was saying something to Charles and wasn't watching.

He didn't see the car's passenger side door open and a man in a dark gray overcoat and wearing black leather gloves put one foot out on the pavement.

The man raised his left arm.

In his hand he held a pistol.

Two holes surrounded by what looked like spider webs appeared in the glass doors.

Shards spewed inward, tinkling musically as they scattered across the marble floor.

Gavin grabbed Johnny's coat collar.

He yanked Johnny backwards as hard as he could, pulling him off his feet and onto the marble floor.

"What the hell are you doing?" Johnny asked, starting to get up.

The doorman, on his way to open the door lurched sideways.

He slumped against the stainless-steel elevator doors.

He left a smear of blood as he slid to the white marble floor.

Gavin's heart was racing.

He crouched beside Johnny and watched.

The gunman stepped up on the curb.

He crossed the sidewalk to the locked door and grabbed the big ornate handles trying to get in.

Gavin quickly scrambled backward on his hands and knees, dragging Johnny by the collar of the cashmere coat.

He pulled him across the blood-slick floor to take cover behind the doorman's counter.

Johnny's face was covered in blood.

Shards of glass were sticking out of his forehead and cheeks.

His suit, the cashmere topcoat, his shirt, and tie were all soaked.

"What the hell just happened?" Johnny cried, starting to wipe the blood out of his eyes.

"Somebody shot the doorman. Don't touch yourself. You've got glass stuck in your face," Gavin said, looking around frantically. "Let's try to get you back inside your apartment and call the cops."

Then he remembered.

The phone in the apartment didn't work.

He peered around the side of the doorman's counter.

The man with the gun walked back to the car.

He got in.

The car drove off.

Gavin remembered the phone on the counter.

Still huddled on the marble floor, he grabbed the phone cord and pulled the whole unit off the countertop down to the floor beside him.

He picked up the receiver and dialed the operator.

"Get me the police!"

"What precinct?" the operator asked.

What did she mean, "What precinct?" What the hell is a 'precinct?'

Just then, the elevator doors opened, and a well-dressed man and woman stepped out.

"What the hell's going on here?" asked the man. Spotting the doorman's body and all the blood he pulled the woman back into the elevator without waiting for an answer.

The doors slid shut and they were gone as suddenly as they'd appeared.

Again, Gavin was alone in the lobby with Johnny and the doorman.

He heard the disembodied voice from the receiver repeat, "What precinct?"

He turned to ask Johnny, but Johnny's eyes were glazing over. He was trembling, bleeding bad and seemed to be going into shock.

"I don't know. We're at 78th Street near the museum, right off Fifth Avenue across from the park."

"Hold the line, please."

The white marble lobby was quiet, just the sound of Johnny's labored breathing. Gavin desperately hoped the gunman had not just gone around the block and was on his way back. After what seemed like hours a policeman came on the line.

"What seems to be the problem, sir?"

Gavin explained what had happened and where they were. The cop told him to stay on the line so they could trace the call and that officers were on their way.

Blood was pooling on the floor under Johnny. He seemed to be getting paler. Gavin cradled the phone with his shoulder and edged away.

He did not want to get blood on his suit or the mohair coat.

Sirens echoed. They stopped in the street in front of the building. Cautiously Gavin peered around the doorman's counter.

The rotating lights on the roof of a NYPD squad car bathed the lobby in red.

Two police officers with their guns drawn hurried toward the door. Gavin hoped that meant it was safe for him to leave his place behind the counter. Careful to avoid the glass shards, he crawled on his hands and knees over to the doorman. He rummaged through the doorman's pockets. He found the keys, stood, and went to the heavy glass doors to let the cops in.

"What the hell happened here?" said the older of the two.

Gavin tried to explain again as best he could. He turned and said to the younger copy bending over the doorman's body, "I don't think there's much you can do for him, I'm pretty sure he's dead."

Another squad car pulled up, and two more policemen rushed in, their guns drawn.

Gavin looked at the older cop's name badge.

"Officer O'Brian, I think my friend here could use an ambulance," he said pointing at Johnny half-hidden behind the counter.

The officer looked, nodded, and picked up the phone to call for an ambulance and the coroner.

"Jesus Jesus Jesus Jesus," Johnny was repeating over and over. He was shaking hard and seemed oblivious to what was going on, the cops moving about, taking notes, and talking.

"What's your friend's name?" O'Brian asked after he hung up.

"Johnny Monreale. His folks own this apartment here and live in Utica. Why would anybody want to shoot a doorman?"

"They weren't trying to shoot the doorman." O'Brian said. He turned to the other three in the lobby and nodded his head toward Johnny. "You guys, I think this kid is Gianni Monreale's son."

181

The policemen all suddenly stopped what they were doing and turned to stare at Johnny.

I do not like the looks of this, Gavin thought.

An ambulance arrived, edged past the police cars, and stopped. By this time, the lobby was crowded with cops. They cleared a way for the paramedics, Johnny was lifted onto a gurney and quickly wheeled it out into the cold night.

The wail of the ambulance's siren echoed in the canyon of apartments lining the narrow street.

In seconds they were gone.

Gavin turned to one of the policemen. "Where are they taking him?"

"To the Lenox Hill Hospital's Emergency Room. It's only a few blocks down Fifth Avenue." He put his hand on Gavin's shoulder. "C'mon. We gotta go to the station and get your report on all this." He looked Gavin over. "That is some mohair coat you got there."

He shook his head. "Wonder you didn't get any blood on it."

Gavin's interview at the police precinct was more like an interrogation with frequent interruptions.

They were finally through around three a.m. and one of the younger detectives offered to run Gavin over to Fifth Avenue and Lenox Hill Hospital.

The dark, empty streets of the Upper East Side were bitter cold and now it was beginning to snow.

Before dropping him off at the hospital entrance the cop had tried to pump him about his friend, but Gavin could only refer to the Johnny he knew as a roommate at school. It never occurred to him that there was another side to his roommate, Johnny Monreale.

The emergency room receptionist gave him directions to Johnny's room.

Gavin's footsteps were the only sound in the brightly lit, empty hallway.

Ahead, leaning against the wall was a large, middle-aged man in a pin striped suit, a man as broad as he was tall. The man was positioned just about where Gavin figured Johnny's room would be.

He glared as Gavin approached.

It occurred to Gavin that the man looked like something right out of a Damon Runyon novel. He was even wearing a black shirt with a white tie. All that was lacking was for him to be flipping a silver dollar.

"Good morning," Gavin offered.

"Depends," said the man.

Gavin turned and paused at the door to Johnny's room.

"Where do you think you are going?" asked the man.

"I'm here to see Johnny Monreale."

"He is not seeing no one at this time." With his tongue he slowly moved the well-chewed match to the other side of his mouth. "Come back later."

Tired as he was at this god-awful hour of the morning, Gavin was not going to press the issue. "Oh well. Please tell him Gavin came by and that I've gone back to Cambridge."

The man cocked his head. "Hold on. I will see if he is awake."

He pushed himself away from the wall and turned to lean in the doorway. Keeping his eyes on Gavin he spoke softly into the room.

"There is a person here to see Little Johnny. Says his name is Gavin."

From inside the room Gavin heard Johnny's voice; "Gavin! Christ, let him in. He's my pal! He saved my life!"

The big man stepped aside. Gavin edged past to enter the room. Johnny was propped up in bed, an almost empty I.V. bottle attached to his arm. He had bandages all over his face and covering one eye. Another man, also wearing a pin striped suit, black shirt, and bright yellow tie was standing by the bed.

His hand was inside his jacket.

"Well, what do you think of New York so far?" Johnny asked, his voice muffled by his bandages. "By the way, this is Uncle Benny. I guess you met my cousin Willy in the hall."

Almost hysterical from exhaustion and the comical circumstances Gavin had to suppress a laugh at this whole scene. He was half expecting George Raft to walk in.

"Well, I've seen all I need to for now. I think I'll just go back to Cambridge."

183

"Aww, stick around. I'm being released as soon as the doctor gets back. He says it's mostly superficial. I lost some blood from the cuts, but they gave me a transfusion, so I'll be all right. You can ride back in the car with Uncle Benny and Cousin Willy and me."

"Certainly," said Uncle Benny. "You are more than welcome to join us." He stepped around the bed to face Gavin. "This is a very nice overcoat." He gently touched the lapel. "Mohair, is it not?"

Johnny was discharged just before 5 a.m. Willy, carrying a hospital bag with the ruined cashmere topcoat and Johnny's clothes went on ahead to get the car.

Benny followed close behind, pushing Johnny in a wheelchair. Johnny, wearing the hospital's blue gown and covered by a blanket, complained the whole time that he could walk just fine. They waited just inside the doors until two matching black 1961 Lincoln sedans pulled in front of the emergency room entrance.

The lead car was driven by Willy.

In the front seat of the second car were two large men.

Gavin, Johnny, and Benny left the warmth of the hospital for the bitter cold of the New York dawn.

Gavin, exhausted and wondering where all this was going to take him, opened the door to the back seat and got in. Benny opened the other door and helped Johnny out of the wheelchair and into the car.

Willy started down the hospital drive and the second Lincoln fell in behind.

There was little traffic at this hour and the gentle turns as the big car negotiated Manhattan's empty streets were lulling Gavin to sleep.

He must have dozed for almost an hour when he heard Johnny say groggily, "Willy, this doesn't look like the Massachusetts Turnpike. Where are we going?"

Benny, in the front seat, turned and answered, "We are not going to Cambridge, Little Johnny. We have been instructed to take you home to your father."

Johnny shrugged, snuggled into his blanket, and went back to sleep.

The Lincoln made its way north on the New York Thruway. Gavin rested his forehead against the car's cold glass window and watched the passing snow-covered fields. In the distance, stark, leafless trees were silhouetted against the cold grey February sky.

The woods are lovely, dark, and deep.

But I have promises to keep,

And miles to go before I sleep,

And miles to go before I sleep.

Except for the 'lovely' part. With apologies to Robert Frost, Gavin could not help wondering why anyone would willingly live in such an inhospitable, God-forsaken place. He sighed and stretched his legs in the roomy back seat, half listening to Benny in front.

Benny was going on and on, telling Willy all about his being married to an older woman, a woman almost 10 years his senior. It sounded to Gavin like the guy thought everyone else was indebted to him for marrying an older woman.

The Lincoln continued past the Utica exit, prompting Gavin to peek over the back of the front seat at the dashboard clock. It had been almost five hours since they had left Manhattan and he had to pee. They just had to be getting close to wherever they were going, he thought. The empty, snow covered fields were a constant reminder of how cold it was outside. He sure as hell did not want to ask Willy to stop so he could pee alongside the road. He wasn't even sure he could do it, cold as it was.

He didn't think he could hold it much longer, when at last the car left the New York Thruway at the River Road Exit.

It turned right on County Road 30 headed north.

Johnny stirred a little but didn't awake and Benny and Willy in front seemed to have forgotten Gavin was in the car.

There was no other traffic and now they were truly in the middle of nowhere. Gavin shifted in his seat. That seemed to help a little with his bladder problem.

Finally, he asked, "Could we pull over for a minute? I really have to take a leak."

"Sure," Willy replied, pulling to the side of the road. "We're almost there anyway, but I guess it wouldn't be polite of you to make a mad dash for the john as soon as you walked in the door."

Gavin got out of the back and the cold hit him, engulfed him. He walked around to the rear of the car and stood above the ditch that ran alongside the road.

Off to his left, a mile or so further along was a group of large homes, maybe even a settlement of some kind, perched on a snow-covered hill and enclosed by a high masonry wall.

Very fortress-like.

Gavin finished his business and returned to the car. Willy put the Lincoln in gear, and they pulled back onto the deserted road, only to turn just minutes later into the short drive that led to the walled compound on the hill.

A guard in a shelter gave them a wave and heavy gates opened to let them through.

Johnny stirred awake. "Home at last. Now you'll meet my family. We live in the second house from the entrance," he explained, excitedly grabbing the back of the front seat and leaning forward. "My Grandfather and my uncles and their families live in the other three houses. Grandpa's is the big house on the end, up ahead at the turn around."

The car pulled up the driveway and parked under the carport of the second house on the right, a large, two-story Colonial. Willy turned to Gavin and said, "Here we are."

They hurried from the car into a large utilitarian-looking room lined with coat racks hung with wet weather gear. In the middle of the room, a big pot bellied stove glowed red, making it almost uncomfortably warm.

Standing near the stove, wearing dark brown slacks and a tan sweater was a good looking, extremely well-groomed man. Gavin thought the man could have been Johnny's older brother but guessed from his angry look that the man was his father.

"What did you think you were doing? Why did you go to the apartment?"

"Now Dad," began Johnny.

"What the hell am I going to tell your mother?"

Johnny's father moved toward him and continued. "Look at you. You look like one of the walking wounded! God knows how your grandpa's going to take this!"

"Dad, I...." Johnny started again.

"Why can't you just stay in Cambridge and go to Harvard?"

Turning to Benny, Johnny's father asked, "Just how bad is it?"

"Doctor said Little Johnny was hit by flying glass. His injuries are superficial. One shard hit his eye, but the doctor said he was successful in removing it. He should recover completely, but he will have to wear a patch for a few days." Benny paused and looked down at his hands. "Your favorite cashmere coat is finished and so is your favorite doorman."

"It wasn't my favorite coat, and I can get another doorman," Gianni replied. "I wouldn't have worn that coat to a dog show and the doorman was only my wife's second cousin."

Motioning toward Gavin, he asked, "Who the hell is this guy?"

"He saved my life, Dad," Johnny answered.

"Yeah, Mr. Monreale. If this guy hadn't grabbed Little Johnny and pulled him out of the way the kid would have got it for sure."

"My name is Gianni Monreale," the man said, turning to Gavin and extending his hand. "That is a very nice mohair coat you have there."

"Thank you, sir." Gavin replied. "Nice to meet you, sir."

Gianni Monreale returned his attention to his son. "I'll have to come up with something to tell your mother. Maybe something about an accident playing sports at school or something. I should be thankful it isn't worse. First, we gotta report to grandpa. He knows all about it by now anyway."

"If you do not need us anymore, we will take our leave," Benny said to the senior Monreale. "I do not want to be around when Don Gianpoalo gets here."

With that, Benny and Willy went out into the gray Utica day.

"Dad, we've both been up all night," said Johnny. "Can we take a nap? This warm room is really putting me to sleep."

"Yeah, go ahead. But before you get comfortable, show your friend to the guest room. I'll beard the lion in his den and call grandpa."

Turning to Gavin, Johnny's father said, "Please make yourself at home. It appears my family is deeply indebted to you."

Johnny led Gavin through the living room and up a broad staircase. He pointed out his own room in case Gavin needed anything, then led him down the hall to the guest bedroom. "You have your own bath and shower when you get ready to use it. I'll come and get you for dinner."

187

The room was in the back of the house. It was nicely furnished, had a full bath and even a television set. A balcony outside the glass doors looked down on a deserted yard and an empty swimming pool. Beyond the high wall surrounding the compound, vacant, snow-covered fields stretched away to the woods.

Gavin carefully took off his clothes and hung them in the closet along with his mohair topcoat, took a long hot shower, then fell on the bed. He was out like a light.

At six o'clock there was a knock and through the door Johnny said, "We'll be eating dinner in about an hour. My grandpa will be joining us. He's here now, and he and Dad want to meet you in the library before dinner."

"Come on in while I shave and get ready," Gavin replied.

When Johnny entered Gavin thought he seemed subdued, anything but his usual rambunctious self. He'd changed into slacks and a sweater, but the bandage on his head made his hair stick out and his left eye was still covered by a patch.

He walked over to the dresser and looked at himself in the mirror.

"Did you want to tell me something or brief me about your family or anything?" Gavin asked.

"I don't know."

Gavin went into the bathroom, leaving Johnny, lost in thought, staring at his reflection in the mirror on the dresser. This is totally unlike him, Gavin thought. This is the longest he's gone without saying something or making some kind of noise since I've known him.

Gavin finished in the bathroom and came back into the bedroom to begin dressing.

Johnny, with his back to him, was still silently looking in the mirror, fingering his bandage.

Finally, he said softly, "Since Grandma died, grandpa has lived alone in the big house at the end of the street. He has a live-in butler, or whatever you want to call him, named Max. Max is like one of the family. We all love Max, and Max is utterly devoted to us. He drives for grandpa and generally does everything for grandpa that the gardeners or the maids don't do." Johnny turned from the mirror and looked at Gavin. "The house directly across from us belongs to his oldest son, my uncle Tony. My cousin Leo and his family live in the other house. Grandpa joins us for dinner occasionally. Quite often, in fact."

188

Johnny was beginning to sound a little more relaxed. "Dad says grandpa especially wants to meet you before we sit down to dinner with mom and my little sister. I don't think Grandpa and Dad want to talk about what happened at the apartment in front of them."

"I can imagine," Gavin said.

Johnny took a breath. "Well, if you're ready, let's go," he said, opening the door to the hallway.

Johnny led the way to the stairs and down, toward the front of the house. From somewhere came the sound of someone playing the piano. Beethoven's Tempe di Menuetto.

The library was large, with floor to ceiling windows looking out on the cul de sac and the houses across the way. The walls were lined floor to ceiling with bookshelves. There were five big, overstuffed chairs placed in a semi-circle in front of a fireplace.

Dressed in a dark suit and tie and seated at the piano near the windows was a distinguished looking older man with white-hair and a neatly trimmed moustache.

Obviously, the mature version of the Monreale male.

Johnny's father stood beside him, his hand on the older man's shoulder. Nodding toward Gavin he said "Padre, this is Little Johnny's friend, Gavin, the one we've been telling you about."

The older man stopped playing, rose from the piano bench, and extended his hand to introduce himself. "Gianpoalo Monreale. I am Little Johnny's grandfather. I am informed that your trip to New York was more adventurous than perhaps you expected."

"Yes, sir," Gavin replied.

"Please sit and tell me all about it," Gianpoalo said, motioning to the leather chairs at the fireplace.

"Can I offer you something to drink?" Johnny's father asked.

"Perhaps a coke? Or just some water."

"Gavin doesn't drink," Johnny interjected.

"Well, after what you've been through perhaps today you might want to make an exception," suggested Gianpoalo.

"No, thank you just the same," Gavin replied. "I just can't seem to develop a taste for it."

"To explain the bandages and all, we have told Little Johnny's mother and his sister that his accident was caused by a broken mirror," Johnny's father said, nodding to his son. "In order to make his appearance less alarming to his mother I've suggested we eat by candlelight."

"I see."

"Little Johnny has told us that you two were leaving the apartment to go out on the town and someone in the street started shooting. We understand your quick thinking saved our Johnny's life. Would you please recount for us your version of last night's events?"

Gavin had told his story to the police two or three times, and it had gotten to the point where he was just repeating himself rather than reliving the events. But the two older Monreales eagerly leaned forward in their chairs, so he went over the whole incident as if for the first time.

When he finished, Gianpoalo turned to Johnny and asked, "How did you happen to be wearing that cashmere coat?"

"When we got ready to go out, Gavin put on a beautiful mohair topcoat. All I had was a London fog, grandpa. I thought dad wouldn't mind if I wore his cashmere," Johnny explained.

Gianpoalo looked over to Gianni and said, "That cashmere topcoat your brother Tony gave you was very conspicuous. He told me it was meant from the heart, and he hoped you'd like it." Then he turned to Johnny. "The two of you must have looked like a couple of pimps."

Gianni leaned forward in his chair, turned to Gianpoalo and said in Italian, "My guess, father, is that someone must have mistaken Johnny for me wearing that damn thing." He leaned back in the chair, thought a moment and added, "Thing is, I've never worn it."

Gianpoalo put his fingertips together and answered, also in Italian, "It sounds like we have the beginnings of a problem."

Crap! The Monreales seemed oblivious to the fact that since he is majoring in law and had to learn Latin, Gavin could understand enough Italian to figure out what they were saying. And all this time he thought Monreale was a French name.

At this point, also speaking Italian, Johnny chimed in "Perche qualcuno desiderebbe sparario, padre?" (Why would anyone want to harm you, father?")

190

"Lascalili opinione che qiasta e 'una disputa di affair'. Sarabbe meglio se quello e a che cosa diciamo al vostro amica qui," (Someone with a disputed claim," He nodded toward Gavin. "At least that's what we're going to tell your friend here."

Gianni turned to Gavin. "We were just saying it appears you two may have been caught up in a business dispute involving perhaps an unhappy insured. You see, I am in the insurance business. Sometimes customers are not satisfied with the way their claims are handled."

Gianpoalo nodded in agreement.

Gavin thought, okay, if that is their story, I'll go along with it at least long enough to get the hell out of here. "I can imagine. I understand that it is tough doing business here in the east."

Gianni looked to Gianpoalo, nodded, and turned back to Gavin, "Yes, it is very tough -here in the east."

Gianni rose from his chair. "Perhaps I can show you my home? I am something of a collector. Are you interested in Roman artifacts?"

"I find remnants of early civilizations fascinating," answered Gavin.

Nodding to his son, Gianni said, "Johnny, why don't you stay here with your grandfather? He has something he wants to discuss with you. We meet the women for dinner in half an hour, and we are not to keep them waiting."

Gianni led Gavin from the library through the large home toward the rear of the house, showing him the formal dining room, living room and game room.

Gavin thought the insurance business must be very good indeed to afford all this.

"I want to introduce you to my pride and joy," Gianni said, ushering him into his office. It was at least as large as the library, beautifully and very tastefully furnished in browns and tans, very masculine.

A high-backed leather swivel chair behind a large mahogany desk was situated in front of floor to ceiling windows that looked out on a private garden.

A bookcase filled one wall of Gianni's office, and built-in display cases occupied the other walls, their contents illuminated by overhead spotlights.

The display case was filled with carefully placed Early Roman artifacts.

Artwork, statuettes, busts, coins, amphora.

In a corner, on a marble pedestal, stood a weathered and obviously ancient bust of Julius Caesar.

Gianni opened the glass door to one of the cabinets and removed a bronze helmet.

Holding it carefully, he turned to Gavin. "I recently acquired this, the newest addition to my collection, from associates in Italy. It was recovered near Pavia and is from about the time of the Carthaginian invasion from the north. It could have been worn by a legionnaire that saw Hannibal and his elephants."

Impressed, Gavin said, "Mr. Monreale, this is just beautiful."

"Here, you may hold it, see how heavy it is."

"No, no, I couldn't take the chance that I might drop and damage so precious an object."

"I see you have an appreciation for beauty. Our family is very conscious of our heritage, and I find Roman history fascinating. To me, our past comes alive through these objects. I have spent many years collecting and assembling this small shrine to my ancestors."

"It is a beautiful and impressive collection. Have you considered putting it on public display?"

"Not really. Mostly I just like to study them, handle them, and imagine the life that was taking place around them at the time they were in use. I consider myself blessed to be their 'temporary custodian."

Setting the helmet back on the shelf Gianni said, "But now I am afraid we must go on to the dining room or risk incurring the wrath of the women for being tardy."

The dining room was large and formal- with a two-story vaulted ceiling. As they entered, a very beautiful woman, probably about the same age as Gianni, but looking no more than thirty, was lighting candles in a centerpiece.

She turned and extended her hand. "Gina Monreale. I'm Johnny's mother. I hope you don't mind dining by candlelight," she said. She went to the switch on the wall and turned off the lights.

Now, the room was almost dark, lit only by the flickering glow of the candles.

She turned to Gavin. "Having Johnny home from school is a special occasion for us. I cannot bear to see him all bandaged up."

Gianpoalo and Johnny entered, and Johnny pulled the chair back for the senior Monreale to take his place at the head of the table.

A teenage girl, kind of gangly Gavin thought from what he could see in the dim light, came bounding into the room. She screeched and threw her arms around Johnny. Johnny untangled himself and introduced her as his kid sister, Caterina.

From what little Gavin could see of her, she looked a little like an adolescent version of her mother, long brown hair and big brown eyes.

When everyone was seated, they all began chattering excitedly that Catarina would finally be getting her braces off just before she was to graduate from high school.

Tired as he must be, Gavin thought that Johnny seemed uncharacteristically quiet. No wise cracking or boasting. The others apparently didn't notice, but Gavin thought Johnny seemed subdued, looking down at his plate and contributing little to the conversation.

After dinner, Gianpoalo, Gianni, Johnny, and Gavin all adjourned to the game room and played pool until late. Throughout the entire evening Johnny still had little to say. By about 11:30 Gavin was about to fall on his face from exhaustion, Gianpoalo offered to have his man Max drive him back to Cambridge the next day. It had been decided that Johnny would remain home in the family doctor's care for a few days; at least until the eye patch was removed.

A week later, an entirely different Johnny returned to Harvard and the dorm.

# Chapter Forty Five

## Tommy "Mr. Thomas" Huber

## March 1961

Mr. Thomas's Antiques of Beverly Hills was enjoying a banner year, especially the rental operation. Antiques that Tommy picked up on his trips east, considered mostly just old used furniture and junk in New England were gold in Beverly Hills and West L.A. Would-be producers and directors, the nouveau riche and Wilshire Boulevard attorneys all thought that antiques in their offices signified taste and substance.

"Mr. Thomas" was having a field day. Now, he dressed carefully in European styles to give the impression of worldliness and sophistication. Tailored suits, silk shirts with an ascot or a scarf, his hair groomed and highlighted by a hairdresser on Canon Drive.

The rent for the big store cost a fortune, but he could easily afford it. He was even considering opening a store on California Street in San Francisco and had flown back and forth several times scouting out locations.

San Francisco had the same type of potential customers, phonies trying to impress. But if anything, they were even more snobbish and pretentious than the L.A. and Hollywood crowd. Mr. Thomas was confident they would really go for the idea of renting antiques, especially since most of them couldn't afford to buy the stuff at the prices he charged.

Tommy used Gavin as a bank, borrowing to stock the store and expand, and from time to time owed him as much as five hundred thousand dollars. But he easily covered the debt plus interest.

In addition, he was able to support a lavish lifestyle. Mr. Thomas lived in a big prestigious new condominium in Brentwood and drove a leased Bentley convertible.

All this to project an image of a successful, educated young man with taste.

But Tommy Huber from Inglewood, California could not let go of his past.

No, the time spent on the street kept calling him back. The thrill, the anticipation, the excitement of not knowing if a john would come up with a new sexual twist, one he had not tried or even considered.

So, more and more often, during the week or on weekends Mr. Thomas would wash the styling gel out of his hair. He would put on ordinary clothes and leaving the Bentley in the condo's garage he would take a bus to Beverly Boulevard.

Here he was Tommy the Streetwalker again, hustling the johns that cruise the boulevard at night looking for action.

It was early in the year, March, and chilly. A stiff wind from the ocean blew across West L.A., whipping the tall palm trees.

The night that he and Chucky were standing on the corner watching traffic, 'trolling for brown-eye' was downright cold. Chucky, a guy about Tommy's size but perhaps a bit heavier, was barely an acquaintance. The two had a drink and done a line once or twice in the head at The Erector Set, a 'small guys bar' on Santa Monica Boulevard. The Erector Set was not just a bar for small guys. It was a small bar that catered to gays, maybe small gays, but no bikers or bears.

Truth be told, Tommy really didn't know Chucky, had never had any sort of "relations" or been on a trick with him.

There were other guys walking the dark sidewalk alongside Beverly Boulevard.

Some of them were alone, and some traveled in pairs in case a john wanted a threesome. Each of them though, were independent contractors as it were, on their own, in business for themselves. Whether they were friends or not, they never greeted each other on the street as they passed by, never said hello or acknowledged one another in any way.

And, despite their insistence that they were all individuals, most of them were very similar to one another in appearance.

Late teens or early twenties, almost always with well-trimmed blond or brown hair, almost always with a mustache, and almost all were under 5'9" or so.

Here on Beverly Boulevard, at night and in the dark, Tommy felt at home, felt like he was among his own kind.

The glare of the headlights as a car approached made it difficult to see who was driving until the car stopped at the curb next to them. For Tommy, that was one of the most exciting parts of this game. It was almost always a surprise, like opening a Christmas present and discovering what was inside. He never knew what he was getting until the car stopped, the window on the curb side lowered, and the driver said something.

Would it be some clumsy line? Would the john immediately get to the point and come right out and say what he wanted? Would it be something interesting? Something new?

For a gay streetwalker, it was almost always something new.

A late model Cadillac separated itself from traffic and pulled over to the curb next to the pair. The passenger side window lowered, and the driver asked, "You boys want to party?"

Tommy and Chucky bent to look in the car. The man seemed okay, maybe in his late thirties to mid forties, nice looking and well dressed.

"Could be," replied Chucky. "Where?"

"My place. Off Franklin, above Grauman's Chinese."

"Sounds good," said Chucky. He turned to Tommy. "Are you game?"

"Yes," Tommy replied.

The man leaned across the seat to open the door, and Chucky got in the front. Tommy opened the back door, got in, and the man eased the Caddy back into traffic.

Through Hollywood to Franklyn, then with a turn off Franklyn onto one of the narrow winding roads, the car began to climb the hill.

Near the top, the john pushed a button on the sun visor to open a garage door for one of the houses perched precariously on the steep hillside.

He pulled the car in, and the garage door closed behind them.

A door in the garage led directly into the house.

Once inside, Tommy saw the place was larger than it appeared to be from the road. On the far side of a nicely furnished living room, a big window looked out on the lights of Hollywood and Los Angeles. The john turned on a table lamp. Now Tommy could see that some of the furnishings were fairly valuable. Paintings, antiques, and other items indicated the john had an interest in collecting and knew what he was doing.

"Would either of you like a drink?"

Chucky piped up. "I'll take a beer if you have it."

"Would you object to a joint?" Tommy asked. He thought a little marijuana really heightened the sensation when it came to sex.

"Not at all," replied the john. "If you'll share it, I'll join you." Taking off his leather jacket and throwing it on the couch he motioned, "Follow me. I'll show you around." He led them toward a hallway. Over his shoulder he said, "I'll get right to the point. I like it rough. I like being bound for forced sex."

Chucky took a drink from the bottle. "Sounds good to me," he said, wiping his mouth with the back of his hand.

Tommy thought that sounded real good. It was one of his favorites, although he was usually too cautious to agree unless he knew the other participants fairly well. But the grass and the moment and even as slightly as he knew Chucky, he felt at ease just enough to go along with the idea.

"Come," said the john. "I'll show you the rumpus room where we can really raise a rumpus." He grinned, began unbuttoning his shirt and led them to a door at the end of the hall. He opened the door with a flourish and Tommy looked in. It was a good-sized room with dark brown carpeting that extended halfway up the walls. Where the carpeting ended, mirrors were mounted at an angle to reflect everything that happened in the room. Spotlights in the ceiling made it all very theatrical. On the floor in the middle of the room was a padded rubber mat about ten feet square.

Chucky took another drink of beer and said, "Let's get the business out of the way. What's your trick so we can work out a deal?"

"I want to be bound, wrists to ankles, on my knees, with him tied up in front of me," replied the john.

"How about $25 each? That okay with you, Tommy?"

"Sounds fair enough."

The three took off all their clothes. Tommy had one long drag on the joint. Chucky proceeded to tie the john and Tommy as instructed, a little too tightly, Tommy thought. But on the other hand, that should heighten the fantasy. As requested, he positioned himself in front of the john.

Chucky moved around behind him.

197

It made this fantasy even better to see that naked, Chucky had a pretty good build and so did the john.

Suddenly, without any warning Chucky raised his arms and brought both his doubled fists down on the back of the john's head, stunning him. The john rolled sideways.

Chucky hit the guy again.

Tommy was so stoned he did not immediately grasp what was going on right in front of him.

Then Chucky turned and hit Tommy full in the face, knocking him backward off the mat.

When Tommy's head hit the floor, everything went black.

The next thing he knew the john was standing over him, screaming and shaking him awake.

His head hurt.

He was still stoned.

The john had him by the neck and was yelling in his face. "Wake up, asshole!"

"What are you doing? What happened?"

"You tell me, you prick! You and your friend set me up to clean me out!"

"What do you mean?"

"You know damn well what I mean! Your friend beat me up and robbed me."

"I don't know anything about this."

"The hell you don't, Mr. Thomas," said the john.

It was then that Tommy saw the john had gone through his clothes and had his wallet in his hands. "I know who you are and where you live and why you wanted my stuff," the john yelled. He shook Tommy's wallet so hard the credit cards flew all over the room. "You planned to sell my stuff in your store, you son of a bitch! But your partner double-crossed you and left you holding the bag."

"He isn't my partner, I swear!"

"Bullshit!" the john said, stepping back a pace. "Here's the way this going to play out, Mr. Thomas. You are going to repay me for every damn thing your partner took." He reached down and grabbed Tommy by his hair. He dragged him, crawling, and trying frantically to get to his feet into the living room. The room was a shambles. The paintings and other artwork, even the color television set, was gone. Not loosening his grip on his hair, the john twisted Tommy's head, again bringing him to his knees. "I figure I'm out at least $300,000. You will repay me at the rate of $10,000 a week. I will be in your store every Friday afternoon to collect until you have me paid off. I can turn you over to the police and ruin you."

With that, the john pulled Tommy across the floor and opened the front door. He pushed Tommy, still naked and with his hands tied behind his back, out into the night and slammed the door.

Suddenly the door opened again. "Oh, and here's your pants, asshole. I wouldn't want you to catch cold."

"What about my wallet and the rest of my clothes?" Tommy whined.

"Fuck you! I'm keeping them!" screamed the john, slamming the door again.

Tommy found himself standing on the porch at the side of the narrow road, shivering in the dark. He sat his bare ass down on the cold concrete step. By pulling his knees up, he worked his tied wrists around in front of him.

Then he struggled to his feet so he could try to get his pants on.

It was pitch dark, so dark he could not see the black asphalt road beneath his feet. The john had kept his belt, so he had to hold his pants up with his tied hands He started stumbling down the hill, guessing where the road was.

He stepped on a stone, he collided with a mailbox, a dog started barking.

Finally, he rounded a bend in the road. Now the lights of Hollywood appeared, spread out below. The sounds of traffic, sirens, buses, cars, the sounds of the city at night were lifted up on the cold breeze.

The unbroken stream of traffic rushing by in both directions on Franklyn.

How was he going to cross that street in all that traffic? How far through Hollywood could he get, barefoot, wearing only his pants with his hands tied before the police picked him up?

Not very far, as it turned out.

# Chapter Forty Six

## March 1961

## Gavin Keller

Gavin thought his business partner's voice sounded strained during their weekly phone conversation.

"What's going on? The antique business slowing down?"

"No, no, nothing like that." Tommy sneezed, blew his nose and continued unsteadily, "By the way, Johnny told me he doesn't want to continue his involvement in the film rental business. He said if it got out that he was involved with porn it could cause embarrassment to his family."

Gavin thought for a minute. "I guess I better tell you what happened when we went to New York." He filled Tommy in about the shooting, the George Raft-type bodyguards, the weekend in the Utica compound and Johnny's family.

"I would have thought Monreale was a French name. Are we talking real gangsters?"

"I think so. I did a little research. First Boston does have a file on the Monreales. Gianni Monreale is in the insurance business, all right. He collects "premiums" from small stores and shops in New York, mostly Italians, to assure that their businesses don't catch fire, or they don't get their legs broken. And insurance does not seem to be the Monreale's only business, not by a long shot."

"Christ, what's next?"

"Nothing, I hope. It's school and work as usual."

"I think we should just let the East Coast film business go," Tommy said. "We made plenty off Johnny's efforts while it lasted."

"I agree. I'll keep my eyes open for a replacement, but for now I want to put some distance between myself and the Monreales."

Winter gradually tried to become spring, and for the next few weeks Gavin concentrated on his studies and work. He and Johnny had very different schedules, so they rarely saw each other.

Johnny was at the desk studying when Gavin came in from work late one afternoon. Johnny looked up from his book, put his finger on the page to mark his place and asked, "Are you going home for Easter?"

"No. It would take a day just to get to California and another day to get back and that's if I flew. By staying here, I'll get to work a full week at First Boston."

Johnny got up from the chair and stretched. He turned to Gavin. "My family asked me to invite you to join us for a week in Bermuda."

The invitation took Gavin by surprise. The last thing he wanted to do was spend any time with the Monreales.

But Bermuda?

"It's warm there this time of year," Johnny continued, "and it's a very beautiful place. We go every year and stay at a really great hotel, the Hamilton Princess. It's right on Pitt Bay. You can swim or go sailing in the bay or do anything you want."

He paused. "My parents and grandpa would be very disappointed if you couldn't make it."

It was too tempting. "That is a very tempting offer. I'll try to get a week off from First Boston and let you know."

Gavin had mixed emotions about this whole thing and halfway hoped that Stone wouldn't let him off work.

But Stone said, "You've worked hard. Take a break. Go. Have a great time."

⁂

The flight in the old DC3 was a nightmare, noisier and bumpier than the flight in the DC7 from California. By the time they landed at Bermuda's tiny airport, Gavin thought seriously of just giving up any career plans and staying on the little island for the rest of his life, rather than ever getting back on that damn plane again.

It was late in the evening when they arrived at the elegant old hotel, so both boys decided to just turn in and start fresh in the morning.

Gavin had been assigned a first floor "garden" room. It had a sliding glass door opening on a semi-private patio. All the rooms on the first floor had a small patio bounded by the high wall that separated the grounds from the street that ran alongside the hotel.

Since he was an early riser, by seven thirty the next morning he was up, dressed and ready to go exploring.

It was a beautiful sunny morning, cool but promising to get nice and warm. A slight breeze ruffled the smooth blue surface of the bay. He thought he could really learn to like this place. After the blasts of the freezing winter wind blowing whitecaps on Boston Harbor, this was paradise.

Gianni and Gianpoalo were strolling alongside the low wall on the path by the salt-water pool.

"Good morning," greeted Gianni. "I see you, too, are a morning person."

"Yes sir. I want to thank you very much for inviting me here," Gavin said, taking a deep breath of the salt air. "I would never have had the opportunity to see this wonderful place."

"I'm glad you are enjoying it," Gianni said, smiling.

"And I'm glad we caught you this morning," added Gianpoalo. "We were hoping for some time alone with you, to get to know you better. We will forever be in your debt for saving our Johnny."

"I am very flattered. But please rest assured your kindness and hospitality is more than enough repayment. Besides, had the circumstances been different, I'm sure Johnny would have done the same for me."

"Perhaps," said Gianpoalo. "Come, walk with us through Hamilton. It is such a small town you can practically throw a rock from one side to the other." He chuckled before continuing. "Something you may feel inclined to do after you have been here a few days."

As they walked along the quay past the cruise ship terminal, Gianni said, "Johnny tells me you work for an insurance company."

"Yes, sir. I was lucky enough to land a job in the legal department at First Boston the day I arrived in Cambridge."

"How do you like it?" Gianni asked.

"I find it fits in well with my major at Harvard. I also thoroughly enjoy the work and the people."

"Good, good," Gianni said. "It is truly the fortunate one that enjoys his work."

202

"Little Johnny tells me you are from California," Gianpoalo said. "I myself have never been to California. I have only been as far west as Las Vegas, in Nevada. We have been exploring business opportunities there."

During the rest of the walk, they asked questions about Gavin's family and his life in California.

By mid morning, the three of them were back at the hotel where they found Johnny stretched out on a chaise near the salt-water pool. Johnny told his father that Gina and Catarina had gone into town to do some shopping.

"We will leave you two young bucks alone to evaluate the flora and fauna," Gianni said with a grin. The two senior Monreales left to play a round of golf.

"Well?" Johnny said to Gavin as soon as they were alone.

"Well, what?"

"Well, what did the three of you talk about?"

"Just about school, my job, and California. Why?"

Johnny stretched and closed his eyes. "No reason."

"I think I'll go to my room, get some swimming trunks, and come back and join you."

"It's well worth it," Johnny said opening one eye to gaze at two blond German girls in two-piece swimsuits.

Gavin had not realized how much he needed a break like this. He looked forward to swimming in salt water again after months Harvard's heavily chlorinated indoor pool.

He really felt pretty good about himself and things in general. And too, it was a real boost to get the attention of some of the hotel's female guests when he returned to join Johnny by the pool.

He was half dozing. The rippling waters of Pitt Bay sparkled in the sunshine. In the distance little white houses with odd pyramid shaped roofs peeked from the tropical foliage. Screeching seagulls came swooping down from the blue sky, diving into the water for fish.

The warm sun had just about put him to sleep when he heard a husky female voice. "Are you two studs looking for a good time?"

He turned his head and with eyes half closed looked to see who it was. Because of the bright sunlight it took him a moment to focus.

But when he did, he saw standing right there next to Johnny, the most stunning girl he had ever seen in his life.

She was about five foot four inches tall, long brown hair shimmering in the sunshine, big brown eyes, long legs, and a heart stopping body.

For the first time in his life, Gavin Keller was speechless.

Johnny said, "Any time, any place, toots."

Horrified at Johnny's response, Gavin thought for god's sake show a little respect in the presence of this goddess. She could bolt, run away. It would be just like fate for a treasure like this to show herself just long enough to prove she existed, then slip away, disappear forever, leaving him only the memory of her image.

He swallowed. He tried to gather his wits and get to his feet.

His foot got caught in the webbing of the chaise and he almost fell on his face.

His legs seemed to have turned to water.

Before he could stand up straight, he had to grab his towel to hold it in front of him.

He felt clumsy, awkward, completely flustered. Nothing like this had ever happened to him before.

She turned and looked to him with those big brown eyes, a wry smile on her full lips.

In a wonderful, throaty, and unbelievably sexy voice she said, "Hiya, big boy."

Those words finished him off.

He was in love.

Now he did not need to hold the towel. It could just hang there by itself.

"Gavin, you remember my sister Catarina, don't you?" Johnny said, getting to his feet.

Gavin was paralyzed, dumbstruck.

This was Johnny's sister?

This was the girl–child he met with the family in Utica?

It could not be.

Where were the braces?

The screeching voice?

Could Johnny have more than one sister?

Two sisters named Catarina?

"Well, aren't you going to say hello?" she asked. She was completely at ease, confident, the way Gavin usually was around women.

He gulped and stammered, "Hello."

"You're welcome to join us," Johnny said, gesturing to a chaise.

"You're sure I won't cramp your style?" she asked.

"No, not at all," Johnny replied. "Gavin and I have it all going for us. Having you here won't discourage beautiful women from throwing themselves at us. Right Gavin?"

"Uh, sure," he said, trying desperately to pull himself together, gain some semblance of composure. "Here, take my seat, I mean chaise. I'll pull up another one."

Catarina smiled and Gavin could swear her perfect white teeth sparkled in the sun. With a graceful, cat-like motion she spread her towel on the chaise he had been using and slowly lowered herself onto it.

Her every move, her every gesture was sensuous, like a dance, a ballet.

And when she spoke, when she spoke or laughed, the sound of her husky, seductive voice ensnared him further.

Oh my God. What was she, sixteen, seventeen years old?

She seemed perfectly at ease with the two of them, not the least bit self conscious or awkward.

No, for the first time in his life, it was the girl who was in complete control. He was afraid if he tried to say something, he would stammer like a schoolboy.

She turned to him. Was she saying something?

"Huh?" he said stupidly.

"Gavin, could you please spread some of this suntan lotion on my back?"

He stared at her dumbly. Spread some suntan lotion on her back? He would die for her. Spreading suntan lotion on her back would mean touching her.

She handed him the tube of lotion. Sea and Ski.

Pull yourself together for god's sake, he told himself. This is becoming embarrassing. He was a twenty-three-year-old college student, and she was at most seventeen.

He fumbled opening the tube. The familiar smell of the lotion reminded him of California, the beach, and home.

He put some on his hand and began to rub her back. Her light brown skin was warm from the sun, and soft. But underneath he could feel her firm young muscles.

Her aroma and the aroma of the suntan lotion made an irresistible combination.

He couldn't think of a damn thing to say.

He finished rubbing the lotion and lay back on the chaise next to her, his mind racing. She lay still on her stomach, facing him but with her eyes closed.

He hoped neither she nor her brother would catch him sneaking looks at her, watching her breathe, studying her face, her body.

He dreaded the thought that this moment had to eventually end.

His heart stopped; alarmed that she might be leaving when she got up from the chaise. But she only walked over to the pool and dove in. He could not stop staring when she emerged from the pool, the saltwater dripping from her glistening brown body.

She smiled. Just a little smile, a Mona Lisa smile. A knowing smile, as if she had some little secret.

What does this mean? Was he supposed to say something? He was completely at a loss as to what to do. Should he offer to put more Sea and Ski on her back?

By two o'clock in the afternoon it was downright hot, and Gavin knew he was getting sunburned. But Johnny and Catarina just seemed to be getting browner. Reluctantly, Gavin finally had to excuse himself to go to his room for a shower.

The arrangement was to meet at seven for dinner.

He found the Monreale family, chatting and looking relaxed, standing in the lobby waiting. They seemed to be the perfect image of the All-American family. The two senior Monreales dressed in suits were handsome, grey haired and prosperous looking. Mrs. Monreale was

206

downright beautiful in a bright yellow dress that really showed off her figure and her magnificent coloring.

And Johnny, now tanned and handsome, looked like the romantic lead in a Hollywood movie.

Catarina. Catarina was wearing a pale blue summer dress, her long brown hair framing her beautiful, flawless face. She smiled as he approached and stunned at her beauty he almost stopped in his tracks.

People passing through the lobby, especially the men, but even the women were turning to get a second look.

Gavin was able to maneuver a seat at the table directly across from her. She was endlessly captivating. Her every gesture, her every move, everything she said and did thrilled him.

When they finished dinner, Gina, Gianni and Gianpoalo went to a nearby hotel to see some old Brit's slide show of his trip to Egypt.

Gavin, Johnny and Catarina begged off, saying after the long day in the sun they were too tired to join them. They decided to make an early evening of it.

Gavin returned to his room, took another shower, opened the sliding door and lay down on the bed.

He half-dozed, thinking about the fantastic Catarina. How could he try to make something work with her? Clearly, she was too young for him, but he couldn't help himself. He could not get her out of his mind. The sound of her voice, the aroma of the suntan lotion lingered with him still.

"Are you going to ask me in?"

He looked up, startled. Her almost transparent gown did not hide the silhouette of her body framed in the doorway to the dark patio.

The warm breeze brought the aroma of the Sea and Ski into the room.

"Please do come in," he replied softly.

She left the doorway, and graceful as a cat, approached the bed, letting her gown fall silently to the floor as she came to him. She leaned over the bed, held his face in her hands, and kissed him full on the lips, hungrily as if she were trying to take him all in, absorb him. He responded instantly, holding her shoulders and gently pulling her closer against him, on top of him.

Two hours later she whispered, "*Amante, devo lasciarlo ora saro indientro*", and slipped out of the bed.

She put on her gown and left the way she had come in--through the sliding glass door to the little patio and into the night.

The next day he was up at seven thirty and feeling wonderful.

He was dying to see Catarina again and was by the pool lying on the chaise at ten o'clock sharp waiting for her.

It occurred to him dying might be an appropriate word for what he'd done. If the Monreale patriarchy didn't approve of a twenty-three-year-old man sleeping with their teenage daughter, dying might very well be in the cards. What was wrong with him? He had already decided to distance himself from the Monreales. What about his plans? His career?

Oh God, what had he done?

But then, Catarina and Johnny came around the corner of the hotel, laughing and talking, and none of those things mattered to him anymore.

Oh Christ. She is absolutely gorgeous. She's wearing a different bathing suit today, even skimpier than yesterday's, emphasizing her long legs, her narrow hips, flat stomach, her breasts.

Oh my God I don't think I dare stand up to greet them.

"Good morning, handsome. Are you ready to Sea and Ski me?" she asked in her incredibly sexy voice.

*Oh, shit, am I*. Aloud he replied. "Ready any time you are."

She and Johnny spread towels on their chaises and settled in.

Handing him the lotion, she turned over on her stomach and said, "This time undo my top, will you?"

*With my teeth if it wouldn't get me killed*. But aloud he said, "Certainly, madam."

He felt great. Young, strong, healthy, confident, and full of energy. He had never been so alive, so relaxed, or had such a good time just being with other people.

Johnny had changed, and it was not just that Gavin was seeing him in a new light. He was quieter and seemed to be more mature and have more depth.

His roommate had become interesting, entertaining.

The day passed quickly, too quickly, without any awkwardness or any reference to the night before.

Dinner again that night with the Monreale clan, this time at the Lobster Pot on Queen Street, just up from the hotel. It was crowded and noisy, but fun. They were back at the hotel by nine-thirty. Gianpoalo and Gianni went on into the hotel bar for a prolonged nightcap, and the rest of the party called it a night.

Returning to his room, Gavin showered, turned off the light, opened the sliding glass door, and stretched out on the bed.

He did not have to wait long.

A slight sound, the faint scent, the outline of her body against the darkness outside. With a quick movement she was across the room, out of her gown and into his arms. Wordlessly they were all over each other, and he was in her. She moaned, and with her hands on his buttocks, pulled him further inside.

Afterwards she slid out of bed, into her gown and was gone.

This routine repeated itself every single night of their stay in Bermuda.

He wished it could go on forever, but too soon the break was over, the family had to return home, and he and Johnny had to return to school. How would he ever manage to see her again? Outwardly, she showed no sign of any particular affection for him. She was certainly friendly enough, but it was as if they were just three good pals: she, her bother Johnny, and Gavin.

Gavin, in love, off balance and thoroughly confused.

The return to Cambridge was a nightmare. The flight back to New York in that noisy little plane was, if anything, worse than the flight to the island had been the week before.

And then he was back in Cambridge. No more warm sunny days for him.

Just the cold, damp New England spring.

# Chapter Forty Seven

## June 1961

Gavin was oblivious to the arrival of spring. The lawns around Harvard turned green, the leaves returned to the trees, blossoms everywhere.

He saw none of this.

Catarina was all he could think about.

The sound of her voice, her laugh, her firm young body. How was he ever going to see her again?

Catarina Monreale never left his thoughts.

He tried to focus on his schoolwork, but he couldn't. He had barely passed the last exam, and that was totally unlike him.

Having Johnny as a roommate made it worse.

No, it made it better.

No, no, it made it worse. Johnny's presence only reminded him of Catarina.

But he could not ask Johnny about her, not even in the most innocent way. That would almost certainly risk tipping off how he felt.

And if Johnny guessed how he felt, there would be no turning back.

Endless days became endless weeks.

A month went by.

Two months. Two months of school, of work at First Boston. Two months of returning at the end of the day to the dorm room. Two months filled with a huge longing for this person, this Catarina who for Gavin had not even existed at all until a couple of months ago. In only that one short, intense week in Bermuda she had filled his being, made him complete.

And now that she wasn't there, he was left with an aching emptiness.

Both Gavin and Johnny had signed up for summer school. Gavin because he wanted to stay in the east on the off chance he could somehow see Catarina again, and Johnny, to make up for courses he had failed in the past.

Johnny was in the dorm room more often now. He didn't go out at night, not even on the weekends. He was studying. It was hard to imagine that this was the same pushy, loudmouth guy Gavin and Tommy put into the business of renting out dirty movies.

Gavin returned to the dorm late one afternoon in June to find Johnny seated at the desk studying. He threw his briefcase on the bed and turned toward his roommate. Just as he started to break down and ask him about his family, Johnny turned the book he'd been reading over on its face, got up from the chair and stretched.

He yawned and turned toward Gavin. "The family will be spending a week at the shore, in the Hamptons," he said, running his fingers through his hair. "They asked me to invite you to join us for the weekend."

He touched the small scar on his forehead. "After what happened in New York, Dad sold the apartment and bought a house on the beach. If you can go, we can drive down Friday afternoon. Next week is the Fourth of July and they're having a housewarming party. You may have an opportunity to meet some interesting people." He sat on the edge of the desk and continued. "Catarina will be there with Mother to start planning her marriage to Peter Ruffalo."

Gavin tried to hide his reaction to this bit of news. He sat on the edge of his bed and thumbed through a book trying to cover his shock.

Doing his best to sound indifferent, to feign only polite interest he asked without looking up, "Who's Peter Ruffalo?"

"Her childhood sweetheart. The three of us grew up together. His family and ours have been close for many years. Peter is the son of one of father's oldest business associates."

Johnny walked past Gavin and into the bathroom to take a leak, and then ran some water in the sink. He splashed cold water on his face, then turned and said through the door, "If you can make it, we can get there after school Friday evening, stay through Tuesday, and be back in Cambridge Tuesday night."

Gavin was desperate to see Catarina. He set aside the disconcerting news of her marriage plans, suppressed it as if it had not been mentioned at all. He didn't care. It meant nothing to him. He wouldn't let it.

"I'd love to see your family again, and I could sure use the break."

Gavin and Johnny arrived at the beach house mid afternoon on Friday. Gianni greeted them both with a hug, including Gavin as if he were his own son.

He proudly gave them a tour. The house, a large New England style home with a widow's walk had verandas in front and back, on both the first and second floor. Scattered around the downstairs veranda facing the ocean were a dozen or so rocking chairs and a hammock.

Gavin and Johnny's rooms were on the second floor, looking down on the lawn bordering the beach and the ocean.

Gavin and Johnny spent all day Saturday swimming, touching up their tans and staying out of the way of the party preparations.

Around noon, caterers and a crew arrived to set up a large tent with tables and chairs, a bar, and a bandstand along with a dance floor.

At twilight the guests began to arrive, and the two senior Monreale's, Gianpoalo and Gianni, along with Johnny and Gavin stationed themselves at the front door.

Gianni included Gavin in the introductions as Johnny's roommate at Harvard and a close family friend. It crossed Gavin's mind that while he was in the company of gangsters, at last he was making the contacts he had hoped for by attending a prestigious eastern school.

A Congressman and his wife and a New York State Senator all brought housewarming gifts.

One gentleman, wearing a dark grey pin-striped suit, dark grey shirt and light grey tie arrived alone. Gianni and Gianpoalo seemed to know him well.

"Boys, I want you to meet Antonio Urbanus," Gianni announced, affectionately putting his arm around the man's shoulders. "Antonio is one of my oldest friends. I have always wanted him to join my organization. But he disappointed me and chose to work for my dear friend Ruffalo."

Urbanus smiled and shook hands all around. "It is so good to see you both again and to meet your son and his friend." Turning to Gianpoalo he added, "It is apparent that good looks are an uninterrupted Monreale family trait."

Gianpoalo bowed. "Grazie, grazie."

"Mr. and Mrs. Ruffalo and young Peter express their sincerest regrets at being unable to attend your housewarming," Urbanus said apologetically, handing Gianni a carefully wrapped package. "But knowing of your interest in Roman art, the family offers this token of his esteem."

Gavin was all ears. Ruffalo. Urbanus must be connected with Catarina's fiancé's family. From his size and his pin-striped suit, Gavin guessed Urbanus was to Ruffalo what Willy and Benny were to the Monreales.

A cousin with a gun.

Gianni carefully unwrapped the package. Inside, in a wooden box stuffed with padding was a small marble bust of a woman. The bust was obviously very old, the nose slightly damaged and the back of the head lost long ago. Gianni gingerly took it out of the box and held it up to look at it. Gavin could see that his host was moved almost to tears.

"Again, Mr. Ruffalo and his family regret their inability to attend. They hope you will accept this small token by way of apology."

Gianni stared at the bust for a long moment. Finally, without taking his eyes from it, he said, "I cannot tell you how much I appreciate this wonderful gift. It shall be the crown jewel of my collection. I already know exactly where I shall position it, with a special light to display it to its fullest advantage. Please," he said clutching the marble figure reverently to his breast and touching Urbanus's arm. "Come, join us for dinner. We will have music and dancing afterward."

Urbanus bowed and backed away, edging toward the door. "No, no, I must get back to the city. Besides, I am here without my wife, so I would be the odd man out. But thank you for the invitation."

Gavin watched Urbanus walk down the steps, get in his car, and leave.

Deep in thought, he only half heard Gianni saying, "I am blessed to have such wonderful friends. This is a truly touching gift—very, very valuable and to me very, very beautiful. What do you think of it?" he asked Gavin, holding it carefully. "This I will not offer for you to hold, for if it were damaged, it would be a great tragedy."

With his hands clasped behind his back, Gavin bent forward to look at it carefully. Then he stepped back a pace.

"May I speak frankly, Mr. Monreale?"

213

"Of course, why not?"

"The bust is not Roman, it is Etruscan. Third century B.C."

Gavin continued. "It is quite valuable, but unfortunately it was stolen from a private museum in Boston three years ago."

"How the hell do you know so much about Roman art?" Gianni said, his voice rising.

"I don't," said Gavin. "But I recognize this piece from a photograph of stolen items insured by First Boston for which a claim was presented. First Boston suspected fraud since the theft appeared to be an inside job. This piece is very hot and every police department in the United States along with the FBI and Interpol are on the lookout for it."

Gianni, Gianpoalo, and Johnny stood motionless. Gavin swallowed hard but plunged ahead. "I also noticed that Mr. Urbanus is left-handed. It was very dark, and it all happened very quickly, but that night at your apartment in New York I did see that the man who shot at us was left-handed."

Gianni, holding the bust, stared into Gavin's eyes. Faces grim, Gianpoalo and Johnny both moved to Gianni's side.

Finally, Gianpoalo spoke in a low, carefully measured tone. "Perhaps you could excuse us, my young friend. I think we, my son and grandson and I need to consider your comments in private."

"I understand. I sincerely hope that I haven't upset you, but I felt I had to say something. You've treated me like one of the family and I felt that I could not remain silent knowing this. I'll go and join the party."

Trying to keep from shaking, he left the group in the foyer and went to look for somewhere else, anywhere else to be.

Gavin had made a move, his *Latvian Gambit* as they say in chess, and he could only pray that Caïssa would watch over him. From here on, other moves would be made by other players.

But his move had set the stage for the rest of this game.

He passed through the house to the back veranda and lawn where the guests were gathered around the bar and the hor d'oeuvre tables. Gina was moving from group to group mingling with her guests. Waiters and waitresses were carrying cocktail trays and the small orchestra was setting up their instruments.

Shaking hands and smiling he made his way through the party, then across the lawn to the top of the little rise where the grass bordered the sand. Standing there alone in the shadows, the sounds of the guests talking and the musicians tuning their instruments behind him were faint, covered by the gentle swish of the luminous waves breaking on the beach.

He felt a tug on his coat and a soft, husky voice asked, "Got chewing gum, Joe?"

He turned.

At last, standing there beside him was the incredible Catarina.

Even though he had tried to prepare for this moment, tried to rehearse what he would say, how he would act, all that was lost. He couldn't help it, he was speechless. She looked up at him, smiling. She was wearing a white strapless dress. The reflections from the flickering light of the torches sparkled in the depths of her brown eyes and gave a golden glow to her suntanned shoulders, the gentle breeze from the ocean stirred her hair.

He swallowed and was finally able to manage a response. "No, but I'm available for a Sea and Ski treatment."

"I could do with a Sea and Ski treatment."

"How have you been?" he asked, starting to relax a little.

"I've been just fine, thank you. How about you?"

"I haven't been back to Bermuda, and I certainly haven't been back to New York City," he replied. "What's new with you?"

"Against all odds and contrary to my parent's predictions, I graduated from high school." She stepped back and did a turn. "And today is my eighteenth birthday. "Did you get me a present?"

"I will be sure to get you one tomorrow."

"What about tonight?"

"See that moon way out there over the ocean?" he said with a sweeping gesture. "If it were a full moon, I would wrench it from it's place in the heavens and give it to you. But since it's only a quarter moon, it isn't worthy of you."

"Perhaps something will come up," she teased. "Come, its time to dine with the masses."

There were almost ninety guests milling around, standing at the bar, and exploring the house and beach. Most seemed to know each other, the conversations were light and friendly with lots of laughter. At eight o'clock all the guests began taking their places at the tables for dinner.

Gavin watched Gianni, Gianpoalo, and Johnny carefully. They seemed relaxed, the perfect hosts. They gave no sign that anything might be wrong. Gina and Catarina were kept busy, so Gavin mingled, chatting with the senator and the mayor and several corporate executives.

By midnight, the party was going strong, the alcohol had kicked in, and the guests were starting to show it. Gavin, knowing he wouldn't be missed, snuck away to his room, showered and went to bed. After an hour went by, he sensed a slight change in the warm breeze coming through the partially open French doors leading to the veranda.

He was pretty sure he had a visitor. He raised his head to look.

For a moment she stood framed in the doorway, her beautiful body a silhouette in the moonlight. Her nightgown fell silently to the floor. With a smooth, graceful movement she was across the room to the bed and on him. Hungrily she pulled the sheet from his body and climbed astride him.

He was ready. He was more than ready.

She was firm and strong and agile. First on top, then she moved forward and lowered herself onto his face, his mouth. Again and again. She was light. She was tireless.

At last exhausted. they fell asleep in each other's arms.

He didn't know when she left.

He had never, ever had a night like that.

Sunday morning breakfast was late. The Monreales had had a long night and so, in his own way, had Gavin. He was so sore he didn't think he could walk at all.

The three Monreale males, Gianpoalo, Gianni and Johnny were seated at the breakfast table, all wearing dark suits and ties.

Gianni turned to Gavin and said, "Today we are going to leave the care of our womenfolk in your hands. Gianpoalo and I have to make a quick trip into the city, and Johnny is going with us. We will return late tonight or tomorrow."

"That is a shame," said Gavin. "Is there anything I can do to help?"

"Just keep our ladies entertained," Gianni replied.

"How about a walk on the beach after breakfast?" Gavin suggested, turning to Gina and Catarina.

Gina looked around at the chaos left by the previous night's party. "You two go," she said with a tired sigh. "I have to stay and supervise cleaning up this mess."

After breakfast, Gavin and Catarina put on their swimsuits, grabbed a couple of towels, and started walking down the beach.

"I still have to figure out how to get into town to get your birthday present," he said.

"You gave me my birthday present last night," she replied, swatting him on the butt with her towel. "Practically all night, in fact."

"You gave as good as you got, so I still owe you a present," he said, rubbing the spot where the towel had smacked him.

It really hurt. He glanced at her face, her expression. She was watching him. There was a glint of excitement in her eye. Then she licked her lips and grinned, kind of a mischievous grin.

But there was also a look of something else. Curiosity? Lust, perhaps? His heart skipped a beat. Was there yet another side to Catarina?

He was getting an erection. Maybe there was another side to him, too.

She draped the towel around her neck and stooped to pick up a stone. "This is probably going to have to be my last fling," she said, straightening up and throwing the stone. It skipped along the water retreating from the wet sand ahead of them.

"Oh?" responded Gavin. "Why do you say that?"

"It has been planned since we were children that Peter Ruffalo and I will be married. He is two years older than me, the son of one of my father's business associates. We grew up together. Ever since we were little children, I have planned to be his wife. Our families have always assumed we would be together. Now that I am 18, the plans for a wedding will be set in motion."

She paused to look out over the waves and then turned to Gavin. "I know he and I will be happy together," she said moving close to him and slowly, sensuously drawing her finger down his chest. "But since my days of being single are nearing an end, with your participation I intend to make the most of them."

217

# Chapter Forty Eight

## New York City

## Sunday, July 2, 1961

To avoid the group being recognized, it was Max that went into Idlewild Airport's arriving passenger area. He went directly to a car rental agency and arranged for a nondescript sedan. The Gianpoalo's Cadillac was left in the parking lot, and with Max at the wheel of a rented Ford they were in Manhattan by mid afternoon. Max drove past 51st Street and parked at the curb on 7th Avenue to drop the Monreale's off. They entered the hotel by the side door rather than through the main entrance.

A suite had been prearranged under an assumed name, a large suite as there were going to be eight people, all men, attending this meeting.

The Monreales already knew the room number, so they went quickly past the lobby to the elevators and directly up to the eighth floor.

Gianni knocked softly. Willy opened the door almost immediately. After the three slipped in he carefully locked it again.

The draperies were pulled closed, and the room was almost dark. Uncle Benny and Harry were sitting on the couch and Marty was perched on the arm.

An older man was seated in an easy chair next to the lamp on the end table. The light illuminated the words "82nd Street Shoe Repair" on the bag he had in his lap. The man was dressed in a cream-colored suit, a suit that was badly in need of pressing and hadn't been in style for a very long time.

Gianni immediately opened the meeting. "First," he said, putting his hand on his son's shoulder, "I want you all to know that my son Johnny, Little Johnny, is now a part of our enterprise."

Marty, Benny, Harry and Willy all stood to shake Johnny's hand and welcome him to the group.

The white-haired gentleman did not get up from the easy chair.

Everyone but Gianni, Gianpoalo and Johnny seated themselves on the couch or leaned against the fireplace. Johnny, his arms folded, stood behind his father. Gianpoalo was on Johnny's right. Facing the men, Gianni continued. "Johnny made this decision on his own after the incident at the apartment. We, my father and I are proud of Johnny and intend to involve him in all aspects of the organization."

Gianni turned to Gianpoalo who nodded in agreement. "My father and I are confident that Johnny can make an important contribution."

Gianni then turned to his son. "Do you want to say anything, Johnny?"

"I don't have much to say this soon, other than the attack at the apartment was a wakeup call to me," he said stepping forward and scanning the men's faces. "That night and what I have learned since has been a revelation not only about the effort and risk my family, my father and grandfather live with. But it brought home to me who we are and what the people, you men we share our lives with, mean to us. I realize now I must shoulder my share of the responsibility and become a part of that."

Gianpoalo moved forward to stand next to his grandson.

"The event at my son's apartment warned us that our enemies are on the move. We had tried to make a truce," he said, spreading his hands and shaking his head as if in regret, "a compromise we hoped would allow our competing interests to exist in peace."

He paused and searched the faces of each of the men. "But we now know for certain what we suspected all along." His voice took on a hard edge. "Our enemy made another move last night, this one much more subtle, more insidious, but every bit as deadly and potentially destructive to us as the attack at the apartment could have been."

The men leaned forward, expectantly. The man in the cream-colored suit sat quietly, unmoving.

"Last night at my son's housewarming party, our enemy's emissary delivered a gift. A gift he knew would touch the heart of my son as a collector of antiquities." He paused and glanced toward Johnny. "We discovered immediately that this 'gift' was a trap, a stolen object of such immense value that a thief would not be able to fence it normally, an object on the list of every law enforcement agency in the world. Our enemy's plan had to be for my son to take this item into his

219

home and put it on display with his collection. The next step in that plan would surely be to anonymously notify the authorities to obtain a search warrant and "discover" this item in my son's possession. Naturally, he would be arrested and jailed, and you can guess the rest."

"Where do we go from here?" asked Benny.

"Anticipating that our efforts for a lasting truce might be futile, several weeks ago I had contracted with our esteemed friend here," Gianpoalo said, nodding to the older gentleman in the easy chair. "I called him last night. Fortunately, he was available and flew in this morning to deal with this. Regrettably, now I'm afraid we must put our plan into motion. Mr. Ehlers, whom all of you except Little Johnny already know, will be our instrument."

He paused and turned to his grandson. "Johnny, will you take it from here?"

Holding a slip of paper, Johnny stepped forward and nodding to the man in the cream-colored suit said, "We strike tonight. Benny, you, Willy, Harry and Marty will assist Mr. Ehlers here in carrying out the plan as has previously been discussed. My grandfather, my father and I will await your telephone call with confirmation of success."

Johnny handed Benny the slip of paper. "Here is the phone number of the public telephone you are to call to confirm success."

Benny took the note. "I think we can have this wrapped up by six thirty or so.

Turning to the elderly gentleman, he asked. "Do you agree, Mr. Ehlers?"

"For a job well done, one should not be rushed," the man in the cream-colored suit replied, folding shut the top of the paper bag in his lap, "but from your description of the layout and the circumstances, I am confident I can make it happen as you desire."

"It is two thirty now. We can wait three or four hours, and plan on making our move at six," Benny said. "Does that make sense to everyone?"

Gianni and Gianpoalo looked at each other and nodded in agreement.

Johnny, his face impassive, said nothing.

The black Lincoln sedan with five men in it was just another car in the Sunday evening traffic on Mulberry Street. After waiting for pedestrians, it turned right onto Hester and stopped, double parked. One of the men in the back seat, a thin white-haired old man in a wrinkled cream-colored suit got out.

He was carrying a paper bag.

The black Lincoln merged back into the Hester Street traffic and disappeared.

The old man, left standing in the street, made his way between the parked cars to the curb.

Once onto the sidewalk he strolled along Hester Street looking in shop windows. He paused to look in the window of a deli, then resumed strolling to the corner of Mulberry and turned left.

Mulberry Street, off Hester, is a narrow one-way street lined with old three, four and five story buildings, some brick, and some brownstones. Mostly restaurants, but some shops and other businesses occupied the ground floors. Cars were parked at the curb on both sides. It was a warm summer evening, and customers were eating outdoors, under awnings and umbrellas on the busy sidewalk in front of the restaurants.

From somewhere, an upstairs window perhaps, someone was playing a scratchy old recording of Caruso's Core N'grato.

It was as if Mulberry Street on the island of Manhattan, New York were a small village somewhere in Italy. The air was filled with the sound of laughter and conversations, the aroma of garlic, of focaccia with herbs for bread and pizza.

Because it was Sunday, all the restaurants were open, but some of the shops were closed. The tailor shop and the dry cleaners were closed, but the newspaper stand, and a small liquor store were open.

The old man carrying the paper bag moved along with the other strollers on the sidewalk. He seemed in no hurry and paused occasionally to look in a shop window or to read the menu posted on a restaurant's door.

When he reached Mama Ruffalo's Southern Italian Cuisine, he stopped and looked around as if trying to decide whether or not to enter. The restaurant's entrance was down two steps from the sidewalk level. He paused to look at the menu displayed on a sandwich board in front. Reluctantly, as if not completely convinced the food would suit him, he descended the steps, opened the door, and entered.

Just inside was a small bar, so small there were only three stools. Two of the stools were empty. The third stool was occupied by a lone man drinking beer and looking out the window, watching passersby on the sidewalk and the traffic on Mulberry.

The restaurant itself was exactly as it had been carefully described to the man in the cream-colored suit, brightly lit and busy.

Much deeper than wide, there were diners eating and talking in booths along both walls and down the center of the room, running from the front to the back. Pen and ink drawings of actors and actresses and other celebrities lined the walls. In the center of the room, right there in front near the entrance, a man in a tuxedo sat at a piano playing Broadway show tunes.

A short, heavy-set gentleman, obviously the head waiter, spotted the old man. He hurried over to show him to a booth. When the head waiter offered to take the paper bag the old man held, the man declined, saying for the waiter not to trouble himself, he could just hang on to it.

He was led to an empty booth about a quarter of the way down the wall on the left side.

None of the other diners paid any attention to the old man with the paper bag. Rather than sit looking toward the entrance, as most lone diners would, he lowered himself into the booth facing the rear of the restaurant.

Waiters scurried to and from the kitchen bringing food, clearing tables and taking orders. One, in a hurry to get an order in, paused and asked the old man if he wanted anything from the bar.

"I would like a glass of milk and a shot glass of scotch, Johnny Walker Black if you have it," said the man. "And" he added as if in afterthought, "directions to your men's room, if you please."

"Yes sir," said the waiter. "I'll put your order in at the bar. The men's room is there in the back, in the hallway on the way to the kitchen. It's the second door on the left."

The waiter hurried off and the old man got to his feet. He picked up the paper bag, bumping the diners in the booth behind him as he stood. He stepped aside for waiters with trays of food and drinks and made his way toward the rear of the restaurant.

No one paid any particular attention to him.

He reached the short hallway that led to the kitchen and the restrooms. He entered the men's room where he opened the paper bag. From it he took a long string of firecrackers, the kind sold in Chinatown to celebrate the New Year.

The pianist was almost halfway through a rousing rendition of "Lullaby of Broadway," when the man in the cream-colored suit stepped back into the hall.

He lit the fuse and flung the string of firecrackers into the center of the dining room.

Then, just as they started going off, he drew a .22 caliber Ruger automatic equipped with a silencer from a holster under his left arm. He leaned from the hallway toward the booth in the corner on the left.

Two gentlemen were seated facing each other, eating, and talking. One of them wrapped his linguine neatly around his fork with his left hand while passing the breadbasket across the table with his right.

Just as the firecrackers began exploding, the man in the cream-colored suit shot the one nearest, the one seated with his back to the wall, at point blank range.

Two quick shots into the side of the man's head, just above the right ear.

Then, in a smooth motion, he swiveled and fired two more times into the forehead of the man, breadbasket still in hand, sitting across the table.

Both bullets entered just above the man's left eye.

By now the restaurant was in turmoil.

Panicked diners were screaming and diving under the tables, frantically trying to take cover, to get as far as they could from the smoking, popping firecrackers.

The old man calmly put the pistol back in its holster and briskly pushed his way down the aisle to the front of the restaurant.

He opened the door, went up the two steps to the sidewalk on Mulberry Street, joined the strollers and was gone.

The muted gunshots from the .22 caliber pistol had added little to the noise in the restaurant. The fireworks had caused such chaos and distraction that most of the patrons missed the killings in the back booth.

No one paid any attention to the man in the cream-colored suit.

A waiter with a tray of dishes coming up the aisle toward the kitchen saw it all, but someone jostled his tray causing him to drop it. He had fallen to his knees as the gunman passed by and could not provide a description.

Johnny Monreale answered the payphone ringing in the lobby of the McGraw Hill building on Avenue of the Americas.

A voice said, "We owe Mr. E $25,000," and hung up.

Johnny left by the building's West 49th Street entrance and walked to the Ford parked at the curb.

He opened the door and got in the front.

"It's done," he said, turning to his father and grandfather in the back seat.

Max put the car in drive. They pulled into traffic, turned right on Avenue of the Americas. He drove on to 50th street, turned right, then right again on Second Avenue, then turned left onto the onramp for the Queens Uptown Tunnel.

"It's still early enough for us to turn in this rental. We can still get back to the Hampton's and your family tonight," Gianpoalo said, looking out the window.

"Yes," replied Gianni.

Turning from the passenger seat to face his father and grandfather in the back, Johnny said, "If I may be presumptuous, I would like to point out that our success this evening relied on the predictability of Ruffalo's habits. Knowing he held court at the same table in his mother's restaurant every Sunday night allowed us to successfully execute the plan."

Gianpoalo turned his attention from the window.

Johnny continued. "However, we, you two especially, may have the same vulnerability. By having established routines and living within them, you give potential enemies the same advantage we just enjoyed over Ruffalo."

The two in the back seat were silent.

Finally, Gianpoalo said, "Gianni, I'm afraid our Johnny is quite correct. We must give this matter our attention; take steps to vary our routines. We must become more random and less predictable in our ways. Your son's observation is a valuable one. I am thankful he has joined us." He adjusted his necktie, and then looked down at his manicured fingernails.

"Max, let's see if we can get back to the Hamptons and Gianni's new beach house by a decent hour."

"Another comment, if you please," Johnny said, still facing the two. "This may only be step one in the plan to consolidate our position in Manhattan. It may not be the final, decisive move. Our competitors may guess our ultimate objective. They may attempt a flanking action or retaliate. Others know mother and Catarina are in the Hamptons. Shouldn't we stop and call ahead to warn them we are on our way, that they should be ready to leave with us to return to Utica? It strikes me that the place on the beach would be more difficult to make secure than the compound."

Gianpoalo thought for a moment. "Another point well taken. However, to vacate the Hamptons so soon after the housewarming may hint at our involvement with this evening's proceedings. We best tough it out there for the weekend because that is what we would ordinarily do. We can bring in some extra muscle for protection and beef up security at the compound in Utica. Max, at your earliest opportunity, please pull over and find a phone so we can make some calls." He rubbed his chin and mused, "At least, in all likelihood, we have prevented Caterina from marrying that Ruffalo kid. I never did like him, and the thought of his becoming a family member gave me the creeps. Your roommate's comments provided all the excuse we needed. If she raises hell, we can blame it on him," he said, chuckling.

"I'm not sure she was really all that nuts about Peter Ruffalo anyway, Grandpa." Johnny replied. "Maybe we did her a favor."

"I have to admit that for a while I had my doubts about your getting anything out of going to Harvard, but now I see your major in business will pay off." Gianni said smiling. "I suppose the goal you have outlined for us is what might be called a 'hostile takeover."

Turning to Gianpoalo sitting next to him, he continued, "After the successful execution of Johnny's plan, I am now a little depressed to find the younger generation is at least as smart and capable as we. I feel like I will be soon set aside, left behind by a quicker, smarter youth."

Gianpoalo chuckled. "Now you can appreciate how I have felt about you," he said, nudging his son with his elbow.

"But then, what are we to do?" he said, sighing. "Times, they are a-changing. As they always have. I imagine my own father, your grandfather and Johnny's great grandfather thought the same about me when I was young and coming up in the family."

225

The rented Ford with three generations of Monreales, Max driving, sped onward through the early evening, away from Manhattan and on toward Idlewild Airport and the car rental agency.

⁂

With the Monreale males off to New York City and Gina busy with the household, Gavin had Catarina to himself all day Sunday.

They spent the morning on the beach. For the first time he was alone with her during the day. This was his opportunity to really take her in, study her in the daylight without being afraid that her brother or someone else in the family would catch him at it.

She was just drop-dead gorgeous. From every angle, in any position, standing, sitting, running in the surf, dry or dripping wet. He had never seen anyone quite like her.

Or had he?

Something nagged at him. Somehow, he thought he had, had seen someone like Catarina.

When she caught him staring, she just laughed. She was so comfortable with herself, so confident. He realized that she knew he idolized her, and she was completely at ease with that, as if she wouldn't have expected anything less.

Late in the morning Catarina borrowed her mother's car, a white Oldsmobile convertible, and she and Gavin drove into Southampton for lunch. This would be Gavin's chance to shop for her birthday present.

Driving, as with everything else, Catarina seemed to know only one speed, flat out. After a hair rising ride along the coast, she made a screeching turn off Dune Road and onto Main Street. She turned onto Jobs Lane and parked in the shade of the trees lining the sidewalk, directly in front of a jewelry store.

It was early afternoon, and the day was very hot, very muggy, and sticky. Church was just letting out. Locals dressed in their Sunday best were strolling along the sidewalk. Some stared disapprovingly at the sweating, sunburned tourists, window shopping in their shorts and flip-flops.

Catarina grabbed Gavin's hand and led him across the sidewalk toward the store. "Let's go in here and cool off," she said over her shoulder.

There were no customers in the cool, quiet jewelry store. A woman stood behind a counter in the rear. Two ceiling fans turned slowly overhead.

226

Catarina went from display case to display case, inspecting the jewelry as if she were a serious shopper looking for a wedding or an engagement ring. Gavin wondered what she had in mind. Supposedly she was already engaged, engaged to Peter Ruffalo. They would have already chosen their rings. Some of the stuff she was looking at was really expensive. What he had in mind for her present was more like a nice little charm bracelet, maybe even with her name engraved on it or something.

The clerk approached them and asked if she could be of assistance.

Catarina said she wanted to see some women's watches.

The clerk brought a tray of Pateks, Rolexes and other brands to look at.

Catarina was taking them out, inspecting them, trying them on, and then dropping them back into the black felt-lined tray.

Gavin was standing next to her, idly looking in the mirror behind the counter.

He knew he was pretty good looking and knew he turned a few heads. But Catarina had an electrifying effect on everyone everywhere she went. Today she was wearing a summer blouse, a 'peasant blouse', white, with little strawberry red roses around the low-cut top, and a short matching skirt that showed off her long, tanned legs.

Reflected in the mirror he could see that there were actually people stopping on the sidewalk outside, looking through the store's window at Catarina.

Out of the corner of his eye he saw Catarina take one of the watches off her wrist and slip it into the pocket of her skirt. The look on her face in the mirror was the same kind of excited, aroused look that he had seen earlier in the day, the look she had at the beach when she swatted him with her towel.

Lust? Wasn't it lust?

The clerk was standing nearby, watching. Gavin knew she saw Catarina take the watch. From her expression it seemed that the woman was torn as to whether to do something about it or not.

After a moment, the clerk said, "Young lady, that watch is a Patek and sells for $4,500.

"What watch?" Catarina said innocently.

"The watch you put in your pocket," the clerk said hesitantly, as if she really feared accusing Catarina of anything.

"Here, let me get that," Gavin said, hoping to avoid a really embarrassing situation. Smiling at the clerk he pulled his wallet out and said, "It's her birthday."

"The watch costs $4,500," repeated the clerk.

"That's all right," Gavin said, handing the clerk his credit card.

"I'll have to call this in," the clerk said, looking at the card suspiciously.

When the clerk went to the back of the store to call the credit card company, Catarina asked, "Aren't we going to make a run for it?"

Gavin looked into her face, her eyes. She licked her lips. She was really turned on.

"Why don't you let me buy this for you?" he said. "It's your birthday, and the watch will make a very nice present, won't it?"

"Why certainly," she said, pressing against him. He could feel her firm breasts, her hard nipples through the thin fabric of the blouse.

"And all this time I thought you were just a poor college student."

"What made you think that?" he asked.

"I dunno," she said. "Is it possible there's more to you than meets the eye?"

About that time the clerk returned, shaking her head as if in disbelief. "Thank you very much for your patience, Mr. Keller. The purchase has been approved. Would you like it gift wrapped?"

"Don't bother," Catarina said, retrieving the watch from her pocket and setting it on the counter. "I've changed my mind." She shook her hair petulantly. "I don't want it."

She grabbed Gavin's arm and turned to leave the store. "What I really want for my birthday is a croissant," she said, pointing toward a bakery across the street.

The clerk handed Gavin his card back. He was relieved - not so much for the money but because he might have had to explain to the Monreales why he bought their teenage daughter a $4,500 watch.

Admittedly, Catarina's shoplifting stunt had unnerved him. In the car on the way back to the house he asked her. "Do you often steal things?"

They were on Dune, the two-lane asphalt road that runs along the ocean. Mecox Bay was on the left, and on the right, set well away from the road, large, oceanfront homes were scattered along the beach.

She was driving fast, maybe 90 miles an hour or more. The telephone poles alongside the road were flashing by like pickets in a picket fence. The top was down.

She took her eyes off the road to look at him. "No," she said, almost shouting over the roar. "That was my first time, and I don't think I'll do it again. Once was fun, exciting. I like excitement." She laughed. "Twice, as Voltaire said, is perversion."

Voltaire, Gavin thought? Where the hell did that come from? What other surprises does she hide?

They got back to the beach house just after 6:00 p.m.

He followed Catarina up the steps to the front porch. Over her shoulder, all the way through the house to the back, Gina was coming up from the beach, maybe 150 feet away and wearing a very brief yellow bikini. She had been swimming, and her wet body glistened in the late afternoon sun.

She bent to pick up a towel at the edge of the lawn, then stood and began drying her hair with it. From where he was standing in the dark house, the very beautiful Gina Monreale looked like a more voluptuous version of her daughter Catarina.

Catarina, standing next to him, said softly, "She's really gorgeous, isn't she?"

He didn't know how to respond to that, and even if he did know, he couldn't have.

He was speechless. A revelation, like the dawn breaking, had swept over him.

He could only hope that in the hallway's dim light neither of the women could see his stunned expression.

Gina, smiling and with the towel draped around her neck, crossed the veranda.

Catarina, standing quietly at his side.

They both looked exactly like a young version and a slightly more mature version of the only other person he'd ever really loved, loved all his life.

His sister Val.

The resemblance had been there the whole time he'd known them, the whole time he'd been in love with Catarina.

Why hadn't he recognized it before?

It had been several years since Gavin had seen Val. She had left home when she was eighteen to join the Navy six years or so ago. They wrote each other, but he had not seen her in all this time.

Catarina looked so much like Val the last time he'd seen her that they could be sisters.

Later, by the time everyone had showered and changed it was twilight, almost dark. The maid had a table set up on the veranda looking out on the ocean. Hanging from the rafters, a hurricane lamp swung gently back and forth in the breeze, casting dancing shadows on the porch and the lawn below. The three of them, Gina, Catarina and Gavin, chatted and laughed about the housewarming party and the antics of some of the guests.

From the front of the house came the sound of a car on the gravel drive. Catarina rose from her rocking chair and looked. "They must have finished in New York early."

Gina was almost to the door when Gianni opened it. He came in, followed by Gianpoalo and Johnny. Behind them were Willy, Benny, Marty and Harry.

"I didn't expect you home tonight. What happened? Did everything work out all right?" she asked.

"Yes, we believe it did. I have invited the men to stay with us until we return to Utica," Gianni explained, gesturing toward the group behind him.

Coming up the steps, Benny was going on and on to Marty and Harry about how he loved his wife, although she was "an older woman." Harry, following silently behind Benny, rolled his eyes. He had the expression on his face that seemed to say he had heard this countless times before.

Benny and Willy shook Gavin's hand and greeted him as if he were part of the family. More like part of the gang, Gavin thought.

The Monreales, Gianpoalo, Gianni and Johnny, along with the four 'cousins' and 'uncles' adjourned to the living room. The men were making themselves comfortable in the chairs and sofas.

For a moment it occurred to Gavin to ask Catarina if she felt like a late-night walk on the beach, but something warned him he was not to be a part of this group.

He excused himself instead, explaining he was going to turn in. He glanced over Gianni's shoulder.

Johnny, dressed in a dark suit and tie, stood resting his arm on the fireplace mantle. He had really changed, changed in nearly every way. He not only carried himself much differently, much more poised and mature, he even looked different.

Now, the careless, immature Johnny Monreale was completely gone, replaced by a junior edition of Gianpoalo and Gianni.

And there was a touch of something else, something more.

Johnny Monreale, Gavin thought, looked like someone you really would not want to fuck with.

Gavin started up the stairs. Gianni, still standing at the living room's big double doors said, "I should tell you, Willy has trouble sleeping. Don't pay any attention if you hear him out on the veranda all night."

Gianni was looking up at him, watching him. He smiled and stepped aside to let Catarina enter the living room. Then he turned, followed her in and closed the big double doors.

Gavin heard the lock click.

That night Gavin had no visitor.

Once, during the long night, Gavin quietly got up and looked out the French doors. Down below on the dark lawn, one of the others was walking back and forth, smoking a cigarette.

Damn Willy walked back and forth on the veranda all night. When he was not pacing up and down, he sat in one of the rocking chairs, watching the lawn and the beach.

Monday morning and the atmosphere in the beach house had become tense and uncomfortable. Benny and Willy and the other two were constantly on the move, popping up at every corner.

Gavin was anxious to get away from there. But how would he see Catarina again? He would be left hanging, hoping for another Monreale invitation of some sort.

At breakfast Johnny mentioned it might be well for him and Gavin to leave a day early to avoid the holiday traffic. Gavin had mixed emotions but given the changed and now charged atmosphere in the house, he saw no hope for further liaisons with Catarina. He mentioned he would like to squeeze in one last walk on the beach, hoping Catarina would say she'd like to join him.

231

But she didn't. She was talking to her brother at the other end of the table and did not even look up.

In the car on the way back to Cambridge, Gavin thought about how much Catarina resembled his sister Val. The thing that must have thrown him off was, of course, Catarina's unique, sexy voice. Then, too, Val was maybe an inch or two taller and had always kept her hair cut short.

Gavin and Val had been very close when they were kids, played together, rode their bikes together. He had never thought of Val as a girl at all.

Or had he?

Gavin watched the passing towns and open fields.

Does this change his feelings about Catarina? No, not one bit. He was as crazy about her as ever.

Johnny said quietly, "I don't know if I'll be continuing at Harvard next semester. I've decided to join my father's business."

Crap! Another surprise. If Johnny isn't there, Gavin would lose his contact with Catarina completely.

"You only have two years to go, and they'll pass quickly. Besides, the Harvard education, the diploma and the contacts you'll make will certainly be a valuable asset to your family's business."

Miles went by before Johnny responded. "You have a point. I guess I should discuss this further with my father and grandfather."

Gavin didn't know what else to say. Neither of the two spoke for the rest of the trip.

# Chapter Forty Nine

## Catarina Monreale

## July 2, 1961

Her father shut the big double doors, locked them, and then moved to the middle of the room, his hands clasped behind him.

"Pietro Ruffalo and his companion, Antonio Urbanus were killed this evening," he announced.

Willy, Benny, Marty and Harry took the news with no show of emotion. They mumbled what Catarina thought was kind of a sheepish, perfunctory regret. Marty, looking down at his hands folded in his lap, said something about having heard about it on the car radio on the way to the Hamptons.

Her father and mother and her brother Johnny looked toward her as if concerned, more like curious about her reaction.

Catarina wasn't particularly shocked or surprised. Friends and business associates had met sudden, untimely deaths in the past. Her family and their immediate circle had always been unscathed. Nothing like that had happened to any of them. As for Peter's father, she barely knew him. Sure, he'd been there all those years, but he was a remote figure, always in the background. Unlike her own father Gianni, Pietro Ruffalo had not been an involved family man.

That was all that was said on the subject, but Catarina was fairly sure they knew a lot more and maybe even had a hand in it.

The real topic of the meeting was the difficulty of making the house on the beach secure. It was pretty much decided that the place was not going to work out for them. It would be put up for sale as quickly as possible.

Catarina, her parents and the uncles and cousins stayed there the rest of the week. When they did return to Utica, it was only two days before her parents and her grandfather, along with Max left for Las Vegas.

Now Catarina was alone in the big empty house. Bored, she roamed the rooms, finally drifting into her father's office to look out the window on the street and the other homes in the cul de sac.

Across the street was Uncle Tony's house. Even in this heat, a gardener was mowing the lawn. Uncle Tony was just backing his car down the drive. After he turned and started toward the gate to the compound, the gardener paused, mopped his brow, and stooped to tie his shoe. Then he stood and watched the car leave the compound.

Next door to Uncle Tony's, Cousin Leo's kids were out on the front lawn running and playing in the sprinkler. Cousin Leo's was the only house in the compound that did not have a swimming pool. He thought his kids were too young, so he was afraid to have a pool installed.

She turned from the window and wandered toward the back of the house, wondering just what the hell was she going to do now?

Where did this leave her and Peter? No funeral arrangements had been announced. Gina had urged her to try to contact her fiancé to console him and make plans to proceed with the wedding. Catarina did call, she lost track of how many times, all through the rest of the week while they were at the Hamptons. Not once did anyone answer the phone.

It did occur to her that her mother's pushing her to try to reach Peter might be to cover her family's probable involvement in the murders, to further the impression that they'd had nothing to do with it.

She had been to the Ruffalo's' many times, and she knew there were always plenty of people about. Just like her parents' home, the Ruffalos had household staff, a maid, and a cook. There were always plenty of cousins or uncles around, also. She and her brother Johnny were familiar with these men, and they knew what their fathers and their families really did.

Benny, Willy, and the others were relatives from the old country. They still, out of tradition and habit, dressed in pinstriped suits, hung around all the time, ran errands, and accompanied their parents wherever they went.

When Catarina was thirteen and Little Johnny was sixteen, the two of them had a long talk about their families and their lives. There was no denying that other kids did not live the way the Monreales and the Ruffalos did. There was the obvious deference and respect, earned or not, that everyone always gave them, especially the other kids at school.

Of course, with this deference came distance, so other than Peter Ruffalo, Catarina and Little Johnny had no friends. At school or at church, no one ever teased them or kidded around with them. Other than Peter Ruffalo, no one ever asked Catarina out on dates. Peter was bright and good-looking, and as they grew up, he became a handsome young man. It seemed to her that she had always thought she was in love with Peter.

Maybe she would've loved him even if she'd had other boyfriends and hadn't been so isolated.

But then, there really was no way to know that, was there?

Where was he now? Despite the death of his father, he still should've called her. He would've called her unless he and his people suspected her family had a hand in his father's murder.

Oh well, what the hell. That plan was not going the way it was supposed to.

In fact, as far as Catarina Monreale was concerned there was no plan.

She wandered through the house and found herself in the kitchen, near the rack where the keys to the cars were kept. The keys for Gina's Olds convertible were hanging there. She took them off the rack, pushed the button to open the garage door and went to the car.

Across the street, the gardener was just coming back around to the front of Uncle Tony's house. He got in his truck just as she started the Olds.

By the time she was on the street the gardener was leaving the compound, turning right onto County Road 30. She was going to go by the Ruffalo's place, so she too turned right.

County Road 30, a two-lane asphalt road through the rural countryside was deserted. No traffic as far as she could see ahead or behind her. No traffic at all except for two vehicles pulled off the road next to a utility pole. A large white AT&T van, and behind it, the gardener's truck.

Without changing speed or glancing at the parked trucks, she drove on by.

But she made a mental note to mention to her parents or her brother that it looked like the Feds had bugged Uncle Tony's house.

What was her plan? She was out of high school now and it looked like she would end up just killing time until, until what?

Her lifelong companion, her beloved brother Little Johnny was away at school in Cambridge. Crap, he wasn't *Little* Johnny anymore. Somehow when she wasn't looking, Little Johnny had grown up. Now he was a handsome, intelligent young man, a leader. He was involved in the family's business, making suggestions, decisions, changing the whole way the family went about things.

He seemed to have become Gianpoalo and Gianni's equal, if not the new idea man.

From what she had learned in the Hamptons, Johnny's grand design was for the family to become more legitimate. His vision was for her father, mother and grandfather to evolve to businesses centered in and around Las Vegas.

Hotels, casinos, gambling.

During Little Johnny's last year or two at Harvard, they would ease him into taking over the family's New York and New Jersey operations. Over time he would liquidate these operations or sell them to one or more of the other "families."

This was a family enterprise. She was part of the family. Now that she was an adult, she was in on all the conversations and meetings.

But she was not really a participant.

Grandpa Gianpoalo was to take a less active role or maybe even retire altogether and move to Phoenix, Arizona. Gianni and Gina would become semi-permanent, if not permanent residents of Las Vegas. No mention had been made of a place for Catarina in all this. At eighteen years of age and out of high school she was too old to accompany her parents or her grandfather all the time, and without Peter, she had no one else.

She was driving 90 miles an hour down County Road 30 in her mother's convertible when she decided to tell her parents she wanted to go to college, to follow her brother to Cambridge.

Returning to the compound, she saw the AT&T truck still there, still parked at the side of the road by the same utility pole. At the top of the pole was a canvas shelter, the kind used by the linemen to shield themselves from the elements.

The gardener's truck was gone.

Gina called her daughter every night to check on her when they were away. During that night's conversation Catarina told her mother she'd like to drive up to Harvard to see Johnny.

"While I'm there" she said, "I'd like to look into enrolling at Lesley."

"Lesley what?" asked her mother.

"Lesley University," she replied. "It's there in Cambridge. Since it doesn't look like I'm going to get married right away, I would like to continue my education."

Thankfully, she was talking to her mother on the phone. She would not want to tell her a lie like that face to face. During her senior year in high school, colleges and universities had sent around pamphlets with their curricula and Catarina had taken a look. There were plenty of courses that looked easy and maybe even fun.

"That sounds like a good idea," her mother replied. "We can have Benny drive you up there whenever you want."

"No, no, I want to drive myself, so I can scout around. I might even stay overnight in a hotel so I can really check the place out."

"You can take my car," Gina offered.

"I'll call Johnny and tell him I'm coming."

She hesitated before hanging up, sorely tempted to tell her mother about Uncle Tony's house being bugged. But she thought better of it. The phones in her own house might possibly be bugged. She'd just tell Johnny when she saw him.

Gavin answered when Catarina called Johnny's dorm room.

"Are you alone?"

"No, Johnny's right here studying. Would you like to talk to him?"

"Yes. I want to tell him I'm coming up. I'm thinking about enrolling at Lesley."

"Now THAT is good news," Gavin said. "I'll hand the phone to Johnny."

"I'll call you at your office tomorrow."

"Great! Here's your brother."

Catarina arrived in Cambridge late Monday afternoon and checked into a hotel on Franklin, a block from Batterymarch.

She called Gavin at First Boston.

"I'm in room 415 at the Langham. Why don't you come by and welcome me to Boston?"

"I'll be there in seconds."

Hearing his knock, Catarina opened the door, reached out and grabbing him by the necktie, pulled him into the room.

She closed and locked the door behind him.

237

She was nude.

Gavin stared at her, at first unable to move. She pushed him back against the wall in the hallway, dropped to her knees in front of him and began unbuckling his belt.

She'd left the curtains open.

Outside were the office buildings of downtown Boston. Knowing that hundreds of people might see them through the window was a real turn-on.

Gavin didn't take long.

"I'll expect you not to be so quick next time," she said, rising to her feet.

"I'll reciprocate as soon as I have a chance to recover," he said smiling and taking off the rest of his clothes.

Catarina spent the next day driving around Cambridge and exploring Lesley University's facilities. There were several dormitories, but the one Catarina decided she must live in was Cuellen House. It was an old turn-of-the-century residence with accommodations for a limited number of students. Although it was more expensive, she knew she would prefer this to a big dorm with dozens or even hundreds of other students.

She introduced herself to the house counselor and asked about availability.

"We have two possibilities," the counselor explained. "You can choose between a double and a four-person room."

"What about the single? The brochure shows you have a single room upstairs in the corner of the house, facing the street."

"That room has already been taken," replied the counselor.

"What would it take to get that room?"

"I can put your name on the waiting list. Since the rate for the single is more than for the dorm rooms, no one else is on standby. You would be next in line."

"Please sign me up for the double room and put me down on the list for the single."

Catarina learned that the occupant of Cuellen House's single room was a senior, a very nice girl named Geri Greene. Geri was due to graduate, but she intended to go on and get her Master's Degree.

She had no plans to give up her room.

Catarina wanted that room.

Catarina was used to getting what she wanted.

She enrolled in Lesley, taking easy subjects and spent every available moment having sex with Gavin. They checked into various hotels and motels in and around Boston and were careful to keep their meetings secret, especially from Johnny. Because parking her mother's car was a hassle and she walked to and from school, she returned it to the house in Utica.

For the next two months she shared the double she was given with a whiney little blond from Springfield. The little shit had never been away from home and cried herself to sleep every night. Catarina felt like strangling her, but that would not get her the single, and Cuellen House would probably just replace the little blond with somebody worse.

She turned her attention to Geri--her habits, her routine, her comings, and goings. Catarina noted that while most of Geri's classes were during the day, she did have one night class on Wednesdays. After that class, at around nine p.m., Geri walked back from the campus to Cuellen House alone.

In the dark.

It was now almost October. The leaves had turned and were beginning to fall. The nights were chilly and the streets, sidewalks, lawns, everything was damp with dew.

One Wednesday, Catarina took the express train all the way to Manhattan and rented a car, a nice, heavy Chrysler Imperial sedan. It was late afternoon by the time she got back to Cambridge. She parked the rented Chrysler in a public lot in town and took a bus back to the dorm. At eight o'clock that evening, Catarina took the bus to a stop near the parking lot and walked the rest of the way to retrieve the rented Chrysler.

She drove to Wendell Street and parked halfway down the block, facing Massachusetts Avenue She turned off the headlights but left the engine running.

At a little after nine o'clock, there was Geri, right on time, walking back from her night class. She was all bundled up against the cold, her books clutched to her chest.

As Geri stepped off the curb, Catarina put the Chrysler's transmission in drive and pressed the accelerator hard to the floor. Tires screeching, the Chrysler reached the intersection in less than

239

three seconds. Catarina gripped the steering wheel firmly to be sure the big car found its target. She both heard the thump and felt the impact through the steering wheel.

She turned right onto Massachusetts Avenue, slowed down, and glanced in the rearview mirror.

Receding from view behind her and scattered on the dark, wet street a few feet from the curb, just at the edge of a circle of light from a streetlamp, were some books and what looked like a bundle of rags.

A big bundle of rags, a bundle of rags about the size of a human body.

Nearby was a smashed backpack, the kind students use to carry their homework.

A notebook had broken open and its pages had come loose. The speeding Chrysler's wake had caught the notebook's pages, making them swirl and flutter along the gutter and the street.

To Catarina, the loose pages looked like little white doves trying to take flight.

Catarina was so turned on she had to make an effort to control her excitement.

She drove on up Massachusetts Avenue past Porter Square until she picked up the Massachusetts Turnpike.

She headed for Utica, as aroused as she would be if she were having great sex.

It was not just that everything was going exactly as planned.

It was not just the thought that she would be getting her own room.

No, it was more, much more than that.

It thrilled her to discover she had the ability to control things, to end a person's life. The realization that she had that power in her hands was as satisfying as anything she had ever experienced.

She arrived in Utica in the early morning hours, parked the car in her parent's garage and went to bed in her own room. Her parents were again in Las Vegas and only the maid was home. She woke the next day around 10:00 a.m. and called Uncle Willy.

"I have a small problem, and I hope you can help me."

"Anything at all, Catarina".

"Well, I had a little accident, and I don't want my parents to know about it."

"How bad?"

"I rented a car and I think I hit a dog or something. I don't think the damage is too bad. Can you help me?"

"Where are you?"

"I'm at home here in Utica."

"I'll come right over, and we'll see what needs to be done. Things happen."

When she got back to Cuellen House late that afternoon she found everyone in mourning. One of the dorm mates, Geri Greene, had died from a massive head injury in a hit and run accident.

Catarina expressed her shock and deepest sympathy.

A few days later Geri's parents came to Cuellen House and cleared out their daughter's belongings.

The next day the counselor told Catarina the room was hers.

⁂

Early the week before Christmas, 1961, Uncle Benny and Willy were sent to Cambridge in the big black Lincoln to bring Johnny and Catarina home for the holidays. It had snowed off and on all week. The rolling hills and the half-buried farm buildings scattered along the white countryside looked like a picture for a Christmas Card.

They had been driving for over three hours and were past Schenectady on Route 90. So far, the New York State Thruway was clear of snow and the occasional flurries melted as they hit the car.

Traffic was light, the ride long and monotonous. The low humming of the tires on the smooth pavement lulled Catarina and Johnny in the back seat of the warm car.

Benny, driving with one hand and gesturing with the other, droned on and on, telling Willy again about his wife and the advantages of being married to an older woman, a woman almost 10 years his senior. Benny never missed a chance to tell everyone about his being younger than his wife. He seemed to believe that because older women outnumbered men, his having married one and taking her off the market meant the rest of the men owed him for it.

Johnny and Catarina and the rest of the family had met Benny's wife, Darlene, many times. While Darlene may have been a little older than Benny, in the 11 years they had been married he

241

was aging faster than she. He was catching up with her. In fact, after all these years she didn't look a day older. Benny, however, had put on some weight and lost some hair.

Now, if anything, he looked older than Darlene.

Benny and Willy had been around as long as Johnny and Catarina could remember. Willy, like an uncle, always there when he was needed.

Through half closed eyes, Catarina looked past her brother, dozing in the seat next to her.

A blue Pontiac sedan pulled alongside on the left.

It matched their speed.

The back window lowered.

A man inside, wearing a dark grey turtleneck sweater and knit cap, aimed a pistol.

Two quick flashes, two loud gunshots and the Lincoln's driver side window exploded in flying glass.

Uncle Benny, hit in the side of the head, died instantly.

He was thrown from behind the wheel and against Willy.

The cruise control was set, and the Lincoln continued driverless along the New York State Thruway. Willy quickly reached for the wheel, at the same time struggling to draw his gun from its holster. But the holster was under his left arm. The weight of Benny's body against him blocked his movements long enough for a third shot from the Pontiac to hit Willy in the neck.

Now the gunman seemed to be having trouble with his pistol. He was trying unsuccessfully to fire it again, pulling at the slide, then thumbing the hammer frantically.

The weapon was jammed.

Johnny lunged forward from his place in the back seat and attempted to push Benny's body out of the way. Struggling to climb over the seat, he grabbed the steering wheel, and using his foot against the side of Benny's face pushed as hard as he could, he cleared a way for himself.

Catarina leaned forward, grabbed Benny's collar, and pulled, at the same time wresting the .45 caliber Colt automatic from his shoulder holster.

She cocked the gun.

A cartridge moved into the chamber.

She slid across the back seat behind Johnny.

The other driver tried to pull away, but the Lincoln was still within a car length of the accelerating Pontiac.

Catarina got to her knees on the seat, lowered the rear window, and leaned out.

Her body was half out of the car.

Fighting the icy wind, she held the heavy .45 in both hands and aimed carefully, forcing herself to take her time. With her first shot she hit her target, the Pontiac's right rear tire. The tire went flat and began to come apart. As it did, the rear of the Pontiac dropped to the pavement. The tire began to unravel, disintegrate, some of the flying rubber striking the Lincoln's grill and windshield. Streaming sparks from the car's bare steel rim in the concrete pavement.

The crippled Pontiac was forced to slow. The Lincoln passed it and began pulling ahead. Catarina, still on her knees, shifted around on the seat.

She was looking back, watching the Pontiac fall behind.

Again, she leaned out the window. Gripping the gun with both hands, she lined the sights down the barrel carefully.

The Lincoln was going 80 miles an hour.

She was partially blinded by her hair blowing in her face.

One second, one moment, one opportunity for a clear shot.

Anticipating the gun's recoil, she slowly, gently squeezed the trigger. The .45 bucked.

A hole appeared in the right side of the Pontiac's windshield, eight inches above the hood.

The driver's head snapped back, and then fell against the steering wheel.

The Pontiac abruptly swerved left.

It violently struck the thruway's center divider, bounced back, scattering hood, grill, and parts of the car along the pavement.

Then it rolled backward across two lanes of the thruway directly into the path of a semi truck and trailer.

Still on her knees in the back seat, Catarina closed the side window and turned to watch out the rear.

The semi hit the Pontiac, slamming it into the concrete support for the Paradise Road Overpass.

The blue sedan exploded in flames. Burning gasoline began spreading across three lanes of the New York State Thruway. Westbound traffic was blocked completely. Motorists headed east were slowing, drawn by the pillar of smoke ahead of them at the overpass.

Satisfied there could be no survivors, Catarina moved to the other side of the Lincoln, leaned over the back of the front seat and maneuvered Willy's body down to the floor under the dashboard. Then, with Johnny pushing, she pulled and tugged at Benny's body and pushed hit off the seat onto Willy so it could not be seen from outside.

The Lincoln with the Monreale siblings and two dead uncles sped onward, away from the scene.

Johnny was driving to match the speed of the other traffic. They continued to Utica as if nothing had happened.

But even with the driver's side window gone and the car's interior close to freezing, Catarina was hot with excitement. She snuggled in her coat, grinning to herself.

She was feeling the same exhilaration as she had the night she killed Geri.

God, is something wrong with me? But there can't be. How can anything that makes me feel so alive, so vital, be wrong?

Neither of them said a word until they were almost home.

Finally, Johnny said "You seem to have a knack."

"I think I've found my calling," she said from the back seat.

He watched her in the rear-view mirror, studying her face. She calmly and carefully released the hammer, removed the clip and ejected the live round from the firing chamber of Uncle Benny's .45.

She inspected the bullet curiously, holding it between her thumb and forefinger, then reinserted it in the clip and replaced the clip in the pistol's grip with a firm, practiced slap of her palm.

They drove to the County Road 30 turnoff and on through the rural countryside to the compound. When they reached the house, Johnny pulled up the driveway past the carport and around to the back, out of sight from the street.

Gianni, wearing an ankle length topcoat came hurrying out to meet them.

244

"What's going on? Why did you park back here? Where's Benny and Willy?"

Johnny opened the door to get out. Shards of glass from the Lincoln's window fell on the concrete parking pad.

"Dad, this is going to take some explaining."

Relaxed and composed as if the trip had been uneventful, Catarina opened the rear door of the Lincoln. She got out, straightened her jacket, and walked around the car to the passenger side.

She opened the front door.

Willy's limp arm fell out.

Gianni, his hands stuffed deep in the pockets of his topcoat for warmth, walked forward and bent to look inside.

"Well?" he said, looking down at Benny's body lying partly on the passenger seat, partly on top of Willy on the floor.

The car's front seat and the bodies of Benny and Willy were soaked with blood.

Johnny and Catarina were composed, unscathed.

Johnny rubbed his gloved hands together for warmth and calmly recounted the entire episode. He emphasized his telling of Catarina's quick thinking and extremely efficient dispatching of the attackers.

Gianni Monreale looked into the faces of his son and daughter. Then bent to gently lift Willy's limp arm and reverently place it over his body.

Johnny started to add something, and then thought better of it. For a moment, the three stood silently.

Catarina broke the silence" Can I keep Uncle Benny's gun? As a souvenir?"

Without answering, Gianni turned on his heel. His hands stuffed deep in his pockets he started for the house. The other two fell in step behind him.

Over his shoulder he said, "I have to call Grandpa and tell him what happened. We will make arrangements to take care of Benny and Willy. And the car. Come inside and say hello to your mother."

An hour or so later a big tractor trailer, diesel engine roaring and belching exhaust smoke into the cold crisp air, drove into the quiet cul de sac. It stopped in front of Gianni and Gina Monreale's house and noisily backed up the driveway.

After it left, Catarina looked out to the back of the house. The blood-soaked Lincoln with the missing driver's side window along Uncle Benny and Willy were not there anymore.

Before dinner that night Gianpoalo, Gianni, Gina, Catarina, and Johnny gathered in the darkened library. The subject of the conversation was the assault.

Gianpoalo, leaning back in the big leather chair, turned to Gianni and Gina. "I am again surprised at your offspring and their calm capabilities."

Catarina got up from the easy chair and moved silently to the window. She looked out on the dark street. Wearing a tight black jumpsuit, she was only a silhouette merging with the curtains.

Cousin Leo's house, all lit up with a big tree in the window and a wreath on the front door, looked warm and inviting. The snow-covered roofs and lawns, the lights along the eaves.

Catarina did not seem to feel the mood of the group in the darkened living room. They looked solemn, thoughtful, concerned.

Catarina tingled with excitement, ready for whatever was coming.

Behind her, Johnny broke the silence, "Why would anyone want to kill Benny and Willy knowing that would cause an outbreak of war?"

"I had planned to ride up with Benny and Willy and accompany the two of you on the trip home," Gianni said from his chair next to the fireplace.

"Who knew of your plan?" Johnny asked softly, so softly and quietly he could barely be heard.

Still standing at the window with her forehead pressed against the cold glass, Catarina's attention went to the next house in the compound, the house that belonged to her Uncle Tony, Gianpoalo's second son.

The windows were dark, only the porch light was on.

Nobody home, she thought. She knew Uncle Tony ran the family's imports from Central and South America. She did not need to be told what that meant. Uncle Tony was huge, weighing maybe 285 or more but only 5'7" tall. Tony Monreale was referred to as "Fat Tony" by his business associates, employees, and everyone else.

246

"I only mentioned it to the immediate family here in the compound," Gianni replied. "At the last minute I couldn't get away."

"We can conclude that our enemies are on the move," Johnny said softly. "The game of chess begins."

Catarina turned from the window. The fire in the fireplace crackled. Gianpoalo rose from his chair, picked up a poker and stirred the embers.

Gina, standing behind her husband, spoke for the first time. "Christmas dinner with the family will proceed as planned."

The next night, Christmas dinner at Gianpoalo Monreale's house at the head of the cul de sac was subdued. For the sake of the children, Gianni and Gina, Johnny and Catarina along with the cousins and aunts and uncles avoided any mention of Benny and Willy.

It was as if nothing had happened.

Everyone was there. Everyone except Benny and his wife Darlene and Cousin Willy.

And Uncle Tony.

The rest of the week before New Years passed quietly, but Gianpoalo, Gianni, Gina. Johnny and Catarina had a lot to talk about. Changes in the family.

And, at last, changes for Catarina, a plan, a purpose.

Christmas break ended, and Max drove Catarina and Johnny back to school.

They were almost to Cambridge before either spoke.

Max was just turning off the Massachusetts Turnpike onto the Cambridge Street when Catarina finally whispered, "I think Uncle Tony is our man."

"So do I," Johnny replied quietly, still looking out the window.

Neither said another word until Max stopped the Cadillac in front of Cuellen House. "Let me walk my sister to the door, Max. You just stay here in the warm car and relax."

Johnny and Catarina walked up to the porch steps and stood facing each other in front of the old Victorian house. It was three o'clock in the afternoon and just above freezing.

"We have a lot more to talk about," Johnny said.

"Yes, I guess we do."

"I'll call you to set up a time and place. I would just as soon you didn't call me at the dorm. Remember, I have a roommate."

"I'll wait to hear from you."

"Our lives have changed, Catarina."

"I know."

Johnny turned and started back to the car. Catarina climbed the steps and went to her single room on the second floor in the front of the house. By the time she looked out her window, the Cadillac with Max and Johnny were gone.

Before taking off her coat, she turned, hands still in her pockets, and looked around the room.

Linen curtains, white and yellow flowers on a cream background that matched the wallpaper, a floor lamp next to an easy chair upholstered to match.

On the bed was the bedspread she'd had since she was ten, and on the dresser, her grandmother's antique silver hairbrush. The room was warm and inviting and seemed only slightly feminine despite the decor.

She pulled the curtains shut and locked the door. After hanging her heavy coat in her closet, she returned to the bed where she'd thrown her purse.

She opened it and took out Uncle Benny's .45 automatic.

Holding it in both hands, it felt heavy and cool.

She slid the clip out of the grip.

There were five bullets left.

"I'll have to get some ammo" she said softly.

# Chapter Fifty

## Gavin Keller

## January 1, 1962

Gavin was on his bed reading when Johnny returned.

"Did you have a Merry Christmas and a Happy New Year?" he asked, looking up from his book.

"Yes."

That was rather an abrupt answer, even for the new Johnny. But he was becoming accustomed to his roommate's new, taciturn self.

The last couple of weeks had been a little hard for Gavin, being alone and away from home during Christmas. In the past, Christmas had never meant much to him, not even the presents, really. His family, his mother and father, that is, were nice people and he liked them o.k. However, he was never 'close' to them, not even his mother. The only person he'd ever been close to was his sister Val. No, until Catarina came into his life, Christmas, the holidays, were just like any other time of year in California. Like spring for instance. There was no real change in the weather, no snow, no nasty freezing slush; no shapeless people all bundled up against the cold.

It was Catarina that had made the difference.

He really missed her. Somehow, he had this fantasy of the two of them together, holding each other for warmth against the cold, strolling happily along decorated streets, celebrating the Christmas Season.

In reality though he knew that something like that could never, ever happen.

"How's the family? All well I hope?"

"Yes, everyone is fine," Johnny answered quietly, hanging his coat in the closet.

"How's your grandfather Gianpoalo?"

"Grandpa Gianpoalo is fine, mother and father are fine, and Catarina is fine. Everyone is just fine."

Johnny went to the window and looked out on the street.

It was just getting dark, and Gavin knew well what Johnny was seeing. The neighborhood was just bordering on tacky. Pretty much as to be expected for a street of student dorms and fraternity and sorority houses.

Had he detected a note of impatience in Johnny's tone? His own mood of the last two weeks, a mood of depression and loneliness had lifted with his roommate's return.

But now, seeing him standing silently at the window of the little dorm room, it was all coming back.

The cheap beat-up furniture, the drab, depressing little room that had been his home the whole time he'd been in Cambridge.

Without Catarina, he saw himself and his life for what it really was.

Bleak and empty. Empty like a monk's cell.

School, work, and home, the dorm room.

If the dorm room could be considered a home.

And it couldn't, it couldn't be considered a home. It was a cell. He had to shake this feeling. He had to re-establish contact with the only person that gave meaning to his life. He had to reestablish contact with Catarina, and he had to do that as soon as possible.

Seeing that his probing was going nowhere, Gavin tried to concentrate on the book, but he could not. The letters on the page just seemed to dance and swim.

Catarina. Where was she? What was she doing? What was she thinking?

Was she thinking of him?

He didn't even know exactly where she lived here in Cambridge. All he knew was that it was somewhere near Leslie.

He'd have to wait until she called him at the office. Could he wait? Could he? What else could he do but wait?

Classes started again on Monday and then there was more work at First Boston. All day at the office, whenever the phone rang Gavin grabbed at it, hoping it was Catarina.

But she didn't call.

He tried calling her, but the number had been disconnected.

Why? What was that all about?

Three weeks went by with still no word from Catarina. Before Christmas they had spent almost every evening and every weekend together. Having Johnny right there in the dorm every night made it worse. His roommate was a constant reminder of her. He thought about her all the time. As the days went by it did not get any better.

No call came, though. What had happened? Had Peter come back? Was there someone else? Maybe she didn't love him anymore.

But then he couldn't recall her ever actually saying that she did love him. Was it possible that she did not love him? Was it possible that after all the passion, all the wild times they had spent together, she didn't love him at all, didn't have the same feelings about him that he had about her? Girls had always fallen for him. Once, when they were in their teens, Gavin's sister Valerie had told him that when a woman said they loved him, she was his. That was the way it had always worked with girls.

Just get them to say they loved him.

But Catarina had never said she loved him. If she felt the same about him, or even missed him at all, she would have called.

# Chapter Fifty One

## February, 1962

Another week passed.

February, New England style, arrived with a howling, bitter cold snowstorm. Most students at Harvard skipped classes and many office workers in Boston decided that braving the elements was just too difficult.

Not Gavin. Gavin doggedly went to all his classes and sat there for the whole period, even when the professors didn't show up. In the afternoons he braved the trip to Batterymarch and First Boston's almost empty office.

The snow piled along the streets had been churned by the cars and buses into disgusting black slush. It was nearly impossible to hop from the bus to the sidewalk without getting his shoes, socks, and pants wet with the dirty, nasty ice-cold water. He was quite sure that the bus drivers deliberately stopped well away from the curb.

He began to really hate this place. Daylight was gone by four thirty in the afternoon. By the time he got back to the damn little dorm room it was dark.

He had no place to go and nothing to do.

The days passed. School and the office helped to occupy and distract him from thinking about Catarina all the time. That sick, empty feeling lingered.

By the middle of March, the freezing snow was replaced by freezing rain and the wind blew all the time.

Returning to the dorm room Thursday night he found Johnny packing. "What's up?" he asked, hoping Johnny's family was going to Bermuda or someplace and would invite him along.

"I'm moving out. I've rented an apartment, so now you have the whole place to yourself. That is, unless they find you another roommate mid semester."

Panicked, Gavin asked, "Why? Is something wrong?"

"Nothing's wrong. Nothing at all," Johnny said closing his suitcase. "I just decided to get out on my own. We only have another year or so of school and I've already more or less joined the family business. I'm working now. It's time I got my own place. Besides," he said turning to face Gavin, "I just don't like dorm life anymore. I haven't for quite a while."

"Where? Where is it?" asked Gavin.

"It's not far from here. I'll still be attending classes. But my new place is bigger, much bigger than this little room. I'll have some privacy and a garage to park the car."

"Would you like a roommate? You know, to share expenses?" Gavin asked, trying to control his voice. "I don't like dorm life either. I would just as soon leave this dump, too."

"No, its time I got out on my own."

Oh God, Gavin thought, Johnny was his last link to Catarina. What the hell was he going to do?

"I know I still owe you for that night in New York," Johnny said, putting on his London Fog. "If there's ever anything I can do for you, look me up and let me know."

With that, he picked up his bags and headed toward the door.

"Wait. I, uh…" started Gavin.

"What?"

"Uh, how could I get in touch with you, you know, if I needed to or something?"

"I'll call you and give you my number as soon as they install the phone."

Johnny gently but firmly pulled the door shut behind him and was gone.

The sound of the door closing seemed to echo in the now bleak, depressing little dorm room. Gavin sat on the edge of his bed and looked around. Now he was completely alone. Granted, Johnny had not been much company since the New York trip, but at least he'd been here. Without Catarina, aside from Rob Stone at the office, Johnny was the only companionship Gavin had in Boston. He was familiar, and most of all, he was a link to Catarina. There'd always been the chance she might call Johnny and Gavin would be the one to answer the phone, or that Johnny might say something about her.

But nothing like that had happened.

The phone in the dorm room had not rung once since Johnny came back from the holidays. The only time it was used at all was when Gavin called to check in with his porn-partner, Tommy Huber in California.

Out in the hallway guys were laughing and yelling and running up and down, going on about beer, having a "kegger" and just making a racket.

What a bunch of assholes.

Lonely, depressed, bored. Get real, Gavin, he told himself. Catarina isn't going to call. Johnny and the Monreales had moved on. They are out of your life.

He began to resent them all deeply. He, too, was going to have to move on, force himself to come up with something else.

At the moment the only thing on his plate were the files he worked on at First Boston. Files that told of pathetic little attempts at small frauds by little people, people like Sol Jamaica. He could write a book about the stupid things some people tried.

It wouldn't be a very good book.

Occasionally, though, someone pulled off a really big scam, a dodge worth millions. In those cases, the insurance companies were slow to catch on, their initial reaction being disbelief that something so large was happening or had happened. In those cases, by the time they did have to face up to it, the perpetrators had disappeared.

Gavin had learned a lot about big frauds from First Boston's files. If he could come up with an idea, a scheme he could implement on a worthy scale and be as invisible as he'd been in the porn film business, what the hell? Why not?

A plan had already formed in his mind, and he began to think it through.

The next day was Friday, classes till noon.

On his way to work, he stopped at a shop on Tremont Street and had a fake driver's license and passport made up in the name of "Anthony Monreale."

Then onward to at Massachusetts Bank and Trust. There he opened an account in the name of The Liberal Mutual Insurance Company, a name similar to that of a large, reputable insurance company located right there in Boston. When the clerk pushed the signature card in front of him, he filled it in using a made-up address he intended to have the bank correct later.

He signed the cards, "Anthony Monreale, President," the same name he had used for the passport and drivers license He studied the looping letters of the name.

Perfect. Just perfect.

After class on Monday, he took the bus to Beacon Hill. There he rented the smallest, least expensive office he could find, an office near Anderson Street and Philips.

He signed the lease Anthony Monreale, President of the Liberal Mutual Insurance Company. For the deposit and first month's rent he used the temporary checks provided by the bank for The Liberal Mutual Insurance Company account.

He needed an address in Boston's financial district, an address with a 02110 Zip Code for this plan. During a break at work, he stopped in the post office and picked up the forms for renting a box.

When he did finally get to his desk that day, he called the phone company. He ordered a phone installed in the Beacon Hill office, a phone in the name of the Liberal Mutual Insurance Company.

Later that day, as the other First Boston employees left for home, Gavin Keller lingered at his desk. When he was sure everyone was gone, he got to work on his project.

Carefully cutting and pasting, he created a letterhead for The Liberal Mutual Insurance Company. The letterhead even included a logo using a picture he'd cut out of a book, a picture of an eagle clutching arrows. He used the address of the rented office and the phone number assigned by the telephone company.

Gavin then went to the file room and used First Boston's brand-new Xerox 914 photocopy machine to print a generous supply of letterheads. The stationery looked flawless, perfectly authentic. Returning to his desk he completed the application for a post office box in the name of The Liberal Mutual Insurance Company.

When he finally left the office, he stopped at the mailbox on Batterymarch and mailed the application along with a cover letter.

He used a postage stamp rather than First Boston's postage machine.

Then he went on home to his empty dorm room.

Throughout the rest of the week, Gavin went by the little Beacon Hill office and checked for mail. Wednesday a letter arrived from the post office addressed to Anthony Monreale.

255

The letter confirmed the post office box number.

On Thursday, the phone company installed the phone. Gavin arranged for an answering service to answer the phone, "Liberal Mutual." He instructed the service to tell callers that the person they wanted was out, but to leave their number and the call would be returned when they got back.

Gavin stayed after work the next day. When he was sure he had the place to himself, he sat at one of the typist's desks with The Liberal Mutual letterheads. He wrote a letter to a retail insurance agent in Tacoma, Washington. The letter said that Liberal Mutual understood the agent had recently written insurance on a bridge. Because of the agent's experience and expertise in the field, Liberal Mutual was interested in appointing the agent. The letter offered to make the agent Liberty's exclusive representative to write property insurance on bridges throughout the United States.

Gavin signed the letter Anthony Monreale, Vice President of Underwriting.

Next, he wrote to Cuttersfield Bank in Bermuda requesting forms for establishing banking relationships and an account in the name of Liberal Mutual Insurance Company, P.O. Box 20409, Batterymarch Station, Boston, MA. 02110.

By this time, it was quite late. He walked through the empty offices to the room where policy forms and supplies were stored. He took one complete First Boston policy blank along with a First Boston application for property insurance. He carefully placed all this in his briefcase, along with the scraps of letterheads and other wastepaper he'd used in creating Liberal Mutual and left the office.

It was almost midnight, cold and threatening to rain again. He'd missed the last bus back to Cambridge, so he walked over to the Langham and caught a cab. When he got to his dorm room, he stayed up all night working on the policy form, application, and the endorsements. Cutting and pasting, he changed the name to Liberal Mutual wherever the First Boston name appeared. He planned to stay after work one night the following week to run off a generous supply of Liberal Mutual policies on First Boston's Xerox machine.

The answer from the Tacoma agent was in the post office box the following Friday. Oh yes, the agent would accept Liberal Mutual Insurance Company's offer. The agent was indeed an "expert" in writing insurance on bridges. He was confident that not only did he know everything there was to know about insuring bridges he could suggest the premium that should be charged based on a percentage of the total value of the bridge.

Gavin, not wanting Vice President of Underwriting, Anthony Monreale to appear as if he had nothing else to do, waited a few days before replying. Then he wrote back confirming the appointment of the Tacoma Agent as the exclusive representative of The Liberal Mutual Insurance Company. He enclosed in the envelope a "Producers Agreement," along with a supply of The Liberal Mutual Insurance Company Applications for Bridge Insurance.

Few insurers cover bridges. Premiums for insuring bridges are substantial, amounting to as much as 1% of the total value of the structure. Since the agent was to receive a 10% commission from Liberal Mutual on the premiums, Gavin was confident the Tacoma agent would contact all governmental entities in the State of Washington and probably other states, announcing his new facility for insuring bridges, and solicit their business.

Checking with the answering service, Gavin got a message that the agent had been invited to meet with the State Department of Transportation to quote coverage on a small bridge valued at $11,000,000. A week later, the completed application for coverage arrived in the post office box, accompanied by the agent's letter suggesting that the rate be .75% of the value of the bridge, or $83,500.

Underwriter Monreale wrote back that Liberal Mutual's quoted rate would be 1%, developing a premium of $110,000.

The agent presented the quote to the State Department of Transportation and got the order. Gavin was sure he had the agent's attention now. A premium of that size meant the agent would receive an easy commission of $11,000 on just this one transaction.

Thirty days later a check from the Tacoma agent in the net amount of $99,000 payable to The Liberal Mutual Insurance Company appeared in the post office box. Gavin endorsed the check using the name of Anthony Monreale with Massachusetts Bank and Trust and deposited the check in the Liberal Mutual account.

Soon, the post office box was receiving applications almost every day addressed to Anthony Monreale for underwriting. In order to appear to be a legitimate insurance company with underwriting standards, Gavin, acting as Vice President of Underwriting Monreale, agreed with the agent's suggested premiums on some, offered counter quotes on others and some he 'declined to insure.'

Within months, the agent was getting rich. Gavin was getting a lot richer. As the premiums were received, Gavin deposited them into the account at Massachusetts Bank and Trust. He periodically transferred portions of the money to Cuttersfield Bank in Bermuda.

The months passed and the wound left by Catarina began to fade.

Gavin's routine consisted of school, now nearing graduation, his work at First Boston, and his "duties" as chief executive officer, underwriter, policy typist, and everything else for The Liberal Mutual Insurance Company. The bridge insurance business was doing so well he had to arrange with an outside policy typing service to type the policies.

By the end of the year Liberal Mutual's account at Massachusetts Bank and Trust held over $22,000,000 and the Cuttersfield account contained $7,500,000.

# Chapter Fifty Two

## January 1963

Another holiday season, another Christmas and New Years spent alone. Soon Gavin would be graduating and could start planning on returning to California. He'd continued living alone in the dorm for the remainder of his stay at Harvard, and he'd continued working with Rob Stone at First Boston.

He hadn't heard from Caterina or Johnny Monreale, not even once.

There were never any claims in the bridge insurance business.

Well, hardly ever.

But finally, not three weeks before he was to graduate from Harvard, the inevitable happened.

Gavin was studying at the beat-up old desk in his dorm room. To keep himself company, he had the little T.V. on the bedside table turned on. The words "dangerous bridge collapse" caught his attention. He turned in time to catch the news clip of a bridge swaying comically back and forth, almost as if it were made of rubber. An old car was dangling precariously halfway across.

At last, the bridge just disassembled itself and fell into the chasm below.

Gavin knew it was a bridge supposedly insured by Liberal Mutual, and he knew it was time to pull the plug. He reached for the telephone and called a travel agency to book the next available flight from La Guardia to Bermuda. One left at seven the next morning. He packed one small bag, then bent and got from under his bed the two large, beat-up suitcases he'd picked up from a thrift shop.

The most dangerous step lay ahead: the payoff, the payoff for all preparation and work of running his scheme.

When he arrived at Penn Central Station he ran, coattails trailing behind him, up the stairs to the street and hailed a cab to La Guardia. By 3:00 a.m. he was sitting in a plastic chair in the departing passengers' terminal, trying vainly to get comfortable. He had a four-hour wait for boarding.

It was mid afternoon by the time he arrived in Bermuda.

Gavin was operating on nerves. He checked into the Hamilton Princess and went directly to his room. Before doing anything else he called Cuttersfield Bank and made an appointment to see the bank's president, John Taylor. Then he unpacked the smaller of the bags, took a quick shower and put on a fresh suit. He put the other two bags on the bed, left the room and walked across Front Street into Hamilton, headed for Cuttersfield Bank. He approached a teller and told her he was there to see the bank's president.

Shortly, a tall, slender gentleman dressed very formally in the style of a Brit but wearing Bermuda shorts emerged from an office in the rear of the bank.

"John Taylor," he said, holding out his hand.

Gavin introduced himself as Anthony Monreale." So nice to meet you after all these months," Gavin went on. "Our company has enjoyed our relationship with your bank. The service has always been impeccable."

He then explained he had to begin the process for withdrawal of a small portion of Liberal Mutual's funds, $5,000,000 in cash as part of a reinsurance recovery to pay a large claim. He verified his identity with the phony driver's license and passport and by using the same signature he used signing the card on file with the bank. Mr. Taylor carefully checked the signatures, held up the phony Tony Monreale driver's license and passport with Gavin's picture on it and looked him over. "I shall begin the process immediately, Mr. Monreale." He got to his feet and extending his hand. "It should take no more than twenty-four hours to confirm the transaction and assemble the funds."

Gavin stood. These were tense moments and he had to steel himself to remain calm. He had expected there would be formalities and he expected he'd be nervous when the time came for him to actually step up for the payoff.

He was almost there. "I understand," he said, shaking the bank president's hand. "I will be staying in room 118 at the Hamilton Princess Hotel. Please contact me when funds are available."

Leaving the bank, he returned to the hotel and to his room to change back into his traveling clothes. He wanted to keep his suit fresh and unwrinkled for his next meeting with Taylor. He left his room and returned to the front of the hotel, stopped under the canopy, and hailed the first cab in line. The next twenty-four hours were crucial. Would Bank President John Taylor get suspicious? Suspicious of Gavin? Suspicious of the large amount of money to be taken in cash? Would this thing really work?

It was midnight by the time he arrived back in Manhattan. He took the night train to Boston, then a cab to the empty office in Beacon Hill and collapsed on the musty old carpet next to the phone.

It was almost dawn.

Aching. Aching was the first thing that came to mind when he was forced awake by the shrill ringing of the phone on the floor next to him. He was aching all over. Sleeping on the dirty old carpet was even more uncomfortable than he had guessed it might be. He felt anything but rested. And it was imperative that for the next few hours he be at the top of his game. He rolled over on his stomach and holding his nose to attempt what he hoped was a nasal voice, answered the phone.

"Liberal Mutual Insurance, Mr. Monreale's office. Can I help you?"

A voice on the phone said "This is the overseas operator. I have a call from Bermuda for Mr. Monreale."

"Mr. Monreale is away on business. Can I help you?"

Another voice came on the line and said, "Operator, can I speak to the person answering?"

"Go ahead, sir," said the operator.

"This is John Taylor, President of Cuttersfield Bank in Bermuda. I'm calling to verify the withdrawal of a substantial amount of money from Liberal Mutual's account. Is there anyone there with whom I can speak?"

"Let me transfer you, sir."

Gavin set the phone down on the floor, got to his feet and went down the hallway to the public bathroom to splash cold water on his face. Then he went to the paper towel dispenser and tore off a small bit. He wadded it and stuffed it in his cheeks, between his lower front teeth and his lower lip.

He walked back down the hall to the empty office, closed the door and locked it.

He picked up the phone.

"This is Dick Schmitt, Vice President of Claims," he said in as pompous a tone as he could muster, his voice muffled by the paper. "Can I be of assistance?"

261

"Mr. Schmitt, this is John Taylor at Cuttersfield's here in Bermuda. A Mr. Monreale has presented a draft for payment of $5,000,000 in cash. We require confirmation of his authority to receive this payment."

"I can assure you, Mr. Monreale has the authority to receive payment," said Gavin. "Will it be necessary to confirm by telex?"

"Yes, if you please. The authorization code is 51439 along with the account number. Our telex address is CuttersfieldsBrmda."

"I'll see to it you have the authorization overnight, Mr. Taylor."

"Thank you for your understanding and cooperation."

"Not at all, Mr. Taylor. We at Liberal Mutual appreciate your caution. It pays to be careful."

Gavin hung up, carefully wiped the phone with a handkerchief, and left the Beacon Hill office for the last time. He took the bus to Cambridge and headed straight for his dorm room to try to catch up on his sleep. At 3:00 that afternoon he got up, dressed, and took the bus to the city and First Boston's offices. He got there, arriving for work at his usual time. Around 4:30, employees began leaving for the day. Gavin remained at his desk pretending to work until after 6:00.

He had to be damn sure he had the place to himself.

When he was absolutely sure everyone was gone, he went to First Boston's telex room. Using the yellow telex tape, he carefully prepared a message prefixed with "libmutbos" for Liberal Mutual Boston, then typed the text. *"This will serve as authorization for release of funds in the amount of $5,000,000 in the currency of the United States to our representative Anthony Monreale for the full and final payment of claims relating to the Washington Bridge incident.* He signed it, "Richard Schmitt, Vice President Claims, co-signed by James Huber, Chief Financial Officer, Liberal Mutual Insurance Company."

Gavin reread the message several times to be certain it was letter perfect. Only then did he dial the telex number for Cuttersfield's. He waited for their answerback and when it came, pushed the telex machine's transmit lever.

The clatter of the machine in the empty office as the yellow tape began feeding through sounded to him as loud as a freight train. He looked around nervously. If anyone did happen in, there would be no possible excuse for him using the machine at this hour. The jig would be up.

Finally, the machine finished sending. He stopped the tape and triggered the answerback from Cuttersfield's machine. When it came through, he let the rest of his tape continue, sending the answerback for "libmutbos" that he had included on the tape. Then he disconnected, removed the tape, tore the printout off the machine and left the room.

Outside the building, Gavin paused and took a deep breath of Boston air. Despite the exhausting flights, the tension and lack of sleep, he had to press on. He walked over to the Langham to catch a cab for the train station. He was back in a plastic seat in the departing passengers' terminal at LaGuardia by 1:00 a. m., hoping to get some sleep before the plane left for Bermuda at seven.

Boston to New York to Bermuda, then back to New York, then Boston. Then repeating the five-leg journey, all in 24 hours. And soon he would be doing it all one last time.

He desperately needed a good night's sleep and a shower and shave.

The desk clerk saw him passing through the now familiar lobby of the Hamilton Princess.

"You have a message, Mr. Monreale," the clerk said, handing him a note.

It was from John Taylor.

So far, so good.

As soon as he got to his room, he dialed the number for the bank.

"We are prepared to complete your transaction, Mr. Monreale," Mr. Taylor's voice said on the phone.

Trying not to sound too eager, Gavin replied "I'll swing by as soon as I finish here." He showered, shaved, and put on the suit he'd left in the room. There was just enough time to get to the bank before it closed. He checked out of the hotel and flagged a cab, declining the bellhop's offer of help with the two empty suitcases. He had the cab go up the hill away from the bank, park and wait at Trott Road and Church Street. Leaving the smaller bag with his clothes in the cab, he took the two empty suitcases and walked back down to Front Street and around the corner to the bank.

It was almost three in the afternoon by the time he arrived at the bank. Mr. Taylor showed him to the private room used by the bank's clients for accessing their safety deposit boxes. There, carefully stacked on a highly polished mahogany table were bundles and bundles of one-hundred-dollar bills, each wrapped in purple paper bands marked "Cuttersfield Bank."

Trying to appear as if this were to him a routine chore, he carefully packed the two suitcases. He was anxious to get off the island as fast as he could. He was fairly sure he would never be able to come back to Bermuda, ever. Sooner or later, all hell was going to break loose when the claim for the bridge was submitted and Liberal Mutual was discovered to be a sham, front to back.

It was only after he left the bank, rounded the corner, and started up the hill on Church Street carrying the two heavy suitcases that he started to relax a little.

It had been another beautiful day in Bermuda.

Life was good.

When he finally returned home to the dorm, he called and arranged storage for the two suitcases with a moving and storage company in South Boston.

By that time, he was exhausted.

But his scheme, the planning, the preparation and the outcome had been a complete success.

⁂

# Chapter Fifty Three

## June 1963

Only the most promising students in the graduating class were invited to the cocktail party at Professor Alexander's home, a cocktail party that would be attended by recruiters from law firms and Fortune 500 corporations from around the country.

Gavin was one of them.

There is nothing like having a ton of money to give a person self-confidence. Gavin, with his new-found but secret wealth, was at ease and self assured. He mixed well with the guests, moving from group to group in the spacious living room, smiling easily and listening avidly.

A tall, distinguished gentleman was holding court over a group standing near the fireplace. During a momentary lull in the conversation Gavin introduced himself. On hearing his name, the white-haired gentleman raised an eyebrow. He was almost rude to the other graduate students, saying he wanted to have a private conversation with Gavin. He introduced himself as Jonathan Bland, Chief Litigator for Greater Energy Corporation. He said he'd heard much about Gavin from Dean Alexander, and he wanted to have a serious conversation with him about a position with his firm. Great pay, prestigious position, Fortune 500 Company.

Gavin agreed to meet with Bland for lunch the next day in the dining room of the Copley Plaza. The two struck it off immediately, and Bland offered him a job. Having no pressure financially, Gavin aggressively negotiated an advantageous salary and was able to stipulate that he would work in the Los Angeles corporate offices.

Graduation came at last. Gavin had already said his goodbyes to Rob Stone at First Boston. His parents, minus his sister Val, in the Navy and unable to get leave, flew to Boston for the ceremony. His dad had rented a car. The three of them, his mom and dad and Gavin, cleared his belongings from the Spartan little dorm room, went by the storage facility in South Boston where he had stored the two suitcases, then headed to the airport for the flight home.

There was a slight twinge when the porter took the two beat up old suitcases to check them through to L.A. Gavin had crudely tied them shut, wrapping them both with twine. He no longer trusted their rusty old latches, but also wanted to make them look more pathetic and less of a temptation for someone to steal.

If they didn't show up in L.A., all that work would be for nothing.

He did, however, still have plenty of money in the bank and he was still, after all these years, making a bundle on his and Tommy's porn rental business.

He had never forgotten that endless, miserable flight from California in the DC7. He'd dreaded the flight home the whole time he'd been in the east.

But the return trip with his folks was in a jet and much faster, not nearly as bad as he was afraid it would be. His sense of relief was complete when he retrieved the two ratty old suitcases at the turnstile in LAX.

His dad, in a rare paternal gesture, grabbed one of them and tried to lift it to carry it out to the car. "What the hell is in this thing?" he asked, surprised at its weight.

"Books," Gavin replied, picking up the other. The two suitcases weighed almost 50 pounds apiece.

∴

He started his job at Greater Energy that Monday and within a month bought a car and rented a nice apartment, explaining to his folks that he'd received a substantial signing bonus for taking the job.

There had been very little in the way of office politics at First Boston.

But when Gavin settled in at Greater Energy, he found a battleground of ambitious personalities, nepotism and cutthroat maneuverings for position and power that involved everyone in the company.

It was a challenge worthy of Gavin Keller's Machiavellian talents.

Because of his stint with First Boston, he was soon assigned to an insurance company subsidiary, Entrepreneur.

Entrepreneur, an old established company, had only recently been acquired by Greater Energy.

Gavin quickly saw that Entrepreneur, overstaffed, and badly managed only got by because of its sheer size. Because of its entrenched, stodgy old management along with huge claims for everything from fire to liability losses, it was spewing capital in a torrent like the break in a dam. Entrepreneur's value as a Greater Energy asset was shrinking rapidly.

This was a major embarrassment to the Chairman of the Board, a vain man who fancied himself the king of mergers and acquisitions.

Greater Energy had several dozen corporate counsels, all slick, buttoned down young men about Gavin's age or older. All political animals, they assumed that Gavin's assignment to Entrepreneur would either be a dead end that would get him out of the picture or a no-win situation that would quickly damage his career with the parent company.

But Gavin didn't see it that way.

No, Gavin saw it as an opportunity, a chance to out-flank the competition and jumpstart a career with the parent, Greater Energy.

He began by reviewing the company's claim handling practices. Sensing Greater Energy would sell or spin off Entrepreneur as soon as it could, Gavin realized it would not hurt to bring a new style to the table. His approach would not include any concern for Entrepreneur's customers, or it's long established and carefully nurtured reputation in the marketplace. Staying in the office late into the night, he gathered files for large losses, starting with claims exceeding $10,000,000. He began reviewing each one to find ways to avoid paying or reducing the company's obligations—by any means. Retaining outside counsel rather than involving his competitors, Greater Energy or Entrepreneur's in-house attorneys, he assigned them to investigate every possible aspect of each file. The policyholder, the underwriting information, anything large or small including the personal lives of the claimants that could provide a way to avoid paying the claim.

He even sued the company's own producers, claiming the misrepresentation of the policyholder's exposure.

If all else failed, he sought to tie claims up in court until in desperation the claimant agreed to a reduced settlement.

Hungry, trying to get more work from Entrepreneur and hopefully even Greater Energy, outside counsels eagerly joined Gavin's efforts to beat the claims.

In Gavin's view he had nothing to lose. Entrepreneur Insurance Company was to Greater Energy a mistake anyway. A mistake that unless dramatically turned around, could only be corrected by disposing of an acquisition that appeared to have been made impulsively to begin with.

Gavin's tactics worked. He saved Entrepreneur $54,000,000 in claim payments in the first six months. This was not lost on Greater Energy's chief financial officer, and shortly thereafter, the Greater Energy chairman himself.

The outcome was so much better than anticipated that in 1964, Greater Energy promoted Gavin to Executive Vice President of what had now become their most profitable subsidiary. Rather than a dog, Entrepreneur Insurance Company had become a successful turnaround, a "tribute to Greater Energy's management expertise," as the now vindicated chairman stated at the Annual Shareholders' Meeting.

At age twenty-nine, Gavin was the youngest man in the company to ever hold the title of Executive Vice President.

He was awarded a substantial bonus and with the money paid cash for a spacious home high in the hills above Encino, California.

⁂

The State of Washington submitted a claim for a little over $24,000,000 to the retail agent in Tacoma for the lost bridge. The retail agent promptly sent it onward to the Liberal Mutual Insurance Company, Attention Claims Department, P O Box 20409, Batterymarch Station, Boston, MA 02110. Over the next several months, the state and the agent sent repeated follow-ups for service on the claim.

There was no response.

The State of Washington Department of Transportation and the state treasurer's office referred the matter to the state's department of insurance. The state insurance department assigned an investigator.

The investigator found no record of any Liberal Mutual Insurance Company.

The investigator paid a visit to the retail agent in Tacoma.

By this time, almost a year had passed. No one had picked up the mail from Post Office Box 20409, and the rent for the box hadn't been paid since April of the previous year. The Batterymarch Station of the Post Office began returning mail to the senders.

Eventually the box was rented to a company that sold dog-grooming products.

The State of Washington Department of Insurance issued a cease and desist order against the Tacoma insurance agent and the Liberal Mutual Insurance Company and requested an arrest warrant for the Tacoma insurance agent along with one Anthony Monreale, whereabouts unknown and co-conspirators unknown.

Arriving at the home of the Tacoma insurance agent, Washington State Marshals found a new Rolls Royce parked in the circular drive way in front of the agent's new mansion. The agent submitted to arrest peacefully and cooperated fully with investigators, admitting he had never personally met anyone from the Liberal Mutual Insurance Company. Furthermore, after the bridge incident, he never heard a word from them on any of the other applications or anything else. No one answered the phone, and no one returned his calls. When asked if that lack of response didn't cause him concern, he admitted he suspected he had a real big problem, but what could he do? He turned over all his records including copies of policies issued to all insureds and copies of his cancelled checks paying premiums to Liberal Mutual Insurance Company for deposit to the company's bank account at Massachusetts Bank and Trust. Investigators from the State Department of Insurance contacted the Commonwealth of Massachusetts Department of Insurance and the Commonwealth of Massachusetts Attorney General's office who in turn served Massachusetts Bank and Trust with a subpoena for records pertaining to the Liberal Mutual Insurance Company.

Massachusetts Bank and Trust disclosed there was just under $64,000,000 on deposit in the account of Liberal Mutual. Records showed no withdrawals other than $10,536 for phone bills, rent payments for a small office in Boston's Beacon Hill section, rent on the post office box, and transfers totaling $31,665,000 to Cuttersfield Bank of Hamilton, Bermuda.

The Massachusetts Attorney General froze the account of the Liberal Mutual at Massachusetts Bank and Trust pending further investigation. The US Attorney's office became involved.

Cuttersfield Bank President John Taylor cooperated fully and disclosed there had been a substantial withdrawal some months prior, but no activity since. He stated that there was still just over $27,000,000 in the account. He was able to give authorities the phone number in Boston that he had called for verification. The names of the men who authorized the withdrawal, Vice President Richard Schmitt and Chief Financial Officer James Huber, were obviously fictitious.

269

Without pictures or fingerprints, there were too many Richard Schmitts and James Hubers around the country to bother looking.

The name Anthony Monreale though, was not made up. Anthony Monreale was well known to the FBI.

Bermuda authorities froze the Cuttersfield account and forwarded a report of a probable fraud to Interpol.

The U.S. Attorney's office traced the phone number to the office in Beacon Hill. The current occupant, a Certified Public Accountant, had only been there for six months and didn't know anything about the previous tenant. He stated that when he moved in the place had been vacant for many months, and the phone had been taken out. The landlord checked his records and said a nice-looking young man representing Liberal Mutual Insurance had paid three months rent in advance. He never saw the young man again and never saw anyone come or go. Like clockwork, the rent checks drawn on Massachusetts Bank and Trust had arrived in the mail on the first of every month for almost a year. The checks stopped abruptly almost a year ago. The landlord went on to say that a few weeks later a man from the phone company came and took out the phone, saying it was disconnected for non pay.

# Chapter Fifty Four

## Catarina Monreale

## 1964

The arrest of Anthony "Fat Tony" Monreale in connection with an international insurance fraud came as a big surprise to the Monreale clan, especially to Tony himself.

Insurance, if the protection racket could be called insurance, had always been Gianni's franchise, not Tony's. Gianpoalo and Gianni were staggered by the size, scope, and sheer audacity of the scheme as details unfolded in the newspapers and on television.

There had been no further bridge losses, so most of the premiums were recovered from the Liberal Mutual bank accounts in Massachusetts Bank and Trust and at Cuttersfield's in Bermuda. That, plus the liquidation of the Tacoma agent's assets left only a relatively small part of the cash missing, so it was difficult to rally interest from the State of Washington to carry on a prolonged, expensive civil trial against the agent and others.

The thought that Fat Tony had been, or seemed to have been, involved in the insurance scam, and her near certainty that he was involved in the attack that killed Willy and Benny, nagged at Catarina.

She called Johnny and asked to meet in the restaurant in the Copley Plaza.

"Tony just doesn't have the brains to pull off something this complicated," she told her brother after they were seated.

"I agree with you," Johnny replied softly. "I don't think he did it, either. From what I've read in the newspapers, there was a great deal of money left in the bank accounts. If Uncle Tony did dream up a scheme like that, he certainly wouldn't have left any money behind. No," he said, draping his napkin in his lap, "I think someone set him up. But I must say the scale is impressive."

Catarina rested her elbows on the table, leaned forward and said quietly, "Whether Uncle Tony did it or not, it's an embarrassment to the family. Then, too, there's our suspicion that he was behind the failed hit on Papa that took out Willie and Benny."

"I've suspected he was jealous of Papa for a long time, "Johnny said, "I don't think he has the interests of the whole family at heart."

He looked around the room, then back at his sister and grinned. "But I think we can set him up, trick him so we can see how far he's willing to go and how far he's gone already."

"Good." She took a drink of water. The dining room was beginning to fill with customers, couples, families all dressed for a nice dinner in a nice restaurant.

She turned her attention back to her brother.

"As an aside," she continued, "I'd like to learn all I can about the insurance scam…for us, just for future reference."

"So, now your ambition is showing," Johnny said smiling. "Interesting. And again, I agree. It's well worth looking into as a possible opportunity for us. Let's make you a full partner, put you on salary plus expenses."

# Chapter Fifty Five

## Anthony "Fat Tony" Monreale

## 1964

Tony Monreale was surprised and curious when he got a telephone call from his nephew, Little Johnny. It was a request, a respectful request for a meeting.

Out on bail, the now embattled Tony's first reaction was, "screw you, you snot-nosed kid." But then he realized that before he shot his mouth off, it might be better to find out what had been going on while he was in stir.

He agreed to a meeting at eight in the evening in a suite on the 43rd floor of the Hilton in mid Manhattan.

No lights were on in the room when Johnny opened the door to let him in, but the drapes were open. The glow from the city provided just enough illumination to see.

Johnny motioned to a coffee table with a tray of drinks, and then settled himself on one of two small couches facing each other across the table.

"Please sit and make yourself comfortable, Uncle Tony," he said quietly.

The couch was lower than Tony had judged it to be, and he dropped heavily, sinking into the soft cushions. Facing his young nephew, he adjusted his clothes, trying to get comfortable, and then poured himself a shot of whiskey.

"What's this all about?" he demanded. Not waiting for Johnny's reply, he finished the shot in one swallow, and then leaned forward to pour himself another, as if he didn't really care what the answer was going to be.

"I thought you might want to be brought up to date. There have been some changes during your absence."

Johnny was speaking so softly Tony had trouble hearing him. He leaned forward. "What? Say that again."

"I simply said, I thought that since you've been away you might want to be briefed on recent developments," Johnny said in the same quiet voice.

"Oh? Like what?"

"My parents and Grandpa Gianpoalo have pretty much moved away from Utica. They are thinking about selling their houses in the compound."

"Oh?" Tony said, thinking maybe that meant they were going to stay out west. With them gone he could easily muscle in on the eastern operations.

"They are curious about your interest in the insurance business."

Tony thought Johnny was referring to his recent troubles with the State of Washington, the FBI and Interpol. With a quick flash of anger, he started to say he had no damn interest in the insurance business.

Then it occurred to him that maybe this little shit was referring to Gianni's protection racket. If that was it, then he was interested. That was an integral part of the family's east coast operations. Maybe that was what this meeting was all about. Maybe they did mean to turn the business over to him and make him the boss. Well, it was about time.

He tried to contain his temper and replied, "If you mean my interest in the insurance business that some phony bastards accused me of, I have absolutely no knowledge of that. I had nothing to do with it."

Then he caught himself. Why should he explain anything to this little asshole?

Leaning forward to pour himself another drink, he strained to hear what Johnny was saying. The kid was speaking so softly he could barely hear him.

"We are inclined to believe you. It would have been odd to let your own name be connected with it."

What the hell did this skinny little bastard mean, "We are inclined?" Who the hell does he think he is? For two cents, I'd kill him right here in this hotel room.

"The family is considering offering you a deal."

Now he really wanted to hear what Johnny had to say. He was leaning so far forward he was all but perched on the edge of the cushion.

"What? What? Speak up."

"The family would like to offer to turn over the East Coast operations, sell them to you outright."

"Sell the operations to me?"

274

"Yes," Little Johnny leaned further back in the couch. He turned and looked toward the window and the lights of Manhattan.

So softly he might have been talking to himself, his nephew continued, "The deal would include all of the family's interest in your current operations plus all of their own operations including the unions, the liquor, protections and the gambling."

He turned back to face Tony. "They wish to liquidate and relocate out west. They are willing to agree to a non-compete in any activities east of Chicago."

"For how much?" Tony asked, a little too loudly, a little too anxiously.

"$16,000,000 cash."

"$16,000,000? Where the hell am I going to get $16,000,000?" Tony asked, almost shouting.

"You can borrow it from the union pension fund."

"The union pension fund? The union pension fund? Is that what you said?"

"Yes, the union pension fund. Income from operations would repay the debt, if you decided to repay it, within two years at most."

"How the hell am I going to get the union to loan me $16,000,000?"

"We will see to it that you are elected president of the union."

Johnny shifted his position on the couch and continued, almost in a whisper. "You will then authorize a loan for the construction of a hotel in Miami. The construction cost will be $44,000,000 including the land. The loan will be for $60,000,000. The $16,000,000 difference will just disappear."

Tony was dumfounded, his mind racing. He strained to hear what his nephew was saying. His dream of becoming the head of the whole operation could be coming true, and out of the blue, at that. This young fuck sitting across from him was outlining a huge, complex financial transaction that he wasn't even sure he understood. He wondered if he was being outsmarted somehow, that someone was trying to pull a fast one.

"I'll have to think about it," he said. He could just take over. Who is going to stop him, this fucking little weasel? Papa Gianpoalo was out in fricking Arizona somewhere and brother Gianni and his smart-ass wife Gina looked like they were in Las Vegas to stay.

"I'll have to think this over," he said, struggling to get up from the couch.

"Shall we say by the first of the month?" asked Johnny, remaining seated. "We would have to set in motion your nomination and campaign to get you elected president of the union. The election is only three months away,"

"I told you I'd let you know," he said sharply. He was breathing heavily from the effort of getting to his feet.

He was startled when he heard a husky female voice coming from the dark corner of the hotel room, opposite the windows.

"We missed you at the family's Christmas dinner, Uncle Tony."

He had not been aware there was anyone else in the room.

But there in the shadows was Catarina. She was almost hidden, sitting in a high back chair, dressed in a dark pants suit, her long legs crossed, her hands out of sight under a jacket in her lap.

Suddenly he felt very cold.

There was a long pause. The only sound was the traffic on 6$^{th}$ Avenue, forty-three floors below. Trying to regain control, he turned and said, "I'll get back to you, *Little* Johnny."

"By the first of the month," Johnny said, still seated on the couch.

"Sure, sure," he said, backing toward the door.

Guido and Lorenzo were waiting for him in the lobby when, wiping his brow he pushed his way out of the crowded elevator.

Guido asked, "What's the matter, boss? You look like you seen a ghost."

"Shut up and go get the car," Tony said, hurrying toward the escalators to the garage and his limo.

# Chapter Fifty Six

## Catarina Monreale

## 1964

Catarina and her brother Johnny stayed seated for several moments after Uncle Tony left, Catarina in the high back chair and Johnny on the couch.

Finally, Catarina rose to her feet, dropped the jacket on the chair and unscrewed the silencer from the .38 caliber revolver she had been holding in her lap. She slipped the silencer into a pocket in her jumpsuit and returned the pistol to its place in her shoulder holster.

Then she stepped to the hotel room door to set the deadbolt and turned to her brother.

He bent forward, fished one of the short swizzle sticks from the drinks tray on the table, leaned back and expertly sailed it into the empty shot glass Uncle Tony had been using.

Catarina walked to the window and looked down.

Below, the brightly lit intersection of 6th Avenue and 54th Street teemed with people and traffic. Reflected in the window's dark glass she watched her brother, still deep in thought, methodically leaning forward to pick up another swizzle stick, carefully take aim and flip it into the empty shot glass.

"Where'd you happen to learn that little trick and when did you find time to perfect it?"

"Harvard," he replied. "When I stopped fucking around, I had to find something to do besides study."

Catarina quickly reached to the back of her neck. In one smooth motion she drew a throwing knife from a sheath between her shoulders, spun and threw it across the room. The knife buried itself halfway to its hilt, just at eye level in the doorjamb.

Startled, her brother asked, "Where'd you happen to learn a trick like that?"

"Martial Arts and Self Defense School in Boston," she answered, moving to the door to retrieve the knife. "After I stopped fucking around, I had to find something to do, too."

She pulled the knife free, and then turned to face him.

"With the family pretty much out west permanently and you living in New York, there isn't any reason for me to stay in Cambridge. I'm just wasting my time at Lesley." She returned the knife to its scabbard behind her neck.

"I'm considering a move to a warmer climate. But first I'll dig into the insurance scam."

⁘

Catarina returned to Boston the day following the meeting with Uncle Tony.

She first visited the manager of the shabby old building in the Beacon Hill section that had supposedly housed the offices of the Liberal Mutual Insurance Company. The man only remembered that the gentleman who had rented the place was young and good looking. Dark, maybe tan complexion, the man said. Five foot eight or nine. Maybe from out west, the little man told her. "California maybe. Yeah, Mr. Monreale sounded like he might be from California."

When she checked the post office and the phone company, she found that no one at either place remembered ever actually meeting "Anthony Monreale."

Catarina had read all she could about the bridge insurance fraud. She found that according to the Tacoma insurance agent's testimony, he had never actually met Anthony Monreale or anyone else at Liberal Mutual. He testified that all communications had been by phone or by mail.

She telephoned Johnny to update him. "Someone covered their tracks well, but Boston certainly looks like it was the base of operations. Now I've got to go to Bermuda."

⁘

When she checked into the Hamilton Princess, she found many of the same people were still with the hotel that had worked there back when she and her family had been frequent guests.

The desk clerk even greeted her by name when she checked in.

"How nice to see you again, Miss Monreale. It's been several years since we have had the pleasure of serving your family."

"My parents and grandfather have moved out west, and my brother and I have been busy finishing school," she explained with a smile.

"Well, it was nice to have had the pleasure of serving your other brother recently," said the desk clerk, handing her the room key.

278

"My other brother?"

"Why, yes, your brother Tony. He spent two, maybe three days with us only a year or so ago," continued the clerk.

"Gee, I don't think I recall him mentioning that. Was the little devil alone?"

"Oh yes. And this visit was all business," said the clerk. "He didn't spend any time around the pool during this visit. Not like he did with you and your brother Johnny when your family was here last."

Well, son of a bitch, she thought.

Catarina returned to Boston the next day. She called First Boston Insurance and Reinsurance and asked for Gavin. The switchboard operator remembered Gavin but told her he was no longer with the firm.

"Is there anyone else that could help you?" asked the operator.

"Perhaps. Is there someone else in that department?"

"I'll put you through to Mr. Stone," replied the operator.

When Rob Stone came on the line, Catarina introduced herself as Francesca Armerina. She explained that she knew Gavin and that she was a student at Lesley and writing her thesis on insurance.

"I hoped I could meet with my friend Gavin or someone else there at First Boston to get some background about how the business works from inside the company."

Mr. Stone, friendly and willing to help, invited her to come by any time.

"I'll take you up on your offer. Can I drop by and spend an hour with you tomorrow?"

Catarina knew as soon as she met Rob Stone that he was going to be putty in her hands. He was all but drooling after the brief interview. He eagerly suggested that she intern with First Boston for a few weeks or longer if necessary.

"That would be wonderful, but would I be able to spend some time doing research for my thesis?"

"Of course, Miss Armerina…"

"Call me Francesca."

279

"Of course, Francesca. You can look up anything you need for your paper. And please call me Rob."

True to his word, Rob Stone gave Catarina complete access to all the company's files, including those that Gavin had worked on. She even reviewed the files they had on Anthony, Gianni, and Gianpoalo Monreale. Gavin obviously knew a lot about the family. On top of that he had access to every variety of insurance scam.

He probably knew them all inside out. Within First Boston's files, Catarina saw that Gavin Keller had all the reference material necessary to become a real pro.

She spent two weeks with First Boston. It was obvious Rob Stone was very sorry to see her go.

She called Johnny and asked to have dinner with him in Manhattan. "I'll take the express train and meet you. How about the Stanhope Hotel dining room at eight o'clock?"

Catarina was already seated when her brother come in. He was followed closely by two other men dressed in the familiar pinstriped suits, dark shirts and light ties. The two men were shown to a table against the wall.

Johnny handed his London Fog to the hat check girl and came toward Caterina's table.

"What's the latest?" he asked as he approached.

"Sit first. Have a drink. I've got plenty to report."

"Like what?" Johnny flagged the waiter and gave his order.

"I know who the Tony Monreale imposter was."

"I am all ears. Anyone we know?"

She leaned back in her chair and paused for effect.

"Your old roommate, Gavin Keller."

Johnny sat stunned for a moment. "Son of a bitch."

Catarina laughed. "My sentiments exactly."

"I totally underestimated him. I thought he was just an obsequious little law student. If only he hadn't saved my life," he said with a wry grin. "He covered his tracks really well. I doubt if he's still at Harvard."

Catarina took a drink of water. "I'll find him. But first things first."

"Uncle Tony?"

"Uncle Tony. Let's take care of him together."

# Chapter Fifty Seven

## Johnny Monreale

## 1964

It was late afternoon, almost dusk when Johnny, standing in front of the Guggenheim, spotted Fat Tony's limo. It was easing its way through the Fifth Avenue traffic toward the curb.

The car stopped next to Johnny.

The heavily tinted back window lowered. The setting sun was reflected by the museum's glass doors. Squinting from the glare, Fat Tony Monreale peered out.

"Is that you, Little Johnny?"

Johnny stepped to the door.

Fat Tony pushed open the limousine's door and yelled, "Well, get in." Then, bending awkwardly to avoid hitting his head on the roof of his own limo, he lumbered forward and turned around to sit next to another man facing the rear of the car.

Johnny got in and sat down facing the two. "Nice to see you, Uncle Tony. Well, well, it's a pleasant surprise to see you too, Peter, after all this time."

The car pulled away from the curb and into traffic. Tony snorted. "You might not think it's so nice when I tell you Peter here is going to be my new partner. To get right to the point, I have no intention of buying anything. We're taking over."

Smirking, he drew a pistol from an armpit holster and laid it on his lap.

"Is that so? And how did this new partnership come about?"

Peter Ruffalo leaned forward. "I'll answer that," he said between clenched teeth. "I've been waiting a long time for the chance to repay you for my father's murder. This night will be the beginning."

"You think I had something to do with the death of your father?"

"I know full well that you, your father, and your grandfather planned and orchestrated the whole thing. The only thing I don't know is why."

"Let me see if we can shorten this," Johnny said, leaning back in the seat. "Your father's man attempted to kill my father at the New York apartment but almost got me instead. At the

282

housewarming for my parents' new place in the Hamptons, your father had a red-hot gift delivered to my father with the intent of framing him for possession of stolen property. This, in the face of the truce our families had agreed to for years."

"I assure you my father never even considered breaking the truce. And he most certainly never had anything to do with the attack at your family' New York apartment."

Grinning, Fat Tony interrupted. "No, that was me."

"And" Peter continued. "The gift was a genuine artifact that my father went to great lengths to acquire legitimately. He contacted relatives working the archeological excavation of a Roman settlement near Milan. The object was sold properly through official channels. The papers authenticating it were on their way for your father's records. What made you think it was stolen?"

By this time the sun had gone down. The car had left Manhattan's traffic, passed through the Lincoln Tunnel and was on the New Jersey side of the Hudson. They bounced and rattled, hitting every pothole in the old two-lane road that ran along the river.

They were headed for the old building near North Bergen that served as Fat Tony's base of operations.

There was no moon this night.

There were no businesses, no homes, nothing but the dark hulk of an occasional abandoned warehouse along this beat-up stretch of asphalt.

The only illumination was the car's headlights and the lights of Manhattan across the river.

The Cadillac pulled up the drive into the dark garage under the building.

When it came to a stop, without the sound of the engine all was quiet.

Next, the headlights were turned off.

Now the garage was plunged into darkness.

With a hissing sound, the partition separating the passengers and the limo's driver lowered.

From the front, a husky female voice said, "End of the line, gentlemen."

The cold barrel of a pistol pressed against Fat Tony's head just at the top of his neck. Another gun pinched Peter Ruffalo's left ear. Catarina, on her knees in the front seat, leaned part of the way through the open partition. She pushed Tony's head forward with the barrel of the .45-caliber automatic. "Nice to see you again, Uncle Tony. Remember Uncle Benny? This is his old gun. Hello to you, too, Peter. This reunion will be short."

Tony snarled. "Fuck. Why couldn't they have done you two in on the thruway."

Johnny leaned forward and lifted the pistol from Fat Tony's lap. "Got anything to contribute, Peter? If you do, it would be best if you came clean."

Peter Ruffalo fished a snubbed nosed .38 revolver from an armpit holster. Holding it gingerly by the butt between thumb and forefinger he carefully handed it to Johnny.

"What happened to Guido and Lorenzo?" asked Tony.

"They were persuaded to switch alliances," replied Catarina. "For the sake of irony, Uncle Benny's widow Darlene, offered herself as bait. She lured them out of the car while they were waiting for you to come down from your office to go meet Johnny." She chuckled. "And in return for a bonus, they agreed to give me the car and the itinerary along with your instructions for tonight's festivities. They're on our team now."

She licked her lips and grinned. "As you know, thanks to you we were short two men."

Johnny got out of the back of the big car, leaving the rear door open behind him. There were two quick muffled pops from inside the car.

Then the driver's door opened, and Catarina slid out.

Johnny watched her walk around to the rear door, lean in and remove Peter Ruffalo's necktie.

"I stashed the bicycles about a mile from here, behind an old warehouse," she said over her shoulder. Then she leaned across her late fiancé's body and rummaged through Fat Tony's coat pockets until she found his cigar lighter.

She stepped back from the car, straightened up and began slipping out of her black pants suit. Underneath, she was wearing bicycle shorts and top. She turned to face her brother and said with a grin, "I hope the bikes are still there. This is a terrible neighborhood. The crime rate must be awful. Some crook might have stolen them."

Johnny smiled, took a carefully folded plastic garbage bag out of his pocket and started to undress. Under his clothes, he too wore bicycling gear.

While he dropped his suit and shirt in the bag, Catarina popped open the car's gas tank filler lid. She removed the cap and stuffed Peter Ruffalo's tie halfway into the pipe. Using her late Uncle Tony's Zippo, she lit the end of the tie and waited till it caught fire.

When she was satisfied that it would not go out, she turned and with a little skip, joined her brother,

The two Monreale siblings, Johnny and Catarina left the dark garage and started walking down the drive to the two-lane road along the river.

"Peter was looking well," Johnny said conversationally, looking up at the stars.

"I think he was wearing his hair too long," Catarina replied. "I wasn't entirely sure just where his ear was."

They reached the road just as an explosion lit the night sky. Very quickly the old office building near North Bergen was fully engulfed in flames.

Walking carefully to avoid stumbling on the road's uneven surface, Johnny shifted the garbage bag and said, "Too bad we were misled about the Roman artifact."

"Gavin," Catarina said, looking across the river toward Manhattan.

"Gavin," her brother agreed.

# Chapter Fifty Eight

## Tommy Huber

## Fall, 1965

Tommy Huber sat alone in his darkened office in the rear of the Beverly Hills store. The only light came from the antique bronze and glass Handel desk lamp, the only sound the low hum of the air conditioning and the ticking of the grandfather clock standing in the corner.

Softly the old clock chimed six times. It was Thursday evening and not one single customer had come into the store all day.

Mr. Thomas's antique business was hard hit by the recession. Promoting the new store in San Francisco's high rent district had cost a fortune. Mr. Thomas realized he'd made a mistake boasting of his success in L.A. San Francisco people considered L.A. backward, crude, and unsophisticated. Anything south of Santa Barbara was considered by them to be suspect and sneered upon.

The San Francisco store "laid an egg big time" as his Hollywood friends put it.

On top of that, the L.A. crowd seemed to have moved away from antiques. They now preferred modern styles with lots of ugly chrome.

And as if all that weren't enough, a warehouse type antique store opened on Washington Boulevard in Culver City. It copied Tommy's antique rental idea, further eroding what was left of Mr. Thomas's market.

With a warehouse full of unsold and unrented antiques, he was in well over his head.

Today had not been the only day no customers came into the Beverly Hills store. It scared the crap out of him when he thought about the drain of the overhead and his dwindled resources. His flashy lifestyle, the entertaining, the clothes, the condo in Brentwood, and the Bentley—all to keep up the pretense of success and wealth—cost a fortune.

All that, plus the blackmail he paid to the john Chucky robbed were finishing him off.

Christ, he owed Gavin almost a million dollars. Since Gavin had always been a ready source of funds, Tommy had never bothered establishing credit with banks. Now it was too late. He knew he couldn't approach conventional lenders to seek a substantial loan to cover operating losses for a failing business.

As Tommy saw it, he had three fundamental problems.

One: the john was costing him $10,000 a week. There was no longer any pretense that the money was repayment for the items stolen from the john's home.

It was simple blackmail.

Two: his debt to Gavin. Gavin had already said flat out that he wasn't going to extend Tommy any further credit. Not until the business showed some signs of turning around.

Three: turning the business around. Tommy would have to reinvent Mr. Thomas and change the type of stock he sold. His whole persona, his whole image was as a sophisticated dealer in antiques. He'd have to completely revamp, redecorate and restock his store with furniture of the style now in fashion. He had to start selling modern stuff or something else.

That would cost a fortune.

Mr. Thomas's Antiques employed three salesmen during the week and six on weekends. He got up from his desk and walked to a large armoire that was against the wall. He opened the double doors that hid the one-way glass and looked out into the store.

His three salesmen were alone there on the sales floor, playing liars' poker. From inside the store, the one-way glass was disguised as an antique mirror.

Customers often stopped and stared at themselves in that mirror, not knowing Tommy was looking right at their stupid faces from the other side. Some of the Hollywood types, even the men, were so vain they couldn't pass a mirror without stopping and peering at their reflection, adjusting their hair or their clothes, searching for wrinkles or blemishes.

Tommy would laugh at them from inside his soundproofed office, but he knew his clientele. He'd lit the store carefully using no neon lighting. His customers saw themselves and the furniture at their best in the mirrors scattered around the store.

He turned and walked back to his desk, opened a drawer, and took out a tiny brown bottle, a mirror, a two-inch piece of soda straw and a razor blade.

Another expensive luxury.

But he told himself he could quit any time. Any time he wanted. It was just that the crowd, the potential customers, and the others he mingled with, all used coke.

It was like drinking, they all told each other, only it didn't smell.

287

Besides, he could use both the coke and drink if he wanted to. Scotch loosened him up and the coke made his mind race. He got his really great ideas when he had some coke. He sighed and wished he had some grass. That was one of the great ironies, he thought as he snorted a line. Coke was much more expensive and harder to get than grass. But he was out of grass and had plenty of coke.

On the other hand, grass brought him down, made him paranoid. If he had a joint along with the coke, his worries about money would really kick in.

He glanced out the one-way glass again. The salesmen were still alone in the store, still playing liars' poker with one-dollar bills. Goddamn it, they could at least try to look busy! There was a fine layer of dust on everything. The least they could do was wipe all that stuff off! He ought to fire the lot of them! Run the store by himself! Sons of bitches! He started to leap out of his chair and run out the door right then and there. Be done with it once and for all.

But maybe just one more line would help clear his head, really light him up.

That damn john up there in the hills, bleeding him dry. Week after week, for years now, paying that bastard for nothing.

Lay out another pile of white powder on the mirror. Chop it carefully with the razor blade. Tap tap tap on the mirror. Make a long thin line, a really long line this time.

Tommy bent over with the straw in his nostril.

Looking back at him, reflected in the dusty mirror he could see part of his face, his eye, his nose.

His face was puffy and seemed to be loose, sagging.

The eye looking back from the mirror was blood shot, red rimmed, the nose a road map of little ruptured vessels.

I'm only thirty and I look like shit. More cocaine, that's what I need! Then I'll spring into action! Go up that hill behind Grauman's Chinese to that son of a bitch john's house and confront that bastard and tell him NO MORE! I'll tell that bastard that I'm not paying another damn dime!

Another line. Pressing one finger against the side of his nose he drew deep from the straw into his nostril, deep and hard, hard enough to feel the powder burn the back of his nose, his throat.

288

Holding his breath as if he'd taken a drag of a joint and didn't want to waste any, he got up out of his leather desk chair. He stumbled to the ornate antique sideboard he'd had gutted and fitted with a small refrigerator.

He took out a bottle of Scotch along with a frosted glass and had a straight shot.

That was just the ticket.

The shot of ice-cold Scotch washed down the coke clinging to the back of his throat and warmed his belly.

He'd left the cabinet doors open. Tommy looked again at the three salesmen out in the store, still screwing around playing liars' poker. He was so disgusted he didn't think he could speak to them coherently.

He slipped the little brown bottle of coke into his shirt pocket, put on his coat, and carrying the bottle of Scotch by its neck left his private office by the back door.

The Santa Ana winds were blowing. Although it was November, the weather was hot and dry.

His Bentley was parked right there, right in his own parking space behind the store. Someone, kids probably, had written an obscenity in the fine layer of dust on the hood. He backed carefully out into the alley. He knew he was stoned, and the scotch was probably hitting him right about now.

Wouldn't do to have an accident, not when he was about to take charge, bring things under control.

Traffic in Beverly Hills was heavy. There's plenty of people out shopping, just not in his store, damn them!

He remembered parking was a real problem on the narrow winding road to the john's house.

The Bentley would stand out like a sore thumb.

Tommy parked in the public lot between Hollywood Boulevard and Franklyn, left the bottle of Scotch in the car and started walking.

He dodged traffic crossing Franklin, reached the other side and in the inky darkness began the climb up the road. On his left the steep hillside reached up to the Magic Castle and Yamashiro's. On his right, the little houses bordering the road clung to the hillside, blocking all but an occasional glimpse of the lights of Los Angeles and Hollywood.

The exertion was making his heart beat hard, circulating the coke and the Scotch in his blood and making everything seem clear and decided.

At last, he was taking action.

Soon he'd be free.

He reached the house, strode onto the small porch next to the vine-covered garage and pounded on the door. He hadn't felt this charged up since he played football in high school.

After a minute or so the door opened.

There he stood, his nemesis.

The john was breathing hard; his hair was mussed, sticking straight up in back. With his hairy white legs showing beneath a short, black silk robe, he looked like some kind of a bird, a big, grotesque bird.

"What the hell do you want?" the john demanded, bracing the door partially open with his bare foot.

Tommy lost it. Without answering, he kicked the door with all his might. The john howled in pain.

Tommy charged on inside.

"You son of a bitchin' bastard! It's over, do you hear? It's over! I'll never give you another rotten dime."

The john was hopping backwards, holding his foot.

"Wait! Wait!" he yelled. "Stop!"

Tommy could see by the light coming through the big window that the living room had been redecorated since the night of the debacle. Now it was in an African style, statuettes of natives, woven wicker chairs. Large masks and shields hung on fabric covered walls.

The john grabbed an ornamental spear that was propped against a sideboard. He started thrusting it at him.

"Get your sorry ass out of here or I'll……"

Tommy picked up a wicker chair. He held it in front of him as lion tamers do and ran at the john.

The john hobbled, stumbled backwards, trying to fend him off with the spear.

Tommy charged at him.

The chair collided with the john and knocked the spear away.

The impact propelled the john against the big plate glass window.

The window broke.

The john fell backward out in a shower of broken glass.

The hills echoed his scream, cut short with the sound of an impact.

Suddenly calm, Tommy stepped over to the window, now open to the remnants of the day's hot, dry breeze.

Twenty feet below, sprawled at an impossible angle on a neighbor's Spanish tile roof, the john lay still.

A little gust picked up his silk robe for a moment, filling and billowing the material like a sail, exposing his flaccid white body.

Then the breeze moved on, releasing the robe to collapse onto the roof's tiles.

From the position of the body, it was clear to Tommy Huber that the fall had broken the man's neck.

Tommy took a deep breath.

Someone, some guy's voice called from the back of the house.

"What the hell's going on out there?"

The voice came from the john's rumpus room.

The voice sounded familiar.

Tommy's instinct was to get the hell out. The combination of Scotch and coke was making time go by very slowly, but the whole encounter seemed to take no time at all. What would it hurt if he took a moment to look in the rumpus room? He walked down the short hall to the open door and looked in.

Hogtied on the rubber mat in the center of the floor was a guy.

Next to the guy, on the mat was a tube of KY jelly.

The guy was blindfolded.

291

The guy was Chucky.

Tommy saw now that these two had duped him for all these years, set him up.

"What's going on?" Chucky whined. "What are you doing? What was that crashing sound?"

Tommy gazed silently at the scene. He knew Chucky sensed his presence, knew someone was there in the doorway.

But now Tommy could hear sirens approaching on the street below the house.

Without making a sound he backed from the rumpus room, made his way to the front door and slipped out. The neighbor below must have heard the scream and the impact, gone out to see what had happened and called the cops when he saw what was on his roof.

Even as coked up and drunk as he was, Tommy knew this was a real good time not to be here.

He walked briskly back down the dark hill toward Franklin Avenue and his car.

"All in all, that went pretty well. I almost wish I could be there when the cops find Chucky."

# Chapter Fifty Nine

## Catarina Monreale

## Fall, 1965

Only 9:30 in the morning and it was hot. Hot and dry and dusty

Catarina, wearing high-top boots, worn jeans and plaid shirt, edged her way around the stand of oaks by the lake and scanned the hilltop looming above, trying to see in the shadows between the big white boulders scattered at its crest.

She had her left hand on her pistol to prevent it bouncing out of the holster if she had to start running. In her right hand she held a coiled rope.

She was doing one of the things she enjoyed most.

She was in pursuit.

"Patience," Mr. Ehlers had taught her during the months she'd spent learning her craft from him. "Take it slow and easy," the old hit man had said over and over. "Learn your prey's habits. You'll find that it's like fixing an elaborate meal. Half the enjoyment is in the preparation. You must learn to consider the chase as important as its outcome," he'd told her.

This morning she was putting that lesson into practice.

Her family had recognized Catarina's particular talent and realized she was going to pursue it with or without their approval, they had sent her to Ehlers in Chicago.

From him she'd learned how to be a successful assassin.

There! Just a quick movement in the shadows between two huge rocks glaring white in the early morning sun.

In a crouch now, she edged her way up the slope, slipping from boulder to clump of sage brush, staying on the soft sand to muffle any sound of her approach.

Some of the boulders scattered at the very top of the hill were as big as houses.

She loosened the coiled rope until the lasso end was almost dragging in the dirt.

Slipping around the biggest of the rocks she came face to face with her quarry, Rondo, out of Comanche Station, the most beautiful quarter horse she had ever seen.

"Game over, big boy," she said, slipping the riata around the horse's neck.

This wasn't the first time the beautiful jet-black yearling had managed to slip out of the corral. He seemed to know he was special, seemed to know he was her favorite. He enjoyed this game of his, playing it for the fun of having her track him.

Truth be told, Catarina, caught up in his little game enjoyed it too. She rubbed the white spot on his forehead, just there in the grove above his eyes and fed him the carrot she had hidden in her Stetson.

Side by side the two started walking back down the slope toward the ranch's corrals and the barns.

Intended at first as a retreat, her family had purchased this sprawling 400 acre horse ranch in a remote area of the Santa Ynez Valley, just east of Santa Barbara, California. The ranch provided complete privacy, a good retreat for family meetings and was potentially a good investment.

Catarina had planned that her stay here be only temporary, just until she found where in the west she really wanted to live.

But once she settled in and took over the running of the place, she found she really loved horses.

Her Grandfather and his man Max had relocated to Scottsdale, near Phoenix, and her mother and father had developed an elaborate hotel casino complex near Las Vegas. For now, her brother Johnny was remaining behind in New York, liquidating the eastern operations.

Only a month or so ago, during the family's Columbus Day get together here at the ranch, Grandpa Gianpoalo had brought up the conversation that had taken place in Tony's limo. In particular, he was disturbed about what Peter Ruffalo had said concerning the gift, the artifact Peter's father had given Gianni and Gina for the housewarming.

Why had Gavin Keller deceived them?

"What was his game?" Grandpa Gianpoalo had asked, looking around the table. "To cause trouble between our family and the Ruffalos? Why? Why would he do that?" Gianpoalo had asked. No one had any answers.

Of course, they didn't know about Catarina and Gavin, and she certainly wasn't going to 'fess up now.

294

Gavin had caused a lot of trouble by using dear departed Uncle Tony's name in his insurance scam. That meant trouble for the whole family. Gavin's statement about the artifact being stolen had led to the deaths of Pietro Ruffalo, his man Urbanus, Uncle Tony, and even Peter. It had brought an end Catarina's lifelong plan to marry the only man she ever thought she loved. Of course, at this point she realized she had never loved Peter.

He'd just been handy.

What if someone in her family sent someone, one of the uncles or cousins after Gavin and when they caught up with him, he shot his mouth off about their affair?

No, I can't have that. That would not do at all, she concluded.

Catarina and the pony were back at the corral. She opened the gate and led him inside. She gently removed the lasso and said quietly in his ear, "Rondo, my young friend, our Gavin won't be too hard to find. He's here in California, down in Los Angeles someplace. I'm sure he isn't trying to hide. He's probably even listed in the phonebook."

She patted the horse on its rump and turned to close the gate.

"I'll just do the same thing I do when I'm tracking you. I'll learn his habits, discover his favorite places, and figure out how he thinks."

She removed her Stetson, slapped it against her thigh to knock the dust off and started walking back to the ranch house.

# Chapter Sixty

## Tom Larson

## Fall, 1965

A four-car accident had resulted in not one but two fatalities, right there at the corner of Torrance Boulevard and Crenshaw, right where he used to sit on his bike waiting for traffic offenders.

Tom Larson had stood in the heat and the dust directing traffic for almost three hours this afternoon. The hot sun beating down on the intersection burned the hell out of his face and the back of his neck. The dust and grit brought by the Santa Ana winds found its way into his uniform. His collar rubbed his sunburned skin raw.

Maddening. The God damn Santa Ana's were maddening. They blew all the time, day and night.

He'd promised last night to sit with Millie this evening and watch some old movie on TV, some damned old war movie made ten years ago.

Now it was all he could do to hide his irritable mood, his discomfort in the presence of the one person he loved, the one person that needed his patience and understanding, the one person that needed him. Because he was stuck with that damned accident till way after his shift ended, he hadn't been able to get away early enough to get home and shower. He'd had to show up at Millie's this evening still wearing his heavy, dirty, dusty dark blue uniform, sunburned, tired, irritable.

The movie, *From Here to Eternity*, picked him up and took him back to '42, back when he shipped out, and in the film the bully, Sergeant 'Fatso' Judson, became Sweeny the Weenie, the bully Larson killed and stuffed in the ship's boiler.

In the flickering black and white images on the screen he saw himself and the others on their way to war, all over again.

The movie was still going, but Millie had fallen asleep, her head resting on his shoulder. He knew if he moved even a little bit it would wake her. He'd held the same position for so long it felt like his right arm had been wrenched from its socket and jammed back into place.

Millie.

Mille and what was left of her family. With her husband's passing back in '54, her oldest son Dick gone all these years, her daughter Marcia living clear up in San Francisco, and poor Timothy dead, Tom Larson was about all she had here in Torrance.

Timothy, Millie's boy Timothy, her youngest, the apple of her eye. Timothy Schmitt, shot to death not six months ago, right here in the trailer park, here at his mother's home, just outside the door on the porch steps of this very trailer.

Gavin Keller.

All those years ago, ever since 1954 when Ralph Beeman, the family's doctor, confided to Larson that he thought young Timothy had been raped, Larson had been obsessed with Gavin Keller. Larson was convinced Gavin Keller did it.

Gavin Keller's mother was a nurse.

Gavin probably had access to anesthetics.

Gavin could've used anesthetics to put Timothy out, causing damage to the poor boy's brain.

Yes, in his own mind, Larson had pretty much tried and convicted Gavin Keller. He remembered the young man's face clearly enough, although he had seen the kid only a few times ten or twelve years ago. He remembered Gavin was a good-looking kid, too good looking in fact.

Larson had known for years that sooner or later he was going to track Gavin Keller down. Otherwise, Gavin would just go on, Scot free, unpunished.

Well, not if Larson had anything to do about it.

Yesterday, before he got off duty, Larson had used the Torrance Police Department's computer to access the driver's license records on file with the State of California Department of Motor Vehicles. If Gavin Keller was alive, lived in this state and drove a car, Larson would find him.

Sure enough, there he was, right there in the DMV records.

Gavin Keller lived in Encino, California, not an hour's drive away.

# Chapter Sixty One

## Marcia Schmitt

## Fall, 1965

It had been a long day and Marcia Schmitt was tired, tired, but not quite ready for sleep. Only an hour ago she'd returned to the hotel from a dinner date with her agent, Tevye, "Turnip" Green and his wife Sophia. They'd spent the night squiring a handsome actor that the studio was making every effort to present to the public as being straight.

"A hopeless challenge," Sophia had pointed out when Marcia and she had gone to the lady's room. "This guy's fruitier than a pitcher of Sangria."

Marcia's role was as the guy's beard this evening, pretending they were on a date.

But there were limits. In the booth at Chasen's, Marsha had pulled away when he leaned over as if to kiss her. Screw that. God knows where that mouth of his had been.

Now after 1:00 a.m. She was alone in the studio's suite at the Beverly Hilton, curled up on the couch and reading a script. The script was for a remake of *The Trojan Wars*. Bleary-eyed, she set the script down on the coffee table and looked toward the sliding glass doors that led to the balcony. The Santa Ana's had cleared the air and a sparkling carpet of lights spread out below all the way to the black void that was the Pacific Ocean.

Tomorrow Marcia was scheduled to report for work at the lot in Culver City. While filming here in Southern California the studio always made this suite of rooms available for her. It was almost like a second home. Gyms, masseuse, the concierge arranged all sorts of conveniences.

Marcia had become at ease with all the little extras that came with being an important star.

She got up from the couch and walked to the balcony doors, her mind still on the script. Marcia's role was as Cassandra, a part that called for a very difficult and emotional scene with the actress playing her mother, Hecuba and how they both had dealt with the tragic life and death of her brother Troilus.

Marcia could not help but draw a parallel with the sad life and tragic death of Troilus and that of her brother Timothy.

The rape, the decline, the death.

Neither Hecuba nor Cassandra had been in a position to avenge Troilus's death. Was there any way Marcia could avenge Timothy's death?

She slid the glass door to the balcony open a few inches. The warm dry air of the Santa Ana wind touched her, took her back to when she was young and lived here in Southern California.

At five-thirty yesterday morning her favorite driver, Jeffrey, had waited as usual in the studio's limo in the circular drive at the entrance to the hotel to take her to work. The studio's chauffeurs doubled as bodyguards for the talent. Marcia always requested Jeffrey as her driver. In his mid forties, he was a former private detective, married, with two teenage daughters. Marcia knew his job with the studio sometimes involved "extra" duties. Discretion was a very important part of a studio driver's job. Celebrities have been known to misbehave, drinking too much or indulging in drugs or sex and a limousine is often the setting for some of their more outrageous behavior.

If a driver wanted to keep his job, he would keep his mouth shut about anything that happened in the back seat short of murder.

Marcia had become pretty good friends with Jeffrey. Such good friends in fact that she was helping pay for his oldest daughter's college education.

As the limo pulled into traffic on Santa Monica Boulevard she'd leaned forward.

"Jeffrey," she'd asked, "I wonder if you could do me a little favor and see if you can track down an old school friend of mine. Without him knowing it, of course," she quickly added. "I might want to look him up and then again I might change my mind, so I wouldn't want him to know I was curious."

Glancing back at her in the rear-view mirror, Jeffrey replied, "No trouble at all, Miss Schmitt."

"His name is Gavin Keller," she continued, and proceeded to tell Jeffrey as much as she could recall about Gavin. Where he'd lived in her old neighborhood, his family moving to Inglewood and everything else she could remember.

"I realize it isn't much to go on and if you can't do it that's all right. It's not really important and I'll just forget about it."

"If he's alive, I'm sure I can find him. I may not have anything for you by the time I pick you up this afternoon, but I should have something for you tomorrow morning."

Marcia came down to the hotel entrance early the next morning and Jeffrey and the car were waiting as usual. When he opened the door for her a manila file folder waited on the seat.

She'd slid in and opened the folder.

There was the information she had requested about Gavin Keller.

For Jeffrey's benefit she made herself appear detached, only mildly curious about its contents.

| | |
|---|---|
| Name | Gavin Keller |
| Address | Encino, California |
| DOB | May 11, 1935 |
| Occupation | Corporate attorney |
| Education | Four years high school |
| | Two years junior college |
| | Four years Harvard law school |
| Religion | None |
| Clubs | Jonathan Club, Los Angeles |
| | Encino Tennis Club |
| | California State Bar |
| Marital status | Single |
| Income 1965: | |
| Salary | $125,000 plus bonus estimated |
| | $50,000 additional |

Half owner and silent partner in antique rental and sales business

| | |
|---|---|
| Investments income | $200,000 |
| Rental income | $45,000 |
| Dividends | $11,500 |
| Sale of stock | $22,900 |
| Assets House | $75,000 |
| Antique store | $550,000 |

| Car | $10,000 |
| Bank account | $71,000 savings |
| Bank account | $15,000 checking |
| Stocks | $835,750 |
| Stock options | $10,000 |
| Real estate | $11,000 undeveloped |
| Real estate | $40,000 developed |

Without taking his attention from driving, Jeffrey explained that he'd need more time to develop information about business practices, reputation, social life, routines and sexual preferences.

Marcia thumbed through photographs of Gavin's house. There were interior photos showing the living room, all four bedrooms and a den. Jeffrey had even included a hand drawn floor plan of the place.

She felt a pang when she saw the photographs of Gavin walking along Wilshire Boulevard near his office.

He hadn't changed much.

There were also photographs of Gavin driving his Jaguar convertible, Gavin having lunch with two other men described in the report as a coworker and a subordinate, even some candid pictures taken inside Gavin's office.

There was no denying Gavin was as good looking as she remembered. She felt a perverse vindication, as if she were at least a little justified for the way she had thrown herself at him ten, twelve years ago. This vindication was quickly replaced by the hate she had suppressed all those years and the hot desire for avenging what Tom Larson had told her he thought Gavin had done to her poor little brother Timothy as a child.

"How did you get the interiors?"

Jeffrey grinned proudly. "It's a quiet neighborhood and neighbors aren't suspicious of a gas company meter reader. I was in and out of the place before anyone could notice. Used a credit card to trip the lock on a sliding glass door by the pool. As for his office, I was a UPS man with a camera hidden in a package."

301

Jeffrey was silent for most of the rest of the drive to the studio.

Finally, looking back at her in the rear-view mirror he asked, "Is this what you wanted?"

"This is all I wanted and more."

# Chapter Sixty Two

## Dick Schmitt

## Fall, 1965

Customs Inspector Richard Schmitt did not drink alcohol, did not drink alcohol at all.

Not even wine or beer.

But finally, after years of panic, years of sweat-soaked sheets and sleepless nights, he did something he had never done before in all his thirty-three years. Desperate for relief from his nightmares, he stopped in a liquor store, Jerome's on Fillmore, and asked the owner for a bottle of the best gin.

"Oh," the man behind the counter said, turning to the shelf behind him, "that would be Tangueray, sir. Frank Sinatra's favorite."

Smiling, he set a bottle on the counter. "Will there be anything else, sir?"

Dick rubbed his face with his palms, trying to clear his head, trying to think.

"Gimme everything I need for a martini."

The man set the bottle of Tangueray, a bottle of Cinzano vermouth, a jar of picked onions, a cocktail shaker and two martini glasses on the counter.

He started to ring up the purchase.

"I'll only need one," Dick said, pushing one of the martini glasses away.

"Remember," the man said as Dick turned to walk out the door into the night, "shake, don't stir."

When he got back to his apartment he went directly to the bedroom, took off the Customs and Immigration uniform and carefully hung it in the closet with the others.

He changed into gray slacks, matching sweater and loafers.

Before closing the closet door, he searched for and found a little slip of paper he'd left in the pants pocket of his uniform. This he stuffed into the front pocket of his slacks.

He turned off the light, left the bedroom and went to the kitchen to make a martini according to the man in the liquor store's instructions.

303

He took a sip. The gin tasted awful, but the vermouth was even worse.

He emptied the drink down the drain, filled the shaker with gin and ice and poured some into the martini glass. He dropped a little cocktail onion in the glass and cautiously took a sip.

The onion floated against his tongue. It seemed to him that the onion took some of the edge off the harsh taste of the straight gin.

With the shaker of gin and the jar of onions in one hand and the martini glass in the other, he went to the dark living room to sit in the rocking chair next to the bay window.

Tentatively, he took another sip of the gin.

He grimaced. Goddamn, it tasted just plain awful.

Slowly, keeping time with the ticking of the schoolhouse clock in the dining room, he rocked back and forth in the chair.

He stared out the window at the street below, stared as he did every night, watching, waiting.

Maybe this night, with the gin's help, he would just pass out, fall into a dreamless sleep, a sleep not cruelly interrupted by the nightmare.

Outside, wisps of fog carried by the soft breeze from the bay drifted like a slow, graceful parade of gossamer ghosts, swirling, touching everything, then moving on. The light from the lamppost across the way competed feebly with the thick dark of the night and cast long shadows on the damp street, the sidewalk, and the parked cars.

An hour passed, then two. The gin was becoming easier to get down, or at least he was no longer gagging. The mist thickened, the light from the lamppost became more and more indistinct. Finally, it was only a glow in the gray world of fog.

Below his window, a woman in a heavy coat and winter hat passed by. She was walking a dog, its fur wet and straggly from the damp. In the silent darkness Dick could hear her footsteps receding on the sidewalk long after the woman and her dog disappeared in the mist.

Cars were parked along the curb on both sides of the street. His poor old T Bird, dirty, dripping with moisture, was hemmed in. If he wanted to go anywhere, he would have to get out of the space by slowly going forward until he hit the car in front, then back to hit the car behind, little by little working the T Bird out into the street.

He sipped the ice-cold gin. Friday night. Ahead of him stretched two bleak, empty days off work.

In order for the Customs and Immigration inspectors to check the passports of arriving passengers, each inspector's table had recently been equipped with a computer linked to the Service's mainframe in Washington D.C. That afternoon, using the terminal at his workstation he accessed the database.

Dick was going to try to find Gavin Keller in the system. If Gavin had a passport, Dick could easily find out where Gavin lived.

It was Gavin Keller who was entirely responsible for his years of constant terror, his years of sleepless nights.

It had been Gavin Keller who picked up the girls at the drag races that led to the sex orgies in the car.

It had been Gavin Keller who had suggested moving the orgies to the motel.

All this led to the compromising pictures.

Dick knew Gavin had a hand in creating those pictures.

Connie and he, Dick Schmitt, killed the motel manager because of those pictures.

For how many years now had Dick lived in fear of the knock on the door of his apartment or the arrival at work of the police, come to arrest him, arrest him as an accessory to that murder?

He started to feel the numbing, levitating effects of the alcohol. Fumbling, he pulled the little slip of paper from his pocket. Yes. Gavin's name, his address, his passport information had appeared on the computer monitor at work.

Gavin had traveled to Bermuda.

Dick had written it all down on the little scrap of paper he held in his hands. Now that he knew where Gavin lived, he no longer had any excuse for putting it off.

Gavin was within reach, accessible.

If Dick Schmitt was ever going to do something, anything at all, now, now was the time.

# Chapter Sixty Three

## Gavin Keller

## November 19, 1965

Friday.

Although the wind and dust put everyone else on edge, Gavin was in a great mood. The defendants in a $14,000,000 suit he'd brought looked like they were on the run. The defendant's attorney, a large Los Angeles insurance company defense firm had obviously recommended that their client settle.

Gavin had banked on their concluding that continuing would become increasingly expensive.

There was always the chance, given the California court system that the defendant could lose, despite his innocence and strong defense.

The real indication had been their ready agreement to arbitration.

Gavin knew that if they were determined to slug it out, they would've never agreed to that. He knew he had them worried, knew their resolve was wavering. Let them worry. Let them stew in their own juices over the weekend. It would make them all the more anxious, wondering whether he'd negotiate a compromise or not. By Monday, the defendant would be a nervous wreck.

Then Gavin would move in for the kill.

He'd cleared his desk, getting ready to go home when he saw the message light for his private phone line blinking. He started to push the button to see who'd called.

No, it was probably just Tommy Huber. Undoubtedly Tommy had run out of money again.

Gavin had already decided that keeping Mr. Thomas's Antiques afloat was hopeless. On his way home Monday, he planned to drop in on Tommy at the store and offer $10,000 to buy him out, lock stock and barrel. It was obvious to Gavin that the antique furniture market had tanked. In all likelihood Tommy would refuse to sell, even as desperate as his situation was. But Tommy Huber had no choice.

Gavin could call the note, force Tommy Huber and the business into bankruptcy. That would be that. Tommy would lose everything, and Gavin would become debtor in possession.

Tommy didn't know that Gavin, as mortgagee, had taken out an insurance policy for an amount far in excess of the actual value of the contents of the store. With his access to Entrepreneur Insurance Company and its records, particularly those pertaining to arson losses, Gavin knew who to contact to arrange a fire. He had already made those arrangements. It was a done deal, the die was cast and one way or the other, in a couple of weeks he'd be waiting for a check from an insurance company.

The check would be in settlement of claims arising out of a fire loss at Mr. Thomas's Antiques of Beverly Hills.

Screw it. He wasn't going to return Tommy's phone call. It was the weekend. Gavin was anxious to get home.

He wanted to celebrate.

Alone.

Gavin had no girlfriend or boyfriend, no romantic attachments of any kind.

Other than himself, of course.

Oh, he always had a string of women, all attractive, that he could take on dates. But they were just for show, for taking to business dinners or parties connected with his work. They could and would be replaced or rotated without any emotional attachment, at least not on his part. He was more or less straight, but he knew that, being in his thirties and single in L.A, his competitors at work would spread rumors.

At Greater Energy, rumors that he might be gay would most certainly damage his career.

Gavin Keller was careful not to get too close to anyone, especially women.

It was career first, last, and always.

Ah, but tonight, tonight he was going to have one of his private little celebrations all by himself.

He deserved it.

He'd worked hard. He'd outmaneuvered or sabotaged the other ambitious young men trying to get ahead at Greater Energy. He'd made his dreams come true all on his own, letting nothing get in the way.

He was successful, gaining the power he'd aspired to, the power to command.

Gavin had made himself rich and he was on his way to becoming a lot richer.

Just like Cary Grant in that movie he had seen years ago, wearing beautiful, expensive suits, surrounded and admired by beautiful, expensive women.

Busy. Barking orders. Important.

Gavin's craving to belong in the big city life of money and power was only matched by his craving for intense, high-voltage sex. If he weren't so dedicated to his career, he could have done some really bizarre things.

But being smart and cautious, he never openly did anything sexual with another person that was out of the ordinary.

He'd had to find other ways to satisfy his appetite for the extreme. For that, he'd outfitted the basement under his hilltop home in Encino for his own private, solitary games.

Like most L.A. commuters, he pretty much negotiated freeway traffic on autopilot. He arrived at his home barely conscious that he'd made the drive.

He parked the Jag in the garage and entered the house. He slipped out of his shoes, set his briefcase and keys on the kitchen counter, and walked down the hall to his bedroom.

Just inside the bedroom door, a bookcase lined one entire wall, lined it all the way to the sliding glass doors that led to the patio and swimming pool.

He paused there, just inside and reached toward the bookcase as if to pull a volume of Shakespearean tragedies from the shelf.

He stopped himself, dropped his hand before he touched it.

"Patience," he whispered. "Dinner first."

# Chapter Sixty Four

## Tommy Huber

## November 19, 1965

11:33 p.m.

Tommy Huber lay in bed, his eyes wide open, open and staring at the ceiling. His mind raced, his thoughts bouncing around in his head like the marble in a pinball machine.

Still wired from the coke, he shook, shook uncontrollably.

How long had it been since he had last eaten anything? He knew he didn't eat anything all day yesterday or last night and he wasn't entirely sure about the day before that.

The high, the elation he had felt earlier when his number one problem solved itself was now replaced with uncertainty, fear that was quickly turning to panic.

His number one problem hadn't "solved itself." What happened at the john's house couldn't, wouldn't be called an accident.

Tommy Huber murdered the man, pushed him out the window with a chair and killed him.

Not only was he a hopelessly bankrupt homosexual coke addict, but Tommy Huber was also now a murderer.

Did anyone see him walking up the hill to the john's house or back to his car?

What if the john had shouted his name? Had he?

Tommy couldn't remember for certain. He didn't think so, but he wasn't absolutely sure, it all happened so fast, and he'd been so stoned.

What if the john had yelled his name and what if Chucky hogtied and blindfolded in the Rumpus Room heard?

Would that son of a bitch Chucky know it had been Tommy in the house?

Tommy looked at the clock next to his bed.

What seemed like hours ago, it had been 11:33.

Now the clock said 11:36.

What if he'd left something, some clue there in the john's house?

What if, in the course of the scuffle, he'd said something to the john and Chucky heard him, recognized his voice?

What if someone saw him get into his car in the parking lot?

What if? What if? What if?

He couldn't think clearly, couldn't focus his drug and alcohol-soaked brain. He had to get up, get out of bed, get dressed, and get going.

Going? Going where? It's almost midnight. Where the hell could he go? He sure as hell did not want to go to the store.

Not now, not in the middle of the night.

In fact, not ever.

The thought of the store, the failing business abruptly brought on a heavy, black depression.

His life was sinking, had sunk, in fact. He'd run out of cash two months ago and had been living on credit.

On top of not being able to pay any of his bills, Tommy had agreed to pay Gavin something on account last Friday, a week ago today. $25,000 or $50,000 against the almost $1,000,000 he owed.

It might as well be the whole million.

He lay there in that bed between cold and clammy silk sheets, staring up at the ceiling and turning his head to look at the clock every ten seconds.

All the stuff he had and all the stuff he did now seemed to him a horror, a nightmare. Sure, there'd been some highs, some moments or hours of—what was it? Pleasure? Excitement? Thrills?

But those moments were so brief, so fleeting. In no way could all that have been worth what he was going through. Was this what being happy was supposed to be?

Scared. He was scared all the time. Not just now, not just because of the john. He worried all the time about the store, about the loans, about the payroll, the taxes, about everything.

He could not remember the last time he hadn't been worried.

How the hell had it all come to this? Where had it begun? He'd done all right as a kid in high school, well liked with plenty of friends, good enough grades. He'd have graduated, got a job, and lived an uncomplicated, "happy" life like everyone else from Inglewood, California.

The turning point had been that one sunny afternoon when he and the other guys were standing there by the football field between classes. What had they talked about?

Football? Girls? Cars?

Someone walked up and stood beside him.

Gavin Keller.

Damn, Gavin Keller. Problem number two.

Tommy remembered that afternoon as if it were only yesterday. Gavin introduced himself and got Tommy away from his friends. They went for a walk, a walk across the campus. Gavin had told Tommy that he knew about his secret Hollywood life. Knowing that, Gavin had been able to coerce him to rent out dirty movies.

The next thing he knew he was in the porn business and the porn business led to the antique business.

It had been Gavin who talked Tommy into flying back east and it had been Gavin who introduced Tommy to the New England junk antique market. That caused Tommy's nice little business to really take off and become the monster that ruled his life today.

Gavin loaned him more and more money, loaned him money to the point where Tommy became hopelessly in debt to him.

He looked at the clock again. 11:45.

What the hell was he going to do?

Should he run away?

Leave the store, the Brentwood condo, everything and just go?

But where? And how? In the rented Bentley, for Christ's sake?

He didn't have enough cash on him to get very far.

But he had to get up, get dressed, and get the hell out of here. It was Friday and he could not make the payroll, couldn't even pay his stupid, worthless employees.

Dizzy, joints aching, he struggled to get out of bed. He stumbled, reeled to the bathroom. He had to try to shave, try to pull himself together.

He turned on the bathroom light.

Christ! There, right there in the bathroom, a pale, ugly cadaver!

Startled, his first reaction was "Who the hell is that?"

But then he realized it was he, he himself, Tommy Huber.

It was his own reflection in the mirror looking back at him.

The image was of a half-dead human wreck, like something that had been in the ocean for a long time and finally washed up on the beach.

Bloodshot eyes, pale, sunken face deeply lined with wrinkles, swollen nose crisscrossed with hundreds of tiny red vessels.

He'd always been a good-looking guy. When he really felt down, he'd always been able to look in the mirror and cheer himself with that thought.

He started shaking and sobbing so hard he had to grab hold of the sink for support.

He vomited till he dry heaved.

When he raised his head, the face in the mirror again looked back at him, an ugly disaster with stained yellow teeth.

He bent to watch the water swirling down the drain, rinsing the sink. He held a washrag under the faucet, and then pressed it to the back of his neck.

Maybe a line of coke would give him a jolt, steady him, and get him going.

Yeah. That would definitely help.

Without bothering to grab a towel to dry his face he stumbled to his bedroom. He fished the little brown bottle out of the pocket of his jacket along with the straw and the little mirror. He spilled out a pile and without stopping to chop it up took a big snort.

He closed his eyes. That was a little better. His head was clearing, and he could think.

Okay. What next? Get dressed. Get car. Get gas. Get going.

First, he had to go see Gavin. He had to get Gavin to let him have some more money, or else.

312

Or else what? Or else the business would go under, and Tommy would lose everything. And so would Gavin.

Tommy had made the trip to Gavin's house many times.

Fucking Gavin had it knocked. Unlike Tommy, Gavin never had any worries. Gavin's life was so ordered, so comfortable, not a care in the world. Whenever Tommy showed up needing money to buy stock for the store or for expansion, Gavin always had it right there on hand. No matter how much it was, Gavin never said 'I'll have to go to the bank'.

And it was always in one hundred-dollar bills. Gavin must have money stashed somewhere in that house of his, maybe thousands and thousands of dollars.

In cash.

The bottle of Scotch stood on the sideboard. Tommy grabbed it, unscrewed the lid, and took a long pull. It burned all the way down, but it warmed him, made him feel like he might come back to life.

He pressed his clenched fist against his forehead. He had to find some way to get Gavin to give him money. But how?

What he needed was another line. That would put him right. He had a whole zip-lock bag of coke hidden behind a picture hanging in his bedroom. He took it out, intending to refill the little brown bottle.

Screw it. He decided to have one monumental line first. He spilled a pile of the powder onto the little mirror and tried to chop it with the razor. His hand shook so badly he kept missing and hitting the countertop.

Another pull on the Scotch and try again. This time he didn't bother trying to cut the coke with the razor. He just stuck the straw up his nose and drew in all he could in one snort.

He filled the little jar and stuck it in his pocket, grabbed the Scotch and went down the elevator to the garage and the Bentley.

# Chapter Sixty Five

## Catarina Monreale

## November 19, 1965

It's always quiet in this valley.

No sirens, no horns honking. From late afternoon until the crowing of the rooster the next morning, just the chirping of crickets and the distant, barely audible hum of the ranch's generator.

Catarina was sitting on the porch step, her dog Shadow beside her. He leaned against her and let her rub the spot on his lower back, the spot just above his tail, the one spot he couldn't quite reach himself.

The sun had dropped behind the mountains to the west and very soon the evening would turn chilly. The ranch hands were putting equipment away for the night, backing the new tractor into the garage next to the barn and checking on the horses in their stalls.

It had been a hot day, even hotter than is usual for the valley.

Santa Ana's. That's what the ranch hands called the winds that brought the heat and the dust from the high desert to the north.

The Santa Ana Winds.

Real ranchers seldom had occasion to go out at night, and Catarina Monreale had become a real rancher.

Tonight though, she would be going out.

She stayed on the porch step long enough to watch Gustavo turn off the light and close and lock the barn.

Now the ranch was dark except for the rectangle of light from the dining room window shining on the big yard in front of the house.

She got up from the step. With Shadow following, she went through the house to her bedroom.

She turned on the light and Shadow jumped up on the bed and made himself comfortable, his chin resting on his paws. His eyes followed her around the room, watching her. She went to the dresser, opened the bottom drawer and gathered a black pullover top, black jeans, and black boots.

She put the clothes in a small suitcase, then moved to the cabinet in the bed's headboard and took out a shoulder holster.

The dog watched curiously when she picked up poor Uncle Benny's old Colt .45 automatic. She hefted it, and then reluctantly returned it to its place.

Too bad. Uncle Benny would have appreciated the gesture, but the .45 was just too big, too heavy. Too loud.

Instead, Catarina chose the .38-caliber revolver with a silencer. She put the revolver and the holster along with a box of ammunition in the suitcase.

She turned and looked down at Shadow, laying on the bed looking up at her.

Shadow was a new addition to her little family here at the ranch. They'd met only a couple of weeks ago. She'd been on her way back on Foxen Canyon Road, doing maybe 90 miles an hour. Ahead, a mile or so, she saw a dark spot. Maybe it was just a shadow in the middle of the pavement. She slowed. When she got closer, she saw it was a dog, a young German shepherd.

He seemed to be waiting for someone, and it turned out he had been.

He'd been waiting just for her.

She stopped at the side of the road, off the pavement on the shoulder. Without saying a word, she reached over and opened the passenger side door.

The dog got up from his place on the asphalt, ran around in front of the car, and jumped up on the passenger seat.

Her hand was resting on the floor shift. He licked it and sat down, looking ahead through the windshield as if he'd been in that seat before and was anxiously waiting to see where they would be going this time.

 From that moment on he'd been always at her side.

Catarina had taken to deliberately letting her pony Rondo loose to play their little game. When she went chasing after him Shadow tagged along, silent so's he wouldn't tip the yearling off that they were on the chase.

She took off her riding boots and stripped out of her jeans and work shirt. She took a long, hot shower, and then returned to her bedroom. From her closet she took a new business suit. Grey slacks, short matching jacket, white blouse and low-heeled shoes.

She put her throwing knife into its scabbard and slipped her arms through its straps. When it was comfortably in place behind her neck, she finished dressing.

Studying herself in the mirror, she looked the picture of a young professional woman.

She did a little pirouette, one final look, then went to the bed, sat down next to Shadow and scratched him behind his ears.

"You stay here nice and comfortable, mi compañero. I'll be back later."

She picked up the suitcase and walked out of the bedroom, down the hall through the living room and out the door to the porch. She paused for a moment looking up at the star-filled sky.

Then down the steps and across the yard to the garage and the ranch's Ford station wagon. Next to it was her favorite car, a red Corvette.

But the Corvette would be way too conspicuous to use tonight.

The mountains made for poor reception, so she left the radio off driving over the San Marcos Pass. She didn't turn it on until she passed Santa Barbara, headed south on 101.

When she got to Los Angeles International Airport, she parked the station wagon in the public lot and entered the terminal carrying the suitcase as if she were one of the airlines arriving passengers. She went to the car rental booths and using one of the many phony ID's Johnny had given her, she rented a four door Chevrolet.

"Have a nice stay in Los Angeles, Ms. Armerina," the car rental agent said, handing her the keys.

She was on her way to Encino, and not for the first time. She'd already thoroughly scouted out Gavin's neighborhood twice during the day when she'd been certain Gavin would be at work.

She'd even been inside his house.

She'd even discovered his secret lair.

# Chapter Sixty Seven

## Tom Larson

## November 19, 1965

Tom Larson awoke with a start.

It was late Friday night, almost eleven. Millie slept at his side on the couch, her head resting on his arm. The television set was still on.

Millie was a good woman. A good woman and a good mother.

He stared blankly in the direction of the television, thinking about all that had happened to this woman, to this family over the years.

"Millie," Larson said softly, "I gotta be going on home now. Can I help you to bed?"

A muffled response, but she got to her feet, gave Larson a quick kiss on the cheek and started down the hall. He watched as she turned on the light in her bedroom in the back of the trailer.

He put on his leather jacket and went out on the porch, locking the door behind him.

Pausing for a moment, he looked down at the steps, the steps where Millie's son Timothy died.

Even as late as it was, Larson could not relax. Tonight, sitting inside with Millie, his thoughts kept going back to Timothy's tragic life and the pain it had caused this woman he cared so much about.

He suspected that young Marcia had also suffered, judging by the look in her face when he told her what he thought had happened to Timothy as a child and his suspicions about Gavin Keller.

Suspicions?

Hell, he didn't suspect. He was as certain that Gavin was the root cause of all this as he was certain that Gavin had been the peeper and had molested Timothy.

Going home to his dark, empty house didn't usually bother Larson.

But tonight he was just too keyed up, too angry. Maybe if he drove around a little, unwound and tired himself out enough, he could get to sleep.

He got into his car and made a left turn out of the trailer park and across the unpaved median.

He headed north on Western Avenue. This took him toward his house in Torrance.

However, when he got to Sepulveda, rather than turning he kept on going straight.

He wasn't going home. Instead, he drove all the way up Western Avenue to Manchester, then east on Manchester to pick up the northbound Harbor Freeway.

The Northbound Harbor Freeway to the Downtown Interchange, then eastbound on the Hollywood Freeway to Encino.

# Chapter Sixty Eight

## Marcia Schmitt

## November 19, 1965

Actors didn't always want to use limousines, so the studio kept a new car, currently a nondescript 1965 Buick sedan parked in the employee parking section of the Beverly Hilton Hotel's garage. It was just for the use of the talent staying in the studio's suite in case one needed to make a quick, discrete trip or simply run an errand.

The car's keys were hanging inside the closet door, off the foyer to the left of the formal entrance to the suite.

Marcia sat in front of the makeup mirror in the large dressing room, a room outfitted with the same equipment and supplies as a dressing room at the studio.

She carefully applied eye shadow, powder to hide her high cheekbones and other little tricks to alter her appearance. She added a little theatrical appliance, a skin-colored rubber item that, once applied and covered with makeup, matched her complexion perfectly. A little more eyebrow, a salt-and-pepper wig, and within minutes she looked twenty pounds heavier and more like forty-five than twenty-five years old.

She'd visited a second had clothing store on Melrose and picked up a wash-and-wear dress, a frayed old plastic purse and a pair of worn and scuffed flat shoes.

She dressed carefully to look careless.

Satisfied that she looked properly dumpy, she went to the suite's little kitchenette. From the drawer next to the sink, she took a razor-sharp butcher's knife and slipped it into the old purse.

She paused at the door before leaving the suite and looked back toward the glass doors to the balcony and the view.

The movie script was where she had left it, right under the light from the lamp.

"The Trojan War.

"Cassandra."

"Hecuba and Troilus."

She took the car keys off the hook in the closet and left.

Friday night. The hotel was usually busy on weekends, but no one passed her in the hall, and no one saw her in the elevator or in the employee parking area of the garage.

It wouldn't have mattered, though. No one would have recognized her.

Marcia went to the grey Buick sedan backed into its parking space, unlocked the door, and got in. She started the car, headed for the Wilshire Boulevard exit, turned right, and headed east, then left onto Santa Monica Boulevard and Beverly Hills.

Working her way through traffic to Laurel Canyon she drove up the winding road through the dark hills and down to the lights of the San Fernando Valley.

# Chapter Sixty Nine

## Dick Schmitt

## November 19, 1965

It was so, so relaxing, rocking slowly back and forth in the chair next to the bay window and Dick was so tired, his eyelids so heavy.

He couldn't help it. He dozed off.

Again, for what must be the one millionth time he wrenched awake at the blast of the gun, the gun in Connie's hand in the motel manager's office.

Christ, it was so loud! Didn't anyone else hear it? Couldn't others in the apartment building hear it? Couldn't they hear it downstairs? Out there in the street?

From where he sat, he could look down on the street.

It was empty.

Once again, he got up from the rocking chair, walked to his door, opened it, and looked down the hallway.

As usual, it was empty.

He'd jumped out of bed or leapt up from the rocking chair hundreds of times, thousands of times and run to the hallway to see if anyone else heard the roar of gunshot.

There'd never been anyone in the hallway.

Friday.

He hated Fridays. All week long the seconds, the minutes, ticked away, bringing the end of the work week closer.

And once again, here it was.

He just didn't see how he could face another hellish weekend alone with his thoughts, his demons. He returned to the chair, sat down and unscrewed the top on the Tangueray bottle. He no longer bothered to pour the gin into the martini glass, no longer bothered to drop the little onion in the glass, no longer chilled it in the shaker.

Now he was considering not even screwing the top back on the bottle.

"I can't take it! I just cannot take it anymore!" he blurted aloud.

Startled by the sudden sound of his own voice in the empty apartment, he covered his face with his hands and began to sob.

He had to eliminate the person, the cause of his life coming to this.

Connie? It wasn't Connie. Connie wasn't a threat. Connie was in it deeper than he.

No, the threat was Gavin Keller.

Gavin is that unknown, that unpredictable element; Gavin is that threat. Gavin had led him to this. Gavin had planned the whole motor court thing, the porn, and the blackmail.

Gavin's the only one that could hurt him without being hurt at the same time.

Dick Schmitt had to do something, anything.

Bracing his hands on the arms of the rocking chair he rose to his feet.

Now! Now the time had come to put The Plan into action, The Plan he'd gone over so many, many times.

He felt dizzy, queasy from the gin and the abrupt movement.

Losing his balance he sat back down in the rocking chair, sat down so hard it broke under his weight.

He collapsed to the floor.

Using the little table next to the broken chair for support he awkwardly got back to his feet. He jammed his hand into his pocket to pull the worn and crumpled yellow lined note paper from his jumpsuit.

Folded and unfolded so many times it was in tatters.

The list of instructions for The Plan.

He lifted the bottle of gin to his lips and took a long drink. It was warm but he'd gotten used to the taste. It no longer bothered him, no longer made him almost gag.

He turned on the little table lamp and bent to smooth the yellow lined paper on the tabletop to read it yet again.

The Plan.

The Plan he'd found excuses to put off, to delay for one reason or another all this time.

One- Dress and retrieve the carefully assembled essentials. Clothing in closet.

Two- Drive his T Bird into the city.

Three- Park in a public parking lot.

Four. Walk to one of the car rental places down on Market Street and

rent a car.

Five- Take 101 Highway and head south, south to Los Angeles.

After that the notes on the paper had been erased and crossed out so many, many times it had become impossible to read. In fact, there weren't any instructions after number five. He didn't know what he would do after number five.

Another pull on the bottle.

"Now," he proclaimed loudly, turning toward his bedroom. "Now is the time!"

The room started to spin. He grabbed the wall near the bay window for support. Yellow lined paper in one hand, gin bottle held in the other in a gesture like a general holding his sword to lead his troops into battle, he propelled himself toward his bedroom.

"No turning back now," he slurred.

He would not be dressing in the Customs and Immigration Service uniform tonight.

No, no Customs and Immigration uniform.

But as The Plan instructed, he would dress carefully. Holding the half full bottle of gin in one hand, he reached with the other for a shopping bag on the top shelf of his closet. A large box fell out, hitting him in the face and then falling to the floor.

He dropped the gin bottle.

It hit the hardwood floor next to the box and shattered.

He kicked the glass shards under his bed as best he could, picked up the box, now wet with the spilt gin. He set it on the dresser and opened it, tearing away the tissue paper. Inside was the pair of neatly folded gabardine slacks and a navy-blue dress shirt he had bought two years ago as part of The Plan.

He dressed and checked himself in the mirror on the closet door. He hated what he saw. The slacks, the shirt was not at all to his usual tastes.

He turned back to the closet. Next to where the bag had been was a shoebox. In it were the loafers he'd bought at the same time he bought the slacks and shirt, bought as part of The Plan.

By God, he would carry out The Plan this very night.

He put the loafers on and stepped back to look in the mirror. He looked strange wearing these clothes and these loafers. Not at all like Customs Inspector Dick Schmitt. No, the image in the mirror looked to him like someone else altogether.

This part of The Plan was complete.

Now, from the bottom drawer, the drawer where he kept the old clothes that he used for fixing the constantly stopped up drain in the bathroom, he took an old pair of stained and torn jeans and a sweater.

These he put in a shopping bag.

He turned out the light, went to the apartment's little kitchen. There he took two unopened bottles of gin from the fridge and slipped them into the bag with the old clothes.

He went to the door to the hallway, carefully looked around the apartment one last time, and turned off the light.

Making sure the door was locked behind him he started down the three flights of stairs to the damp, foggy street and his car.

He felt both relief and regret when the old T-Bird started. No, now there would be no changing his mind, no backing out. He was committed. Gently he worked the old T-Bird forward until it hit the car ahead and then backed till it touched the car behind him, back and forth until he was out of the parking space and on his way down the hill.

It was a little foggy, so he turned the on the wipers. Now the headlights of oncoming traffic glared through the dirt-smeared windshield.

Traffic was light nearing the bay. The fog closed in on the T-Bird, intensifying his feeling of isolation in the car's dark interior.

Forty-five minutes later he reached Market Street in the Embarcadero District.

The Plan. Keep to The Plan. So far it had gone just as he'd written it down on the yellow lined paper, just as he'd played it out in his mind—over and over.

He parked in a public lot on Market. Carrying the paper bag, he walked two blocks to a car rental office next to one of the hotels and marched in. He approached the counter, gripped it tightly to steady himself and spoke to the clerk carefully, enunciating his words clearly.

He didn't want the rental agent to know he'd been drinking; know he was carrying out The Plan.

The rental agent looked at him suspiciously, but shaking his head, he rented Dick a new Chevrolet business coupe, $19-a-day plus 10 cents a mile.

With this step in The Plan behind him and he was in the car, he started driving, headed south out of the city.

Away from the bay the fog lifted. After a half hour or so he pulled the car off the main road onto a side street in a light industrial area. He found a driveway for a closed business and drove partially onto the top of the curb so that the front and back wheels on the right side were up off the street. Now he had ample space under the car. He turned off the engine and headlights and slid across the seat to the passenger side. He got the jeans and sweater from the shopping bag. Working as best as he could in the car's cramped interior, he put them on.

Breathing hard from exertion he opened the door and slid out of the front seat, went around to the back of the car, and crawled under.

On his back he worked his way along the gutter until he was all the way under the rented car. Groping in the dark he located the speedometer cable where it connected to the transmission, unscrewed it and draped the cable over the car's frame so it wouldn't drag on the road.

Then he worked his way back out from under the car and got in the passenger side to change back into his other clothes. He returned the jeans and sweater to the shopping bag to use again later when he reconnected the speedometer cable.

Now there would be no way to tell how many miles the car had been driven tonight, no evidence that Dick Schmidt had taken a long trip.

He slid behind the wheel and used a Kleenex to wipe a little gritty oil off his hands.

Before leaning forward to turn the key and start the car he took a long pull on the gin.

"Next stop Encino, California," he said aloud, settling in for the long drive south.

# Chapter Seventy

## Gavin Keller

## November 19, 1965

Gavin was alone in the dark quiet house. He liked it that way. He'd already taken a long hot shower.

Finally, it was time.

Nude, dragging his terrycloth robe behind him he went to his bedroom. He turned to the bookshelf and reached for the volume of Shakespeare.

He tipped the book forward.

Silently, smoothly, a section of the bookcase swung open. Concealed behind it, the alcove and the stairway that led down to his den, his play world.

He descended the steps to the hidden room beneath the house.

Secret, secure, utterly soundproof, the perfect setting to play out his fantasy.

At the bottom of the steps, he touched the dimmer switch on the wall and adjusted the overhead lights.

The room became almost dark, indistinct, dreamlike.

Dark brown wall-to-wall carpeting.

Mirrors everywhere.

Facing a motion picture screen, two projectors, all set up, ready for use.

In a closet behind hidden panel, he'd stored an extensive collection of pornography along with every sexual device available.

Fighting to contain his excitement, he walked to a sideboard, opened the cabinet door and retrieved one of two elaborately carved, matching canisters. He took two sticks of incense from one of the canisters, placed them on a dish and lit them.

He replaced the canister and retrieved a hookah. This he proceeded to load with marijuana from the other canister.

Step by step, he slowly, meticulously made his preparations. Anticipation and preparation were everything.

He lit the hookah and took a deep drag, just one.

It was Maui Wowee. Very good, very smooth.

One drag transported him.

More than one drag would be too much.

He moved under one of the spotlights recessed in the ceiling. His naked body was reflected in the mirrors around the room. Staying in shape and taking care of himself paid off.

He was finally ready to enjoy this Friday night celebration.

Between two sections of ceiling mirrors was a large stainless-steel hook.

He walked to a cabinet, got a bottle of baby oil and began rubbing it all over himself, slowly, sensuously.

Don't get in a hurry. Don't get impatient. Make it last.

He left the baby oil on the bar, went to another cabinet. From it he took a coiled length of thick white nylon rope prepared with a perfect hangman's noose.

His excitement grew and his heart beat hard and fast.

First, a film. Something really outrageous, really perverted. Maybe violence. Maybe something with a very beautiful and very young and frightened victim.

The vision of terror along with the sensation of strangulation would be beyond ecstasy.

Gavin caressed his naked body with the coil of rope.

Wait. Wait. Slow down.

He wanted it to last a nice long time.

It did.

# Chapter Seventy One

## Office of Western Dispute Resolutions

## Wilshire Boulevard, Los Angeles, California

## November 22, 1965

The initial arbitration meeting in the matter of Greater Energy subsidiary Entrepreneur Insurance versus Defendant James Edwards and Company and Others had been scheduled for nine o'clock Monday morning in downtown Los Angeles.

The outside attorney representing Entrepreneur Insurance Company had been shown to the conference room reserved for him and Gavin.

Defendants and their attorneys were shown to a separate conference room.

Nine-thirty came, and Gavin hadn't appeared. Greater Energy's attorney decided to wing it, assuming Gavin had been held up in traffic and would be arriving shortly.

The arbitrator, a retired judge, met with the defendants. Afterward, at around 10:30, he came to the room assigned to Entrepreneur. Counsel was still alone, sitting with his back to the window, his file on the table in front of him.

"Still no Gavin?" asked the arbitrator.

"No, but I'm confident I can relay the plaintiff's position. We demand payment of the full $14,000,000."

"The defendants offer $2,000,000 without prejudice and that's it," said the arbitrator. "They say they are prepared to go to trial."

"I have no authority to settle for anything less than our initial demand. I hope we can wait another hour for Gavin. If he doesn't show, you can reschedule."

Counsel was charging $350 an hour plus travel. He'd come from Minneapolis, so he didn't really care if Gavin showed up or not.

The arbitration conference broke up at noon with the agreement to reconvene after counsel conferred with Gavin. Counsel called Gavin's office repeatedly through the rest of the day and all day Tuesday to see when Gavin wanted to reschedule.

But his assistant told him she hadn't heard from Gavin. She'd tried repeatedly to reach him by phone at his home but there'd been no answer.

This information had been passed on to the President of the division. He decided that if Gavin didn't show up the next day, he'd send someone out to Gavin's home to see what was up.

On Wednesday, November 25th, 1965, Jack Hayward, a paralegal in Greater Energy's Office of Corporate Counsel was sent to Gavin's home in Encino.

Hayward arrived at the house midmorning, parked, went to the wrought iron gate and rang the bell. There'd been no answer, so he walked along the high wall to the gate leading to the side of the house, the patio and pool area.

The gate wasn't latched, so he pushed it open and entered the back yard.

As he disappeared behind the privacy wall inside the gate, Leo Kramer, a neighbor watching from across the street called the Valley Division of the Los Angeles Police Department.

Now inside the enclosed pool area, Hayward paused, hoping Gavin would be in the house and would see him.

There'd been no sound or movement. Other than the birds chirping in the trees and the distant hum of traffic far below on Ventura Boulevard, all was quiet.

Jack started toward the house, toward the sliding glass door just as a unit of the LAPD Valley Division pulled up in front.

The neighbor saw the patrol car arrive and crossed the street to meet the officers.

"I'm Leo Kramer, the one who called you. You guys got here fast."

"I'm Officer Drake. We were already in the neighborhood following up on a car wreck last Friday night."

The younger of the two officers piped up excitedly, "I'm Officer Delgado. Yeah, some cokehead crashed his Bentley into a telephone pole. Scotch and coke all over the inside of the car."

Drake frowned. "It's an ongoing investigation. We don't have all the evidence yet." He turned back to Kramer. "So, what's going on?"

"I haven't seen the guy that lives here, Gavin Keller, for several days. Just now a stranger drove up and went in the back entrance. That's his car there at the curb," Kramer said, gesturing to Hayward's Volkswagen. "I have a feeling something's wrong."

The three of them walked through the open gate.

Jack Hayward stood by the pool, looking at the partially open sliding glass door.

"I'm Officer Drake of the Los Angeles Police Department. What are you doing here?"

"I'm from Greater Energy, where Gavin Keller works," Jack replied, handing the officer his business card. "He hasn't come to work since last Friday and they sent me out to see what's going on."

"Did you figure on breaking in?" Delgado asked.

"No, of course not."

"The door's open."

"I didn't open it. I just got here."

"That's true," Kramer interjected. "He hasn't been here that long."

Drake moved toward the door, and then reeled backward. "Wow. What's that smell? I sure don't like the looks of this." He turned to the other officer. "Delgado, I think you'd better call downtown for a detective."

The two policemen, the neighbor Kramer and Jack from Gavin's office stood around on the patio deck, hesitant to go inside the house.

It took almost an hour before a detective, smelling slightly of whiskey showed up.

Well overweight, wearing a rumpled old suit and looking a little like W.C. Fields but not as healthy, he introduced himself.

"I'm Detective Sergeant Elliot from Central Division Homicide," the old guy said, gasping for breath as if he'd just climbed a hill.

"What's the story here?"

The uniformed officers brought him up to date.

"Well, let's see what this is all about," Elliott said. He lumbered over to the sliding glass door and pushed it all the way open.

Now a stink, a vile stench came from the house.

"Phew!" the detective said, recoiling. "I'm afraid I recognize that smell." Holding a handkerchief to his nose, he stepped inside. The others, trapped by their own curiosity, followed. Each held something to his nose—a palm, a handkerchief, or a shirttail.

They entered a beautifully furnished master bedroom, a room right out of *Better Homes and Gardens*, a room that appeared as if it were professionally decorated. A king-sized bed faced the sliding glass doors and the pool. To the left of the bed, a sitting area with three leather covered swivel chairs arranged around a low mahogany table.

Detective Elliott opened the drapes behind the sitting area, flooding the room with sunlight. More floor-to-ceiling glass doors leading to another deck overlooking the San Fernando Valley.

On the other side of the room, to the right of the bed was a large bookcase. Next to that, a doorway led to the rest of the house.

Unmindful of the stench, Detective Elliott stood near the foot of the bed and scanned the room. To the others the old detective's attention seemed mostly focused on the bookcase, as if the extensive library were the most curious and interesting aspect of the room.

Law books, American, International and Maritime Law, the complete Encyclopedia Britannica.

Detective Elliott walked around the foot of the bed, past the bookcase and started toward the doorway to the hall.

He paused and turned back into the room.

"Something odd here," he muttered. "The books on this shelf are all law or reference books, all except these two."

He pulled a soiled handkerchief from his back pocket, wiped the perspiration from his forehead and studied the matching volumes at the end of the bottom shelf.

"It seems to me the smell is strongest here, here in this area." He bent and looked closely. "There's a gap behind this section of the bookcase. It isn't flush with the wall."

He tried shaking the case, then felt up and down along its sides.

Finally, he straightened and stared at the two books.

Shakespeare's Tragedies, Parts One and Two.

The only books on the shelves that didn't deal with law or weren't technical.

One of the volumes protruded slightly.

He pulled on it.

The section of the bookcase silently and easily swung open.

Looking pleased, Detective Elliott stepped back for a moment, then leaned into the opening and looked around. He gingerly stepped onto the small landing and cautiously started down the stairs.

"Boy, the smells a lot worse now," the neighbor said, clearly torn between curiosity and revulsion.

"What's that flapping noise?" someone asked. "It sounds like there's bats down there."

With the portly old Detective Elliott leading, the group slowly descended the stairs. At the bottom they found themselves in a large, dimly lit room.

Lush carpet, mirrored walls and ceiling, small bar with one leather barstool, a leather sofa.

A blank movie screen glowed, lit by the beam from one of two motion picture projectors. On the projector, a spent reel was spinning round and round, the end of the film slapping against its casing over and over.

Young Officer Delgado felt something brush against his back and when he turned, became the first to discover Gavin Keller.

There, right behind him, Gavin Keller, hanging by the neck from a rope strung through a hook in the ceiling.

Gavin Keller, completely naked, bloated and dead.

On the floor, in the shadows just out of reach of his dangling feet, an overturned leather footstool.

Delgado threw up.

With that, everyone except Sergeant Elliott felt they'd seen enough and scrambled hastily halfway up the stairs.

"You'll never make it as a homicide detective," Elliott shouted after them. "The first rule is not to contaminate the evidence at a crime scene."

He stepped carefully around the mess left by Delgado and looked at the body.

332

Old Detective Elliott had been sitting relaxed on the sofa, still unbothered by the smell that had driven everyone else from the room when the coroner came down the stairs.

Followed by his assistant carrying a rubber body bag slung over his shoulders, the coroner greeted the detective like an old friend.

"Well, Elliott, every time I run into you there's a dead body somewhere nearby. I guess that's the nature of our relationship," he said, turning his attention to the late Gavin Keller.

"My guess is he's been dead for five or six days, judging by the settling of the blood in his lower extremities. And the smell."

Without taking his attention from the body he told his assistant to spread the big rubber bag on the floor and start taking pictures.

Using the countertop for support Elliot struggled to get up from the couch. He pulled the soiled handkerchief from his pocket and wiped his brow. Still gripping the countertop for support the detective knelt stiffly and felt the carpet around the base of the bar near the stairs. He ran his fingers over a spot and sniffed it, then straightened up with a grunt. "It's damp and flattened here." He turned to the group on the stairs.

"Are his shoes down here?"

"No, sir, Detective Elliot," Officer Drake replied. "They're by the kitchen door."

The coroner and his assistant lowered the body and removed the noose. Elliott wandered around the room making notes on his pad. He found the cabinets with the porn, all neatly sorted by category. He glanced at the terrycloth robe on the stool. Again, like an old dog on the hunt, he scanned the room, sniffing the air as if he could separate any other odor from that of the late Gavin Keller.

"Any sign of a woman?"

"Like what, sir?"

Elliot looked at the officer with mild exasperation.

"Lipstick on a glass. Panties. Perfume."

"No sir. Not that anyone could smell perfume in here…."

Detective Elliot cleared his throat, spit into his handkerchief and sank back down onto the sofa. He sighed wearily, touched the sharpened end of his pencil to his tongue and thumbed through his notepad.

"You say you found the sliding glass door to the bedroom open?" he asked no one in particular.

"Yes sir," Officer Drake answered from the steps. "That's how the man from the victim's office found it."

"Footprints in the yard?"

"It's all concrete and tile deck around the pool and to the house, sir."

"Car stolen or tampered with?"

"No sir. It's a Jag and it's locked in the garage."

"Money taken?"

"We found his wallet on the kitchen counter. It has over $500 in it."

"Rich man, eh?"

"Apparently. An insurance company attorney."

The old detective exhaled dismissively.

"Insurance companies *and* a lawyer." He took his handkerchief from his pocket and started to mop his brow again, then thought better of it and put it back.

"A plethora of motives, my friends, a veritable cornucopia of reasons for the multitudes to do the bastard in."

The coroner and his assistant maneuvered the body into the rubber bag.

The others still gathered on the stairs waited for Elliott to pronounce his verdict as to what had gone on here in this strange place.

Finally, as if to himself Elliot began speaking,

"I've only seen something like this twice in my thirty-five years on the force."

He got to his feet and looked at the white rope, now lying loose on the floor.

"A guy will hang himself as he masturbates," he began, his hands in is coat pockets. "Steps off a stool or chair just as he's about to climax. It's supposed to heighten the whole sensation. All these mirrors around the room and the way the place is lit may have been part of his thing, a big

334

production just for his own personal benefit." He looked up at the ceiling, thinking, then looked back at the body bag.

"Autoerotic Asphyxiation, I think it's called."

He caught a look at Gavin's face as the coroner's assistant pulled the zipper shut on the bag.

"Looks like a nice enough looking guy when he was alive."

"Yes sir," interjected Jack. "He'd always been very conscious of his appearance, a very careful dresser, real popular with the girls at the office."

"Always dressed well around the neighborhood, too," added Leo Kramer. "All the young housewives had an eye for him."

The old detective turned to the group on the stairway.

"I'm sure he wouldn't want anyone to see what he looks like now." He squinted and stared at the ceiling. "So, where was I? Ah yes. It looks to me like Keller got good and stoned, strung himself up, and accidentally knocked over the footstool he was standing on. Then again," he scratched his nose with the pencil, "why would he have left the sliding glass door to the bedroom unlocked?"

The others in the room looked at each other as if someone among them should know the answer.

"Screw it. I'm putting this down as Death from Suspicious Circumstances," Elliott declared with finality.

As he and his assistant lifted the body bag to carry it up the stairs, the coroner turned and said over his shoulder, "It might have been suicide, Detective."

There was a moment of silence.

Then Elliott shrugged. "Whatever," he said, flipping his notebook closed.

# Chapter Seventy Two

### *Don't Play with*

## The Girl down the Street

## Valerie Keller

## March 1966

When my little brother Gavin and I were kids, back in 1946 or so, our family set out on what seemed like an endless cross-country motor trip in an old, thoroughly unreliable 1939 Plymouth.

We had almost no money, so staying in hotels or motels was not an option.

At night, like thousands of other young families at the time, we'd just make camp alongside the road. We had an old Coleman stove and some food in the car's trunk, so we ate all our meals "al fresco." That's a fancy term for sitting in the car or on a rock or log and eating peanut butter and jelly sandwiches or, with a plastic fork, eating cold pork and beans from a can.

Mom would sleep on the front seat. Gavin and I would sleep in the back, one of us on the seat and the other on an old steamer trunk covered with blankets. Dad would sleep outside in a sleeping bag.

At some point during that old Plymouth's past someone had thrown up in it and after a few days on the road the car's interior began to smell even worse from all of us being in it 24 hours a day.

Mom and dad took turns driving during the day. Gavin and I would pass the time in the back seat looking out the windows and making up games.

I remember we were crossing the flat farmlands of Kansas or Nebraska when Gavin and I went from counting the different makes of cars going by to dreaming about our futures.

It started with, "What are you going to be when you grow up?"

I must have been around 13 at the time and Gavin 10 or so. Since both of us intended to be wildly successful, the game quickly became a question as to what we would do with all our wealth. Gavin, slouched down in the seat, vowed solemnly that if anything happened to him in the course of his adventurous life, he would leave me everything he owned.

Naturally, I reciprocated. What the hell. It was the least I could do.

That had been 20 years ago. I'm 34 now, still single and sitting in an attorney's office listening to an old man drone on and on reading my little brother Gavin's will.

On my left, looking awkward and out of place were my parents. Dad dressed in his old blue suit, my mom in her black dress, hat and veil.

Mom dabbed at a tear, and then looked startled when the old attorney told them their son Gavin had left them $100,000.

I reached over to put my hand on hers. By my reckoning, that amounted to three times their combined annual incomes. I was glad for them, and the thought that Gavin could and did make so generous a provision was really very nice. I was impressed.

The attorney then turned and began reading the part of the will that pertained to me.

"To my beloved sister Valerie Keller, I bequeath the remainder of my estate and all my worldly possessions."

The attorney then proceeded to read an itemization of assets including life insurance, cash, stocks and investments.

My younger brother had been more than just well off.

He'd been rich.

And, he hadn't forgotten the vow he'd made as a child in the back seat of that old Plymouth.

From the tone of his voice, I could tell the old attorney must be finally winding down. I stifled a yawn and stretched as discreetly as I could, then turned and glanced outside the glass wall that separated the big law firm's conference room from the rest of its offices.

There was aggressive energy in the sharp looking and ambitious young men and women hurrying to and fro. It struck me that this world, the world my brother had inhabited and thrived in had to be indeed a jungle of sorts, a jungle filled with smart, hungry animals.

"Death under suspicious circumstances."

That's what the folks had said when they called me to tell me about Gavin's death.

That's what the coroner's report said when I used my pull as a Commander in Naval Intelligence to get a copy.

Death under suspicious circumstances?  What the hell was that supposed to mean?  This offhanded dismissal of my brother's death would not be enough for me. I knew that until I settled in my own mind what actually happened, I would not rest.

Death under suspicious circumstances?

This is 1966.

This is L.A. for God's sake.

Where's Dragnet? Where's Jack Webb? Sergeant Joe Friday?

Did the Los Angeles Police Department think they could just leave it at that? Gavin had been only 30 years old when he died. From what I saw in the police report he could have been murdered for all they knew.

Or cared.

Could Gavin's success have given someone in this world of his a motive to kill him?

Could he have been murdered?

The elevator ride with the folks passed in silence. When we reached the steps outside the building we stopped for a moment-dad, his hands in his pockets, looking down at his feet and trying to think of what to say, mom dabbing at her red-rimmed eyes with a handkerchief, oblivious to the hundreds of office workers hurrying by.

"You always expect your children to outlive you," dad finally muttered.

After a moment mom stepped forward and gave me a hug. "Please stay in touch now, will you? It's taken this to show us how much we've drifted apart."

"I will, mom. I promise."

Dad took mom by the arm. "Call us when you get to his house and let us know everything is o.k."

I watched them walk toward the parking garage.

The folks had started to show their age, dad kind of stooped and walking almost with a shuffle. They both seemed resigned to Gavin's death, not showing any sign of dissatisfaction at that half-assed explanation, just acceptance.

But I wasn't buying this "Death under Suspicious Circumstances" for one minute.

I retrieved the grey Navy pool car from the lot and headed for the valley.

The directions provided me to reach Gavin's house were to turn off the freeway at White Oak and head on up into the hills.

Near the top, the road began to wind through an up-scale neighborhood of larger homes on large lots.

Gavin's house was at the very crest of the hill and had a sweeping view of the entire San Fernando Valley.

The last one on the right, it was set back from a steep hill, almost a cliff and was enclosed on the other three sides by an eight-foot-high white masonry wall. Five decorative pots, each almost three feet high were spaced at intervals along the wall, the Fichus plants in them were dead from lack of watering. An iron gate guarded the driveway to a two-car garage, another gate set in the middle of the long wall and a third gate at the far end, all in a matching wrought iron design.

Set back on broad, well manicured lawns were a half dozen other very nice homes scattered along the street before it curved to a dead end and a turn-around a hundred yards ahead

I'd tried to mentally prepare myself for what the place would be like, but was still impressed when I saw the house, the setting, and the valley below.

I parked at the curb, got out, took the keys from the manila envelope and went to unlock on the gate.

A flagstone walk scattered with sun-bleached newspapers led to the broad porch and a formal entrance.

On my right, as I faced the house, came the sound of water, perhaps a waterfall or fountain of some sort. It was on the other side of a wall that connected the outer wall to the house itself, with no access from where I stood on the front walk.

To my left, at the other end of the house, another wall that I later discovered enclosed the swimming pool and patio.

Unlocking the heavy oak door, I found myself in a very nicely decorated formal foyer. Dark brown, almost black polished flagstone floor, a large ornately framed mirror on the wall to the right.

To the left, a large, well appointed living room and entertainment area with a big television set. The room had been either decorated by a professional or Gavin had extremely good taste.

Judging from the vacuum cleaner tracks on the carpet, I got the impression this part of the house had been rarely used.

Ahead, a formal dining room, separated from a casual eating area and kitchen by a bar and three stools. The living room and dining room were carpeted in a deep brown and the casual eating area and kitchen were in polished flagstone matching the foyer. The living room's sliding glass doors led outside to a swimming pool and a deck.

More sliding glass doors led from the casual eating area/kitchen to a deck looking out over the San Fernando Valley.

Thus far the house looked more like a model home than a place in which someone actually lived.

Definitely a long way from our childhood home in Torrance.

At this point I hadn't decided whether to keep the place or sell it, but for the time being I intended to take up temporary residence here until I settled his affairs.

And I fully intended to find out what had led him from Beach Street in Torrance to being found hanging nude in a secret room hidden beneath this house.

⁂

For the first week or so after I moved in, I just relaxed around the pool during the day.

By night I prowled the hilltop house and went through Gavin's belongings and his papers.

These nightly explorations really amounted to a treasure hunt. I found I would come across some new item or scrap that might answer one question, only to pose two more.

Certainly, that basement room and all it hinted at were enough to arouse my curiosity.

What kind of games had he played there and with whom?

That hidden place accessed through a secret section of the bookcase in his bedroom led me to think that the house probably held other surprises.

It seemed eerie to me to be suddenly dropped into his life like this. Everything still just as he'd left it, his wallet and keys on the counter in the kitchen, his shoes on the floor just inside the door.

340

I planned to devote at least one full day to each of the ten rooms, and I'd start with Gavin's office.

It was a good-sized room, located in the front of the house, the side facing the street. He'd furnished it with a big mahogany table he probably used as his desk. In the center of the table, a single sheet of paper, a partially completed insurance claim form.

A pen lay on top of the form.

It looked as if he'd only just set it down, got up to get a drink of water and would be right back.

The claim form had been partially completed for a fire loss on an antique store in Beverly Hills. The amount claimed, over $3,000,000 and the claimant, Gavin Keller as loss payable.

The date of loss was left blank.

Since the responsibility to settle his affairs had fallen on me, this had to be one of the many things I'd have to look into.

A roll top desk occupied the wall behind the mahogany table and in front of it, a big leather swivel chair.

At the far end of the room, sliding glass doors led outside to a small garden with a pond. In the pond, a statue of a woman endlessly pouring water from a pitcher. This had been the source of the falling water sound I'd heard when I first entered the front gate.

On the wall to the right, shelves held six television monitors along with what looked like six oversized tape recorders.

Next to that, a grouping of framed photographs.

There were two leather swivel chairs and a small table along the wall below the television monitors and the framed pictures.

I guessed that the monitors were for a security system. One monitor showed a view of the street in front of the house, one showed the front door, one showed the pool area, one the master bedroom.

The other two viewed the secret room beneath the house.

The recorders had turned themselves off when all the tapes ran out. I'd have to take some time figuring out how all this worked, but my duties in the Navy had given me some familiarity with surveillance devices. If I needed help, I could always call on a technician from the base in El Segundo or Long Beach.

I decided to start by searching the big roll top desk.

I carefully opened every drawer, removed them and measured their length to see if they matched the depth of the opening in case there might be another compartment behind it. Maybe I was being overly suspicious, but in my work, I was used to looking for secret places where the subjects of my investigations tried to hide things.

I'm a professional and this is what I do.

I methodically emptied each drawer, memorized the contents and carefully replaced everything just as I did on the job when I searched someone's home or office.

Rolodex cards, alphabetized names, addresses and phone numbers. Drawer measurements matched the desk's dimensions.

I found the cards for the cleaning woman and the pool service and set them aside to call later.

I examined the roll top desk drawer by drawer and slot by slot. It did not have any secret compartments. In the larger, lower drawers were carefully filed papers, correspondence, lease agreements on some property he owned, a loan and partnership agreement for the antique store shown on the claim form on the table, and his passport.

Other than several trips to Bermuda, Gavin had not been out of the country.

Starting to relax a little, I swiveled the big leather chair around, leaned back to put my feet up on the mahogany table.

Across the room, on the wall in front of me next to the television monitors and tape recorders were framed photographs of various sizes.

One was a photograph of me, taken probably 20 or so years before, back when Gavin and I were kids and living in Torrance. Another showed the whole family. Our parents and Gavin and I standing beside that damned old '39 Plymouth.

There were 12 pictures in all, some of them of strangers that may have been friends or co-workers. All were in color.

All but one.

That one was a grainy black and white picture that had been cut from a newspaper.

342

It was the only picture of something other than people.

Instead, it showed a bridge.

The bridge seemed to be coming apart in a high wind just as the picture had been taken.

Another photograph drew my attention, a photograph taken in what appeared to be the lobby of a hotel in some tropical place.

Gavin standing with a very attractive family.

An older, distinguished looking gentleman, (from the family resemblance probably the grandfather)-a very striking man and woman, and two younger people that I guessed were the family's very handsome son and very beautiful daughter. The picture had probably been taken by a roving photographer working the hotel.

I got up and stepped around the table to take a closer look.

The young girl, the one I took to be the daughter looked a lot like me, if I do say so myself.

She wore a pale blue summer dress. I'd never had a pale blue summer dress like that, but now that I saw how I'd look I decided to get one.

The lobby looked like The Hamilton Princess in Bermuda, a hotel I had been in once on a stopover to Jamaica. Since Gavin's passport showed he'd traveled to Bermuda I was pretty sure that was it.

But back to the photo of that bridge. It was so out of place among all the glossy color photos of people. Why the hell would a grainy black and white picture from a newspaper be here?

I decided to take it off the wall for a closer look. Maybe on the reverse side there'd be a note or clue as to why it was here.

I tried lifting it, gently at first, but the damn picture, frame and all wouldn't budge. It wasn't just hanging on a nail, and it wasn't coming loose. I tried two of the other pictures. They were just hanging on hooks tacked to the wall.

But the black and white picture of that ill-fated bridge had been securely fastened somehow.

I twisted it. When I turned it to the right, behind me came the barely audible sound of the rollers on the big leather chair moving on the carpet.

I turned quickly.

The roll top desk was swinging away from the wall, pushing the leather chair ahead of it and jamming it against the table.

I walked around the table and pushed the chair out of the way. Now the roll top could continue moving. It came to a stop at a 45-degree angle from the wall.

In the wall behind where it had been there was a locked cabinet door about 36 inches square. The lock looked like a match for an odd key I'd noticed on key chain for the Jag.

I left the room and went to the garage, took the keys out of the Jag's ignition and returned to the den.

The key fit easily.

Inside this hidden space, a metal box, maybe 24 by 30 inches and 14 inches high. I pulled it. The box was heavy, but I managed to slide it out onto the carpet, lift it up to the table and open it.

The box was filled almost to the brim with bundles of one-hundred-dollar bills, all neatly stacked, all in packets of one hundred. All wrapped with grey and purple paper bands printed with the name of Cuttersfield Bank Bermuda.

Scattered on top of the neatly stacked bundles were a considerable number of loose bills.

I got comfortable in the big leather chair and began counting.

The box contained four hundred bundles. The banded bundles totaled Four million dollars in one hundred-dollar bills and the loose bills came to another four hundred and seventy-five thousand dollars.

Gavin had almost five million dollars in this metal box.

I put the lid back on the box, dropped it to the floor and slid it back across the carpet to the hidden cabinet, then shut the door and locked it.

I put the key in the center drawer of the desk, not back on the Jag's keychain.

I planned to get rid of that car as soon as possible.

Returning to the wall I turned the black and white picture of the bridge to the left. The roll top desk silently returned to its place.

The Navy had allowed me a thirty day leave to settle my brother's affairs, so I had plenty of time. Tonight, I planned to figure out how to use that motion picture projector. Then I could watch some of those movies in the secret downstairs room.

That might be a kick.

I only toyed with the salad I'd fixed for myself that evening. I couldn't help thinking how sorry I was that I hadn't stayed in touch with my brother Gavin these last few years, hadn't lived up to all those intentions we'd had as kids.

And sorry that I hadn't known him as an adult.

It looked like he'd turned out to be a very interesting young man.

Finally, I cleared away the dishes, checked that all the doors were locked, and went to the master bedroom.

The coroner's report had warned of a considerable smell, but the air conditioner had been left on, so it really wasn't bad at all.

I found the hidden panel where the films were kept. Inside, shelves filled with row after row of carefully labeled film canisters. I selected one at random and went to the 16-millimeter projector.

A diagram on the projector showing how to thread the film and after a few false starts I got it going, turned off the lights and settled down on the couch to see just what Gavin had going here.

"Oh my," I thought as the film began. "This is really excellent." Two good looking young guys and three really beautiful young girls, naked in what looked like a hotel or motel room, even a mirror on a dresser showing the action from another angle.

Although the room itself looked cheap, the lighting, the film and the cast were certainly first class.

And in color.

Something looked familiar about one of the guys, the slightly younger of the two, but although his face never appeared, it didn't take long for me to figure out who it was.

My brother Gavin, about the time he was in high school.

Controlled, methodical Gavin had his wild side. Or, while at the same time careful not to show his face, wild enough to have a truly enviable five way.

345

I can't deny that this rampaging action, this all-out orgy turned me on. After all my travels and adventures, I'd thought my escapades and other experiments had been daring.

But this was impressive and certainly on par with anything I'd ever done.

Could the other films in his basement collection similar be to this one?

Had he participated in and produced others?

I certainly intended to find out. There were dozens and dozens of film canisters in the cabinet. I wouldn't be able to watch them all tonight, but this would be another side of Gavin that I'd take my time and enjoy exploring.

I decided to slip into something naked and watch the rest of this epic.

I finished twice before the film did.

# Chapter Seventy Three

## Jim Miller

## March 1966

Gavin Keller had been dead for going on six months when he began to change my life.

Until I left to join the LAPD, I'd been the youngest member of the force there in Torrance.

Just a kid.

I thought of myself as pretty tough, thought I knew my way around. The older guys used to tease me, call me "Young Blood."

But I didn't mind.

I thought I was king shit, being a cop in my own hometown.

Yeah, that's what I thought until that hot August day I saw Timothy Schmitt shot and killed.

I'd been part of that team, that group of cops that responded to the "man with a gun" call.

Yeah, I know there wasn't anything I could have done, anything to make it come out any different.

But I know I'll never forget that day.

The yelling,

The gunshots.

The heat.

The Goddamned heat.

And in my mind's eye the image of all of us gathered there in that trailer park, the other guys, the LAPD guys that shot him, cautiously approaching Timothy like they had to sneak up on him.

Dying in the sun he was, dying on the steps to his mother's trailer.

I began to live in dread that I'd have to respond to another call, another situation where I'd have to witness, or worse yet participate in an incident that involved the death of someone I knew.

One of the guys on the force told me of the time he had to respond to an especially horrible traffic accident. When he arrived at the scene, he saw the victim was his own daughter.

What if I had to respond to something like that?

Being a cop in a small town, sooner or later I would.

Sooner or later there would be a traffic accident or some other tragedy that would involve someone I knew or someone close to me, like my sister or my mother.

But what could I do, quit? Quit and get a dead-end job with all my buddies in one of the town's factories or the refinery?

We were still newlyweds, my wife Sharon and I, married less than a year. I knew very well she was, damn it, in awe of the gun and the uniform.

When we were having sex, she really got off fantasizing that I was dominating her, punishing her. Every afternoon when I came home from work, she became aroused just seeing me in the uniform.

If I could have just talked to her, explained to her about the nightmare my job had become.

But knew I couldn't.

I didn't know how.

And I'd been sure she wouldn't understand. In fact, I'd been afraid that if I weren't a cop, it would change things and she wouldn't want me anymore.

Face it. I was crazy about her, and I couldn't risk losing her. She was beautiful and so sexy, a little blond doll and a tigress in bed.

But as the days went by the fear that I would be thrust into another personal tragedy troubled me more and more.

I guess the turning point came the day I got to the station to check in for work and I couldn't make myself get out of my car.

I just sat there, unable to open the door, to get out and walk to the officer's entrance to join the rest of the guys going on duty.

Maybe it would be different if I weren't a cop in my own hometown, the town I'd grown up in and lived in all my life.

Maybe that was it.

Maybe the answer would be to get the hell out of Torrance, somehow get on the force in Los Angeles or even Long Beach where I didn't know everyone.

Without telling Sharon, I finally worked up the courage to try.

I decided to start with the Los Angeles Police Department.

I had Mondays and Tuesdays off, so I made up my mind that first thing Monday morning I would drive into Los Angeles and apply for a job with the LAPD.

I felt kind of sneaky, like I was keeping a secret from Sharon when I got up early that morning, dressed in my best suit and slipped out of the house.

An hour later I was walking up the steps of the Police Administration Building in downtown Los Angeles, still trying to convince myself that they would take me on but scared that they wouldn't.

Twice I started to return to the car, to just give up without even trying.

I sure didn't think I belonged here. I was intimidated by the noise, the traffic, and the crowds of people hurrying by on the sidewalk.

But then I began to feel the energy and excitement of the place and the people, energy and excitement I would never find in a small town.

"Mr. Miller, I see that despite your youth you have some training and a little experience with the force there in Torrance. A fine organization. What brings you to want to join the LAPD?" asked Officer Jack Turner from behind his desk.

I'd been nervous. The smoke from Turner's cigarette rising from the overflowing ashtray had made my eyes water. I'd felt my throat tighten and I'd had to try to choke back a cough. I hadn't wanted to embarrass myself by acting like I couldn't take a little cigarette smoke.

"Sir, I want to be a part of a larger organization and test myself against the challenges of the big city," I lied, thinking I couldn't imagine anyone believing a corny line like that.

But Detective Sergeant Turner did buy my corny line.

He leaned back in his chair and looked me straight in the eyes. "We can send you through our training program at the academy, but your resume says you've had two years of pre-law at El Camino. I'd really like you to consider becoming a detective rather than patrolman or traffic. What would you think of working homicide?"

I'd been flabbergasted. Homicide Detective? Officer Jim Miller, Los Angeles Police Department, Homicide? My God, that sounded really impressive!

And with that kind of duty, I wouldn't be there when someone actually got killed. Homicide detectives came along later when it's all over.

"Six months training, three as a patrolman on the beat and three months reviewing files in the office. Then we'll put you with a partner and let you see some action," he'd said, signing the orders. "Give them your notice in Torrance and check in with these as soon as possible at the training center in Elysian Park." He'd pushed a sheave of papers across the desk. "They'll get you started."

Sharon had been shocked when I got home and told her I would be quitting the force. But her jaw dropped when I told her I'd be a homicide detective with the Los Angeles Police Department.

I'd be Detective Jim Miller, LAPD Homicide, and no longer a small-town cop.

I breezed through the training at Elysian Park. I never thought of myself as being particularly bright, but being tall, I guess I fit the image the department wanted.

Once the training period was behind me, I'd been assigned to partner with a fat, grizzled old coot, a veteran in homicide named Maurice 'Hank' Elliott.

I'll never forget Elliott. Elliott had an immense belly that actually jiggled when he walked.

Everyone in the department called him "Elliott the Bellyot" behind his back.

Elliott was a holdover from the old school, been on the force forever and seen it all, most of it by his account pretty gruesome. He'd been on the scene when they found the Black Dahlia and had been one of the responders when Bugsy Siegel got it.

When I told Sharon about all this she seemed to think of Elliott as a celebrity.

And I, by association, had to be a celebrity too.

The first case for us as a team, Elliott, and me, came the day I joined homicide. At first, I'd been nervous about working with this "Elliott the Bellyot." But he seemed to be barely conscious of my presence, or conscious of much of anything else for that matter. Inside his coat pocket and hidden by his girth, Elliott kept a half pint of P&M. Everyone knew he had it, knew he took nips all day. Christ, you could smell it for miles.

After 35 years on the force with time out for a stint in the army during World War Two, Elliott was nearing retirement. He had all the signs of a chronic alcoholic. Florid complexion, rheumy eyes, and who knew what else. Everyone in the department said if we could just prop him up for another year or so he'd retire and that would be that.

"Got a stiff at the Jonathon Club," he said after Captain Yeager finished introducing us. "Come on, we got to go check it out."

Elliott led the way between the desks, across the floor of the bullpen to the back stairs and down to the garage to check out an unmarked car. "From the report they took over the phone," he was saying over his shoulder, "it doesn't sound like a homicide. Just some old guy drank himself to death and cashed out in one of the rooms. If you'd come along yesterday, you could have seen the mess a suicide with a .38 can make of a new Pontiac."

"Down at Dockweiler Beach," he said, huffing and puffing his way down the stairs.

"Did himself in sometime late the night before last. Beautiful car, white with red velour upholstery. Except for the little hole on the passenger side where the bullet exited, the car looked brand new."

As Elliott got in the passenger side of the unmarked car, he pointed to the roof above the door to show where the bullet hole in the Pontiac had been. "A hole that small could be fixed with body putty. Once you scrape the brains off the headliner you probably wouldn't be able to see the blood stains on that red upholstery. They sell those cars cheap at the insurance company auction," he said, mopping his forehead with a handkerchief he'd pulled from his back pocket.

"Let me know if you're interested. I know a guy."

It seemed like Elliott talked mostly to himself and would have been carrying on a conversation even if he were alone. He just rambled on and on, talking almost non-stop about one ghastly crime or another.

It was probably Elliott's casual, detached attitude toward the endless parade of death, plus the sheer size of the city and the anonymity of all these corpses that helped me get used to this job so quickly and to take all this mayhem in stride.

I quickly figured out that whenever possible, Elliott pronounced the victims as "suicides," or "death under suspicious circumstances." This conclusion, if supported by the coroner's office, meant no lengthy investigations that could delay you for months while your case load backed up.

Unless the victim was a celebrity or well to do, the coroner's office usually went along. No one in that office wanted to work any harder than they had too, either.

I guess that's the nature of being in a large organization. Most people find the easiest way to get by. Only the very few ambitious ones really go that extra mile.

At first the job went the way I thought it would. I hadn't actually been present when anyone got killed. They were already dead, and the body gone by the time Elliott the Bellyot and I got there.

And I never knew any of the victims or the perpetrators.

By the time I'd been in the department for a few months, smart ass that I was, I thought of myself as about as seasoned a homicide detective as I would ever be. Oddly enough, despite having only average grades in school, it turned out I had a real talent, a real aptitude for detective work. I liked methodically researching even the most minor details, I seemed to be effective at interrogating witnesses and I usually got lucky sizing up a crime scene.

Poor Elliott the Bellyot on the other hand was within months of retirement and failing fast.

I usually left for work early to beat the traffic. This got me to the office before Elliott came in.

One morning as I was taking off my jacket and getting settled, Captain Yeager came over and briefed me on a file he'd put on my desk. I took a quick look and when Elliott arrived, I handed the file to him.

"The captain says the department is being pressured by some lady out in the valley to investigate her brother's death a while back."

"Oh?" Elliott said with a rumbling belch. He tossed the file on his desk, shook his head vigorously and rubbed his bloodshot eyes with his palms, trying to come to full consciousness.

Christ, I thought, watching the old timer take off his coat and collapsing in his old swivel chair. His holster is empty. He's either forgotten his gun or lost it again. He's getting worse every day, really falling apart.

"Whatever it is, tell her the case is closed," Elliott muttered, bending over his desk and shuffling the file.

"I'm afraid she's got some pull," I told him. "Captain Yeager says she's a high muckety-muck with Naval Intelligence. Says if we don't do something, she will. Captain checked her out in San Diego, and it seems she's just the person that could."

"Ah screw it," he said impatiently. "What case are we talking about?" he asked, without glancing at the file in front of him. Instead, he looked around the bustling office. Some of the other teams had gathered up their brief cases and were on their way out to crime scenes or to court to testify at trials.

"Guy named Keller. Gavin Keller, an attorney that hanged himself or something out in Encino going on six months ago. Turns out you were on the scene."

Elliott rubbed his stubble and looked longingly toward the door. I knew by now that he was thinking the sooner we got out of here the sooner he could have a hit on that P&M. From the look of him I guessed Elliott wasn't shaving any more often than once a week and the harsh neon lights in homicide made him look like a corpse.

"What'd I say about the investigation?"

I gestured toward the file on his desk in front of him. "Your report says you declared it "death under suspicious circumstances."

"I think I remember that one. Wasn't the stiff found hanging naked in some secret room under his house? Thought at the time it had to have been some weird sex act, masturbation heightened by partial strangulation gone wrong." He pulled the soiled handkerchief from his pocket and blew his nose. "Autoerotic Asphyxia, they call it."

"It looks like you remember correctly, according to your report."

⁀⌃⁀

Working a case in the valley when it's hot is always a bitch.

 Maybe I'm not such an asshole kid anymore, but despite myself, I'd become fond of poor old Hank Elliott. I could see that the heat and the dust really made the old man miserable, so I made sure the car I checked out of the motor pool had air conditioning. I left it on high all the way from downtown out the freeway to Encino. While the cool car was more comfortable for Elliott and he didn't sweat nearly as much, the air conditioner seemed to aggravate his sinus condition.

I, on the other hand, was freezing my ass off.

We left the freeway at White Oak and started up the hill to Keller's house.

"I'm not going to stay in the car for this one," he told me.

In this heat Elliott usually stayed in the car with the engine running and the air conditioner on, letting me do the legwork and handle the interviews.

"I think I remember the neighborhood. When I see the house maybe it'll all come back to me," he said, peering out the window. "I vaguely recall the victim had been a young, good-looking guy."

I parked in front of the walled home and hurried around the car to help Elliott's struggle to get out.

Sick as the old guy was, he didn't seem to be losing any weight. Pulling and tugging, trying to get him out of the car and on his feet was like trying to help a kitten give birth to a calf.

Once I got him on his feet on the sidewalk, I walked to the wrought iron gate in the center of the long wall and pushed the buzzer.

No response.

Elliott, standing unsteadily next to the car remembered the patio entrance and suggested we try the gate toward the far end of the wall.

"Maybe someone's swimming," he offered, mopping his brow. "It's hot enough."

Head down, one hand on the wall to brace himself he shuffled along behind me, we walked to the other gate.

"Anyone home? Los Angeles Police Department Homicide here."

I could hear someone inside, the sound of a deck chair scraping on tile. Shortly, a tall, slender, and tanned young woman in the skimpiest swimsuit I'd ever seen appeared, coming around the privacy wall.

She held a towel in front of her, but it didn't hide a thing.

I was dumb struck.

My wife Sharon is a beautiful blond and I'd seen plenty of good-looking women before. This woman was well beyond anything I'd ever experienced. She wasn't just drop-dead gorgeous. The way she moved, her brown, sun-streaked hair, her voice, the whole package just oozed sex.

Now it wasn't just Elliott sweating there in the sun.

"We're here following up on a case involving one Gavin Keller," I said, introducing myself and Detective Elliott.

"I'm Val Keller, Gavin's sister. Please come inside, gentlemen. You must be boiling, wearing those suits out here in the sun. I have the house's air conditioner on. I'm sure you'll be more comfortable inside," she said, opening the gate. "Follow me."

Watching that ass of hers, I would follow her anywhere. She led us across the deck to a sliding glass door leading to a kitchen and a bar.

"Can I get you a drink? Water perhaps?"

"Water would be fine. Detective Elliott and I are here to assure you that we're continuing to investigate your brother's death."

I nodded toward my partner. "Detective Elliott here had been on the scene at the time."

Miss Keller turned to Elliott and asked, "Why did you label his death "under suspicious circumstances" rather than either suicide or murder?"

Elliott took a drink from the glass, fished his very soiled handkerchief from his pants, looked at it for a moment, and then stuck it back in his pocket.

"There were no signs of forcible entry, and nothing seemed to be missing. His wallet had $500 in cash in it and the car was in the garage. Rather than leap to the conclusion that it was suicide and jeopardize any life insurance beneficiary's chances of collecting, I determined the circumstances to be suspicious, meaning the incident warranted further investigation."

I was relieved to hear Elliott's coherent and logical explanation.

"Yes," I added, "we've been cross checking this file with other, similar incidents to see if there is any match that could lead us to conclude that a crime might have been committed."

"And what did you discover, officers?" Val Keller said softly, leaning her elbows on the counter and looking me directly in the eye. I knew I was blushing. I thought I might even faint, she was having that kind of effect on me.

I'm pretty sure she wasn't buying our story at all. But it was better than any other we could've come up with, aside from telling the truth, that the file had been closed. Until now, the department had no intention of doing anything.

Elliott piped up. "Other incidents of this sort have always been accidental death at the hand of the victim. The evidence in this case even more clearly pointed to this being a solitary sex act that went wrong."

Now we were more or less on the offensive, rather than defending ourselves for not doing anything. Might as well press forward.

"Do you have any reason to suspect that your brother's death was other than an accident?" I asked.

She straightened, turned, and walked to the sink to fill another glass with water. It was distracting, seeing her standing there in profile, looking out the window toward the valley and the mountains beyond. Her waist was so narrow I thought that I could hold her in both hands, fingers and thumbs touching.

She turned to face us. "Perhaps in a great big city like this you have enough unexplained deaths and don't need any more that might have been murders," she began, with a smile that looked like an animal about to eat the belly of its prey. "But this is my brother we're talking about." Now there was an edge to her tone, a tough edge that gave me a chill. "I understand from the police report that the sliding glass door to the master bedroom had been open. The report says the door had been open when the gentleman from Greater Energy came to investigate Gavin's absence from work. The report also says the hidden door in the bookcase had been slightly open." Her eyes narrowed. "I hardly think my brother or anyone else that was preparing to engage in a sex act would leave the doors open."

Thinking there would be no point in getting into an argument, I decided to try to throw oil on the waters in preparation for our retreat. "We do not disagree with you, Miss Keller. There were enough loose ends to warrant keeping this case open in the hopes something would develop. Now that you're here to help, perhaps with your assistance we can make some progress."

"Yes," added Elliott. "Perhaps you could provide us with a list of your brother's friends or contacts and any other information that might be helpful."

At that, she leaned her hip against the counter, another move on her part that I found extremely disconcerting.

"I'll do that. I've begun settling up my brother's affairs and will see what might be in his files that could provide a lead. Presumably you've interviewed his co-workers? Perhaps someone where he worked could shed some light on Gavin's personal or business life that could help."

"We've been preparing to do just that, Miss Keller," Elliott replied.

I'm pretty sure I detected sarcasm in her voice when she asked, "Can I assume you'll keep me informed as to any information you develop?"

"You can be sure of it" I said, rising to leave. "And I hope we can expect the same from you. If you come across anything suspicious, please get in touch with us immediately. Here's my card with my direct extension number."

As we got in the car to leave, I said to Elliott "Well you certainly came alive in there. I think you turned things around and headed off what could have become a rout."

"Don't be so sure, me lad" he said, settling in the passenger seat. "She gave as good as she got. She's going to be a handful and you know it."

"Why do you say that?" I asked, afraid I already knew the answer.

"When we walked to the house your eyes were on that tight ass of hers. But I saw she had a gun wrapped in the towel she was carrying."

He coughed, rolled down the window and spit, and then turned back to me. "It was a High Standard HDM with a silencer."

"You saw that wrapped up in the towel?"

"Yep. I'd recognize that weapon anywhere. Had one just like it when I was with the OSS during the war."

# Chapter Seventy Four

## Tommy Huber

## March 1966

Tommy Huber's hip ached every morning. Sleeping in the cold barn made it much worse. But when he asked his mother if he could come home after he lost his store, his condo and everything else, she got real huffy and told him she wanted the house to herself. Now that his old man was dead and gone, she had a life too, she said. Since Tommy had been such an ambitious little shit, he could fix himself up a place in the barn if he wanted to. That way they would both have some privacy. Shit, she didn't care what he did, just as long as he stayed the hell out of her way.

Tommy figured she had a right to be bitter. Back when he was doing well, he hadn't visited her once or even tried to help her out at all.

Plus, he was pretty sure she had a problem with his being gay.

He was 31 years old now. For a while he had been a real success. Young, good looking, owner of a very successful Beverly Hills antique store.

Had a Bentley and a condo at the Buffington Plaza.

Sex, drugs and rock and roll.

But all that was gone now. He was right back where he started.

Not even that, really.

Now he was banged up and scarred from the accident, a cripple living in a barn behind his mother's house, living in the barn where it had all begun.

Yes, it had been in this barn that he'd started his fortune.

He and Gavin Keller.

He and Gavin's porno movies.

Tommy rolled over and considered the effort involved in getting up and lowering himself from the mattress on the old redwood picnic table. Crippled as he was, it had been a struggle to drag the mattress up there to the tabletop. The mattress had been his dad's and it was old and stained and smelled like cigarettes, bourbon and urine. But he had to get it up off the dirt floor and away from the mice and the spiders that had the run of the old barn.

Tommy had no prospects, no prospects at all.

He'd been broke before he stacked up the Bentley, unable to make the payroll, unable to meet expenses for the store and unable to keep up the condo.

He'd been so certain freeing himself of the john that had been blackmailing him all those years would be the start of solving all his problems.

But it wasn't.

No, his problems went far beyond being blackmailed by the john.

If only Gavin would have loaned him some more money.

But would that have really helped?

Would it?

He really wasn't convinced that it would have. He already owed Gavin almost $1,000,000. More, really, figuring in the 15% interest he and Gavin had agreed on.

No, his "business model," as his accountant put it, just hadn't worked anymore.

Tommy, "Mr. Thomas" didn't know what to do about it.

Well, none of that mattered now.

He had nothing.

He owned nothing.

The store was gone and although insurance paid the leasing company for the wrecked Bentley, he still had to file bankruptcy to hold the IRS off. Failure to pay back taxes and worse yet, failure to pay his employee's withholding tax.

That pretty much meant that if he ever did make anything, the IRS and the State of California would take it.

It really didn't make any sense to even try to rebuild his life. Besides, what could he do? Go back to showing porno movies to teenagers? Try to get a job?

His mother wasn't about to loan him her old Camaro and limping from store to store looking for work with his bad hip during this recession would be hopeless.

He sat up, ran his fingers through his shaggy hair and looked around the dark, dusty old barn.

Shafts of sunlight shining through the cracks in the walls made the rain of dust motes falling from the rafters above look like tiny snowflakes. Every so often he could hear the rustling of the mice or the lizards in the barn's dark recesses.

The old barn still seemed to echo with the catcalls and hooting of the horny teenagers watching porno movies. $5.00 a head he'd charged them, and he and Gavin made pretty good money. Not nearly as much as he made in the antique store, but pretty good just the same.

And tax free at that.

He slid off the table looked around for his pants.

# Chapter Seventy Five

## Dick Schmitt

## March 1966

Using tape and glue and string, Dick had done his best to repair the broken rocking chair.

It looked like shit.

But then, he looked like shit.

He felt like shit.

He sat alone in his dark apartment, sat alone rocking back and forth. He stared as if mesmerized by the glow from the imitation gas streetlight across the damp, empty road below.

3:30 a.m.

He knew from the hundreds of times he'd sat here like this that the streetlight went off at 5:00 a.m. every morning, meaning he had spent another tortured night trying to avoid sleep.

He'd been so certain that he could bring his life under control and that he would be able to sleep again once he knew his nemesis, Gavin Keller was dead.

And Dick was pretty sure Gavin Keller was dead.

At least he thought Gavin Keller was dead. He certainly should be, the son of a bitch.

But that night eight years ago stayed with him still, haunting him, obsessing him.

Every time he dozed off, he wrenched awake at the roar of the gunshot in the motel's little office, wrenched awake shaking and covered with sweat.

Christ! How could he be absolutely sure Gavin Keller was really, really dead? How could he be certain?

Dick's arm hung loosely down the side of the rocking chair. By the tips of his fingers, he held an almost empty gin bottle.

He lifted the bottle to his lips and tried to drink. The remnants of the gin were warm and very bitter. After drinking for 20 straight hours, it tasted beyond ghastly.

He tried to clear his fatigued mind, to push away the ghosts and demons so he could think. He needed to remember every detail of that trip when he drove clear down to Encino to look up Gavin Keller and settle the score.

Had anyone seen him? Was there any way he could be traced through the rented car? He paid cash for gasoline, but would anyone in the gas stations along the way recognize him?

He'd carefully read all the San Francisco newspapers and even bought a copy of the Los Angeles Times from the newsstand off California Street on Kearney, the news stand that carried out of town newspapers. He could find no mention of Gavin's death.

What if the guy at the newsstand had been suspicious and wondered why anyone in San Francisco would want to buy a copy of the Los Angeles Times? Maybe the guy got a good look at Dick and gave the police his description.

He took that one last swallow of gin, finishing off the bottle.

Then he made the mistake of letting his eyes close for just a second.

He was back in that shabby little motel, back in the manager's office. Connie, beautiful blond Connie standing next to him, looking small and young and innocent.

Connie, pretty as a picture, wearing a light pink angora sweater and a white skirt.

Connie holding a big white purse.

Dick, standing there as if paralyzed, watching pretty little Connie take a big gun out of that purse, hold it in both hands, lift it, pull the trigger.

The roar of the gunshot shook the little office. The fat clerk's head jerked back, and he was hurtled across the small space behind the counter and against the file cabinet. Once again, eight years later and 500 miles away, Dick snapped awake, his heart beating in his chest so hard he thought it would burst through his rib cage.

He'd never seen any of the girls again after that night, after they drove back to where he'd left his car. They, Connie at the wheel of that old Cadillac with Michelle and Sandi still in the back seat, drove off into the night and out of Dick's life.

Did Connie tell Michelle and Sandi what happened in that little office? That she, with him standing right next to her, had shot and killed the motel manager while the two of them waited around the corner in that old Caddy?

362

If she did, then two more people, Michelle and Sandi also knew Dick had been in on it, had been an accessory to the murder of the motel clerk. He tried to guess whether women would talk among themselves about something like that. He had no idea. Dick had very little experience with women before he and Gavin got mixed up with Connie and Sandi and Michelle. He had no idea how women thought. Would men talk among themselves about something like that? Dick wanted to believe they wouldn't, that if a man were involved in a crime like that, he'd keep his mouth shut forever.

Certainly, Dick wasn't ever going to tell anyone about it.

Of course, there was always Gavin. Maybe Dick had been mistaken and Gavin wasn't dead. That would mean what Dick thought happened in Encino had been just another addition to his nightmare.

Today was a holiday. Since he was unmarried, he was scheduled to go to work, to spend the day standing at a table in the Customs and Immigration section of the San Francisco International Airport. He'd be rummaging through luggage, processing the travelers arriving from out of the country.

Thinking about the effort it would take to get out of the rocking chair, shave and get dressed to go to work was overwhelming.

# Chapter Seventy Six

## Marcia Schmitt

## March 1966

She hadn't slept much the night before, and because she'd been in only two scenes today, she spent most of her time in her trailer waiting for the director to call.

Like most actors and actresses, for her the waiting was far more tiring than actually performing.

She'd passed the time by reading a story outline for a "lighthearted romp," starring two of Hollywood's legends, a pair of aging, golf-obsessed characters. Rumor had it that one of them always demanded to sleep with the leading lady.

"Turnip" Green had suggested that a break from dramatic roles would be good for her. It would show the industry and her public that she could be a versatile actress with comedic capabilities.

Green had been her agent from the beginning and hadn't steered her wrong yet. So, she agreed, thinking it could be fun sparring with these two old hams.

She'd play one off against the other and stay out of both their beds.

After Jeffrey dropped her off in front of the Hilton, she went directly to the studio's suite on the 7$^{th}$ floor. She really looked forward to a nice hot bath, a quiet meal alone and an early evening in bed watching television. While the water ran in the tub, she called room service, ordered a club sandwich and a copy of the L.A. Times.

She liked to eat a sandwich and read the paper in the bathtub. She wondered if this little secret of hers, eating in the tub, could be considered perverse. She'd been careful to never mention it to anyone for fear they would think she was really screwy.

The last time she'd been here in L.A., back in November, the headlines had been something about the Watts Riots the previous August.

But it wasn't until page three that she'd found the item that she'd been looking for.

A single column headed;

`'Local Attorney Found Dead'`

`Gavin Keller, Vice President and`

`corporate attorney for Greater`

Energy's subsidiary, Entrepreneur
Insurance was found dead in the
basement of his home late yesterday
afternoon.

Homicide investigators say the
victim's employer became concerned
and sent someone to investigate
when Keller failed to show up for
work. A spokesman for Thomas
Noguchi, chief medical
examiner for the Los Angeles County
Coroner's Office said in a release
that preliminary examination
indicated Keller had been dead for
several days. No drugs were found
at the scene. Pending an autopsy
the police ruled it "death under
suspicious circumstances."

Gavin son of a bitch Keller didn't even make the front page.

She didn't find anything particularly interesting in the paper this evening, so she folded it neatly, set it on the floor next to the tub and leaned back. Tomorrow's a holiday, Washington's Birthday. She planned to take the studio's Buick and go to Torrance to spend the day with her mother and Tom Larson.

Marcia Schmitt didn't have a worry in the world.

# Chapter Seventy Seven

## Sergeant Tom Larson

## March 1966

Torrance Police Officer Tom Larson stood at the cashier's counter at Ding How Café in downtown Torrance, waiting for his takeout order. Every time he came here, he wondered who or what a Ding How could be. Could it be a person? If so, was the person still alive?

This place had been in Torrance since before Larson's time, and Larson went back a long, long time.

The little bell above the door jangled and he turned to see who came in. It was his former partner, young Jim Miller, and his pretty little blond wife. "Christ what's her name?" Larson thought, putting a smile on his face for the couple.

Jim spotted Larson and led his wife over to say hello.

"How nice to see you, Sergeant Larson," Jim said. "Sharon, you remember Sergeant Larson, don't you?"

Larson took the young lady's hand and in what he always thought of as his 'warm, friendly' voice said, "Great to see you both. And, young lady, you're even prettier than ever."

Jim had left the force last year. When he'd been Larson's partner, they'd worked traffic. Larson seemed to recall hearing that Jim had joined the LAPD and now worked homicide, for god's sake. That would explain the brown suit and the not too carefully concealed gun and holster inside his coat. The way Jim's wife hung all over him Larson thought she'd have an orgasm.

Larson's takeout came just as they exchanged greetings, so he'd be able to duck getting into a conversation. "Well, it's great to see how well you two youngsters are doing. All the best now".

With that he was out the door and gone, having escaped another potentially awkward moment that required small talk.

Larson was fairly sure it had been witnessing the Timothy Schmitt shooting that drove Jim to quit the force.

# Chapter Seventy Eight

## Catarina Monreale

## March 1966

The Monreale family had gathered in the shade under the grape arbor behind the ranch house. Grandpa Gianpoalo, in a white suit, his shirt open at the neck, and Gina, barefoot in a peasant girl skirt and blouse were twirling and dancing, showing Catarina and Johnny how they dance to the music of Sciacca (Shaka).

Catarina, Johnny and Gianni were laughing and clapping to the beat. The record ended and Gina returned to the table.

Grandpa Gianpoalo went to the record player and began shuffling through the stack of records.

When he turned to his family, he was holding an old Caruso 78. "How wonderful it was to find this old Victrola and all these old records. I hadn't thought of them in many years, not since your dear grandmother passed away."

Facing her across the table, Gianni gave Gina a look. This was the fifth time this afternoon that Grandpa Gianpoalo had said the exact same thing. More and more lately he repeated himself and more and more often he forgot things.

Catarina walked over to him and put her arm around his shoulder. "See Grandpa, if we hadn't left the cold, miserable east we wouldn't have had occasion to pack all your things and find these treasures."

The music of Caruso's *A' Vucchella* in the background, the old don joined his family at the table. Making himself comfortable he began telling them of the problem one of the Chicago families had with their man in Las Vegas.

"Now that the corporations, Hilton and Marriott and the rest are moving into Vegas, Al and his bunch want out. They say they don't think they can change their stripes. In fact, they don't believe we are going to be able to, either." He leaned forward in his chair and took an orange from the bowl of fruit. "They have a problem, though," he continued. "Their front man out here, Frank Greco, seems to have a mind of his own."

Johnny looked up. "That would hardly seem wise, given their history of dealing with dissidents."

Grandpa Gianpoalo nodded in agreement. "On top of that, young Johnny, as a concession to the changing times and a desire to be more subtle in their practices, they have decided to go outside for assistance. Because of our proximity and expertise," he said, nodding toward Catarina, "they have approached us to deal with this nuisance rather than doing it themselves."

Gianni looked toward Catarina, then back at Johnny. "Greco," he added, "is living a disconcertingly visible life in Beverly Hills, running around with celebrities and getting his name in the papers."

"So I've seen," Johnny commented. "From the interviews and word around L.A, he gives the impression he runs things in Vegas. Says he has plans to expand. "Grow with the town," he says."

"That is what he is saying, and that is contrary to the family's goals. They made their money, and they want out before Vegas becomes so legit it draws too much attention from the IRS. They haven't forgotten what brought Capone down," Gianpoalo explained. "They want Greco to be gone, period. They don't want there to be any more Greco." Reaching down to scratch Catarina's dog Shadow behind the ears he concluded, "*Quando la forza con la ragione combata la forzavince e la ragione non basta.*" "When force and reason collide, force wins, reason is not enough."

Catarina remembered Greco. She'd seen him once from a distance, when she'd stayed in Illinois as an apprentice to Mr. Ehlers. Greco, at the time a runner for the Giuliani family, was to meet Mr. Ehlers in a little park on Lake Shore Drive. Since Greco was to deliver a payoff, Mr. Ehlers wanted someone at his back. Catarina had been sitting on a park bench some ways off, pretending to be sunning herself, her late Uncle Benny's .45 under a newspaper on her lap. She remembered Greco as being about 5'11, medium build, and kind of good looking in a fleshy sort of way. He had to be in his mid thirties.

"I'd like to do this job," she said.

"We expected that you would. Al offered $50,000. I assume we can count on you to be especially careful," Gianni said, reaching over and putting his hand on hers. "Please do not take any chances. You are, after all, our only begotten daughter."

"I'll be careful," Catarina replied laughing. "Where can I get all the information about Greco's habits and the layout?"

"Here you go," Gianni said, fishing a sheaf of papers from his breast pocket and handing them to her.

"One other thing," Catarina said, taking the papers and setting them to the side. "I believe I see an opportunity in the insurance business. My time with Gavin Keller's old employer in Boston gave me an idea that could be much bigger than that phony bridge insurance scheme." She leaned forward. "Can we call in a favor from our friends in Chicago, kind of a trade, as it were? It won't cost them anything, just a little cooperation."

"What do you need?" Gianni asked.

"I need to induce or compromise an executive within a good-size insurance company to allow an outsider to make underwriting decisions for that company," she explained. "It's called a Managing General Agency Agreement."

"Before we leave tomorrow, I'll call Chicago and tell them we accept their contract. You can explain your request then," her father assured her.

# Chapter Seventy Nine

## Jim Miller

## April 1966

It was obvious to everyone that Elliott got worse every day. He was fading fast, missing work more and more often. The other guys in homicide thought he should stop coming in altogether.

Ironically, I, his protégé had turned out to be the up and comer in the department. My being partnered with Elliott, even in the twilight of the sick old man's career turned out to be a real break for me. I did listen and I did learn from his endless stories about murders and how they were solved. That, plus my knack for this work prompted the commander to assign the tougher and higher profile cases to the team of Elliott and Miller.

My success in handling these put me on the fast track for promotion.

I'd never been the kind of guy that ran around, and even with the visibility of my job and the temptations that came with it, I hadn't considered straying.

At least not until now.

But I could not get Val Keller in that bikini off my mind. For the first time since I'd met and married Sharon, I found myself fantasizing about another woman.

I was well aware that since we'd reopened the case of Gavin Keller's odd death, sooner or later I'd have to go back out to Encino and the house in the hills.

That prospect both scared and excited me.

Every time I thought of her, I became aroused. I'd never had this happen to me before, never lusted for a woman.

But since more and more often Elliott was in no condition to be seen in public, he just stayed in the car, and I was left to do the legwork. In all likelihood, for my next visit it would be just the two of us, Val Keller and me, alone in that house.

Captain Yeager had been pressing us about the investigation. Unless I got a lead or two, I'd have no choice but to revisit the scene.

I'd interviewed the late Gavin Keller's former co-workers and acquaintances and looked into his background. There were some big blank spots and plenty of questions.

Apparently, Gavin Keller hadn't been the warmest and friendliest guy. Some came right out and said they were glad he was dead. They went on to describe Keller as being a cut-throat competitor who would stop at nothing to get what he wanted.

Given the enemies and potential for enemies, even Elliott had to agree that Keller may well have been murdered.

# Chapter Eighty

## Val Keller

## March 1966

Gavin's house had only three entrances, the driveway gate and door and the main gate to the house's front door that both opened electronically, and the gate to the patio and pool. All were very visible from the street.

Trying to get in by climbing the steep hillside, almost a cliff, would be very difficult. That route would require passing through yards belonging to the homes on the street below, most of which had dogs. If anyone could clamber up that steep hill, it would have to be hand over hand.

A chain link fence halfway up the almost cliff made access from there even less likely.

For anyone short of a professional, the probable choice would be a running jump onto one of the big pottery pots along the front wall and then lever on up and over. Such a maneuver would run the risk of being spotted by nosy old Leo Kramer across the way.

Kramer never missed anything that went on in the neighborhood.

Apparently, he never slept.

I'd finished looking through Gavin's den. It was time to track down the names I found in his files. There weren't that many.

I'd been especially intrigued by the very attractive family in the photograph taken in the lobby of the Hamilton Princess. I dropped it off with Heidi at the Admiral's office in El Segundo. She ran off several high-quality color reproductions using the Navy's professional equipment. When she got them back to me, I mailed copies to my friends and contacts at Interpol, the FBI and the ONI office in Washington, requesting any information they might have.

Researching the black and white photo of the ill-fated bridge turned out to be much easier. Due to a design error the bridge collapsed in a high wind when it had been only a few months old. Newspapers carrying the story further reported that there'd been no insurance on the structure. Somehow the agent, along with persons unknown, had provided a phony insurance policy supposedly covering that bridge plus a number of others throughout the northwest. It had turned out to be a fairly widespread phony insurance scheme. Most of the premiums had disappeared

372

along with the mastermind behind the scheme, leaving the insurance agent to try to explain to authorities what had happened. A full-scale investigation had been launched by the FBI, Interpol, the State of Washington and the Commonwealth of Massachusetts.

One Tony Monreale, an east coast Mafia figure had been arrested. He'd been released for lack of evidence.

Then there was the matter of the antique store. That file showed Gavin was owed a little over $1,000,000 including interest. A debt of that size could certainly provide a motive for murder. Gavin's records showed this Huber guy, or "Mr. Thomas" as he called himself, had been current for several years. Gavin had done pretty well from that investment or loan. But about a year ago Huber started missing payments and finally stopped paying altogether. In the file a copy of a letter to Huber said that Gavin wanted to explore liquidation of the store's stock and assets to the extent necessary to cover the debt. There were notes back from Mr. Thomas promising that things would turn around and Gavin would be repaid. The ledger however showed Gavin had received nothing further.

The antique store's address matched the address on the fire insurance claim form I'd found on the desk in Gavin's den when I first got here. Since the place had burned, Gavin's loans to the guy should be protected by the insurance. It would just be a matter of turning in the claim.

I took the claim form along with the loan agreement and drove into Beverly Hills, parked in a public lot off Wilshire and started looking for the address. When I found it, the place turned out to be a very fancy Persian carpet store.

As soon as I entered, a little man with a heavy beard hurried over, introduced himself as the store's owner, and asked if he could be of assistance. I asked if he knew anything about the antique store that had been at this location. He knew nothing about it, having rented the space when it was vacant, remodeled by the building's owner after a big fire.

"When was the fire?" I asked, thinking I would just go ahead and complete the form to turn in the claim.

"December 11th of last year, in the middle of the holiday shopping season," he answered. "The previous tenant's rent had been in arrears, so the building owner leased me the space a week later."

December 11? That was over two weeks after my brother died. How could Gavin have been filling out a claim form for a fire that hadn't happened?

I asked if he could furnish me with the landlord's phone number, which he did.

The landlord turned out to be more than happy to rat the previous tenant out, since he'd left owing several months rent.

Thomas Huber c/o of Mrs. Barbara Huber, 18436 132nd Street in Gardena, California.

This address had been easy enough to find. I got there just after midday.

It turned out to be a dusty old house in a semi rural neighborhood just south of Rosecrans, between Western and Normandy.

Verging on ramshackle, all of the houses on 132nd Street were small farms or ranches set on large lots, maybe two acres or more, with barns and corrals and chicken coops.

I pulled into the drive and parked behind an old Camaro.

A worn looking woman of at least 50 sat in a rocking chair on the porch. She held a tin-foil reflector under her chin, trying to get a tan. She glared at me and without removing the cigarette in her mouth asked in a raspy voice, "Whatdayawant?"

"I'm looking for Thomas Huber."

"Mr. Thomas," she said sarcastically, "lives in the barn out back." She cleared her throat and spit over the porch railing. "You're welcome to go on back there by your own self if you want." She resumed holding the tin foil reflector under her chin, leaned back in the chair, and with her eyes closed continued rocking. "I sure as shit ain't gonna go get him for ya."

I thanked her for her assistance and walked on past the house towards the barn 50 yards or so away.

# Chapter Eighty One

## Tommy Huber

## March 1966

Tommy Huber sat on an old empty paint can next to the redwood bench that went with the picnic table he used for his bed. Earlier this morning he'd done a little harvesting from the small marijuana patch he had growing behind the barn.

He hunched over the bench rolling a joint.

It was dark in the barn, but Tommy knew what he was doing. He'd rolled joints in the dark many times. He'd even mastered the art of doing it with one hand.

He'd been startled and had no time to hide his stash when the barn door opened, and a sudden shaft of sunlight stabbed across the dirt floor.

A figure stood in the doorway looking at him. The bright sunshine outside made it impossible for him to see who it was, but from the silhouette he knew it wasn't his mother.

It was a woman though, that much was for certain.

At first Tommy had been afraid that it was his mother. She must never find out about the grass. She hated him enough for being a "fucking queer."

The woman asked, "You Thomas Huber?"

"Who wants to know?"

The woman stood there for a moment, then moved into the barn. She pulled the door shut behind her. Now the interior was plunged in darkness. Tommy, his eyes having adjusted to the bright glare from outside had trouble seeing her.

He heard or sensed the woman had moved quickly to his side.

"I asked you a question." Her voice was right next to his ear.

"And I asked who wanted to know?" Tommy replied.

Suddenly his scalp exploded in pain. She'd grabbed a handful of his hair and violently yanked him backward off the paint can and onto the dirt floor of the barn. She was too quick and too strong. He tried desperately to get to his feet and somehow defend himself. But she pulled him backwards by the hair across the barn's dirt floor toward the empty stalls. She didn't seem fazed by the effort, but he gasped for breath. He tried to get to his feet but in a smooth movement she flung him against one of the stalls. Then she squatted on his chest, her knees pinning his arms to the ground.

It all happened so quickly he hadn't been able to catch his breath. She grabbed an ear in each hand and violently slammed the back of his head against the stall's wooden door.

"Now let's have a little lesson in hospitality," she said.

He was stunned, dizzy, disoriented. Still sitting on his chest, she reached up and grabbed an old, dried out bridle that had been draped over the gate to the stall.

She rose to her feet. He watched helplessly, unable to focus, unable to move, to try to defend himself. She stood over him and holding the bridle by the bit whipped him across the face with it as hard as she could.

The pain was instant and unbelievable, and he screamed.

"There, there now, you don't want to make so much noise that the lady in the house out front comes back here to see what's going on, do you?"

Oh God, he thought, I think she broke some teeth, and I may have lost an eye.

He whimpered. He tried to scrunch himself up against the stable door as if he could somehow merge into it, somehow get away from this devil woman.

"What…what do you want?"

She squatted beside him, still holding the bridle. He could smell her perfume, Chanel Number Five.

She leaned close, so close that he felt her breath on his ear. In a very determined voice, she said so quietly he could barely hear, "It is my understanding that you owe a considerable amount of money to one Gavin Keller. I will want that money. I also understand that you had a close relationship with Mr. Keller. I want to know all about it. ALL about it," she said, wrapping the bridle around his neck and cinching it tight for emphasis.

"Gavin was a business partner. There was a fire. The business burned to the ground. I went broke."

The woman tied the bridle around the stall door, tight enough to almost choke him.

She rose easily and walked around to Tommy's feet.

She spread his legs with her booted foot and kicked him in the balls as hard as she could.

The pain was excruciating. His head snapped back, banging against the stall door so hard that he almost blacked out.

"Now let's start from the beginning," she said.

Christ, he's getting his ass kicked real good by a woman. He'd been on the football team in high school. Now he's huddled on the dirt floor of his mother's barn being worked over by a broad. He had to turn this around somehow, get on the offensive. But he was afraid that if he tried, she'd do something else to him.

She knelt with her knee in his groin.

She grabbed a handful of his hair and slammed his head against the stall door four, five, six, he didn't know how many times. The dark barn, the rafters above and the straw on the dirt floor, everything seemed to be spinning.

"You're taking too long."

He couldn't stop shaking. He began to sob.

"Gavin found out about me in high school, Inglewood High. I was a football player. B Team. He'd found out I was gay, turning tricks on Beverly Boulevard at night."

Everything was a blur. Tommy didn't know if it was from the tears that filled his eyes, his being choked by the bridle or the banging his head had received.

She knelt and he felt her lean forward, pressing her weight down on her knee in his groin.

"Go on."

"He offered me a partnership renting and showing a bunch of porno films. We started out just me showing them to guys from school, here in the barn. We made a fortune. When he went off to college, I opened an antique store with my share of the money. It had done fine until I got into trouble. I started borrowing money from Gavin, first to open another store and for stock. Then I had to pay a blackmailer. It just got out of hand. The antique business went downhill. I couldn't turn it around. I didn't know what else to do."

She rose to her feet and stood over him for a moment. "Where were you the night he died?"

"I didn't see him. I swear, I never got to his house." He was gasping now, almost faint. But he was afraid to reach up and try to loosen the bridle that was choking him. He didn't know what she might do. "I was going to. I was going to see if he'd give me an extension on the loan, maybe loan me some more money. Then maybe I could try to restock my store with something that would sell. I started up to his place, but I never got there, I swear. I was drunk and stoned on coke and got in an accident. I never made it.  You can check it out with the police, with the hospital."

Wordlessly the woman rose to her feet and went to the barn door.

She pushed it open and walked out into the bright sunlight without looking back.

Just outside the door stood Tommy's mother looking in, watching him and shaking her head.

# Chapter Eighty Two

## Val Keller

## March 1966

The light on the answering machine in Gavin's den was blinking when I got back from my field trip to Gardena. My friend, Julie, with the FBI in Washington had left a message that she had a make on the family in the picture.

That sure didn't take long, I thought. I picked up the phone to return the call. Must be someone reasonably well known.

"Julie Rodriguez," my friend's voice answered.

"I'm calling to report the assassination of President Lincoln," I said, pretending to disguise my voice. "I figure it was time you people heard about it."

"I'm afraid the party you need to speak to is on vacation for a month. Can I put you on hold till they get back?" she replied.

"I asked for someone with a little authority," I said. "The operator said you had as little as anyone."

"I have a bit of information for you."

"Let's hear it."

"That nice family in the Norman Rockwell picture you sent is the Monreales. Grandpa Don Gianpoalo Monreale, Mama Gina, Papa Gianni, son John and daughter Catarina. The picture is better than our file photos. It's such a damn good picture that we're going to use it instead of the ones we have."

"I think it had been taken by a professional. Maybe I could sell it to you. Who are the Monreales?"

"Only one of the big five New York mob families," Julie replied. "They've pretty much moved out west now, Vegas and along the coast. Gambling casinos, hotels, maybe some prostitution in Nevada. It's legal there, in case you're interested in a career change that wouldn't require any adjustment of your morals. Back east they were into protection rackets, unions, drugs and murder."

"What are they doing out here, the same?"

379

"No, word is they are trying to go legit, or something close to it. The mob in general is moving out of Las Vegas, now that Hughes and the corporations are moving in. The Monreales seem intent to stay and develop the place."

"Is there any possibility that would work?"

"Probably not. Not with the trail of death and destruction they left in the east. The law never forgets."

"Can you elaborate on what they're doing out here?"

"At one time Gianpoalo Monreale had been hell on wheels, as tough a don as there was. He's pretty much out of the picture now, retired and mostly living in Scottsdale.

His son Gianni and Gianni's wife Gina are heading up an effort to expand hotel and casino operations in and around Las Vegas.

The younger guy in the picture, the "movie star," is Johnny Monreale, AKA Little Johnny. He wound down the eastern operations and is developing interests on the West Coast. Lives in Malibu. Keeps pretty much out of the spotlight. Rumors had it that while he was at Harvard, chip off the old block as he was, Little Johnny ran a porno film rental business."

The gorgeous young girl is Catarina. When I first saw the picture, I thought it was you, the two of you look so much alike. We're not sure what she's up to. Lives there in California, on a ranch in the Santa Ynez Valley. People end up dead when she's around. The previous occupant of a room she wanted when she was in college had been mysteriously killed in a hit and run and the driver never found. Her fiancé had been murdered, along with her uncle. There'd been a shootout on the New York Thruway that ended up with two bodies in a flaming wreck. Given that the deceased were gunsels we think Johnny or sweet little Catarina repelled an attempted hit. Two of the family's uncles "disappeared" at the same time."

"She sounds like a real fun person to know."

"Sounds like someone you and I could have a good time with."

I agreed. "Our kind of gal."

"I'll bring my rubber sheet, you get another couple of gallons of baby oil and we'll invite her over for a slumber party. Maybe listen to Frank Sinatra records while we braid each other's hair."

"Now that's an idea I could live with. Can you send me a copy of the dossier on the family? I'd very much like to find out how my brother happened to know them."

"Sure. And don't forget my offer of the rubber sheet if you make contact with her."

As soon as I put the phone back on its cradle it rang.

Detective Miller of L.A.P.D. Homicide, asking if he could arrange to meet with me regarding their investigation into my brother's death.

# Chapter Eighty Three

## Jim Miller

## March 1966

"Is your heart beating like a little girl's?" old Elliott asked from the passenger seat. I slide behind the wheel and fumbled with the keys. Yes, I had to admit, it was.

Poor old Elliott was running out of time. He slumped down in the seat, a little spittle dribbled from the side of his mouth. His eyes were red rimmed and opaque, and his chin rested on his chest. Even as repulsive as he was, I was still glad to have him along.

I'd really been afraid to go to the place where Miss Encino and her bikini dwelled, the place of Val Keller.

And, too, as I said before, I'd become fond of old Elliott, protective even. I warded off the jibes from the guys in the department and helped the poor sick old man any way I could.

The wisecracks had pretty much stopped now that the guys realized that the end was near for old Elliott the Bellyot.

He wasn't going to make it long enough to retire.

Elliott seemed to doze most of the way to Encino. Even when I pulled up in front of Keller's house, the old man didn't stir.

"I better wait in the car," he muttered almost inaudibly. "Tell her I'm standing by out here in case there's a call on the two-way."

I got out and shut the door, leaving the engine running. It was cooler today, but Elliott seemed more comfortable with the car's air conditioner on.

I walked to the gate and pushed the button under the intercom. From it came a voice, Val Keller's voice.

"Please come in."

Noiselessly, the wrought iron gate swung open.

Walking up to the front door I realized that just as old Elliott had teased, my heart was beating like a little girl's. I was as nervous as a kid on his first date with the prom queen.

As I neared the front door it opened and there she stood.

I knew that I was headed for trouble, that this was going to pick me up and carry me with it as if I were caught in a rip tide.

She represented the epitome of cool, languid poise. She wore a simple light blue cotton dress that fit her tight slender body like a second skin. It showed the muscles of her abdomen, the curve of her narrow hips, her nipples.

I knew I had never seen anyone that seductive, that outright desirable in all my life.

She turned and led me into the house.

I swallowed, trying not to betray my runaway nerves.

Following her, I made one last attempt at self control. As firmly and confidently as I could, I said, "Miss Keller, I'm here to bring you up to date on the investigation."

She turned and smiled. It was the smile of a woman who knows she has you.

The closed drapes almost completely blocked the bright sunlight, leaving the interior of the house dark, quiet, remote, as if nothing outside mattered, nothing could intrude on this place.

"Let me show you to the den," she suggested. "There may be something there that can help you with your investigation. Would you like a drink? Water or soft drink?"

"No, no thank you," I said. "I want to assure you that I've taken this case very seriously." And, in truth, I had.

I was truly afraid of where being alone with this woman would take me. At the same time, I was helpless to stop myself from finding out.

"I have to admit I really haven't got very far. I seem to be running out of leads," I said, surprised at my own candor. Usually we try to bullshit the survivors, tell them that we're really on top of things during an investigation and that we're close to a solution.

She led me past a spacious living room and down a short hall. Walking behind her and watching her long legs and tight ass gave me an erection.

"In here," she said, leading the way into the den. She motioned to the two leather swivel chairs.

"Please sit and be comfortable. As you can see from the monitors," she said, gesturing to the wall, "Gavin had some kind of a security system. It should have been difficult for anyone uninvited to access the house."

I thought this was something that could've been important for us to know. Could there be anything else that might shed light on what happened here the night Gavin Keller died?

In the center of the room was a table and a big leather chair and behind that, a roll-top desk. She eased herself into the big chair and leaned back.

Outside, a small garden and a statue were bathed in sunlight, but the partially closed drapes muted the glare. The dark brown carpet, the tan suede wall covering, and the dark browns of the desk and leather chairs made the den feel like a grotto, cool and quiet and safe.

It occurred to me how badly I wanted to leap over the desk and mount her right there in that chair. From the half grin on her face and the way her eyes narrowed slightly, it was as if she read my mind.

"Your brother had a wide circle of acquaintances but few friends," I began. "In fact, none of the people I've talked to so far could be called close friends. I detected animosity, jealousy among his co-workers. And none of them knew anything about your brother's home or social life."

"Do you think any of them could have killed him?"

"I don't know for certain. There's big money involved in the field he was in. That could provide motive enough in some circles. But usually white-collar types don't kill for money or power. They will kill for love, but it would probably take a lot of money to get one to commit murder."

I took a quick look around the den and thought how great it would be to have a place like this. "Have you come across anything around here that might give us a clue?"

Val paused for a long moment. "It's hard for me to say, not being a homicide detective and all. I don't know what it would take to motivate someone to kill."

"Did your brother ever mention anything that might hint he thought he could be in danger? Any enemies?"

"My brother and I had been very close, but in recent years we really didn't talk that much. My job involves a lot of travel, and we just hadn't had an opportunity to keep up with one another."

I twisted in my seat to look at the monitors built into the wall behind me. "What do these things do, exactly?"

"I don't know. He was a big shot at Greater Energy, and their electronics division had developed some new toy or other. I think those things were experimental models of some sort, tape recorders or something they installed to let him test in the field or to play with."

"Have you come across anything that might lead you to believe he could have been a victim of foul play?"

"Well, since I have to settle up his affairs I have been going through his papers. My first priority is to see that his bills are current, that the house is maintained, that sort of thing. Settling up someone's affairs is new to me. I have noticed that his personal address book and Rolodex were practically empty, and there's been a complete absence of phone calls or visitors looking for him or wondering what happened to him. I suppose that supports your theory that he had few friends who really cared about him."

"You haven't found any correspondence or something like a threatening note or anything?"

"No, no I haven't. All the stuff I've gone through is business related or has to do with his personal finances. So far, I haven't seen anything, any correspondence of a personal nature."

"Do you find that odd?" I asked, wondering if I might be pushing the issue.

"I wouldn't know. For my own part, I don't clutter my life with old personal correspondence. If I get a letter from someone, a friend or whatever, unless it should be retained for financial recordkeeping purposes, I just read it and throw it away. I don't keep it. I assume Gavin did the same thing."

I swiveled the chair around and looked at the group of pictures on the wall next to the monitors. "I've noticed that other than these displayed here, your late brother did not have photographs scattered around the house."

"I've noticed that too," Val replied. "I haven't come across any photo albums, and as you say there aren't any pictures in the living room or his bedroom or anywhere else other than the paintings. Those, by the way, are semi valuable and look to me they were chosen mostly for decoration."

"What can you tell me about these?" I asked, looking up at the photographs.

She got up from the big chair and came around the desk to stand next to me in front of the pictures. Her nearness was extremely disturbing. I didn't know whether to get to my feet to stand beside her or to remain seated.

A very good reason to remain seated was beginning to present itself.

"Some of these I can readily identify," she said, looking at the framed photographs. "This one, of course, is of our family; my parents, Gavin and I on a vacation trip, taken probably 15 years ago. The one next to it had been taken when we were kids and lived on Beach Street in Torrance."

I took a chance and got up to stand next to her while she pointed out the pictures. Her nearness was really getting to me. I could not get past the thought that underneath her thin cotton dress she was naked.

I'm maybe four or five inches taller than her. When she turned to look up at me her lips parted slightly. I felt like I was falling, falling into her eyes, her mouth.

This was the moment it could go either way, and she apparently sensed it. With a little amused look, she returned her attention to explaining the photographs.

"My guess is that this picture was taken at some company function," she said, indicating a photo of a group of men and women in casual clothes. "Perhaps you recognize some of them from your having interviewed his co-workers?"

I stepped closer to take a better look. "I think you're right. One or two of them do look familiar. What about this one?" I asked, indicating a picture of a family, an older gentleman, a very attractive couple and Val standing next to a very good-looking young man. Or maybe it wasn't Val, but it was a beautiful young woman that looked an awfully lot like her.

"So far as I know that's a picture of his Harvard roommate's family. It looks like he joined them on a vacation to Bermuda back when he was in school. I believe the picture had been taken maybe five or six years ago in the lobby of the Hamilton Princess Hotel."

I looked more closely at the picture then back at Val. "I would have almost sworn that was you."

"No, I wasn't there, but I agree the resemblance is remarkable. No, I don't know these people at all."

386

It seemed to me that I wasn't getting anywhere today. Then I remembered poor old Elliott waiting out in the car.

"We'll continue questioning his coworkers and following any leads they might give us. As you go through his things, I hope you'll call me if you find anything that might be helpful," I said, again turning to face her.

For a moment she seemed preoccupied, lost in thought looking at the big tape recorders. With a start, she looked up and smiled.

"You can count on it, detective. I still have quite a bit of Gavin's stuff to go through. If I find anything, I'll let you know. Here, let me show you out."

I wondered if it had been me that triggered the almost abrupt conclusion of this meeting or was she suddenly anxious to get me out of the house. I had the feeling that up until now she'd been toying with me.

In fact, when I thought about it, I was sure she'd been toying with me from the moment she first saw me weeks ago, when she opened the gate for me and Elliott. She probably thought I'd be just something she could play with or use any way she wanted to.

I'm afraid she'd be right.

# Chapter Eighty Four

## Val Keller

## March 1966

Julie Rodriguez had called back and left a message to return her call.

When she answered, I said in French "I am calling you about the small child you left behind with us here in Aix-En-Provence. He seems to have a virulent case of crabs that can only be hereditary."

"You have the wrong extension," she replied in that ever-so-helpful tone of hers. "Let me transfer you to that skanky Valerie Keller. That's "K-e-l-l-e-r. She may be getting her shots and not at her desk so leave a message."

"What's new?"

"I checked up further on your brother's life while he was at Harvard and I also expanded on the Monreale connection. I hope you don't mind the invasion of his privacy."

"I think we're past that point," I answered. "I'm fairly sure he was murdered."

"He may well have been, given the company he kept. As I told you before, his roommate for most of the time he'd been at school was Johnny Monreale, AKA Little Johnny. Back then, the Monreales lived in a compound in Utica along with Grandpa. A couple of other family members had homes there, too. Gianni Monreale also had an apartment in Manhattan. According to the NYPD, one night your brother and Little Johnny went down to the city to rip it up and someone tried to whack a Monreale. Probably mistook Johnny for his father. Your brother saved the kid's life, or at least had a major hand in it.

The Monreales seemed to have been very grateful. Our agents first spotted your brother with them there, and then at the Monreale place in Utica. He also accompanied them on vacations from time to time.

"Did you come across anything that might hint at Gavin being killed because of his association with the Monreales?"

"Not directly. But they'd been and so far as we know still are a murderous bunch. How far do you think I should go with this?"

"I hope I can ask you to see it all the way through, until you turn something up or the stories and leads dry up altogether. It doesn't sound like you're at the end of the trail yet. And you may come across something the Bureau can use in pursuing the Monreales."

"I have to agree with you there. In this time frame, Catarina's uncle, her fiancé, the fiancé's father and his man, one Antonio Urbanus got knocked off. We never got a satisfactory explanation as to who did all that or why. Informants do tell us though that the Monreale's had been behind it."

After she hung up, I went over my meeting with Detective Miller. The poor guy really didn't know shit, hadn't turned up much of anything except a whole bunch of people who didn't do it.

But it did give another dimension to my late brother Gavin. Just as I'd surmised during the reading of the will in the attorney's office, he'd been a lone operator that trusted no one, ambitious and ruthless.

For now, I was pretty sure I shouldn't share much of anything with Detective Miller. There could be too many things that might be awkward to explain.

I certainly didn't want Miller or anyone else to find out about that box of cash hidden behind the roll top desk.

Would it be helpful to the murder investigation to let Officer Miller see one of the films? I had no idea who the other participants were. One or more of them could be suspects. Maybe he'd recognize one of them. I was well aware of the effect I had on handsome Jim Miller. I knew watching a porno movie together would quickly progress to sex, not that I was necessarily against that.

Gavin's face not showing in any of the films I'd seen so far could not have been an accident. I was pretty sure he'd been the instigator behind their production and distribution. Tommy Huber said Gavin put them both in the porn business, so when Julie mentioned Johnny Monreale having distributed porn during the time he and Gavin were roommates I immediately made the connection.

Gavin was likely responsible for Little Johnny's getting into the porn business, so it was probably he that had corrupted the Mafia don's grandson.

I had to include Johnny Monreale in my list of people to investigate, but I wouldn't be using the same technique that I used on Tommy Huber.

No, I'd better do a whole lot of research and preparation before I took on the Monreales.

# Chapter Eighty Five

## Jim Miller

## April 1966

Old Elliott said I was like a man lost in a house of mirrors. Everywhere I looked, there I was.

When I got back in the car after my meeting with Val Keller, poor old Elliott turned and gave me a little grin. His all but opaque eyes seemed to almost twinkle a little.

"You weren't in there long enough to have done much other than official business."

"I'm stuck," I responded, "but I still have my honor."

"That is a shame, on both counts," the old cop said. "She's about to pick you up and ride your ass right off. That's what you're afraid of, isn't it? That and the fact you have no case. It must appear to you that I did the right thing when I left the victim's death as "suspicious circumstances." You're beginning to think I might as well have called it accidental even then. You haven't found any evidence of foul play, have you?"

We were still parked in the idling car in front of the Keller house. Elliott's analysis of the situation was the most he had spoken at one time in weeks.

I turned to him. His face showed the effort had taken a lot out of the old cop, worn him out.

I looked back out the windshield.

The picture windows of the expensive homes lining the street looked like sentinels staring unblinking out on the valley below.

"In your later years you have developed an uncanny ability to dissect the situation and present the results clearly and succinctly. Perhaps you would be so kind as to confirm once and for all that at this point in time it is your conclusion Gavin Keller's death had been a self-inflicted accident?"

"No, son, after seeing the circumstances and some of the players from a fresh perspective, and upon further reflection of the results of your inquiries among his co-workers and his conspicuous lack of friends, I'm afraid someone murdered Mr. Keller. Can you run me on home now? I'm tired and I declare my shift to be over for the day. You can sign me out when you get back to the station."

# Chapter Eighty Six

## Tom Larson

## April 29th, 1966

Retirement was not far off for Tom Larson. He'd been a policeman on the force in Torrance since the end of World War Two, Twenty years. Starting as a motorcycle officer and when he got too old to ride the bike, in a patrol car.

In less than five years he'd be 60. He hoped he could go on as he had, spending time with Millie, holidays with her and Marcia.

He hoped nothing would change.

Nothing had changed, not even with Marcia, at least on the surface. But every so often he thought he saw something in her eyes when she looked his way. He wondered if it was because of what he'd told her that night about her high school boyfriend, Gavin Keller, and the attack on her poor little brother Timothy. The only reason he'd told her had been because he hoped she'd be able to shed some light on the subject, say something one way or the other about Keller that supported or rejected his theory.

She didn't.

She didn't even rise to Keller's defense. Now he was sorry that he'd said anything. Other than Marcia, the only people in the world that knew were Doctor Beeman and Tony Giuliani.

This evening Marcia entertained them with gossip about the movie business. As usual she seemed to have an inexhaustible supply of insider stories.

"My agent, Turnip Green's birthday party is coming up and I'm going," she told them. "I never, never go to these things, but he means so much to me I'm going to make an exception. It's a costume party with a 1920's theme. I'm hoping you still have that old flapper hat, that lavender cloche you had in your closet when we lived on Beach Street."

Her mother said she did. She rose from the sofa and went to her bedroom in the back of the trailer, returning shortly carrying a hat box.

Laughing, Marcia took the box. "Turnip Green isn't really his name you know," she said, going to the mirror near the door.

She tried on the cloche. "It's Tevye Greenberg. No one knows how old he really is," she laughed, delighted with her image in the mirror, "but the story is, he was the agent that rounded up all the extras for the Sermon on the Mount. Not the movie, the actual event."

# Chapter Eighty Seven

## Catarina Monreale

## April 29th, 1966

The folks in Chicago had come through for her. They'd compromised some sap insurance executive, tricking him into a gambling debt he wouldn't be able to handle. The phony automobile insurance scam Catarina had created using his influence was going like gangbusters. It would be months before anyone realized that the claims weren't going to get paid.

In the meantime, she would pull out so much money it would be obscene.

Now it was payback time, time for her to drop down to L.A. for the Frank Greco job.

The Hollywood trade magazines had been going on and on about a big costume party that was coming up, a birthday party with a Roaring Twenties theme. Everybody that was anybody would be expected to attend. Greco's appetite for hanging out with celebrities, plus the fascination celebrities had for "dangerous" characters practically assured he'd be there. To get an invitation, Catarina had used her parents' connection with a big shot singer who was regularly booked at their Vegas hotel.

Her plan would be to take Greco out by placing a device in his car while he attended the party. The device would be triggered remotely by the controller for an electric garage door opener. It would be simple enough for her to make.

She figured on leaving the party at the same time Greco did. She'd follow him, staying within the remote controller's range. At the right time, probably as he pulled into his own driveway, she'd push the button on the controller, sending a signal to the device. The receiver for the garage door opener would close a circuit, creating a spark and igniting three sticks of dynamite. The whole package weighed just three pounds and fit easily into a medium size handbag. She planned to carry the handbag in the big, beaded purse that went with the beaded flapper dress she'd picked up at the yard sale in Buellton. A magnet would hold the handbag to Frank Greco's car, inside the rear wheel well near the gas tank.

# Chapter Eighty Eight

## Val Keller

## April 30<sup>th</sup>, 1966

In view of the porn thing and the Monreales penchant for murder, I concluded I needed to get to Little Johnny somehow, especially since he and Gavin had been roommates at school. According to Detective Miller, Gavin wasn't liked by anyone that knew him very well.

How to have a talk with the Monreale's would be the problem. A problem that is, until Julie Rodriguez called with the answer.

"I'm taking a survey on the employment prospects for overly tall ex- call girls with complexion problems," she said when I answered the phone.

"I've got your prospects right here," I replied, "By the way, I'm not overly tall and since I stopped hanging around with you my complexions cleared up."

"I may have a break for you. One of our informants in Las Vegas told us the Monreales went to a lot of trouble to get an invitation to a big Hollywood party."

"Now that IS interesting," I said.

"It's a costume party with a 1920's theme. The invitation is in the name of Francesca Armerina, but we think it's for the daughter, Catarina. If you want to go, we may be able to get an invitation for you, too."

"That would be terrific. If it is for Catarina, I'll work my womanly wiles on her and get her to lead me to her brother."

"You know hearing you threaten to use your womanly wiles turns me on, don't you?"

"Oh yes. That's why I do it."

"You're such a slut. I'll get the invitation couriered to you by Military Air Transport today. You should have it by late afternoon; earlier, if you want to drop down to the base at L.A. International and pick it up."

"That's what I think I'll do. I'll drive down there on my way to the party. I assume it's in Beverly Hills."

"How the hell should I know? What am I, your social secretary? Next, you'll want me to dress you and drive you to it, Little Miss Socialite. I'm sure the address will be on the invitation."

"Thanks. Your heroic efforts will be rewarded in a way that will cause you to be sore in a place only a gynecologist would ever see."

"There you go again, turning me on."

I hung up and left for Hollywood. I had just enough time to swing by Western Costume on Melrose and rent a flapper outfit. Then off to LAX to pick up the invitation from M.A.T.

# Chapter Eighty Nine

## Catarina Monreale

## April 30th, 1966

Lupe, a look of satisfaction on her face, had stepped back to examine her work. She'd fidgeted with her needle and thread, made little adjustments to the beaded flapper dress and the feathered headband.

She finally left the room and Catarina was finally able to remove the dress and placed it along with the headband and beaded purse in a suitcase. Then she put on traveling clothes, slacks and a sweater. She'd already called a rental agency and reserved a Cadillac to be picked up at LAX. She'd wait to change into the flapper outfit when she got to West Hollywood.

Then she'd head for the party in Beverly Hills.

She left the ranch just after 6:00 p.m. She wanted to allow plenty of time for the drive over the San Marcos Pass and the traffic on Pacific Coast Highway in Santa Barbara. When she got to LAX, she'd leave the ranch's station wagon in short term parking, pick up the rental and go on to one of the restaurants on Melrose to change.

No one on Melrose would pay much attention to a woman in a flapper dress.

No one on Melrose would pay much attention to Gandhi riding an elephant down the middle of the sidewalk.

She planned to arrive at the party a little early, 9:30 or 10:00, and wait in the car where she could watch the arriving guests. She was certain Greco would be there, star struck as he was.

# Chapter Ninety

## Marcia Schmitt

## April 30<sup>th</sup>, 1966

## Turnip Green's Birthday Party

Marcia was restless, sitting in the chair in front of the mirror in the suite's dressing room. She felt guilty that she was keeping Jeffrey waiting downstairs in the limo.

Marcia hated to keep anyone waiting.

But the makeup girl, the hairdresser and the wardrobe guy fiddled around until after 9:00 o'clock, finishing her hair and arranging the piece d' resistance, her mother's lavender cloche.

Her arrival at the party had been carefully orchestrated by Green and the studio for maximum effect. Her rare public appearance would be one of the evening's major attractions.

She'd been to the Green's home many times, a lovely three-story mansion set on four acres in a neighborhood of similar homes on a street north of Sunset Boulevard.

She arrived as scheduled, just before 10:00 p.m. Her grand entrance amid the flashbulbs of the paparazzo's cameras went as planned. Gorgeous, untouchable but humble, the big star, Marcia Schmitt, gracefully made her way up the steps to embrace her mentor and agent, Turnip Green. With her hand on his arm, he escorted her to the veranda and on outside to the crowd of partygoers around the large patio near the pool.

A hush fell as all eyes turned to watch her descend the steps to the party.

She maintained her stately dignity.

Her heart, however, actually pounded with excitement. The fact was, she really loved all this adulation. She had to work hard to act this dignified, this aloof or else she'd start to giggle.

She mingled and the conversations among the other guests resumed.

The grounds had been strung with lights and there were propane heaters scattered here and there to ward off the cool night air.

Everyone, including the army of servants with trays of cocktails and hors d'oervres, had dressed in the style of the 1920's.

A photographer moved among the guests taking pictures.

Near one of the bars, the two hams (her co-stars in the comedy she was to appear in) had dressed in red and white candy-striped blazers and straw boaters. They'd gathered an audience with their wisecracking and carrying on. Thankfully they either hadn't spotted her or else they didn't want to share the spotlight. This helped to take the pressure off Marcia as the center of attention. She was able to maneuver her way toward the pool area and avoid getting caught up in their performance.

They were an odd couple, the two old hams. Close personal friends, they'd co-starred together in a bevy of comedies. One was a very nice guy, but the other had been acknowledged as being the biggest asshole in Hollywood.

# Chapter Ninety One

## Catarina Monreale

## April 30th, 1966

## Turnip Green's Birthday Party

Catarina Monreale got stuck in traffic on Robertson and didn't arrive in the neighborhood until after 10:00 p.m. She parked half a block away after reaching the party house and waited. Within a few minutes Greco showed up in his Lincoln Continental. Catarina watched him get out of the car and throw his keys to the valet.

She started her rented Cadillac and waited. The valet drove Greco's car almost to the end of the block and parked it at the curb in front of a line of cars belonging to other partygoers.

When she saw the valet coming back down the sidewalk, she put the rental in gear and headed down the tree lined street.

Away from the party house, it was dark and quiet. There was no one out other than the valets jogging back to the Green's driveway to attend to arriving guest's cars.

She parked around the corner. Although it had been warm during the day, by this time the evening had cooled. Dew had settled on the grass and on the cars parked along the curb.

Approaching Greco's car, she pretended to accidently drop her beaded purse on the grass. As she bent to pick it up, she slipped the smaller handbag out and with a smooth movement stuffed it past the tire and up against the inside of the car's rear fender.

She checked to be certain the magnet held it firmly.

She straightened up, turned and walked on down the street to merge with a group of other arriving guests attending the party.

Her intentions to be as inconspicuous as possible began to go wrong as soon as she entered the big house. A dapper little man ignored the others in the group she'd temporarily attached herself to and turned his attention to her.

"My child, I am Turnip Green, your gracious host," he said with a little bow. Then, turning to the matronly woman standing next to him he said, "This is my wife, Sophia. Sophia, will you look at this beautiful young woman? And that dress. It is perfect for you. You are extraordinarily beautiful. Are you represented?"

"Why thank you sir, but no I am not."

"Now Tevye, it's your birthday and she is our guest. Surely you are not working at your own birthday party. Leave the young lady to enjoy herself," chided Mrs. Green.

"Well, at least let me have your name, my dear, and let me give you my card. I very much want to explore with you a career in motion pictures. Have you ever considered such a thing? Of course, you have. This is Hollywood. Everyone here has."

"I'm a recent transplant to the coast, so I'm new to Hollywood. I had not thought about a career as an actress. My name is Francesca Armerina and I'm pleased to meet you both."

"Francesca Armerina? What an intriguing name. We wouldn't even have to change it."

Mrs. Green interceded. "Let me introduce you to our guest of honor before my husband gets any more excited," she said. "Do you know Marcia Schmitt?"

"No, I do not, but I would love to meet her."

"Well then, come along, Francesca. I think I saw Marcia on the patio, near the pool. Coincidently my sister's name is Francesca. Such a pretty name, but unfortunately not that popular nowadays."

That means I'm going to have to ditch this I.D., Catarina thought. When they start interviewing party guests after Greco's murder, the name Francesca Armerina is going to stand out.

# Chapter Ninety Two

## Val Keller

## April 30th, 1966

## Turnip Green's Birthday Party

I arrived at Turnip Greens party just in time to see an older woman leaving the foyer with what from the back looked like a very attractive young lady in a beaded flapper dress.

A distinguished looking little gentleman who, I assumed, was Turnip Green himself greeted the guests. His head was turned, watching the older woman escorting the young lady down the steps to the garden. When he looked back and saw me his eyes lit up.

"Good evening," he said, extending his hand. "I'm Turnip Green, the birthday boy, and I am your host. May I have the pleasure of escorting you around and introducing you to our guests? I would be honored to have someone as beautiful as you on my arm. It will rankle the other agents here when they see that I have landed yet another great beauty. Are you in the industry? I don't see how I could have missed you if you are."

"Why thank you very much," I replied, holding out my hand. "Valarie Keller."

"Let me introduce you to Marcia Schmitt. THE Marcia Schmitt. She's one of my clients, you know."

"I would be thrilled to meet Marcia Schmitt," I answered, thinking what I really wanted was to meet someone named Monreale.

But I knew there wasn't anyone here who would answer to that name.

No, the person I was looking for tonight would be calling herself Francesca Armerina.

# Chapter Ninety Three

**Marcia Schmitt**

**April 30<sup>th</sup>, 1966**

**Turnip Green's Birthday Party**

The small orchestra stationed in the gazebo on the other side of the pool launched into a very loud Charleston, so Marcia moved away to stand near one of the radiant heaters.

A handful of people, young actors, actresses and a would-be producer with a beard and dirty looking hair had gathered around her. They all chattered away excitedly talking about themselves. In an hour or less one or more of them would start drinking if he or she hadn't already. He or she would say or do something embarrassing, then there'd be the obligatory starlet falling into the pool.

So self absorbed was the group surrounding her that they were the only ones still talking when a hush fell over the rest of the party. Turnip's wife Sophia was making her way through the crowd escorting an especially stunning young woman in a beaded flapper dress. The woman looked to be around Marcia's age, mid twenties or so with brown hair, brown eyes, beautiful face and body.

"Marcia dear, I especially want you to meet this young lady. Her name is Francesca, Francesca Armerina, and she says she doesn't want to be in the movies," Mrs. Green said smiling.

"I must say I'm relieved to hear that," Marcia said extending her hand. "I don't need the competition."

"I hardly think I could compete with you, Miss Schmitt," the young lady said smiling.

"That's a relief. What do you do, Francesca?"

"I dabble in insurance industry related investments."

Despite hearing that Francesca was involved in insurance, a subject Marcia always found unutterably boring, she was fascinated by this young woman. There was something about her, her look or poise or a combination of all that and more. She was genuinely interested in this extraordinary beauty.

Turnip approached with yet another stunning young lady in tow.

"I hate to interrupt but given the unprecedented opportunity to bring together three of the loveliest women in the world, I must do so. It is, after all, my birthday. If I can just see the three of you together, the three most beautiful women I have ever seen in all my years, it will be the pinnacle of my lifelong search for perfection."

The latest arrival to the group extended her hand. "Val Keller, Miss Schmitt. I'm a big fan. The charming Mr. Green certainly has a way with words."

Marcia hid her surprise when she heard the name Keller. My god, who the hell is this, Gavin's sister, Val, Val Keller from Beach Street in Torrance?

# Chapter Ninety Four

## Catarina Monreale

## April 30th, 1966

## Turnip Green's Birthday Party

So far, so good, Catarina thought. She'd spotted Greco. It would be easy to keep an eye on him. Fittingly enough, he wore a 1920's gangster style pin-striped suit and a bowler hat.

She felt she carried herself well in this group. She'd even met a famous movie star with whom she was having a conversation.

Wait until she told Johnny and the rest of the family about this.

Then Mr. Green, accompanied by a gorgeous woman appeared at her side.

The woman introduced herself as Valerie Keller.

Valerie Keller?

Keller?

Keller wasn't that common a name, and the girl's coloring and features were very reminiscent of a Keller she knew, or at least had known.

Looking open mouthed from her to Val Keller, the others in the group fell silent. It could have been an awkward moment if it weren't for Marcia Schmitt.

"You two could be sisters, you look so much alike."

# Chapter Ninety Five

## Val Keller

### April 30<sup>th</sup>, 1966

### Turnip Green's Birthday Party

There was no mistaking Marcia Schmitt. Movie stars are different, I guess.

This one anyway.

She seemed to give off a light of her own, glow in the dark like some kind of mystical being, a goddess. She smiled and extended her hand. I took it in mine.

It felt cool but firm.

I held it maybe just a second longer than I should have.

Our eyes locked.

I felt the presence of the lovely young woman in the beaded dress standing beside me, the girl/woman Marcia Schmitt had been talking to.

For just a moment, there was no one else in the world, just the three of us.

Turnip Green was saying something, something about beautiful women, Marcia Schmitt not needing an introduction and then "…and this young lady is "Francesca Armerina."

I took my eyes off Marcia Schmitt and turned.

There she stood, the murderous Catarina Monreale.

Amused, her eyes twinkled. There's no question that Catarina in person was even more impressive than in the photograph. She could be best described as like a beautiful predatory animal, a panther, sleek, firm, exuding sensuality.

Christ, I wonder if Gavin knew her, and if he did, had he been able to keep his hands off of her.

I was pretty sure I couldn't, given half a chance.

A tall, distinguished looking gentleman approached. He caught Marcia's eye and she looked at her watch. "I have to tell you two I really would like the chance to get to know you, spend more time with you both. Right now, there's a special birthday presentation for Turnip. I'm supposed to say a few words and give him a present. Can we set up a lunch date, just the three of us? Perhaps for the day after tomorrow?"

"You can count me in," I replied.

"That sounds like fun," Catarina agreed.

"How about Thursday noon, the Sand Castle in Malibu?" Marcia suggested over her shoulder as the man started to escort her toward the upper deck.

"It's a deal," Catarina said.

"Thursday it is," I added.

This could be the opportunity I'd waited for, an opportunity to be alone with Catarina.

But the band launched into a loud fanfare and the party guests gathered around to hear Marcia give the guest of honor a birthday tribute.

In the confusion, Catarina and I became separated, and I never saw her again that night.

Thankfully I had a chance to pick up where we left off when we meet for lunch on Thursday.

⁂

The next morning, I was up and awake at 7:30, fixing an orange juice and raw egg drink when the phone rang.

It had to be Julie Rodriguez. Who else would call at this hour?

"I'm looking at a picture of you in Stars and Stripes. You're wearing a T-shirt that says, "Almost a Virgin," Julie said.

"It's an old T-shirt."

"What the hell happened last night?"

"Thanks to you, I went to the party and met up with Catarina Monreale, my bourgeois capitalist lackey."

"Well, I understand it was a major blow out, at least for Frank Greco."

"What happened? Who's Frank Greco? I left around 11:30. I'd been talking to my new buddies, Marcia Schmitt, that's THE Marcia Schmitt and 'Francesca Armerina' as Catarina called herself. Girl talk. You wouldn't understand."

"Girl talk you say? I'll make a note and check that out."

"Why are you calling so early?  Who or what is this about Frank Greco?"

"What do you think?  If Catarina's around someone's likely to get killed. Mr. Frank Greco is, or was an underworld character, a front man for a Chicago mob with interests in Las Vegas. He left the party just after midnight. He didn't get lucky, so he left alone, drove through Hollywood toward Nichols Canyon where he lives." She corrected herself. "Or lived, that is. He got about halfway up the canyon to his house, and on a deserted stretch of the road his Lincoln Continental exploded, killing him instantly and very thoroughly."

"Sounds like a contract hit."

"Sounds like a contract hit, you say? I'll make a note and check that out, too. Yes, it was most definitely a hit, and probably by contract.

"Beautiful Catarina Monreale is not someone to be taken lightly," I said, "In more ways than one."

"Better fill me in. I'm going to put all this in the Monreale file, you know. I have to."

"She is beyond beautiful. She's smart and quick. She has a husky, throaty voice and a way of projecting sexuality. I get the impression that there isn't anything she wouldn't be capable of."

"She's like you, then."

"I don't know how to respond to that."

"I find that hard to believe. You've known how to respond to everything else that's come your way.

And I mean that both figuratively and literally."

"Look who's talking. If you had as many sticking out of you as you've had sticking in you, you'd look like a porcupine. Anyway, I'm having lunch with her and Marcia Schmitt, that's THE Marcia Schmitt, at Thursday noon, at the Sand Castle in Malibu.  If the Bureau's looking for a chance to wire Catarina's car or wants to listen in, this may it."

"I'll pass it on. I'm sure we'll take you up on that."

After we hung up it occurred to me to try to figure out what the tape recorders in the den had to do with the monitors. What with all the house's other devices and toys, I'd put off checking into them for far too long.

# Chapter Ninety Six

## Jim Miller

## Sunday, May 1$^{st}$, 1966

Las Vegas Entrepreneur and investor Frank Greco had been murdered as he drove home from a party in Beverly Hills.

Sergeant Maurice Elliot and I were assigned to the case.

We arrived at the scene early the day after the crime. The Los Angeles County Coroner's office had removed what remains they could find. Positive identification was impossible pending FBI fingerprint analysis. Most of what could be found of the vehicle was in the County impound lot being checked by the forensics team. They thought it had been a Lincoln.

"The coroner's office says a bomb had been placed somewhere near the gas tank in the rear of the vehicle, probably in the trunk or the rear wheel well," Elliott said, reading from the report prepared by the responding officers the night before. "Professional job. Must have been a hell of an explosion."

"There's a crater in the pavement," I added, "the guard rail's gone, and the weeds along the road are burned. Whoever did it wasn't taking any chances that the victim might survive."

I left Elliott in the car and walked to the edge of the ravine where the guard rail had been.

"There's some wreckage down there, too" I yelled back to him. "Think the coroner will come back for it?"

"Naw. The guy was a gangster, and this was a mob hit done by a pro. Nobody much cares, as long as no civilians got injured or killed."

"Think I'll climb down there and see if I can find anything," I yelled back.

I found a place where the drop off wasn't so steep and started down the 35 feet or so. Covered mostly with dusty knee-high weeds, it was much hotter at the bottom of the ravine. In addition to anything that might have to do with what happened last night, I'd better keep an eye out for snakes.

The rear tire and wheel assembly along with the axle had buried itself in the slope twenty or so feet to my left. Hanging from the brush were pieces of cloth and leather, probably the car's upholstery. Some of it had red on it. The victim probably stopped at McDonalds for fries and that was just catsup. At least that's what I wanted to believe, that all that red stuff was catsup.

I spotted a white 3X5 card stuck in a tumble weed and put on my gloves to pick get it.

It was an invitation to the party the victim had attended the night before. Great keepsake.

Something else lay in the dirt under the tumble weed.

A photograph.

I bent forward to take a closer look, then carefully snaked my gloved hand through the stickers and gently lifted it free.

It had been taken at a party, probably the one referred to in the invitation. I had no idea what the victim had looked like, but the picture showed a man in his mid forties or so, maybe 5'11" or 6 feet. He wore a pinstripe suit and a bowler or derby hat. He stood near a swimming pool, smiling at the camera and talking to another, older gentleman. In the background, the movie star Marcia Schmitt stood talking to two other beautiful young women. They both looked an awful lot like Val Keller. One in particular looked just like Val Keller.

In fact, I was pretty sure it was Val Keller.

I looked around a little more. Bits and pieces scattered over a wide area, scraps of the car's body and interior mostly. I really didn't think there'd be anything else down here that would lead to solving the crime.

I decided that rather than stomp around and risk destroying evidence, I'd go on back to the car and radio forensics for a team to go over the whole area with a fine-tooth comb.

As I started to climb back up the bank, I saw a bowler hat in the brush a little way off to my left. I pushed the weeds aside and bent to pick it up.

Under the hat was the head of the man in the photograph.

He wasn't smiling now.

I put the hat back on his head and climbed on up the bank.

Old Elliott was already on the two-way. "I don't think we're doing a very thorough job out here, you guys," he was saying. "There may be more at the bottom of the ravine. Better send a forensic team out to go over the whole area."

"Christ," I thought. "We've gotten to know each other so well we've started to think alike."

"Well, what'd you find, sport?" Elliott asked, trying to inject vitality into his quavering voice.

"An invitation to the party last night," I told him, handing him the 3X5 card. "And this," I said, holding up the 8X10 glossy. "That's him in the picture, the one smiling. His head's down there in the ravine, under that bowler hat he's wearing there in the picture."

"Gee," old Elliott said wiping his mouth with the back of his hand. "A pretty picture of some pretty people."

"Yep," I said, reaching for the car keys. "Look at the people in the background."

Elliott rubbed his eyes and put on his glasses, then held the photo as far away from his face as his arms could reach. "Hollywood party, eh?"

"Don't you think the brunette on the right, the one talking to Marcia Schmitt, looks like our friend Val Keller from Encino?"

"Oh yeah," Elliott replied. "I spotted that right away. I just wasn't going to say anything, for your benefit."

"I think I'm becoming so desperate for a break on the Gavin Keller case that I'm reading clues into every little thing, even this photo taken at a Hollywood party. The Greco killing is clearly a mob hit and couldn't possibly have had anything to do with Keller."

Elliott looked out the window on his side of the car. The steep hill went almost straight up. It was scorched clear to the top from the blast the night before.

"I understand your frustration. I wouldn't suggest this if I didn't, but perhaps you should consider trying to get some assistance from the Feds."

"What can they contribute?"

"I don't know at this point. Let's drop the photo off with them as if you were offering possible evidence that they might find useful to their Organized Crime Unit. Ask them as a matter of course if they can provide you with I.D.s for everyone in the picture, including the party guests in the background."

"Check. I'll go by the house too. We can ask the host if we can have a copy of the guest list. Might as well. We've nothing to lose."

411

# Chapter Ninety Seven

## Catarina Monreale

## May 1ˢᵗ, 1966

The California legislature, in its infinite wisdom, mandated that all California drivers have automobile liability insurance. This law had been passed without regard for the fact that many were such lousy drivers they couldn't afford the premiums legitimate insurers would need to charge to make them an acceptable risk.

Catarina's answer had been simple.

Create an insurer and charge a premium low enough to attract a multitude of drivers, good and bad alike.

Catarina knew from her short internship at First Boston Insurance Company that legitimate insurance companies would not compete for that business. This meant she had that whole class of potential customers to herself. Of course, the premiums charged would not be enough to cover the losses, but she had no intention of paying claims anyway.

During that internship she'd also learned there would be a considerable lag between the time when a claim occurs and when it's turned in to the insurance company. There'd also be a huge lag in the time before a claim is actually paid by the insurer.

This delay between the time a premium is actually collected, and a claim is actually expected to be paid is typically at least a year and a half. Often it can even be much longer than that.

Catarina's policies were being sold through a multitude of retail insurance agents throughout the state. She had been able to jump into the market and capture it quickly. Within the first eight months her agents had produced over $189,000,000 in premiums.

She had to pay commissions to these retail insurance agents. There were various other costs also, such as advertising and policy printing. But by May of 1966 she'd channeled the bulk of the money, over $110,000,000 into accounts she'd set up in the Cayman Islands and the Turks and Caicos.

And she was invisible. The whole thing had been fronted and seemed from all appearances to be masterminded by two characters in San Francisco, two characters that the pigeon, the hapless gambler her friends in Chicago furnished.

# Chapter Ninety Eight

## Val Keller

## Sunday, May 1st, 1966

I really looked forward to my lunch at the Sand Castle with Marcia Schmitt and Catarina Monreale. I couldn't help but wonder how Catarina would continue her "Francesca Armerina" charade. Sooner or later an amateur would screw up. But I had no doubt Catarina Monreale could keep that act going to her grave if she had to. She's a pro, no question about it.

Well, it should be fun.

Today I'd take my time and try to figure out what the tape recorders in Gavin's den had to do with the monitors.

The recorders looked just like the ones sold in electronic stores, except they were somewhat larger. When I took a closer look, I could see the tape in the machines was much wider. I found a lever on the machine connected to the monitor that showed the street in front of the house and turned it to the rewind position.

The picture on the monitor immediately turned to snow and lines. I was afraid perhaps I'd screwed something up, so I quickly turned it back to the neutral position. Again, the image showed the street in front of the house.

I thought I might be getting an understanding of how this worked, that it might indeed be recording the scene that the camera had transmitted to the monitor. I turned the lever to the rewind position again, and this time I let the machine run until the tape rewound completely on the big reel. Then I turned the lever to the "play" position. Now the scene on the monitor showed the street in front of the house at night. At the lower left-hand corner of the screen, it showed the date and time.

11:00 p.m., November 19, 1965, the night my brother Gavin died.

Traffic on the street had been all but nonexistent after 11:00 p.m., but at 11:13 a car drove slowly by with its lights off. It looked like it probably stopped and parked up the street out of the camera's range.

After that, no further activity other than the lights going off at 11:47 in old Leo Kramer's house across the street. No foot traffic on the sidewalk, no one in the neighborhood came out of his home.

The tape ran out at 07:03 a.m. I rewound it to see if I could get a better look at the car. Late model something, probably a Ford.

The next tape recorder I tried was connected to the monitor for the camera showing the front door. The time recorded on the tape was 07:01 a.m., November 20, 1965.

I rewound it. I really didn't expect anything to show up on this one, since the tape of the street showed no activity. I was right. I stopped it where it ran out and removed it.

Gavin must have placed fresh tapes in all the machines at about the same time, around 11:00 p.m. every night. Each tape ran for eight hours. They would all run out about the same time the next morning.

Next, the tape from the pool area monitor. I had some hope for this one. Decorative lights provided some illumination around the pool, and I knew there were a motion detector and a flood light that doubled as a security light above the sliding glass door to the bedroom. Anyone crossing the pool deck or entering the house through the sliding glass door to Gavin's bedroom should set off the flood light and be picked up by this camera.

Then I remembered that when I first came to the house, the switch for the flood light, located just inside the sliding glass door to the master bedroom had been turned off. I'd turned it back on and left it on after I moved in.

In the cabinet under the recorders were seven stacks, each of six tapes, each carefully marked and dated, for each of the monitors. Gavin apparently kept the tapes for seven days, and then recorded over them.

I pulled the one for the patio and pool for the Thursday night before, November 18, 1965, and ran it in the machine. The tape showed that around 11:55 p.m., Gavin, nude, ran out across the deck for a midnight swim. His movement triggered the motion detector for security light.

It came on, and there he was, naked. It was eerie to see him again. He'd still had the body of an eighteen-year-old, right up until the night before he died.

I took the Thursday night tape out and re-inserted the one for Friday night and restarted it where I had left off.

By the clock on the tape, at around 12:10 a.m., it looked like a shadow, a good-sized one, came over the wall at the bottom of the picture on the monitor.

It went right up next to the house, just below the motion detector's range.

The shadow moved quickly and even after rewinding and replaying the tape several times, I still could not make out for certain who or what it was.

It could even have been a shadow cast by a cat running in front of the lights around the pool.

I kept running the tape. A few minutes later, at 12:25 a.m. there was some kind of commotion, again near the wall along the street. Then a figure went to the swimming pool.

It looked like the person washed their foot.

Then the figure approached the house and out of view of the camera.

No more activity until 1:15.

A movement on the far side of the deck, the side of the property overlooking the cliff and the view. This one also moved quickly to the house.

Could it have been a moth fluttering around the front of the camera's lens?

People must have been streaming in and out of the place all night.

I'd been reviewing these tapes now for 12 hours and was getting bleary eyed. I ran this tape through to its end, rewound it and quit for the day. I'd resume this tomorrow or later in the week, after I had lunch with Marcia and Catarina on Thursday.

# Chapter Ninety Nine

## Jim Miller

## Monday, May 2nd, 1966

We dropped by the FBI office in Westwood, Elliott and I, to see if anyone there could identify the others in the photo taken at Turnip Green's birthday party.

As usual, Elliott stayed in the car.

Poor old Elliott tired so easily now that it had become difficult for the two of us, especially him, to pretend in front of the captain that he could still fulfill his duties.

The FBI's office is on the seventh floor of one of the tall buildings lining Wilshire Boulevard. It's on the south side of the street, just before the Veterans Administration Building and almost across from UCLA.

The door had only the suite number, no name plate or marking to identify the office.

I opened the door and entered a small, windowless reception area.

There were two pull-up chairs, and an American flag on a pole in the corner. A Government Issue portrait of President Lyndon Johnson hung on the wall.

Oh, I almost forgot to mention the gorgeous blond, her hair in a tight bun, sitting behind a receptionist's desk.

She looked up and smiled. It was the kind of a smile I don't often get from a woman I'm meeting for the first time, a smile of greeting as if she'd been waiting just for me.

Her name tag said M. Sprout and with her hair like that, she had the cool, efficient look one would expect of a person working for the FBI. I wondered what her hair would look like if it were loose, unpinned and wild, spread on a pillow and framing that beautiful face.

I showed her my badge, set the photograph on her desk and asked if anyone in the office could help me identify the people in the picture.

She glanced at the photo. "Let me take you inside and we'll see if one of the agents can help you."

She started getting up from her chair and I thought whoa, when is this going to stop? She seemed to be unfolding, like one of those wooden carpenters' rulers that scissor open. By the time

417

she was fully upright I saw she had to be six feet tall, perfectly proportioned and with the posture of a Marine Corps Drill Instructor.

I tried to hide my astonishment, but it must have showed, because she gave a little grin as if to say, "follow me, little one, and I'll teach you something new." I thought if she ever got her hands and other things on me, I'd come away very bruised, but very pleased.

Fortunately for my morale and my morals she only led me into the FBI office's inner sanctum and introduced me to the agent on duty, Rob Raymond.

Agent Raymond rose from his chair to shake my hand and I was relieved to see he was only about my size, 5'11" or so. This reassured me that the FBI didn't have some extraordinary height requirement.

"I know that this may be asking a bit much, but can the FBI give me any clues as to who these people are?" I asked, sliding the photo across Raymond's desk. "The photo was taken last night at a party in Beverly Hills, a birthday party for a theatrical agent, Turnip Green."

"Well, I can tell you right off that the guy on the left in the foreground wearing the pin striped suit and the bowler hat had been, until last night, Frank Greco. But I presume you already knew that, and the reason you're here is that you want a make on the others."

"Yes, you presume right. I guess that's why you're with the FBI and make the big bucks."

Raymond chuckled. "Yeah, I'm only here today because my yacht's in dry dock." He turned the picture sideways on his desk so I could see as he pointed out the others. "The guy Greco's talking to is John Hardy, an agent that handles some of the animals used in TV and Movies."

Raymond paused, put on his glasses, then slid the photo under his desk lamp. He bent to look closer. "I see a pretty good shot of Marcia Schmitt there in the background." There was an intake of breath, and then he said, "Wait a minute. These two with her look familiar."

"Don't they though," I said. "They look so much alike they could be twins."

"They might look alike to you," he said, turning the photo so I could see, "and I do admit to a remarkable resemblance, but the one on the left is Catarina Monreale."

"And I'm supposed to know who that is? Is she a famous movie star or something?"

"She's famous all right, at least in my circles. She's Gianni Monreale's daughter and Gianpoalo Monreale's granddaughter."

418

"Oh, THAT Monreale," I said, as if I knew who or what he was talking about.

"What the hell is she doing here in L.A.?" Raymond asked more to himself than as if he expected an answer from me. "Can I have a copy of this?"

"I suppose. I'm on my way to the party house to get a copy of the guest list."

"We already have a copy of the guest list," he said, rummaging through a file on his desk. He retrieved two pages. "I can tell you right now Catarina Monreale's name is not on that list. I don't readily recognize the other woman, the one that looks so much like her. Looks like I'll have to go back out to Turnip Green's house and ask if they can tell me who she is."

"I can tell you that," I said, trying not to sound too smug. "I'll make you a deal. You tell me all about Catarina Monreale and give me a copy of that guest list and I'll tell you who that other woman is and give you a copy of the picture."

"It's a deal. Who is it?"

"Her name is Val Keller. Valerie Keller. She's living in her late brother's house in Encino. He'd been found dead, hanging in his basement a few months ago. Homicide's been investigating his death at her request, more of a demand really. She's determined to find out if he was murdered."

"If Catarina Monreale's anywhere around, in all likelihood it was murder."

"Really? What makes you say that?"

"When Catarina Monreale's in the neighborhood, someone usually ends up dead. Now that I see her near Greco, my suspicion is that she did the hit."

I started up from the chair and held out my hand. "Mr. Raymond, I cannot thank you enough for the information. I promise you I won't tell anyone. We wouldn't want it to get out that our two organizations had cooperated with each other. It would set a dangerous precedent."

Raymond rose from his chair. "I quite agree. Next thing we know, it would be expected of us. I'm going to have to go back out to the Green's house, too. Do you want to tag along?"

"I've got a partner with me out in the car, and he's been really sick lately. Can I follow you?"

We arrived at the Green's residence just as the caterers were leaving. Raymond and I made our way through the confusion and after flashing our badges were shown to the kitchen of the big house where Mrs. Green bustled about supervising the storage of the dishes.

419

Friendly and gracious, in a wash and wear dress she looked like she could be just about anyone's mother.

"Tevye is at the office," she told us after we identified ourselves. "Is there anything I can do to help? I presume this is about Poor Mr. Greco's awful accident."

"Yes ma'am, it is," began Raymond. "The Bureau must investigate the possibility that there might be something wrong with the vehicle that caused this awful mishap."

"Oh, I hope not. Excuse me a moment," she said. Then, speaking to one of the help putting dishes away, she said "No, no dear. Please don't put the punch bowl on the top shelf. I can't reach it clear up there and I use it to feed the dogs."

Then turning back to us she continued. "One of our cars is just like the late Mr. Greco's. Of course, now we should get rid of it. For his birthday last night my husband was given a new Rolls Royce. We won't need the Lincoln anymore."

"Part of our investigation is to identify last night's guests. In speaking to one of them Mr. Greco might have mentioned having trouble with his car."

"Yes," I added. "Can you help us by telling us who this is talking to Marcia Schmitt?"

Mrs. Green took the photo and put on her glasses. "Why yes. The one on the right is Val Keller and the other one is Francesca Armerina. My husband was quite impressed with both of these beautiful young ladies, so impressed that he asked if they were interested in exploring a career in movies."

"Francesca Armerina? Is her name on the guest list?" I asked.

"Yes, it's there," Raymond answered. Mrs. Green nodded her head in agreement. "We'd been asked to include her by an old friend, Frank Fisher, the singer. He's a client of Tevye's. He's been appearing in Las Vegas for the past six weeks."

As Agent Raymond and I left the Green's household we paused at the end of the drive.

"Well, this has been most productive. Your having that photo has given the bureau a real leg up on this."

Yes," I added, "and if we're ever invited to a party at the Green's, don't let them serve you anything from that punchbowl."

That evening after my shift ended, I drove by the Ding How Café in Torrance on the off chance that I might see Tom Larson's car. The last time I'd run into him was there. I just wanted to have a casual, off-the-record word with my former partner and mentor.

I think by this time I'd become a fairly seasoned and passable detective, so I'd picked up an old detective's trait of not liking too many coincidences.

Marcia Schmitt came from Torrance. I'd witnessed her brother's death in the shoot out with the police.

Gavin Keller came from Torrance, and I was investigating his murder.

Val Keller came from Torrance, and she'd been with Catarina Monreale and Marcia Schmitt last night when someone else was murdered. Could there be any connection with Marcia Schmitt's brother Timothy's death, a death both Tom Larson and I had witnessed?

Was Valarie Keller's determination to investigate her brother's death connected with all this?

What about Marcia Schmitt?

And Catarina Monreale? Where did she fit in? Agent Raymond had pretty much concluded that Catarina Monreale was responsible for Frank Greco's death. Why the hell would she be with Marcia Schmitt and Val Keller?

Sarge's car was parked in the red zone in front of the café, so I pulled into the lot, parked and went inside.

He stood waiting at the takeout counter as before.

"Hi, Sergeant Larson. How are you?"

He turned and smiled as if glad to see me. "I'm doing alright," Sarge replied, "Stopped in to get some take out for you and the missus?"

"No, I'm not that fond of Chinese food. Only tolerate it for my wife's sake. I really wanted to talk to you for a moment."

The takeout cartons containing Larson's order arrived and he turned to settle up with the cashier.

"Sure. What's on your mind?" he asked over his shoulder.

"Well, it has to do with the Schmitt's."

There was a noticeable reaction from the Sarge. I couldn't help but wonder what that meant.

He picked up his order. "Here, let me help you with the door," I offered.

We walked out to the sidewalk in front of the café.

"I'm investigating two cases that should be unrelated," I continued. "One happened last night. You probably saw it on the news. A gangster named Frank Greco. The other is an older case that involved a death, a possible murder in Encino several months ago. The Encino victim, Gavin Keller, originally came from here in Torrance. His sister Val Keller is pushing for an investigation. Last night she was with Marcia Schmitt, also a former Torrance resident, in fact Timothy Schmitt's older sister. Do you think it odd, all these people from Torrance showing up together at a party in Hollywood?"

"I can assure you Marcia Schmitt had nothing to do with it!" Larson snapped.

"I didn't mean to imply that I thought she did," I said almost defensively, wondering why Larson would jump to the conclusion that I might head in that direction.

Larson's face reddened "I am very close to the Schmitt's," he said leaning close and continuing slowly and evenly. "I see Millie Schmitt, Marcia's mother, every night, and I see Marcia frequently. She's a wonderful person and wouldn't hurt anyone. The Schmitt's are good people."

"I didn't think anything along those lines," I replied. Here I was an almost seasoned detective, standing up to the fearsome Sergeant Larson, the man I'd always held in awe.

"I came here asking for your help, or at least your input. I hoped you might have some words of wisdom."

"I suggest you turn your attention to the Keller's," he said heatedly. He opened the door to his car. "My food's getting cold." He slammed the car door and drove off, leaving me standing there wondering what I'd said that had set him off like that.

# Hundred

## Tom Larson

## The Evening of May 2$^{nd}$, 1966

After running into Jim Miller in the restaurant, Larson had to force himself to control his anger, to drive calmly and carefully the rest of the way to Millie's place. But he was as angry at himself as he was about anything Jim had said.

Larson knew that Timothy Schmidt's death had been rough on Jim. He was pretty sure that's what drove Jim to quit the force.

But maybe the encounter at the café had been, in fact, official business on Jim's part. Could Jim, now a big shot L.A. homicide detective, be questioning Larson as part of a murder investigation? Could Jim have been saying he suspected Marcia was involved somehow, either with the mob hit or in Gavin Keller's death?

He'd better not be, Larson thought grinding his teeth.

Hindsight is always better than foresight, but Larson could just kick himself for telling Marcia of his suspicions about Gavin Keller. Thinking about her reaction when she walked with him to his car the night he told her, he had to suspect there might have been more to her relationship with Gavin than just dating.

What could it be? If Timothy were 12 or so back then, Marcia would have been 14 or 15. Gavin would have been 17, 18 years old. Could they, would they have had sex? His sweet little 14-year-old Marcia had sex with that son of a bitch Gavin Keller?

Given all the things Larson had seen during his years as a police officer, yes, yes, that son of a bitch Gavin Keller could have taken advantage of poor little Marcia Schmitt when she was only 14 years old.

Larson realized he'd been gripping the steering wheel so hard his knuckles were white. He had to calm down, had to bring himself under control. He was on his way to Millie Schmitt's house even now. Millie Schmitt was one of the most precious, most important things in the world to him, Millie and her daughter Marcia. He most certainly did not want Millie to see him upset. He wanted only to have a nice dinner of Chinese and spend another quiet evening with her in her cozy little home.

Besides, Gavin Keller was dead, may God damn him anyway.

# One Hundred One

## Jim Miller

## May 3$^{rd}$, 1966

It's relatively quiet in the squad room this morning.

Captain Yeager's in his office doing paperwork. Almost all the other detectives in homicide were either out on calls or in court.

I didn't want to get into any more conversations with the captain today. He'd already buttonholed me about the Gavin Keller case and the Frank Greco case.

Worse, he'd asked just how bad off Elliott really was. I didn't tell the captain the truth that Elliott was sick most of the time, so sick that when we went on calls, he rarely even got out of the car.

I had to cover for poor old Elliott more and more.

But as a mentor, the old detective had proven to be invaluable. Time after time, his years of experience and his street smarts jump-started investigations and got me going again, making me look like a very smart detective.

I was sitting at my desk shuffling through all my notes, going from the Keller file to the Greco file, re-reading the coroner's reports, the forensic reports and the evidence taken from the two crime scenes.

There, in the middle of all this, was the photograph taken at the party. Could it be important, or did I think so only because Val Keller was in it?

God, it was hard to keep from thinking about her. I couldn't help but wonder what she looked like naked.

Elliott's desk faced mine and the two were pushed up against each other, forming one good sized work surface. He sat across from me, kind of slumped down in his chair, his chin resting on his chest. He'd been holding the same sheet of paper in his hands for fifteen minutes. I could never quite tell if he was awake or not. Sometimes he just dozed off, and I hated to disturb him.

But his snoring would get so loud I was afraid others would hear, even over the ringing of phones and the other racket in Homicide.

"Elliott," I whispered, "can I talk to you about something?" The encounter with Larson last night was on my mind. I'd really been surprised by the usually reserved Sergeant Larson's angry outburst, and I wanted to run the whole episode by Elliott.

"HHMMMFPT," Elliott said with a start. "I was just studying this report," he said, dropping the paper to his lap. He rubbed his stubble. It took him a moment to focus. "Whadda ya got?"

"I looked up my former partner last night, the guy I worked with when I was on the force in Torrance."

"Yeah? What's bothering you? Homesick?'

"God no, I love this job," I said. "I especially cherish all the intimate moments you and I are alone together."

"That just shows you're human," Elliott said. "What did happen last night? And leave out anything having to do with sex. It only depresses me."

"His name is Tom Larson," I began, "Sergeant Tom Larson. I wanted to ask him about one of the people possibly involved in the Greco case. Marcia Schmitt. It so happens she came from Torrance and that photo with her and Val Keller kind of triggered something in my mind."

"It's hard to see any connection," Elliott said, setting the papers back on his desk.

"I can't argue that. But let me tell you all I know, and maybe in the telling it will become clear to me, or you'll see something I don't. Or maybe I can just put that line of speculation to rest altogether."

"Proceed," he said, leaning back in his chair and lacing his fingers together across his belly.

"I'd only been on the force in Torrance a short time, a year maybe. I'd been partnered with Larson. He's a big man, over 6'4" and weighs maybe 230. A legend on the Torrance Police Force and a very intimidating guy. He never said anything critical or mean to me, but I was very uncomfortable working with him. It was like I walked on eggs all the time. And too, being on the force in my own hometown wasn't all it was cracked up to be. I became scared to death I'd have to respond to an incident involving someone I knew, or worse yet, someone close to me. It finally happened. Larson and I had to answer a call just outside of town, in the L.A. Strip. A man with a gun call. It was a trailer park. We got there just about the time the LAPD guys arrived."

I'd been trying my best to keep my voice even and relate this story as unemotionally as I could.

426

But as I relived that hot August day, I realized I'd been clenching my hands so hard my nails were digging into my palms.

"Larson had been driving. We came tearing into the place just in time to see this guy coming out of one of the trailers."

I swallowed and looked up at the ceiling tiles.

"He had a gun.

The LAPD guys were yelling for him to drop it.

But the guy didn't. He didn't drop the gun.

Right there in front of us they shot him to death with a shotgun."

I looked back at Elliott, looked him in the face hoping my eyes wouldn't tear up.

"I knew the guy. Not well, but well enough to know he was just a harmless guy that wouldn't have hurt anyone."

I had to pause a moment before I could continue.

"The guy just fell on his back and died. Died on the steps to that trailer. His eyes were wide open, looking up at the sky. He looked just like he had when we were growing up."

My throat was tight. I had to pause and pretend to look around the almost deserted office. When I thought I could look Elliott in the face again, I turned back and continued.

"Anyway, Larson ran past the L.A. cops to the porch and into the trailer before anyone else knew what to do next. I don't know how well Larson knew those people. It was a small town and maybe he knew them well. He never said."

I took a deep breath and shifted in my chair. "That was the end of my career with the Torrance PD. The guy that got killed that day was Marcia Schmitt's little brother Timothy, Timothy Schmitt."

I searched Elliott's face. I wasn't sure if he'd been listening or had dozed off again. But after a moment he said, "You thought that because Marcia Schmitt's in the picture taken at the party, this Sergeant Larson might be able to contribute something about her that could help? I'd be more inclined to try to tie Catarina Monreale into all this."

"I don't know what I thought. The Monreale connection is obvious on the Greco case, but does she tie in with the Gavin Keller homicide? Anyway, last night when I tried to talk to Larson about the Schmitt's and Marcia Schmitt being with Val Keller, he immediately got mad and clammed up, acted like I suspected the Schmitt's. Larson wouldn't even talk to me at all. For some reason he suggested I go after the Keller's instead. Before I could even say anything about this Catarina Monreale he got in his car and drove off."

"Which is what you want to do," Elliott said grinning. "Go after Val Keller, I mean."

I sat there looking at a spot in space above Elliott's head, thinking the old guy is right. I am afraid to go back out there. To be honest with myself, I have been avoiding it, hoping something would develop that would take this in another direction so I wouldn't have to see her again, be with her again.

I can't help it. I want to be faithful. I don't want to be just another cheating husband.

But if I had even half a chance, I would take Val Keller. She has an effect on me like no other woman ever has.

# One Hundred Two

## Catarina Monreale

## Thursday, May 5, 1966

Catarina knew she'd be taking a chance, meeting with Marcia Schmitt and Val Keller. But she was too curious, too intrigued not to go through with it. Marcia Schmitt is beautiful and charming.

But impressive as the actress is, it's Val Keller that kept intruding herself into Catarina's thoughts. Certainly, meeting Marcia had been just luck, but could running into Val have been an accident? She felt positive Val was Gavin Keller's sister. Did Val know about Gavin's friendship with Catarina's family and her own affair with him?

She had to be extra careful. The Francesca Armerina alias had begun to get old, too old. Continuing to use it would be asking for trouble. She'd been about to replace it with another before it tripped her up anyway, but now she was stuck with it, at least for today.

An early morning swim in the lake, a leisurely ride back to the ranch house, Shadow running ahead to chase a jackrabbit, and it was time to get ready to drop down to Malibu. She undressed, showered, and afterward stood naked in front of the full-length mirror in her bedroom. Her firm, supple body was tan, tan all over from her daily swims in the lake.

For some reason, no reason, Val Keller again came to mind. Why? Why would Val Keller keep popping into her head?

From her dresser she picked up the little brown jar Lupe had given her, the jar of cream made from the Tepescohuite tree. Despite Lupe's enthusiastic praises, until now Caterina hadn't opened the jar. Lupe told her it was a secret cream from this special tree, a cream discovered by the ancient Mayans. The cream was supposed to make the skin softer, make it seem to glow. Still standing in front of the mirror she slowly and carefully applied it all over her body. Her skin easily absorbed the cream, and she stepped back from the mirror to examine herself.

Lupe and the Mayans had something here. The cream made the sunshine coming through her bedroom window highlight her curves, outlining them and emphasizing her fit, toned body.

She opened her closet and began to carefully choose what she'd wear today. This day she wanted her appearance to be especially impressive.

For Val Keller.

For some reason she wanted to bowl Val Keller over, show her something she would never forget.

Catarina Monreale's particular calling did not permit close friends, but she wanted Val Keller to remember her.

She chose a pale blue summer dress, cotton, one that fit her every curve. She'd only worn it once before, several years ago, in Bermuda.

It still fit her perfectly.

⁂

The restaurant's off the highway, down a shady tree-lined drive, no other roads in or out.

Off to the right, on a knoll some distance away and beyond the far side of the parking lot was a trailer park. There were only a handful of cars, none of them new, near the restaurant's entrance. An older van, a white one without any markings was parked off toward the edge of the parking lot. To the left of the restaurant, a short pier and beyond that a small creek.

She guessed they didn't serve breakfast and it wasn't yet time for the lunch crowd.

Her early arrival at the restaurant had been no accident. She always made it a habit to arrive at places strange to her well in advance of when she was expected. This bit of caution, a lesson taught to her by Mr. Ehlers gave her a chance to familiarize herself with the territory.

This place having only one way in or out disturbed her.

She parked, took a quick walk past the restaurant and the beach, out onto the pier to take look around.

No one was on the beach or the pier.

She returned to the restaurant's entrance and went in.

The interior was in shadows, the only light from the sun shining through the big windows looking out on the waves breaking on the sand. Although she was 45 minutes early and there were few others in the restaurant, she asked the man at the reception if anyone else in the party had arrived.

He told her no; she was the first.

He led her to a table in front, in the corner next to a window looking out on the empty beach and the ocean.

# One Hundred Three

## Marcia Schmitt

## Thursday, May 5$^{th}$, 1966

Others in the business had tried to make friends only to be lured into some sort of compromising situation or end up in a betrayal of some kind, sold out to the scandal magazines. Marcia, almost a recluse, had always been careful about letting anyone get too close.

She had a feeling about Catarina and Val, however. She knew instinctively that both were interesting people. They both shared the same element of something mysterious about them, something hidden.

That fascinated her.

And she was pretty sure whatever their secrets were made them much more vulnerable than anything she had to hide.

They'd obviously been sizing each other up at the party the other night. Like two predators in the wild, wary, but too intrigued, too curious, to drawn to each other to pull away.

Marcia wanted to get to know them better, both of them. She suspected she'd never learn their secrets, what it was they were hiding.

That made them both all the more alluring.

At the very least, she would add the Francesca Armerina and the Val Keller personas, their animal-like grace and aura of controlled power to her repertoire for use in some future role.

Val Keller had to be Gavin's sister for God's sake. She vaguely remembered having seen Val years ago when Marcia had been just a child. But it was only once, and from a distance at that. Why had she turned up in Marcia's life? Could it be only a coincidence, an accident? Or did Val know what Gavin had done to Marcia when she was only fourteen years old? Marcia's thing with Gavin was ten years ago. She thought she'd got over it, that his death closed the door on that unhappy episode, expunged the hate and anger that went with it.

But was she really over it?

Maybe Tom Larson's suspicions about Gavin having raped Timothy were true.

She left the suite at the Beverly Hilton, went down the elevator to the employee's garage where the studio's Buick was hidden and set out for Malibu.

# One Hundred Four

## Val Keller

### Thursday, May 5, 1966

I figured it to be a forty-five-minute drive, so I left the house at about eleven.

I'd got myself a new Corvette, a bright red one, to replace Gavin's fucked-up Jag. I backed it out of the garage and headed for Ventura Boulevard to pick up Topanga Canyon Boulevard.

I'd been waiting for the traffic light to change at Topanga Canyon when a grey Buick sedan went by, headed west on Pacific Coast Highway toward Paradise Cove. Other than that, there'd been no traffic. The Buick turned left into the tree-lined lane leading down to the Sand Castle. I turned left, too and slowed to let the sedan get ahead of me. I wanted to take a look around the place from the little rise just before the road dropped down to the parking lot.

Through the trees I could see that there was only half dozen or so cars in the lot. One was a brand-new Corvette convertible, red, exactly like mine. I put the car in gear and started down the hill as the grey sedan parked and Marcia Schmitt got out.

At the far side of the lot was what I'd kept my eye out for.

A nondescript van, a white one, not new. Julie Rodriguez's people were here.

# One Hundred Five

## Catarina Monreale

## Thursday, May 5th, 1966

The restaurant began to fill with customers. A hush fell over the place at eleven forty-five and she knew without looking that Marcia Schmitt had arrived.

Catarina stood to attract her attention and saw Val Keller come through the door as Marcia was making her way through the restaurant toward her.

"You must create quite a stir everywhere you go," she said as Val joined them.

"I would guess that both of you do too, don't you?" Marcia replied smiling. She slid into the booth next to Catarina.

"I appreciate the attention and the extra service, so I don't complain," Val said laughing.

Hearing Val's easy laugh, Catarina began to relax a little.

Val seated herself in the booth across from Catarina. She looked out the window at the beach and the waves, then turned to Marcia.

"This place is really very nice. Fun. How did you happen to find it?"

Marcia unfolded her napkin and replied "I came here on a date with Dan Ridges, Lloyd Ridge's son. He lives a mile or so up the coast in Malibu. I think the place is great. Occasionally there are others here who are in the business, so I don't create a huge stir. It's much more relaxed than the places in Hollywood and Beverly Hills." She took a sip of her water. "Speaking of business, at the party I understood you to say that you were in investing."

"Yes," replied Catarina. "I dabble in insurance related investments. Safe. Dependable. The public always needs insurance."

Turning to Val, Catarina asked "What do you do to occupy your time, Val. You look like you're in excellent shape. With that tan it must be something outdoors."

Val leaned forward, her elbows on the table. "Currently I'm a woman of leisure. I've come into an inheritance that allows me to avoid work, so I've been doing a lot of swimming and just enjoying myself."

"The both of you should consider taking up acting," Marcia said. "With your looks and with the contact you made with Turnip at the party you have an easy in."

"Sounds way too much like work," Catarina replied. "Memorizing all those lines, all those action scenes. And I understand the hours are pretty awful."

Marcia laughed. "What you say is true, but I really enjoy it. Some of the people I work with are extraordinary and almost all are very interesting in one way or another. If I hadn't been in this business, I wouldn't have met you two, would I?"

The waiter came and took the drink orders. Tea for Marcia, lemonade for Val and for Catarina a Coca Cola.

Catarina wondered if it was curious, the three of them out having a good time and none of them ordering anything alcoholic, not even a glass of wine. She could understand Marcia not drinking. She was a well-known figure, and the public watched every little thing she did. But Val Keller struck her as someone who lived life to the fullest. Among other things, that would include having a drink or two.

"That is a very becoming dress, Francesca," Marcia commented, looking Catarina over. "The color really suits your complexion, your coloring."

"Thank you," Catarina replied." "It's something I've had for several years but only worn once before. My Uncle Emilio in Milan is a designer. He made it just for me.

Val wore a loose-fitting white silk blouse, open at the neck. Every movement she made caused it to slip down her firm, tanned shoulder. When she pulled it back up a bit, the neckline drooped, displaying a tantalizing cleavage. All during the conversation her brown eyes seemed to be searching Catarina's face, sizing her up. Catarina had the same feeling of excitement mingled with curiosity that she got warily circling a wild horse, a bronc, taking its measure before trying to mount it for that first ride. The horse's brown eyes would return her gaze with that same sort of challenge, curiosity. "Try to take me, I dare you," the bronc's eyes would seem to say. Her Mexican ranch hands had told her that the word bronco meant "rough" in Spanish. Were the playful movements of Val's blouse deliberate and directed at her? Catarina definitely felt a tension, a sexual tension building between them.

436

She absently moved her finger slowly around the rim of her water glass and returned Val's gaze.

# One Hundred Six

## Marcia Schmitt

## Thursday, May 5, 1966

Those two really are a pair, Marcia thought while driving back to the hotel. There was something so exciting, so charged with energy about them. She wondered what it would be like to be alone with them somewhere, a beach, maybe. Why did her thoughts go in that direction? In all her life it had never even occurred to her to "experiment," not even when she was a kid, first starting out in the business, when she lived with all the other girls at the Chateau Marmont.

Returning to her room she saw she had a call from Turnip Green. He'd left a message that a homicide detective, a Jim Miller, wanted to talk to her about the party at Turnip's house. In particular, the detective wanted to know if she'd spoken to Frank Greco at the party and how long she had known Val Keller and Catarina Monreale.

Who the heck could Frank Greco be? Who the heck was Catarina Monreale? Marcia didn't recall having spoken to either a Frank Greco or a Catarina Monreale at the party. She didn't think she'd even heard those names before.

She put in a call to the detective at the number Turnip had left and made an appointment to talk to him the next day, Friday.

# One Hundred Seven

## Val Keller

## Thursday, May 5th, 1966

Well, the lunch had come and gone, the moment passed. I really hadn't established a connection with Catarina Monreale, one that could lead me to meeting her brother or to an opportunity to talk to her about Gavin.

Mission not accomplished.

But not to make light of Marcia Schmitt the movie star, Catarina Monreale is really something. I'd tried not to gape during the whole time I sat across from her, not to stare at the young woman who I knew murdered professionally.

But not only is this Catarina gorgeous in a predatory animal way, like a leopard, or better yet, a panther, sleek and fit, she's also bright, quick witted and very intelligent.

I'm fascinated all the more, knowing how dangerous she is.

When I got home, I saw Detective Jim Miller had left a message on the answering machine. He wanted to meet to bring me up to date on his investigation into Gavin's death.

# One Hundred Eight

## Catarina Monreale

## May 5th, 1966

Catarina had given a wrong phone number when they'd said their goodbyes in the parking lot. They'd all promised to get together again real soon, but Catarina knew she had to cut this off right now.

From behind her sunglasses, she'd snuck a look at the far side of the parking lot. The white van had still been there. A guy in clean white coveralls was just climbing in the back. His coveralls had looked brand new, still pressed. His shoes were dress shoes, brown, shiny.

When Catarina put her hand on her car's door handle to open it, she felt, hidden on the inside edge, a tiny sliver of Scotch Tape. She'd stood for a moment next to her car as the other two drove away. Then she got in and left the restaurant's parking area. Watching the rear-view mirror to be certain she wasn't being followed, she'd driven west and north, up Pacific Coast Highway until she got to Encinal Canyon Road.

She'd pulled off the highway into the dirt, parked and got out.

She slipped off her sunglasses and crouching next to her car ran her fingernail inside the door handle. She found and carefully peeled away the small bit of tape. Just as she feared, stuck to the tape was a layer of fine black powder, graphite. While she'd been in the Sand Castle, someone, probably the guy in the van, had dusted her car for fingerprints. That meant that the car had probably been bugged, or that a tracking device had been hidden somewhere in it.

Who'd set her up, tipped off the law, the police or whoever, that she'd be going to that restaurant?

It wouldn't have been Marcia Schmitt.

She put her sunglasses on, took a look around, and then got back in the car.

She continued on north, up Pacific Coast Highway past Port Hueneme, on toward Oxnard. There was no place she could stop and search for whatever had been hidden in the car. She wasn't sure at that point if they knew where she lived, so she couldn't return to the ranch to look for it.

When she got to Oxnard, she stayed on Pacific Coast Highway where it runs along the railroad tracks until she got to the Cooper Road grade crossing. She turned right on Cooper, drove over the tracks, made a u-turn and parked. Leaning across the seat she emptied the registration information and other papers from the glove compartment and put them in her purse.

Then she waited.

It wasn't long, not even ten minutes, before she heard the train whistle. The gates to block traffic came down across Cooper Road.

She started the car, drove around the gates and parked on the tracks.

She got out, stepped carefully across the tracks and started walking briskly along Pacific Coast Highway back to Enterprise Street and the Greyhound Bus Depot.

She'd got about halfway down the long block when the ground shook.

From behind her, the roar of the collision and explosion, locomotive and Corvette. The car's gas tank must have exploded on impact.

She turned to watch the black fireball rise in the dusty blue afternoon sky.

She took the bus to Santa Barbara where she rented a car. When she got back to her ranch, she got rid of Francesca Armerina.

# One Hundred Nine

## Jim Miller

### Friday, May 6, 1966

Old Elliott the Bellyot was roaming around the department giving the other guys a ration of crap and I was at my desk when Marcia Schmitt called.

Joking around and goofing off was really a change from Elliott's behavior for the last few months. I waved to him, and he returned to our desks. I told him Miss Schmitt had agreed to meet and had given me her suite number at the Beverly Hilton. She'd suggested that we talk to her there at the hotel rather than here at the station or the studio. She didn't want to cause a stir. She'd said on the phone she didn't think she could help and wanted to stay out of the limelight but was curious about the Greco matter.

I agreed that if she had no useful information, we wouldn't mention her name to the press.

Marcia Schmitt herself, wearing a form fitting peach colored jump suit and as beautiful in person as she is on the screen met us at the door. After we showed our badges, she invited us in and led us to a sitting area near the veranda looking out over West Los Angeles and the ocean. Two couches faced each other separated by a coffee table. On the coffee table, a silver tray with drinking glasses, ice, soft drinks and a pitcher of water.

Her suite was larger than the apartment I'd lived in before Sharon and I got married. The daily room rate was probably more the month's rent for my old place, too.

"Please be seated and help yourselves to soft drinks or water, gentlemen," she said, gesturing to the couches. "I promise you that I'll help in any way that I can."

"First let me say we are both fans of yours, Miss Schmitt and we really appreciate your willingness to cooperate," I began, taking a seat next to Elliott on one of the couches. "This is just a routine visit. Because you were a guest a Tevye Green's birthday party, we need to ask if you might have spoken to Frank Greco or overheard him say something that might be useful."

"I understand, Detective Miller, although I did not speak to Mr. Greco at the party or at any other time. I'd never met him."

I showed her the photograph. "Perhaps one of the others in your group, Miss Keller or Miss Monreale spoke to him and one of them related something he said?"

"No, nothing like that happened," she said, taking the photo and holding it up to the light, "and who is this Miss Monreale you refer to? These two with me are Val Keller and Francesca Armerina."

"The name of the person on your left is Catarina Monreale, not Francesca Armerina."

Marcia looked confused and I knew it wasn't an act.

"Who is Catarina Monreale?"

"She's under investigation for the murder of Frank Greco," Elliott interjected.

"I don't understand. I thought Mr. Greco's car exploded as he was on his way home."

"It exploded because somebody put a bomb in it. We suspect that somebody was Catarina Monreale."

Surprised, Marcia asked, "Why would she do something like that?"

"That's what Miss Monreale does for a living. She's part of a family of gangsters who moved here from the east."

Then, thinking maybe I'd said too much I added, "We can't tell you more at this time and must ask that you keep this completely confidential. Do not tell anyone."

Marcia still had a stunned look on her face. "I find this very hard to believe. I had lunch with her just yesterday, her and Val at the Sand Castle. You're telling me that beautiful young girl is a murderer?"

"She is a professional murderer," Elliott confirmed, handing her one of his cards. "A professional assassin. If you see or hear from her again, please contact us immediately."

"Miss Schmitt," I said, leaning forward on the couch. "On another subject, I understand that you're originally from Torrance. Coincidently Torrance is my own hometown. The other person you were with at the party, Val Keller is also originally from Torrance. Did you know Val Keller when you lived in Torrance?"

"No, I'd never met her before. The Greens introduced me to Val and Francesca, I mean Catarina Monreale there at the party."

"Miss Schmitt," interjected Elliott with a vigor I hadn't seen him exhibit before, "we also understand you know Tom Larson, Sergeant Tom Larson, a police officer on the force in Torrance. Detective Miller here had a short conversation with Officer Larson the other evening and Larson urged him to pursue leads in the direction of the Keller's. Would you have anything to add as to why he would make such a suggestion?"

I wasn't expecting Elliott to bring up our conversation, or his taking to heart my dismay at Larson's attitude the other night.

But I was even more surprised at the expression on Marcia's face. She looked torn, as if trying to think of a response.

Finally, she replied, "No, I'm afraid I don't know why Tom would say that. I left Torrance almost ten years ago. Other than visiting my mother and getting together for holidays with her and Tom from time to time, I don't see him at all."

"And you didn't know Val Keller when you lived in Torrance?" I asked, picking up on the direction Elliott was taking.

"No."

For some weeks now Old Elliott the Bellyot had been having his bad days and his good days. Today looked like it was going to be one of his very good days. I think I was getting a look at what he must been like back when he'd been a hotshot young detective, back before the cigarettes and booze caught up with him.

He was more than reasonably coherent, presentable and at this moment, alive, alert.

He leaned forward and asked in a compelling, no, a commanding voice that I never knew the old cop had.

"Did you know Gavin Keller when you lived in Torrance?"

Elliott's voice and his question filled the room. I had to hide my surprise at the old man. He was showing a presence I had no idea he possessed.

But more than that was the look on Marcia Schmitt's face. It looked to me as if she'd been dreading Elliott's question.

And now, there it was.

"Yes," she answered softly.

444

I'm afraid I was no longer able to hide my surprise at this sudden turn of events. I thought this interview had been all but over. I'd been getting ready to leave. Now it was taking a whole new turn.

Elliott pressed on, his tone lower, softer now, almost hypnotic. "Would you mind telling us how well you knew the late Mr. Keller?"

I got the impression she was trying to avoid feeling trapped. She reached for a glass, put ice and water in it and took a drink. Then she got up, walked to the sliding glass doors and looked out.

The room was silent except for the low hum of the air conditioner.

It was Elliott's game now. He was in command. We remained seated and waited.

Finally, still facing the closed sliding glass door to the veranda she began to speak in a low, quiet voice, as if recalling something that happened to someone else a long time ago.

"Gavin Keller and I dated for a while. I was 14 and he was 17. He was a junior in high school, and I was a freshman."

She paused, her back still to us, and shook her head as if to clear it.

"Please go on, Miss Schmitt," I said softly, still pressing the advantage Elliott had established for us. "There was more, wasn't there?"

"We were in love. At least I was. He said he loved me." She paused for a moment, "but it turned out he didn't."

She took a deep breath, and then turned to face us. "That's it."

I'd just learned a real lesson in interrogating from old Elliott the Bellyot, the switching to a friendly, reasonable voice that compelled an answer. This was as good a time as any for me to put that lesson to use.

"Miss Schmitt," I began quietly, "I must remind you that Detective Elliott and I are with the Homicide Unit of the Los Angeles Police Department. We are investigating two deaths, one of them certainly murder and the other probably a murder. Frank Greco had been most certainly murdered. The coincidences between the two deaths, unclear as they appear to be at this time, point to Gavin Keller having been murdered. You are seen by us to be a link or connection between the characters in these events, the thread in this play, as it were. We are determined to find out what happened in both of these incidents, and we will. We are paid to do this. It is our job. In order for us to get this job done we will see every lead, every connection through to the point where we either solve these cases or we feel the lead is not taking us to the solution. You will help us by telling us everything you know about Gavin Keller. If we have to find out elsewhere, it may not reflect as favorably upon you as it will if you tell us in your own words."

Out of the corner of my eye I caught Elliott's look of surprise and satisfaction when I concluded that speech.

We, Elliott and I, waited.

Marcia approached the coffee table and picked up a bottle of water, unscrewed the cap and took a long drink, ignoring or oblivious to her glass of ice water already on the table.

Then she turned and looked at us with an expression as if she were trying to decide whether to say something, or if so, how to phrase it.

"Gavin Keller was the worst thing that could have happened to me at age fourteen." she said, bending to set the water bottle on the coffee table. "Or maybe the best," she continued, taking a deep breath, and bringing herself to her full height, "because I came away from my disastrous relationship with him determined to recover and make something of myself. Had he not treated me the way he did, had he done the 'honorable' thing, my life would have turned out much differently."

I looked at Elliott, then back at Marcia. "Do you want to tell us exactly what happened, or would you prefer we fill in the blanks ourselves? We might err on the side of making it sound worse than it really was."

"It couldn't have been much worse. My father had died, and I discovered I was pregnant with Gavin's child. He promised me he'd marry me and take care of me, that everything would turn out all right. Then he ran out on me. His family was moving away, and he didn't even tell me. He just left me flat. I had nowhere to go, no place to turn. My mother had just been through so much with my father's illness and then his death. My older brother, Dick, shunned me as if I was evil, and I began to think that I was.

I miscarried before anyone found out. I've carried that secret with me ever since."

She turned, walked back to the sliding glass doors, and paused. She seemed to be staring toward the ocean six or seven miles away.

"Since this doesn't have anything to do with your investigation into the Greco matter, I hope you'll see no need to include it in your report."

"That remains to be seen. At this point we don't know whether this is important to solving these cases or not, Miss Schmitt."

"But if no one knew, where does Tom Larson come in?" Elliott asked.

She turned from the sliding glass door to face us. "He and mother became very close friends after my dad died. Tom Larson became like a father to us. But by that time, it was too late. I didn't need a father anymore. My little brother Timothy though, had been having trouble in school and finally dropped out, or was expelled. After that he just kicked around, never quite able to get a start in life. It ended with his being killed by the police."

I know," I said. "I was there."

She gave me a kind of curious look and continued. "I went down to Torrance the next day to be with my mother. Larson came by as he did every evening. He'd stop somewhere and pick up something for them to eat. Usually, they'd just stay in and watch television together or he'd take her out somewhere, to a café or something. I'm pretty sure they were each other's entire social life. As he was leaving that night, he asked me to walk him out to his car. I thought maybe he wanted to just take a moment to say something about mother. But when we got to his car, Tom surprised me by saying that he and the family doctor, Doctor Beeman and our old neighbor on Beach Street, a detective named Giuliani, suspected that Gavin Keller had been a peeping tom back in the nineteen fifties. He said they were pretty sure that one night when Timothy was twelve or so, someone drugged and raped him. Larson said Doctor Beeman feared that the experience or the drug that had been used caused brain damage, made Timothy change, and ultimately led to his death. Larson swore me to secrecy. He suspected Gavin. Promised he'd never told anyone and never would. He told me no report had ever been made because he didn't want to see our family and Timothy, at age twelve, put through an interrogation like that. There was no real proof anyway. He said Doctor Beeman had examined Timothy and my brother didn't remember anything, seemed to have blocked out the whole experience. I'd been angry at first for his having kept it from my mother, but I understand why he did."

Elliott and I looked at each other. "This opens up a whole new can of worms," I said." Where do you suppose Val Keller comes in?"

"I have no idea."

Elliott piped up "I think she just butted in because she wanted to find out what really did happen to her beloved brother."

"Miss Schmitt, I really don't know what to say," I began. "In the course of throwing a great deal of light on the Gavin Keller death you've explained a lot but created a whole new batch of questions."

Again, I thought we had all we were going to get from this visit and was about to get up from the couch when Elliott said, "I can understand that you may still be very bitter about Gavin Keller. Did you hate him enough to kill him?" he asked.

"Oh yes. But I didn't. He was already dead when I got there."

"What?" Elliott asked surprised.

I thought this was going to be the shock that would kill the old man.

"Do you mean you went to Gavin Keller's house in Encino the night he died?"

"Yes. I wasn't sure what I would do when I got there. Maybe I'd have killed him. I can't imagine that I would be going there just to talk. It was late at night, and I parked down the block, climbed up on a pot and jumped over the wall. I entered his house through a bedroom door, his bedroom, I guess. It was dark. The sliding glass door had been partially opened. I could hear a noise, a flapping noise. It came from behind a bookcase. Part of the bookcase had been pulled away from the wall. I could see an entranceway down to a basement. I went down the stairs. It was pretty dark, but there was an overhead spotlight in the middle of the room. It was shining on Gavin's body. He was naked, hanging by a rope tied to a hook in the ceiling. I was pretty sure he was dead. To me, it looked like it was probably suicide. I figured maybe his conscience had finally caught up with him. I got out of there as fast as I could."

"You didn't call the police?" I asked.

"What do you think? I'd broken into Gavin's home. He was dead. The papers would have had a field day. What good would it have done? I suppose I could have put in an anonymous phone call, but I didn't."

448

I looked over at Elliott. It had been a long day for the sick old man. I could tell by his pallor it would be best to get him out of there. "This has been extremely helpful. As I'm sure you know, you could be arrested for obstruction of justice or even suspicion of murder, but I think you're telling the truth. And famous as you are, we'll know how to find you if we need you. And we may."

# One Hundred Ten

## Dick Schmitt

## Monday, May 9<sup>th</sup>, 1966

He just had to go back down to Encino, had to find out for certain if Gavin Keller was dead. He thought Gavin had been dead when he left him last, but maybe Dick should have made sure somehow. The fear and pain of that trip stuck in his mind. He rehashed it again, stupid as it was.

It'd been a long drive and he'd been drinking all the way down Highway 5 from San Francisco. He'd to stop twice for gas and three times for gin. It'd been very late by the time he'd located what he thought was Gavin's fancy-ass house.

There were no streetlights, and it was foggy and damp that night, like San Francisco. He'd parked on the next street, took off his shoes and left them in the car. He'd been careful not to make a sound.

But as he moved through the dark neighborhood, turning on to Gavin's street, he stepped in something, something squishy. Whatever it was, he'd felt it soak through his sock. He didn't know at first what it was, mud or something. But whatever it had been, he'd been afraid he would leave footprints on the sidewalk. In a backyard across the street, a dog began to bark, and at the same time an odor became apparent, an unmistakable odor. It had been then that he realized what it was he'd stepped in. He'd steadied himself with a neighbor's ornate wrought-iron fence and carefully peeled off his sock. He'd started to stuff it in his pocket, then thought better of it and draped it over the top of the fence. He'd continued walking, now in one sock, one bare foot on the damp, cold sidewalk, walking toward the walled house, the last house on the street.

He'd been on the road for 6 hours straight and drinking for 10, also straight. He'd been really strung out, shaking like a leaf.

Ahead, in the misty dark, he could just make out the address on the high wall in front of the house. He'd started running toward the big planter pots along the wall, made a mighty leap onto one, and leveraged himself up and over the top.

He'd landed face down on the concrete deck near a swimming pool, bloodying his nose and knocking out one of his front teeth.

450

He'd rolled over on his back. For a few moments he lay marveling at the stars turning slowly overhead. The cold mist settling on his face reminded him it was overcast. There were no stars that night.

Struggling slowly, painfully, he'd gotten to his knees, then to his feet. He'd staggered a little, used the wall to balance himself.

There was a disgusting smell, a smell that almost made him sick.

It came from his one bare foot.

He couldn't stand that smell, that stench. It had made him nauseous. He'd almost thrown up. He'd stumbled toward the swimming pool to rinse his foot. He almost fell in.

Luck had been with him. He'd only gotten his pants wet to his knees.

On one bare foot, cold, wet pants clinging to his legs, Dick made his way to the house.

Except for the little decorative lights by the pool, the place had been pitch dark, so dark he'd had to feel his way along the house's wall until he reached a sliding glass door.

He remembered now that he wondered why, damp as the night had been, the door was partly open.

Then he'd found himself in a bedroom, a big one. He'd heard a flapping sound. Cold, shivering in his wet pants, he'd held on to a bookcase to steady himself, trying his best to think.

His nose hurt.

His mouth hurt.

He needed a drink.

He'd almost turned to leave, abandon this quest.

But after what seemed like hours there was no movement, nothing but the flapping sound. He moved in that direction, feeling his way in the dark along the bookcase until he found where a section of the shelves had been sticking out a little. It was from there that the sound had been coming.

Carefully he'd edged through the opening behind the bookshelf until he'd found himself on a landing at the top of some stairs.

There'd been a glow at the bottom. Dick concluded that Gavin must be up and awake, down there in this basement or whatever it was. He'd slowly, silently descended the stairs, feeling his way down with his left hand along the wall. About halfway down he stubbed his bare toe. He'd fallen headfirst the rest of the way, coming to rest against some bar stools a few feet from the bottom step.

He'd been dazed, disoriented and lying on his back in the dark room. Again, he watched the slowly revolving stars overhead, stars just like the ones he'd seen after jumping over the wall outside.

But how could that be? He was in a basement.

He'd felt and tasted the blood from his nose or his missing tooth, he hadn't known which. He groaned. He ached all over. He tried to find the easiest way to get up, to get to his feet.

It was then that he found he'd broken his toe and twisted his ankle.

He'd had to use one of the bar stools for support so he could look around. The bright white light from a motion picture screen and the light from the projector along with a single light in the ceiling had been shining on something hanging in the middle of the room.

It turned slowly, round and round.

He focused.

The thing hanging there had been a naked body.

"Jesus Christ!"

Without looking back, he turned and ran, scrambled on his hands and knees back up the stairs, twisted ankle and all.

That had been six months ago. The drive down from San Francisco, the drive back, so much of that night was a drunken haze. That had been Gavin Keller hanging there, hadn't it? He was dead, wasn't he? He'd seen Gavin's naked body often enough during the orgies with Connie, Michelle and Sandi to know what it looked like.

He was sure it'd been Gavin.

Wasn't he? Wasn't he sure?

Now it was five thirty in the morning. He just could not sit here in his apartment wondering any longer.

He had to find out for certain somehow.

But how? The only way he could find out for sure would be to drive back down to Encino, go up to that house and knock on the door to see who answered.

If it was Gavin, he'd confront him then and there. If it turned out to be someone else, he'd say he was looking for Gavin.

He'd either be told that Gavin didn't live there anymore, he was dead or whatever.

Wearily Dick shuffled to the refrigerator and got as many bottles of gin as he could carry. He put them in a shopping bag. He wasn't going to bother renting a car this time. Hell, he wasn't even going to bother changing clothes or shaving.

Just get going, get it over with.

He left his apartment, descended the two flights of stairs and crossed the street to his sad old T-Bird. He unlocked the door and got in, setting the shopping bag with the bottles of gin on the passenger seat beside him.

The starter ground a few times and the old 'Bird came to life.

It was raining hard when Richard "Dick" Schmitt, wearing one of his custom fitted Immigration and Naturalization Service uniforms, worked the T-Bird out of the parking space.

He headed down the hill toward The City and the highway south.

# One Hundred Eleven

## Val Keller

### Monday, May 9, 1966

It was the kind of drizzle that tried to turn into rain, but in California rarely does.

I'd been out all morning and was just about to take off my shoulder holster and set it on the desk.

I'd just settled in the den, ready to review the tape from the second camera in the downstairs fun room when the buzzer for the front gate sounded.

I checked the pistol's magazine to see that it was full, slipped my vest back on and went to the monitor for the gate camera.

The drizzle made the picture grey and fuzzy, so I pushed the button that adjusted the camera's lens and zoomed in on the visitor. He wore some kind of government uniform and was getting soaking wet.

I zoomed in some more. Water droplets ran down the man's face, and his hair was matted. He was missing a front tooth and had a broken nose. From the dark circles under his eyes, he looked like he hadn't slept in weeks, months even.

But he was unmistakably the other guy in the porno movies.

I pushed the button for the intercom. "Can I help you?" I asked.

He bent to the microphone and said shakily, "I'm here to see Gavin."

I pushed the button releasing the electric lock on the gate. "Come on up the walk," I replied. "I'll let you in."

I was standing at the front door when he reached the steps to the porch. "What can I do for you?" I asked, holding my vest closed to hide the gun in the shoulder holster.

He stood there on the walkway to the house getting more and more soaked in the almost rain.

He looked up at me with this really pathetic expression.

"I'm looking for Gavin."

"Gavin who?" I asked, prolonging the moment a little. I relished that he was so miserable and so wet.

"Keller, Gavin Keller."

"Gavin Keller's not here right now."

He looked surprised. "You mean you expect him to return?"

"Why don't you come in and dry off. We'll see if we can find out when Gavin might come back." I opened the door and stepped back.

He stood there another moment on the walk, not even on the porch under the eave and out of the drizzle.

He hesitated as if he might decide to just stay where he was, getting wetter and wetter rather than coming inside.

"Well, do you want to come in or not?"

"Uh, sure. If you don't think he'll be too long."

I let him in and shut the door. "I'm Gavin's sister. Why don't you come in and have some coffee or tea? Follow me to the kitchen and I'll fix you something. Which will it be? Tea or coffee? Soft drink?"

He followed me through the foyer past the living room and into the kitchen.

"Have a seat at the counter. What did you say your name was?"

"Schmitt. Dick Schmitt." He looked around. "When did you say you thought Gavin would be back?"

I set a tea kettle on the stove, turned, and walked back to the counter. Resting my elbows on the countertop across from him, I looked directly into his eyes.

"Well, Dick Schmitt, Gavin isn't coming back. Gavin is dead."

He seemed to recoil. "What, what do you mean? I thought you said he was just out for a while."

"No, I don't believe I said exactly that, Dick Schmitt. Why don't you tell me why you're here and what you want with Gavin?"

"I just wanted to see him to talk. But if he's dead I won't take up any more of your time," he said, starting to move off the stool.

"Look, Dick, I don't feel like dicking around with you, Dick. I'll get straight to the point, o.k. Dick? You were a feature player in some really good movies. I want to know all about them. I want to know when they were made, who made them, who the other players were."

He went even whiter than he'd been when he'd showed up at the door.

"I, I don't know what you're talking about."

From the other side of the counter, I hauled off and hit him on the side of the head as hard as I could with the palm of my hand. The force of the blow knocked him off the stool and onto the kitchen's tile floor. Before he could even think about getting back to his feet I was around to his side of the bar with my booted foot on his neck. "Why don't you just stay put for a minute and collect your thoughts, Dick. Maybe then your memory will start to come back."

He made a noise that sounded like "Gaak" and threw up.

I stepped back. "Now you've made a mess of my nice clean floor, for Christ's sake. What kind of a guest are you?"

"I gotta go," he said, trying to get to his knees. I put my boot on the top of his head and gave it a push.

"I don't think you're going anywhere just yet, Dick."

He fell backwards and huddled in the corner where the bar and counter met the wall.

I stepped carefully around the mess he'd made on the floor, crouched in front of him and pulled my vest back so he could see the shoulder holster and the .22.

His eyes got as big as saucers. He looked like he might not be through throwing up.

"The movies, Dick, let's hear all about the movies."

"It was all Gavin's fault." He started shaking uncontrollably. "It was all Gavin's doing. He picked up the girls. He steered us to the motel room in Lomita. He arranged everything, the orgies and everything. He even brought the marijuana. If it hadn't been for him, Connie would never have killed the motel manager."

Dick Schmitt, huddled on the floor in a corner in my late brother Gavin's kitchen, seemed to shrink. He covered his face with his hands and broke down completely, sobbing and gasping for breath.

I stood up and walked around the counter to the sink to get a wet paper towel. I returned and handed him the towel.

"Here, clean up your mess."

Once he'd cleaned up his vomit, I got a clean towel, soaked it in cold water and came back.

I laid the towel across his neck and the back of his head.

I pulled up one of the stools and sat down, watching and waiting for him to pull himself together.

Finally, he reached around and pulled the wet towel from the back of his neck, rubbed his face with it and looked up at me.

"What happens now?"

"That depends entirely on you and on what you have to tell me."

"What happened in the motel manager's office or the movies?"

"Let's start with the movies."

"I didn't know anything about them. I had no idea there were movies, not until the motel manager tried to get us to pay him off, to join in." He shuddered.

"How could you not know that you were being filmed?"

"I had no idea." He bit his lower lip with his one front tooth, and then continued. "There wasn't anyone else in the motel room. There wasn't any camera or anything. It had just been a little room in a little motel that Gavin knew about in Lomita."

"How did this all begin?"

Now he was on a roll, unloading himself. It all spilled out. "At the drag races. Gavin picked them up at the drag races, or they picked us up. I didn't want to. We'd started out partying in Connie's old Cadillac. Then after a while, weeks, months, I don't know, Gavin suggested it would be even better in a room on a bed."

"Who's Connie?"

"One of the girls. There were three of them, Connie, Michelle and Sandie. I didn't want to do it, honest. I just wanted it to be Gavin and me, like it was before. We'd gone to the car show, looked at old cars and stuff. I just wanted to be with him, just the two of us."

457

"What were the girl's last names?"

"I never did know any of their last names. I'm not even sure those were their real first names."

"Did you ever see or hear from any of them again?"

"No. After Connie shot the guy, we left in Connie's old Cadillac and went back to my car. Michelle and Sandi had been waiting in the back seat of that old Cadillac. I don't know if they ever knew what happened in the motel manager's office."

"What did you do then?"

"I went home and got my stuff and got out of town. I never went back."

"And you never heard from Gavin again? Have you ever been to this house before?"

There was a pause, and when he answered, "No," it sounded more like a question, like he was trying it on for size, trying to see if that would work with me.

"Dick Schmitt, I think you're lying. I think you have been to this house before. We're doing so well here, you telling me all this. You don't want to stop now, do you?"

He was a poor, wet, and bedraggled mess, all scrunched up there on the floor in the corner. His bloodshot eyes looked up at me, his wet hair dripping down his face. I tugged at my vest so he could again see my pistol in its holster.

"Yes, yes," he said. "I have been here before. I was here several months ago."

"Why?"

"I was going to confront Gavin somehow. I didn't know what I was going to do. The murder of the motel manager, the films, Gavin was behind all that. He ruined my life".

"What happened when you were here?"

Now it looked as if my wreck of a guest was slipping into a trance. He began to speak in a monotone and his eyes took on a faraway look.

"I'd driven down from San Francisco. I live in San Francisco," he said, looking up at me as if seeking approval.

"I drove straight down here."

He began talking faster and faster now, his words almost running together.

458

"It took almost all night. It must have been after midnight by the time I got here. I parked up the street, climbed the wall and got in the house through an open sliding glass door to a bedroom. I found Gavin, or at least I was pretty sure it was Gavin. He was hanging in some kind of room downstairs. I was scared. I panicked and ran without seeing for sure if it was Gavin, or if he was dead or what."

I got up from the stool, went around the counter into the kitchen area, got a glass of water and brought it back to give to him.

His hand shook when he took it

"What happens now?"

"What do you want to happen?"

"I guess I want to confess or something. I can't go on living like this, keeping it a secret about Connie shooting the motel guy, me being there and all, not reporting it. I'm an accessory, an accessory to murder."

Now his voice became almost a whisper.

"I've been running from that all these years. I can't go on."

"Well, Dick Schmitt, I can see your point. Unfortunately confessing to me will do you no real good. I'm afraid you would have to take all this up with the police."

"What about Gavin?"

"What about Gavin? I don't think you had anything to do with my brother's death, try as you might have if given the chance. If you want to confess to what happened at that motel, I do know a homicide detective. I'm sure he'd want to hear all about it. He's with the Los Angeles Police Department. We can call him from here if you like, or you can just get out of here and never come back."

He looked up at me for a moment, and then using the counter for support lifted himself from the floor. "I've been afraid for so long I'm not sure I know how to quit."

"There's a phone on the wall. Just dial O for the operator and ask for The Los Angeles Police Department Homicide Division. Ask for Jim Miller. Or just walk out of here, get in your car and go back to San Francisco."

Dick Schmitt hesitated, and while he did, the phone rang.

459

# One Hundred Twelve

## Jim Miller

## Monday, May 9th, 1966

Calling on Val Keller was well overdue, a call I just couldn't put off any longer.

In spite of the drizzly and unpromising the afternoon, old Elliot had been having another good day. For this I'd been grateful. That meant he'd be accompanying me into the house rather than waiting in the car. I wouldn't be alone when I bearded the lioness in her den.

I used the two-way radio in the car and had the station patch me through. She answered the phone on the second ring.

"Miss Keller, this is Jim Miller, LAPD Homicide. Elliott and I are just down the hill in Van Nuys. I wondered if we could come by to talk with you for a minute. I want to share what we've discovered and see if you have anything to add."

"Now is as good a time as any," she replied.

"We're on our way."

As I started up the hill toward the Keller house the drizzle turned to sprinkles. Elliott, his head propped against the car's window had been dozing in the passenger seat. He snapped awake when we stopped in front of the house.

On the short walk to the ornate gate, he motioned to an old T-Bird parked at the curb in front. "I always dreamed of having a car like that," he said, pausing to look at the sad old thing. "Well, not just like that. I would have kept it up," he said wistfully. "Now I guess that'll never happen."

I didn't know what to say. I pushed the button under the intercom at the gate.

From the speaker came her voice. "Come on in, gentlemen." The electric lock buzzed, and the gate swung open.

She stood at the front door wearing high heel leather boots, culottes, white blouse and leather vest. She made no effort to conceal her pistol in its shoulder holster. Other than the gun, she looked like she'd stepped right out of a fashion magazine. "Come on in," she invited, with a kind of Cheshire cat like grin, a grin as if she knew something we didn't.

"Follow me to the kitchen. There's someone here I think you'll want to meet."

460

Her saying that kind of took the wind out of my sails. Now I was curious. I'd expected to be the one to furnish information about the death of her brother, intended to confirm to her that it appeared more and more likely that her suspicions had been valid, that indeed he had been murdered.

Entering the kitchen, I was surprised to see a very disheveled male wearing a soaking wet Customs and Immigrations Service uniform. The guy appeared to be in his mid-30's but looked much older.

He was slumped on one of the stools at the counter and looked truly beat.

"Detectives Elliott and Miller," Val said smiling, "I want to introduce you to Dick Schmitt. Dick's from Torrance and is, or was, an old friend of my brother's, right, Mr. Schmitt?"

The guy had been looking down at the counter. He nodded without turning his head to look at us.

I couldn't figure out what this had to do with anything, so I improvised, thinking perhaps I should skirt the issue of Gavin Keller's murder and open the conversation from another direction.

"Detective Elliott and I are also assigned to the Frank Greco murder," I began, "and as part of that investigation we've come into possession of this photograph taken at the birthday party for Turnip Green. It looks like you attended the party. The picture was taken while you were talking to Marcia Schmitt." I took the picture out of my briefcase and slid it across the countertop toward Val.

"Why, so I am," she said, picking it up and looking at it.

Dick Schmitt didn't look at the picture, didn't acknowledge it.

I asked Val, "Do you know who the other person is?

"I met her there at the party. The Greens introduced her as Francesca Armerina."

Introduced her as Francesca Armerina? It was as if Val already knew that wasn't really her name. I continued, "Her name is Catarina Monreale," I said, thinking that would get a rise out of the always composed Val Keller. "She's a suspect in the Frank Greco murder. She could also be a suspect in your brother's murder."

Val didn't bat an eye. "Oh? What makes you say that?" she asked calmly.

461

At this point Elliott joined the conversation. "Miss Monreale is part of an east coast crime family. Your brother met this family through having roomed with Catarina Monreale's brother Johnny, Johnny Monreale while they were both at Harvard. Catarina Monreale has a history of being around people that end up dead."

"So, you think she might have had some reason to kill Gavin?"

"Yes, but we don't know what that reason would be. As our investigation has progressed, rather than eliminating suspects, we're collecting more and more."

I stood at the end of the counter, Elliott in the middle and Dick Schmitt was slouched against the kitchen wall.

Elliott looked at him and asked, "So you lived in Torrance and knew Gavin Keller? How well did you know him? Are you related to Marcia Schmitt? Marcia Schmitt dated Gavin for a while."

Dick Schmitt looked shocked, and Elliott's statement even got a rise out of Val for a second.

"Marcia and Gavin dated?" Schmitt asked in surprise.

"Gavin and Marcia dated?" Val asked, equally surprised.

Elliott looked pleased with himself, having caught them both off guard. "I get the impression neither of you knew that. How about it, Mr. Schmitt? Are you related to Marcia Schmitt?"

"Yes."

"How are you related to her, Mr. Schmitt?"

"She's my sister."

"How about Gavin Keller? How well did you know him?" Elliott asked again.

I watched Schmitt's expression as he looked over at Val. He looked back at Elliott.

"Pretty well, I guess," he answered in almost a whisper.

"Were you close friends when you lived in Torrance?"

"I thought so. I thought so at the time." There was a catch in his voice. "I thought we were pals," he said looking down at the floor.

It occurred to me that the guy might be in the midst of a breakdown.

"But something happened that made you change your mind?" I asked in as friendly and reassuring voice as I could.

462

Again, Schmitt looked to Val, then back at Elliott and me. It seemed like he was trying to say something, but the words just wouldn't come out.

I looked curiously, first at Dick then to Val.

Val had moved across the kitchen and now was leaning against the sink, her arms folded across her chest. She looked relaxed, curious, almost amused.

I turned back to Dick Schmitt. He seemed to shrink into himself. I watched in surprise as he slid off the stool and down the wall to the floor into a squat, his knees to his chest. He covered his face with his hands. He was shaking, sobbing. He began to make a high shrill sound, like he was wailing.

Elliott and I both looked back to Val. She shrugged her shoulders, turned to the sink, and ran cold water on a hand towel. She came back to the counter and handed it to me.

"Here, give him this."

I took the towel and leaned down to give it to the broken man huddled on the floor in the corner.

"Mr. Schmitt. Mr. Schmitt. Can you hear me? Take this towel. Try to pull yourself together. Are you going to be all right? Should we call for paramedics?"

Val came around the end of the counter and pulled a chair from the dining room table. She sat down, crossed her legs and watched.

Elliott turned to her and asked, "What do you know about all this?"

"Nothing," she answered without taking her eyes off Dick Schmitt huddled on the floor. "He showed up about an hour ago looking for Gavin. I never saw him before in my life."

Schmitt had taken the towel I handed him and buried his face in it. He stopped crying long enough to say "I think you'd better take me downtown. I have a confession to make."

"Do you mean you killed Gavin Keller?"

"No no," he replied, looking up at us. His eyes were bloodshot, red as they could be. "I never killed Gavin," he said, shaking his head. "I never killed anyone."

Now his voice broke. "But I was there when Connie killed the motel manager."

"What motel manager? Who's Connie?" I asked, getting up from the stool and stepping around to squat down by him. He was shaking. I put my hand on his shoulder. "Perhaps you'd better start at the beginning. What exactly is it you are confessing? Does it have anything to do with Gavin Keller?"

"Yes, yes, yes. Yes, damn it! It has everything to do with God damn Gavin Keller. It was all his fault."

From his place on the stool Elliott asked, "What was all his fault, Mr. Schmitt?"

"Everything, everything, everything." He was gasping, and his words were running together. "It was all his fault. He picked up the girls. I didn't want to pick up any girls." Now Dick Schmitt's speech slowed, he seemed to gather himself.

"I just wanted to be with him," he continued softly, so quietly it was hard to hear him. "I just wanted us to be pals, to hang around together."

"What girls, Mr. Schmitt?" Elliott probed.

"They said their names were Connie and Michelle and Sandi. Those were the names they gave us. I'm not even sure those were their real names. I never knew their last names. Connie was blond, Sandi had red hair and Michelle was the brunette. We met the girls at the drag races. We had sex in Connie's car. But then Gavin had the bright idea that we should go to a motel. We had drugs, marijuana, and we had sex. We had sex every Saturday night for months in that motel room. Somebody, Gavin and somebody else, the motel manager I guess, took pictures, movies of the whole thing."

Elliott and I let the flood of words run their course and Dick Schmitt needed no further prompting. It just all spilled out that rainy afternoon, right there in the kitchen of the house on the hilltop in Encino, the house that had belonged to the late Gavin Keller.

He started shaking again, wringing his hands. "Gavin told us he and his family were moving to Utah. Me and Connie and Michelle and Sandi, we were to go on with the orgies without him."

He paused, a long pause, so long I thought maybe that was it, that was all he was going to say. But finally, he took a deep breath and continued. "When we went back the motel the next time, when Connie and I went into the little office to get the room, the manager had some pictures. He said he wanted money, was going to blackmail us and that he wanted to join in. He said, "Now

464

that you're one player short." He knew about Gavin. Gavin and Sandi and Michelle always hid in the back of the car until Connie and I got the room."

Now Schmitt ground his teeth and spit out, "That motel manager knew about Gavin all along. That's how I finally figured out Gavin was in on it, was in on filming us all having sex and smoking marijuana. Gavin had to be in on the scheme for the motel manager to blackmail us."

Abruptly Dick stopped shaking and seemed to compose himself. He looked around, as if trying to figure out where he was, get his bearings.

He looked at me, then at Elliot.

"Connie shot him," he blurted out.

"Who's Connie? Connie who? What's her last name?" Elliott asked.

"I don't know. I never knew any of their last names. I didn't know where they lived or anything else about them."

"Where was this motel?"

"It was on a side street in Lomita. Just a little place. There were never any other guests. The parking lot was always empty. We always got the same room, just a cabin really. The place was old, maybe built in the twenties."

"You say a girl named Connie shot him. Exactly what happened?" I asked.

"The manager showed us the photographs. He said he'd taken them from a motion picture film. He wanted money and sex, or he was going to distribute them, send them to the newspapers, the police. Connie and I went back to her car. Sandi and Michelle were waiting in the back seat for us to get the room. I got in, got in the driver's seat. I thought we were going to leave. Connie got something out of the glove compartment. It was dark. I didn't know what she was doing, what it was she was getting. She told me to go with her back to the motel."

Dick Schmitt paused, as if reminiscing.

He went on softly, quietly now. "When we walked back in the door the manager had this little smile on his face. I'll never forget it. He must have thought we were bringing him his money and we were going to agree to his deal, let him join in the orgies."

Suddenly he became animated, almost panicky.

465

"But Connie got a gun out of her purse and before I could do anything, she shot him in the face. She did it, I swear. It wasn't me. I didn't know she was going to do that. I couldn't stop her. I didn't know what to do. What could I do?"

"We have to take you downtown and get a written statement," I said, getting to my feet.

I turned to Val. "I don't believe you're telling us everything you know about your brother's death. I'll have to come back, and next time I hope you will be truthful with Officer Elliott and me, share anything you know that might be helpful in solving that crime."

I turned back to the wreck that had been Dick Schmitt. "Come along, Mr. Schmitt. Inasmuch as you are an accessory to a capital crime, the procedure requires that I put you under restraint."

I helped him to his feet, handcuffed him and we, Dick Schmitt, Elliott and I left the late Gavin Keller's house on the hill in Encino.

 "Well, my boy," old Elliott said getting in the back of the car. He settled in next our collar. "I must say I am very impressed with your handling of that interrogation."

"I'd rather call it an interview or even just a conversation."

Parked at the curb ahead of us was the old Thunderbird.

"That your car?" I asked, catching Schmitt's eye in the rear-view mirror.

He nodded yes. I took the mike from its holder on the dashboard and called the station for a tow truck to have it hauled to impound.

I made my u-turn, and as I did, I glanced again in the rear-view mirror at my passengers in the back. Elliott, slumped down in the seat, craned his neck looking wistfully out the window at the old T Bird.

Dick Schmitt, sitting in the seat next to him, his hands cuffed behind his back, was staring down at his lap.

He didn't look up.

# One Hundred Thirteen

## Catarina Monreale

## Tuesday, May 10<sup>th</sup>, 1966

Finding that her Corvette had been dusted for prints and probably bugged was all the warning Catarina needed. Ironically, everything else seemed to be going just great. The ranch was doing well, she was riding when she wanted to, the insurance scam was going gangbusters.

And the Frank Greco hit went off to everyone's satisfaction. Everyone, except maybe Greco's.

But Catarina knew she'd somehow attracted too much attention from someone, probably the police. Greco had been in the mob, so it could even be the Feds.

Whoever it had been, she was sure she had to make some life-changing decisions.

Val Keller. Val Keller meant trouble. It must have been Val Keller that set her up at the restaurant. Where'd she come from and why?

The beautiful Val intrigued her. Sensing she was dangerous fascinated Catarina all the more.

Like a snake charmer fascinates a cobra.

Or is it the other way around? Is it the cobra's deadly beauty that fascinates the snake charmer?

Val Keller was most likely Gavin Keller's sister. Keller just wasn't that common a name. Besides, there was a very distinct family resemblance. Now that Gavin Keller was dead, and Catarina Monreale knew damn well he was dead, was his sister looking for revenge?

Catarina was standing in the shade just inside the barn, chewing on a piece of straw. She'd watched the dark clouds gathering over the mountains to the north and reluctantly came to the conclusion that it was time to call her brother Johnny.

She had to make a move, and she had to do it soon- now, in fact, or it would be too late.

By 2:00 o'clock that afternoon Catarina and Johnny were sitting in the back of his limo parked in the public lot at Zuma Beach.

"I'm pretty sure I'm in somebody's sights, the FBI or the police," she said quietly.

"Oh? What's up?" Johnny asked.

"My guess is that the Greco hit attracted too much attention," she answered. She stretched her legs and leaned back in the seat. She looked up. Through the car's sunroof, puffy white clouds, precursors of the coming rain, hurried across the blue sky.

She continued quietly, as if talking to herself.

"Something else happened that night. I met the actress, Marcia Schmitt, at that party. While I was talking to her, another woman was introduced to us, name of Val Keller. We arranged to have lunch several days later. While I was in the restaurant someone dusted my car and probably bugged it. I'm guessing that Val Keller's your old roommate's sister and I think she's the one that set me up."

Johnny lowered the window next to him and looked toward the beach. There were some surfers out. At the edge of the otherwise empty lot a handful of old cars were parked close to each other in a group as if huddled together for warmth. Nearby, a bunch of seagulls were dive bombing, wings flapping, making a raucous attack on an overflowing trash can and on each other, scattering wrappers and French fries.

Johnny Monreale turned to face his sister. "I don't like the sound of this," he said, reaching for the button to close the window.

"I have to think of the family, the whole family. We could not afford to have you in the wrong hands."

"I understand and agree. I love living on the ranch, but I think it would be best if I were out of reach-and the sooner the better. I have over $220,000,000 from my insurance scam scattered in offshore accounts all over the Caribbean. I think we should figure on my leaving the country for good."

She turned in the seat and leaned against the door so she could face her brother. "It is very important to me that you take care of my favorite pony, Rondo and my dog Shadow. Once I'm settled somewhere, I'll contact you so you can send them to me. I'm thinking Spain. Spain doesn't have an extradition treaty with the U.S. for white collar crimes. And Spain won't extradite to countries that have a death penalty. I'm very sorry about all this."

# One Hundred Fourteen

## Val Keller

## Tuesday, May 10$^{th}$, 1966

I still hadn't filled in the Johnny Monreale gap in my search for the real story of my brother's life and death. In the course of trying to eliminate suspects, all I'd managed to do had been to come up with more questions.

And one of the less pleasant revelations had been that despite my own feelings about him, most of the rest of the people I'd come across hated Gavin enough to kill him.

The security cameras in and around his house showed a veritable parade of people coming and going the night of his death. Had one of them been Johnny Monreale? Or even Catarina Monreale? Based on my admittedly limited knowledge of Catarina, I didn't think the tawny beauty could care enough about anyone to kill him. Like most pros, she'd only kill to further her and her family's interests or in self-defense. If Catarina did kill Gavin, it probably didn't have anything to do with love.

Maybe Johnny Monreale had been the killer.

According to Tommy Huber, Gavin and Johnny had been roommates for several years. That would have easily been long enough for Gavin to have made an enemy of Johnny. Gavin had made enemies of a host of others in a lot less time than that.

I'd better call Julie in D.C. again. Maybe she could fill me in some more about the Monreales.

"I'm calling to tell you that unfortunately I'm unable to attend your parents wedding," I said, as soon as I heard her answer the phone. "I'm allergic to fried possum."

"I'm sorry to hear that," Julie replied. "You could have been the first in your clan to see a gathering of people wearing shoes and eating cooked meat."

"What do you have on Johnny Monreale, where he lives, habits, weaknesses, anything?"

"Why?" asked Julie. "Are you considering moving up in society?"

"I'm wondering if there's a way to meet him short of dropping in unannounced."

She snorted. "I'd recommend that you be particularly careful with him. Dropping in unannounced would in all likelihood be a fatal mistake.  We have very extensive details on his home. The security is all but impenetrable. And we're pretty sure we don't have the whole picture at that. It's always been assumed that if The Bureau ever decided to go in, it would be a full-frontal assault. We've concluded that a more subtle approach would not succeed without a lot of casualties."

"What do you have?"

"Let me go get his file, I'll be right back."

Julie left me hanging on the phone for five minutes. When she did return, she began describing a setup that should have been incorporated in the Maginot Line. If it had, France's defenses against Germany would've worked. I leaned back, put my feet up on the desk and listened.

"It's a two-story house on the beach in Malibu," Julie began. "The first and second floors facing the beach are sliding glass doors opening onto a deck on the first floor and a balcony on the second. The beach in front is supposed to be accessible to the public, however the homeowners along there all but drive everyone away. Monreale's house is set back from the sand, up on a slight bank. The bank is covered in ivy, poison ivy. And on top of that, it's wired. Random bare copper wires running 220 volts hidden in poison ivy. Floodlights connected to motion detectors aimed everywhere. Two big dogs. Ten-foot walls on the east, west and street side. Did I mention it's a gated neighborhood?"

I could hear her turning pages before continuing.

"Front entrance to the house is two electric gates. The outer gate has to be closed before the inner gate will open. 220-volt cables buried in the drive. Top of the wall also wired. All windows and doors alarmed. Sensors in the carpets, infra-red beams in certain parts of the house, microphones in the ceilings. We got our info from contractors that installed some of this, but there were others we couldn't get to. I can fax or courier you copies of all we have. If you pursue this and survive, you must report back to us with all you find. Of course, if you don't survive, you needn't bother."

I thought a moment, digesting all this, and then said, "I may just start with Catarina. What do you have on her place?"

"The ranch covers 400 acres, and even has a nice lake. The whole place is completely surrounded by a six-foot Cyclone fence, but the fence isn't hot. It's in the Santa Ynez Valley, just

470

over the San Marcos Pass from Santa Barbara. We couldn't get to anyone that's actually been inside. She has six fulltime ranch hands working the grounds and the horses. A man and wife team does the cooking and takes care of the house. The staff also does the shopping, so Catarina doesn't leave the ranch that often. The whole crew is from Mexico and has been with her since she moved there three years ago. They are very loyal. All of them live on the premises in real nice digs. She takes very good care of them. If any of them are sick or injured, she sees to it they get first class treatment.

"Any personal info?"

"As far as Johnny is concerned, he seems to be a workaholic. Doesn't smoke or drink. No girlfriends or boyfriends. Has a live-in man that drives him everywhere in a black limousine, a Lincoln. We don't think Johnny drives at all. Catarina, however, does some traveling and has various I.D.'s."

I could hear Julie turning pages, going through her file. "Catarina rides horses," she continued. "Crack shot. The place is big enough so that she can get in considerable practice. We have telephoto pictures of her practicing with pistols and rifles while on horseback."

There was a sharp intake of breath, and then she continued in an awestruck voice, "Also some really great shots of her swimming nude in her lake. I guess it gets very hot in Santa Ynez."

"You'd think they'd get lonely."

Julie seemed to regain her composure. "You would, wouldn't you? But Catarina and Johnny don't seem to need any company. On the other hand, the parents, Gianni and Gina are Las Vegas' answer to Scott and Zelda."

"Interesting as I'm sure the senior Monreales are, I don't think they're going to shed much light on what happened to my brother."

"Nonetheless, if you find out anything, we expect you to share it with us. How do you want me to send you the dossiers?"

"Same as last time. I'll pick it up from Heidi at the base in El Segundo."

"It'll be there by midnight."

"Thanks and keep taking the pills."

471

# One Hundred Fifteen

## Tom Larson

## Tuesday, May 10th, 1966

Larson was in the locker room getting ready to go off duty when Detective Tony Giuliani walked up and said with a grin, "I understand that your former partner made a big bust yesterday."

"Oh?" Larson replied, pausing at his locker.

"Yes, your boy Jim Miller, LAPD homicide finally got a lead on that old case in Lomita, that motel shooting, years ago."

Giuliani seemed to be relishing his being able to tell Larson something that apparently the Sarge didn't already know. The shooting death of the motel manager had been a local mystery for years. It dated back to a time when serious crimes and especially murders were unknown in the South Bay.

"I haven't heard anything about it," Larson said, taking off his hat and putting it in the top of his locker.

"Well, seems young Jim got a confession out of someone who was actually there, an accessory who claims he didn't pull the trigger, but had been involved."

"Who did pull the trigger?"

"Some girl name of Connie, the guy said. Swears he doesn't know the perp's last name. Claims the motel manager had been about to blackmail them. He had films of the guy and this Connie using drugs and having sex orgies with three others in one of his rooms. That's when this Connie killed him."

Giuliani stepped back with his thumbs hitched in his belt and said with a smirk, "Oh, and guess who the guy is."

"Who?"

"Dick Schmitt."

Larson had only been half listening to Giuliani's gossip, so it took him a minute to connect the name. Dick Schmitt. Dick Schmitt? Millie's oldest boy?

He stopped taking off his gear and turned to Giuliani. "You're telling me that Dick Schmitt had been in on the murder of that motel manager in Lomita eight years ago?"

"Yep," Giuliani looked proud to have been the bearer of such big news.

Larson stared at him, lost in thought. He wondered if Millie knew about this. Dick had just dropped out of her life altogether, back in 58' or 59', right about that time. He never contacted her, not even once. Larson knew she wrote him weekly for years before giving up.

Dick had been all but forgotten in the Schmitt family.

The Schmitt family.

Nowadays that consisted of Millie and her daughter Marcia.

And Larson, so far as it went.

Timothy, dead these last, what was it, eight, nine months? Going on a year almost, and mostly absent even before that. Would that wound ever heal?

And now this news about Dick. Should he try to keep this from her? Or should he be the one to tell her? She'd find out from someone sooner or later, the newspapers or some other way.

"Sarge?"

"Huh?"

"Sarge, you alright?" Giuliani asked, bringing Larson back to the present.

"I was just thinking about Millie," he responded.

"Oh yeah. Millie. Christ. What are you going to do?"

"I don't know," Larson said, turning to put his things away.

# One Hundred Sixteen

## Jim Miller

## Tuesday, May 10th, 1966

As far as the Homicide Division of the Los Angeles Police Department was concerned, the team of Elliott and Miller were the pair to watch. Elliott and I were right on top of the Greco hit and we'd collared a cold case murder that had no leads whatsoever for going on ten years.

Elliott the Bellyot even seemed to be getting better, reveling as he was in our successes and enjoying the synergy of our partnership. It was a synergy that worked both ways.

We were sitting at our desks when Elliott pointed out, "You know what the next step in the Greco case will have to be, don't you?" He paused for effect. "We'll have to pick up Catarina Monreale for questioning."

I leaned back in my chair, laced my fingers together behind my head and looked up at the ceiling. Catarina Monreale. Francesca Armerina. She was some piece of work, according to Rob Raymond.

I came forward, rested my elbows on the desk and looked at Elliott.

He'd shaved. His suit, while old and worn, had been cleaned and pressed. He looked human, almost cocky. Pulled together as he appeared to be, would he be up to something like that?

Would I?

"Do we have a fix on where she lives? I understand it's up in Santa Barbara County somewhere," I asked.

"Yes," Elliott replied with a grin. "She has a big spread in the Santa Ynez Valley, over the mountains from Santa Barbara."

He slid a thick file across the desk. I took a quick look at the dossier. Photos, maps of a ranch, background information on the Monreale clan. For the first time since I'd joined Homicide, I was seeing old Elliott show real interest in a case. He'd actually taken the initiative to do a thorough job of organizing the file on Catarina Monreale.

"Oh Christ," I said under my breath.

"I thought that would get your attention," Elliott said, looking pleased. "And you were already afraid of Val Keller. I'm thinking the women in your life are going to give you a real ride, Youngblood. This is going to be something to watch."

"I think in this case it will behoove me to research Miss Monreale very carefully before we even begin," I said, slowing to take my time reviewing the file. "Have you looked at this?"

"Oh yes, in fact I have" Elliott replied, "and you are absolutely correct. We would sail into a real hurricane if we jumped right in. What do you think about our going back to your friend at the FBI to see what he has to say?"

"Rob Raymond? Yeah, that's a good idea."

# One Hundred Seventeen

## Val Keller

## Wednesday, May 11th, 1966

"Now we're talking," I thought, muscling the mighty Corvette up Highway 154 through the San Marcos Pass. Gavin's damned Jag would have broken down twice before I even got to Santa Barbara.

The roar of the big V8 and the squealing tires on the mountain curves really brought out the adrenalin and sharpened my senses for whatever awaited me.

Catarina Monreale awaited me, although Miss Monreale didn't know it.

I planned to drive on past her ranch and check into a motel in Solvang or Buellton. Tonight, once I settled in, I'd study the FBI's dossier on her and her ranch. I intended to be fresh and fully briefed before I took her on.

All I really hoped to do was to talk to her, to see what she knew about Gavin. I'd play it by ear as far as an introduction to her brother Johnny.

I was pretty sure Catarina wouldn't take too kindly to the fact that I knew her name wasn't Francesca Armerina. Her knowing that would lead to all sorts of other conclusions. My hope was that she might be as intrigued by me as I was by her.

We'll find out tomorrow.

It had been raining in the Santa Ynez Valley for the last day or two, but the weather tomorrow promised to be sunny. I had riding boots and gear, wire cutters to cut through the cyclone fence surrounding the property, binoculars, a cold chicken salad sandwich, six bottles of water, and a 30-30 with a scope.

And, of course, my .22.

I'd be nothing if not prepared.

# One Hundred Eighteen

## Jim Miller

## Wednesday, May 11ᵗʰ, 1966

Rob Raymond slipped us a copy of the FBI's file on Catarina Monreale and her place in Santa Ynez. This went with the understanding that if we turned anything up, we had to share it.

And if there was any action, we had to call him immediately.

Elliott wasn't having a particularly good day. I held him by the arm to help him into the elevator on our way back down to the car.

"Do you think you can make it?" I asked.

"I hope so. I just want to see this case through."

"I'm anxious to get this wrapped up too," I replied. "I'm still convinced Val Keller knows a lot more than she lets on. If we could combine what she knows with what we know, I think we'd be almost home on this."

Elliott propped himself up against the elevator wall and closed his eyes. He rubbed his face with his hand and asked, "Why don't we call and see if we can drop in on Miss Bikini tomorrow? Hopefully, I'll be up to it. Maybe we can get something out of her if we feed her a little of what we have."

"Agreed."

The following day Elliott did seem much better. But after trying Val Keller's number repeatedly and receiving no answer we concluded she was out, perhaps for the day.

That meant going to plan B, a trip to Santa Ynez to call on Catarina Monreale.

# One Hundred Nineteen

## Val Keller

### Thursday, May 12<sup>th</sup>, 1966

The sun was just coming up. I got "something" from the vending machine at the end of the hall. "Something" meant a "sweet roll" when it had been put in the cellophane package back in January. That, along with a cup of coffee I'd make using a plug-in device in the bathroom would be my breakfast.

When I'd checked in last night, I'd told the desk clerk I wanted to go riding this morning. He'd referred me to a stable where I could rent a horse for the day. I planned to be on my way to the ranch by 08:00.

I'd reread the FBI's file. I'd studied the aerial photographs of the ranch and the description of Catarina's habits and routine.

Being extra careful, I reviewed the file again this morning.

Catarina liked riding horses and swimming nude in her lake.

Alone.

Afterward, she liked to ride up a hill on the ranch to some big rocks, dismount and eat her lunch.

Also, alone.

Someone in surveillance had done a pretty good job. It appeared obvious that the FBI figured sooner or later they'd need this information for tactical reasons.

Using the maps and the surveillance photos, I located a trail that meandered along the foothills at the base of the Santa Ynez Mountains.

It was a good six or seven miles from the stable where I rented the horse to the edge of Catarina's ranch. I found a place where the cyclone fence went through a grove of trees, dismounted and used the wire cutters to make an opening large enough for me and the horse.

I thought the rock formation mentioned in the report would be the best place to intercept her. According to the report, that spot was always included in her routine.

The rocks might offer some cover, in case it came to that.

478

# One Hundred Twenty

## Catarina Monreale

## Thursday, May 12<sup>th</sup>, 1966

"God, I'm really going to miss this place" Catarina thought, looking around the ranch house. The weather was always glorious. Even though there were still big patches of mud here and there, left over from the recent rain, they'd dry as the day warmed up.

The ranch hands were rounding up the two new quarter horses, Lupe was dusting and vacuuming and Lupe's husband, Francisco, was painting the eaves.

It was the perfect picture of a successful working ranch.

Catarina wanted to enjoy one last ride. She led Rondo out of the corral and saddled him up. She had a couple of enchiladas Lupe had made for her along with Uncle Benny's old .45 in her saddle bag.

With Shadow at their heels, they left the corral and headed out in the general direction of the lake.

It was hot, humid, maybe 95 degrees by 9:00 a.m.

It would be getting a lot hotter.

# One Hundred Twenty-one

## Val Keller

## Thursday, May 12th, 1966

The crest of this hill was about 100 yards in circumference, sixty or seventy feet higher than the surrounding terrain, covered with wildflowers and littered with huge boulders, some of them big as houses.

I tethered the horse in the shade of an overhang where it should be cooler as the day wore on.

Then I settled myself in the cleft of a rock. I might have a long wait and I wanted to be as comfortable as possible.

There was no one else around, no one within miles of this place. Except for the buzzing of insects, all was quiet.

From here I could see the ranch house, barn and corrals in the distance. In the other direction, off to the left and behind me, the lake's surface glittered in the morning sun.

It was spring, going on summer. There was color everywhere. The whole valley, including the ranch was in bloom.

This really was a beautiful setting.

I scanned the layout with the binoculars and counted the ranch hands.

Catarina, followed by a dog, led a black pony out of the corral. She mounted up, and with the dog running behind, set off at a gallop.

That dog could become a problem for me when the little party reached these rocks.

Once away from the house and barn, Catarina slowed the horse to a canter. I could faintly hear the dog bark in the distance as it ran off in first one direction then another. They were headed toward the lake, and away from where I was.

After a while, the little party started toward the lake, more or less in my direction. The lake was "L" shaped and at its closest, about three hundred yards from the rock formation. As they got closer, I felt more and more like a voyeur, watching them through the binoculars, Catarina and that beautiful pony.

Woman and animal moved in perfect harmony.

She rode slowly through a grove of oak trees along the lake's edge, stopped and dismounted in the shade.

The dog headed straight for the lake and plunged right in.

Catarina sat on a fallen log and pulled off her boots, then her socks.

She stood, unbuttoned her plaid shirt, took it off and draped it over the saddle horn. She wasn't wearing a bra. With a shimmying motion she worked her skintight jeans down to her ankles and stepped out of them.

Now she was completely naked.

I nearly fell off the rock.

Nude, Catarina Monreale was fucking gorgeous.

I was entranced, couldn't take my eyes off of her. She walked the few feet to the water's edge, waded in and swam to the middle of the lake. She turned over to float on her back, looking up at the blue sky, her arms outstretched. Only partially submerged and wet, her firm, tanned breasts and flat stomach glistened in the sunlight.

I could have watched her all day.

The dog had left the water and was chasing a rabbit clear on the other side of the lake when Catarina returned to the shore.

I wished I could be there with a towel to greet her.

She unrolled a saddle blanket, spread it on the ground and lay naked in the sun to dry. Oh my God, I thought, I don't know how much more of this I can take. She sunned herself for 45 minutes, and I was really getting turned on.

When she got up from the blanket, she shook her hair to dry in the warm air, and then bent to pick a spray from the field of purple flowers growing under the trees. She wove the flowers into her hair, slipped into her jeans and put on her socks and boots. She put her shirt back on but didn't button it.

She mounted the pony, gave it a slap on its haunch and headed toward the rock formation where I hid.

I glanced at my watch.

Almost 12:00 o'clock.

This is it, I thought.

High noon in Santa Ynez.

# One Hundred Twenty-two

## Jim Miller

## Thursday, May 12<sup>th</sup>, 1966

Once past Santa Monica, Elliott and I made fairly good time all the way up Pacific Coast Highway and over the San Marcos Pass.

After all the overtime I'd been putting in on the Greco and Gavin Keller cases, and all my calls apologizing to my wife Sharon that I'd be late, I owed her an outing. The Santa Ynez Valley looked like just the place. Maybe next weekend we'd take off and come up here, just the two of us.

It was just after 11:30 in the morning by the time Elliott and I found the Monreale ranch. The gate was closed and locked, but on the gatepost, an intercom and a small sign directing visitors to ring the buzzer for admittance.

A voice with a Latino accent answered. "Sí?"

"Detectives Elliott and Miller from the Los Angeles Police Department. We're here to see Catarina Monreale."

"Señorita Monreale not here," said the voice from the speaker.

"When will she return?" I asked.

"Señorita out riding. Be back two, maybe three hours."

"We'd like to come in and wait for her."

"I must send someone to see identification," the voice on the intercom responded.

"Fine," I said.

"Getting hot," Elliott said, mopping his brow, "and all these weeds are murder on my sinuses. I gotta sit in the car with the a/c on."

"Go ahead. I'll wait here at the gate."

Shading my eyes from the bright sun, I looked up toward the ranch house. A guy in a cowboy hat, jeans and a t-shirt was walking slowly down the drive toward us, big clumps of mud sticking to his boots.

He looked annoyed.

I took my handkerchief from my back pocket and wiped my forehead as he got closer.

"Am I to understand, Señor that you are here to see Señorita Monreale?"

"That is correct," I answered, showing my badge.

"Please come in," the ranch hand invited, opening the gate.

I returned to the car and drove through, then stopped to let the ranch hand, muddy boots and all, ride with us back up the hill to the house.

Elliott, in the front passenger seat turned to face the man in back. "Can you tell us where Miss Monreale might be?"

The man leaned forward over the back of the front seat and pointed through the windshield at a rock formation on top of a hill. It was quite a way off, maybe a mile or more. "By now, Señor, she is probably up there."

"Can we drive up there and meet her?" Elliott asked.

"Sí," he said smiling, "….en un vehiculo de cuatro ruedas."

# One Hundred Twenty-three

## Catarina Monreale

## Thursday, May 12<sup>th</sup>, 1966

Shadow was chasing a rabbit clear on the other side of the lake. Other than the faint sound of his barking it was quiet, just the clop clop of Rondo's hoofs, and the buzzing of insects.

No birds chirping, not even the ones Catarina knew nested here.

Still, she was relaxed and rode at a leisurely gait to the top of the hill. She would sit on a rock in the shade of the largest of the boulders, eat the enchiladas and look out over the valley and the ranch one last time.

This was her favorite spot, this hill. The ground was still damp from the rains; the whole ranch was carpeted with spring grass and wildflowers. The hilltop, with its scattered boulders was beautiful and secluded, yet high enough to provide a sweeping view.

She had quickly acclimated to the warm, dry valley, the scent of the wild mustard plants and the fields of California poppies. According to Lupe, the Indians who once lived in this valley believed that if you held a poppy blossom under your lover's chin and their chin turned golden in the sunlight it meant he loved you.

When she reached the rocks she dismounted, took the saddlebag, and looked around.

Something didn't seem quite right.

Down below, down toward the ranch house, a car was at the gate. One of her ranch hands, she couldn't tell for certain which one, was walking down the drive toward the car.

The car was a plain brown sedan, a Chevrolet like the cop's use.

She made herself comfortable on her favorite rock, opened her saddlebag and unwrapped one of Lupe's enchiladas.

# One Hundred Twenty-four

## Val Keller

## Thursday, May 12th, 1966

Catarina had settled herself on a rock in the shade of a big boulder. I'd moved as quietly as I could to the other side of it when I heard an intake of breath and something warm nuzzle my behind.

Startled, I turned.

It was the black pony. I couldn't stay this close to Catarina very long without her realizing that she had company. Separated by this huge boulder though we were, we were really only a few feet apart.

I could almost hear her breathe.

I edged closer.

Her back was to me.

She got an enchilada out of her saddlebag, unwrapped it and held it up.

Without turning, she asked in that throaty voice of hers, "Want some?"

Catarina knew I was there; knew I was right behind her. This is the time to be extra careful, I thought, putting my hand on my .22.

"No thanks, I have a chicken salad sandwich. Want some water?"

"That might be nice," Catarina replied. "What are you doing here?"

"My dear Miss Monreale, I'm here to see you, of course. Just to talk."

"About what?"

"About my brother, Gavin Keller."

"O.K. What do you want to know?"

"I want to know all I can about him and his relationship with you or your brother or both. But what I really want to know is who killed him."

"It wasn't me," Catarina said, finishing off her enchilada and reaching into her saddlebag. "Sure you don't want one? There's plenty more," she said, getting to her feet and turning to face me.

Before I could decline the offer, quick as lightning she pulled a great big .45 automatic from the saddle bag.

"Ah, the lovely Miss Keller. I really hoped we would be meeting again. But as it happens, this is not an opportune time."

Over her shoulder, way down at the ranch house I could see a car moving up the drive.

She did not turn to look. "I presume you rode here. Where's your horse?"

"On the other side of the rocks."

"Let's take a quick look. And by the way, I didn't kill your brother. I would have, but he was dead when I got there. I don't know who did it."

We walked around to the other side of the rocks and found my horse. She untied it, gave it a smack on the haunch and off it ran.

The horse looked relieved, happy to be running away. It disappeared through the brush and down the muddy hill, along with my hopes for a long and happy life.

I sure wished I were with that horse.

"Now let's go back and wait for developments," Catarina said, motioning with the .45.

She followed me back to the side of the rocks overlooking the ranch house.

In the distance, a ranch hand got out of the car. Then the car started across the open countryside, bumping and bouncing through the puddles and mud toward the small hill where we were.

Behind me I heard her cock the .45. "Why don't you slowly turn around and hand me that .22 you have in your shoulder holster," she said evenly. "Grip it only by the butt with your thumb and forefinger and you might just live through this."

I was pretty sure that was the better of the options I had before me. In fact, I didn't know what my other options were. But to hear that Catarina wasn't going to just kill me right away was encouraging.

I did as I was directed and dropped the pistol.

"Now back up 15 paces," she instructed. When I complied, she moved forward, bent and picked up my pistol. "HDM High Standard with a silencer," she said, looking it over.

"OSS or CIA?" she asked, looking me in the eye.

I didn't answer.

"Doesn't matter," she said. She threw my pistol into the brush without taking her eyes or that big .45 off me.

"Now let's get comfortable and wait for the inevitable."

"And what would that be?" I asked, still fearing the worst.

"For those stupid bastards to get that fucking sedan stuck in the mud," Catarina replied.

Catarina knew her ranch well. It wasn't long before the inevitable happened.

She whistled and the black pony came to her. "Perhaps we'll meet again, Miss Keller," she said.

Still holding the big .45 in one hand, she grabbed the saddle horn in the other, slipped her booted foot in the stirrup and mounted up. She gave a little salute and was off at a gallop, down the hill away from me and the men in the car.

My horse and my gun were gone. Like a dumbass, I was left standing in the hot sun, outflanked by a twenty-six-year-old girl.

# One Hundred Twenty-five

## Jim Miller

## Thursday, May 12th, 1966

It was hotter than hell and I felt stupid for getting the car stuck in the mud. I tried rocking it back and forth, first putting it in drive, then reverse.

But it only dug itself in more and more.

"I knew this car wouldn't make it across open country," Elliott said from the passenger seat. He was looking green, and his head bobbed back and forth with the motion of the car.

"I think I'm going to be sick," he added.

"You could've said something before," I said grinding my teeth.

"About being sick?"

"No, about the goddamn car not making it."

"Somebody's coming," Elliott said, nodding toward the hill. "Maybe they can help."

I stopped trying to free the car and leaned back to watch the approaching figure.

"Oh, swell," I said as they got closer. "Guess who?"

"Who?" Elliott asked, trying to focus his rheumy old eyes.

"Val Keller."

"Now this is embarrassing," Elliott said.

She walked up to the car.

"Howdy boys," she said, hitching her thumbs in her belt. "Need some help?"

"No, Jim here just wanted to get out of the city and get some country air," Elliott replied.

"Would you mind explaining what you're doing here?" I asked.

"Same as you," she answered, looking around as if scanning the countryside. "Just getting some air."

I opened the car door, got out and stood over Val.

"Miss Keller," I said, leaning toward her and grinding my teeth, "in the course of investigating the murder of your brother we have come to the conclusion that you have been less than cooperative. I remind you that it was you who insisted the department reopen this case. Unless you are forthcoming with any and all information you have pertaining to this crime, I am going to charge you with obstruction of justice. Now I ask you again, what are you doing here?"

"You're right," she said, looking down toward her boots as if she were contrite. I'm pretty sure she was pretending.

"I've allowed you to struggle with this case when I could've been more helpful. I came here to confront Catarina Monreale to find out what information she might have about Gavin. I've been informed that she knew Gavin. I know her brother Johnny had been Gavin's roommate in college."

"Are you aware of just who Catarina Monreale is?" I asked.

"Yes. I'm with Naval Intelligence and I have friendly sources in the FBI. I'm well aware of who the Monreales are. My source was kind enough to provide me with all the information they had on her habits and the layout of this ranch."

"What did you think you were going to do here?" I asked.

"What did you think YOU were going to do here?" she countered.

"We simply wanted to learn what Catarina knew. We didn't seriously consider her a suspect in your brother's murder, but she is most certainly a suspect in the murder of Frank Greco. Now why are you here?"

"I meant to get the drop on Catarina when she stopped at those rocks" she said, motioning at the hill behind her. "My information is that she usually stopped during her rides to have lunch up there." Val took off her hat and smacked it against her leg to shake the dust off it. She then put it back on and straightened it.

"She got the drop on me instead, took my gun away and ran my horse off. There. Now are you happy?"

"Hardly. We're stuck in the mud in the middle of nowhere, the two-way radio is out of range and our only option is to walk all the way back to the ranch house and see if they'll let us use the phone to call for help."

I took a deep breath and looked around. "I suppose Catarina is long gone?" I added as an afterthought.

"I think you suppose right. She waited till she saw you were good and stuck, and then she mounted her horse and rode through those trees to the ranch house. A few minutes later she got in a station wagon and left. I don't think she's coming back."

"Swell."

We three walked down the muddy slope to the ranch house where the Mexican woman told us that when Catarina returned, she picked up a travel bag, took a moment to say goodbye to everyone, and left.

It was nine o'clock that night by the time a tow truck showed up from Solvang and our unit was freed from the mud.

Elliott and I gave Val a lift back to her motel in Buellton with the promise that she'd be more forthcoming in the future. Based on the short conversation Val had with her, we three more or less agreed that Catarina Monreale, guilty as she may be of a host of other crimes, did not murder Gavin Keller, or she wouldn't have admitted to being in his house the night he died.

It had been a very long day, well beyond Elliott's capacity. He was exhausted.

We agreed to meet at the Keller house the following morning to combine what we all knew about the murder of Gavin Keller.

Much as I wanted to rehash the day's developments and assimilate what we'd learned from Val so far, I couldn't.

Elliott slept all the way home.

# One Hundred Twenty-six

## Tom Larson

## Thursday, May 12th, 1966

Tonight, was to be a special occasion for his adopted family. Marcia's schedule called for her to be filming in Italy for two months, so she, her mother and Tom planned to have a bon voyage dinner.

He arrived at the little trailer just after six. In the back of his mind was the news Millie's oldest son Dick had been held as an accomplice for a murder. He certainly was not going to tell her that now, or ever, if he could help it.

He'd followed the progress of that re-opened case and reviewed what old files the Torrance Police Department had concerning the matter. He'd even stopped in the library and reviewed the Torrance Herald Newspaper's archives for the period.

With all that, plus his recollection of Dick Schmitt, Larson had his own picture of what happened in that old motel back in 1958.

Dick Schmitt had been a taciturn, rude really, asshole as a boy, bitter and self absorbed. But Larson recalled a change in the guy about that time. He wasn't as deliberately nasty to his mother and the rest of the family. For a while Dick's rare presence among them hadn't been a strain on everyone.

Larson figured it was because Dick Schmitt had been getting laid.

Lost in thought, Larson was staring at without seeing Marcia's portrait hanging over the television set. On top of the T.V., below the portrait was the framed black and white photograph of young Timothy.

Little Timothy was posed dressed in a cowboy hat and vest and wearing a toy gun and holster, trying to look as menacing as a freckle face ten-year-old boy could.

Marcia calling his name brought Larson back to the present. "Tom, are you alright?"

"Hmmm? Oh, yes, I was just admiring your portrait and remembering how heavy it is. We had a struggle getting it up there," he said with a grin. "It was worth it, though."

Marcia laughed and moved close to him. "Well, I'd been in full makeup and wardrobe, so it was a good time to catch me at my best."

He stepped back and looked away, self conscious at being close to her like that. It seemed to him almost provocative. She was like a daughter to him, and her mother almost like a wife. They were his family, his world. He looked out for them, protected them like they were his own.

He would never let anything harm them in any way.

# One Hundred Twenty-seven

## Jim Miller

## Friday, May 13th, 1966

We'd requested that the Santa Barbara Sheriff's Department try to determine Catarina Monreale's movements after leaving the ranch. I received their reply just as Elliott and I left for the Keller house. The sheriff's department reported that at 1:05 p.m. on May 12th, a woman fitting Catarina's description showed up at the small general aviation airport near Solvang. There, using the name Debbie B. Cooper, the woman paid cash to charter a small plane and hire a pilot.

The trail ended at San Francisco International Airport.

Elliott had been having one of his o.k. days, neither good nor bad. Good enough, I guess, for him to be out of the car under his own power and at the wrought iron gate almost before I'd shut the engine off.

The gate swung open. Val stood holding the door for us when we started up the walk. She wore a short print dress, cream colored, sleeveless, with a collar.

I swear that on her it was as sexy and provocative as anything I'd ever seen.

"Follow me to the den, gentlemen," she said, shutting the door behind us. "I don't know how helpful this is going to be," she began, "but Gavin had six closed circuit television cameras installed at various places around the house. They're prototypes, put together by Greater Energy's electronics division and they're connected to video recorders, something like everyday tape recorders. I guess Greater Energy gave or loaned them to Gavin for field testing. Sony, an electronics manufacturer in Japan is expected to have something similar on the market within a year. I've already reviewed the tapes from four of the monitors," she said over her shoulder as she led us down the hall.

"They don't show much."

She ushered us into the den. "We'll see what the last two cameras recorded. Please make yourselves comfortable," she said, gesturing to the two leather swivel chairs in front of the desk.

She stood in the doorway while Elliott and I turned the chairs around to face the six monitors and recorders.

494

Pointing at the equipment, she explained, "The camera for that one is at the front door and is aimed out toward the street. This one shows the street itself. One records the action at the pool and deck, and one is for the bedroom. The last two, the two I haven't looked at yet are for the downstairs room."

She paused and nodded toward the kitchen. "I'm going to get us some water and soft drinks. Watching these tapes will take a while."

She returned with a pitcher of ice water and glasses and set them on the table.

"The recorders taped everything that appeared within the range of the cameras," she began, "and the tapes each ran eight hours. Apparently, my brother reloaded the recorders every evening around 11:00 p.m. He kept each night's tapes for a week, and then recorded over them."

She took a deep breath and for the first time I thought I detected a show of emotion, however fleeting.

"I guess I hoped I could tell what had happened that night from the first four tapes and maybe who the murderer was without having to actually see my brother die. But the ones showing the street don't show anything other than a suspicious car driving by. The one of the deck shows a lot of movement, but no clear image of the several people who came and went that night, and there were several. Gavin's house had been busy the night he died. As you've said before, Gavin had a lot of enemies. Several of them had motive enough and were capable of killing him."

"Yes," Elliott said. "From our interviews it appeared that several people decided to descend on him at one time. You mentioned yesterday you didn't think Catarina Monreale did it?"

"No, I don't think she did. She said she came here to kill Gavin, but he was already dead when she arrived. Because she had a gun on me when she said that and could have easily killed me then and there, I don't think she would have bothered lying. I think she skipped because she figured the law was catching up with her. My guess is that she's left the country by now."

"We're pretty sure you're right," I said. "Please go on, Miss Keller."

"Let's play one of the two tapes showing the downstairs room," she suggested. She was utterly composed. I wondered how she was going to react to viewing the death of her brother, the brother who meant so much to her that she initiated this investigation and worked it so hard on her own. I recalled her mentioning she was with Navy Intelligence, but what was that supposed to mean? What the hell was it she did in Navy Intelligence that made her so indifferent to death?

Whatever it was, apparently, she had to carry a gun to do it.

She closed the drapes to the small garden outside. Now the room was dark. She started the tape. A dimly lit, carpeted room with mirrored walls appeared on the monitor. In the room a movie was being projected on a screen just at the edge of the monitor's field of view.

A nice-looking young guy, naked, erect and with a pretty good build was standing in the middle of the room oiling himself.

Elliott turned to me and said quietly, "That's Gavin Keller."

We three watched Keller climb onto a small stool and fit his head through a noose hanging from the ceiling. He turned to watch the movie and began to masturbate. It was awkward, sitting here with Elliott and especially Val, watching her brother do that.

But it didn't last long.

There was a movement just at the edge of the monitor's screen, near the stairway at the side of the room. Very quickly a figure moved to where Keller was standing on the stool. The figure kicked the stool out from under Keller, and then stepped back. Keller struggled frantically, trying to get free of the noose.

Finally, he stopped trying. Slowly now, his naked body turned under the spotlight in the ceiling.

We three had just witnessed the murder of Gavin Keller.

The killer stood there a few more minutes, and then kicked the stool back toward the body.

We watched the murderer start toward the stairs, pause, then hurry to a darkened corner of the room and out of view.

Now another visitor come down the stairs. This one walked straight to the circle of light, reached out to touch Gavin Keller's nude body, then turned around and left.

The time and date on the monitor's screen showed 12:24 a.m., November 20, 1965.

The tape ran on.

At 1:05 a.m. yet another figure appeared, coming down the stairs. This one stumbled and fell; cartwheeled to the bottom and came to rest against the bar. The person struggled to their feet and looked toward the body hanging under the light, then turned and scrambled back up the stairs.

All this time, visitor number one, the murderer, the person who had kicked the stool out from under Gavin Keller, still hid somewhere in the room. Apparently, every time the murderer thought it might be safe to leave, someone else came down the stairs.

The killer had been trapped in the downstairs room.

Although none of the visitors' faces could be seen and there was no way to identify anyone, there was something slightly familiar about that first figure, the murderer.

Could it be the way the person moved, a gesture perhaps?

"Would you please rewind the tape to where the murderer comes down the stairs?" I asked.

"Certainly," Val replied. As I requested, she rewound and replayed the tape from where the time on the monitor showed 12:12 a.m.

I stood and moved closer to the screen, but I still couldn't tell anything from the shadowy figure. I sat back down. "What else do you have?"

"Well, we have the tape from the other camera in that room. Let's see what's on it," she said.

She pushed the play button on the other recorder and sped it ahead to where the time showed 12:12 a.m. Then she slowed the tape and let it run at normal speed.

This camera recorded the scene in the basement room from the bottom of the stairwell and was focused more on the movie screen. The movie screen itself was again just out of range.

The back of the head of the first visitor to the room appeared on the screen, the murderer coming down the stairs. Again, I thought there seemed something familiar about the person, but what? Once again, the action repeated itself and once again the killer started back toward the stairs to leave, only to be interrupted.

The killer darted to the shadows in the far corner of the room.

At 12:24 a.m., right on cue, the next figure came down the stairs. The person, a middle-aged woman in a print dress spotted the hanging body, walked over and stood looking at it for a moment, then reached out to touch it.

She shook her head and turned to leave, her face clearly visible on the monitor.

497

"Unless I miss my guess," Val said, "that's Marcia Schmitt in makeup, disguised to look 20 years older and 20 pounds heavier."

Val, Elliott and I knew the action wasn't over yet.

We sat quietly watching.

Visitor number three made an entrance, falling down the stairs, stumbling around and spotting the dead body. As in the previous tape, he again turned and scrambled back up the stairs.

It was Dick Schmitt.

I started to say something, but Val held up her hand. "Wait. Let's see it all the way through."

The tape played on.

The time on the monitor showed 1:44 a.m.

Out of nowhere the last figure appeared, almost like a shadow. Dressed in black and wearing black leather gloves and a ski mask, this visitor moved with cat-like grace.

The figure stood for a moment in the circle of light, removed the glove on their right hand and reached out to touch Gavin Keller's body. The person stepped back and looked around the room, then walked calmly to the stairs and left.

"My guess is that's Catarina Monreale behind the ski mask," Val said.

The three of us continued to watch the monitor closely, waiting for the murderer to reemerge. We knew the killer was being extra cautious, waiting to see if any more visitors showed up.

I sneaked a look at Val. She'd leaned back in the big leather chair, holding the remote for the tape player in her hand, her feet up on the desk.

Elliott said, "There he is."

The time on the monitor showed 2:20 a.m.

Out of the shadows, Gavin Keller's murderer stepped into view, took a quick look around, and then started toward the stairs.

When the killer's face appeared on the monitor's screen, Val paused the tape, stopped it in mid-frame.

"Who the hell is that?" Elliott asked.

"Damned if I know," I heard Val reply.

498

I knew exactly who it was.

After a long pause, Val turned to the only one in the room who hadn't responded to seeing the face on the screen.

Me.

"Detective Miller, do you recognize that man?"

I had to shake myself. There, on the monitor was the clear, indisputable image of Torrance Police Officer Tom Larson, passing in front of the camera on his way to the stairs.

Without a shadow of a doubt, it had been Tom Larson who murdered Gavin Keller at 12:15 a.m., Saturday, November 20, 1965.

"I'm afraid I do," I finally answered. "He's a police officer on the force in Torrance."

I added almost in a whisper. "His name is Tom Larson."

Elliott was watching me, a curious, expectant look on his face.

"We'll have to ask you for this tape and the others showing the crime and the other activity pertaining to it along with one of the recorders," I said getting up from chair. "I'll write you a receipt. Detective Elliott here will witness it. We'll try to have the tapes and the machine returned to you, sooner or later."

I looked back to the monitor.

Larson's face, frozen in time, looked almost right into the camera, right into the room.

Right at the three of us.

I'll never forget that image.

Elliott got unsteadily to his feet. He seemed to be trying to say something.

Of the three of us in the den, only Val, leaning back in the big leather chair and toying with the remote for the recorder seemed unperturbed. In one smooth motion she sat forward in the chair, rose to her feet, and broke the thick silence.

"Well, that's that, then. You arrest him, there's a trial, and he's convicted."

I looked over at Elliott, and then back to Val.

"That's pretty much the drill," I said, rubbing my eyes with my palms as if I could blot out the image on the monitor. "We'll have to work with you a bit more on the shooting of the motel

499

manager. I'm afraid we're going to need one or more of the porn films so we can try to identify the shooter and for evidence. Dick Schmitt seems to have told us all he knows, other than providing an I.D. we can use."

Elliot seemed as mesmerized as I by the image on the screen. Finally, he turned to Val and said, "You'll have to excuse us for now. We need to get back to the station to get a warrant for Larson's arrest. Then we start building this case."

We'd started to leave the den and head for the front door when Val asked, "Will you two be in on the collar of this guy Larson?"

"I don't know," I replied, still trying to absorb all this. "Maybe they'll send someone else. I've known Larson for several years. They may think that I might compromise the arrest," I said, opening the door.

We left the house without another word.

It was only after Elliott and I were back in the car that he said, "You're kidding yourself if you don't think they're going to send us to pick Larson up, you know. This has been our case from the beginning, and it'll be our case until the end."

"I know," I replied, still numb.

⁂

Reporting back to the station and bringing the captain up to date on the Gavin Keller case, then getting the arrest warrant for Tom Larson took until after eight o'clock that evening. I called home and told Sharon that I'd be late again, a conversation that was becoming routine.

Despite the long day, Elliott had held up o.k. Adrenalin and nerves must have been keeping him going for the last few steps toward closing this case.

At a little after nine we checked a car out of the motor pool and headed for Torrance.

I was in no hurry. I was pretty sure I knew where I'd find our man. I'd been there before, less than a year ago.

We pulled into the trailer court just after ten, stopped a short distance behind Larson's car and parked with the engine off.

That's where we'd wait for him.

500

The trailer ahead looked the same as I remembered it. In one of the windows, probably the living room, the flickering bluish light of a television reflected on the porch steps where my childhood buddy Timothy Schmitt had died.

At a little after eleven the light from the T.V. went out and a few minutes later the door opened.

Larson came out onto the porch, turned to lock the door and started down the steps.

Abruptly opening the passenger door of the unmarked LAPD car, Elliott said, "I'll take this one."

I started to get out too, but Elliott waved me off. "I want to handle this, Youngblood."

Elliott walked to the front of the car, bracing himself with one hand on the fender, his wallet and badge in the other. As Larson approached, Elliott held up his badge and said quietly, "Tom Larson? Sergeant Elliott, Los Angeles Police Department Homicide. You are under arrest for the murder of Gavin Keller."

Larson stopped and stood still, a big dark presence. Elliott moved toward him, handcuffs in hand.

"I hope you will come quietly."

Larson hesitated, and my heart was in my throat. Then he held both hands out in front of him. Gently, Elliott put the handcuffs on Larson and put his hand on the big guy's shoulder to guide him to our waiting car.

I heard Elliott say, "Thank you, Officer Larson, for your cooperation."

I got out of the driver's seat and hurried around to open the back door.

Larson looked at me.

Without a word, he ducked his head and got in the back of the car.

It was 11:32 p.m., Friday, May 13th, 1966.

No one spoke during the trip up the Harbor Freeway to LAPD Headquarters in downtown Los Angeles.

# Epilogue

## Jim Miller

## Monday, May 16, 1966

The strain of working the Gavin Keller case coupled with the trip to Santa Ynez and the late night bust took about all Elliott had left. He'd pretty much fulfilled his vow to hang on long enough to see this case through. I thought he'd been living on borrowed time for days, if not weeks. Looking at him, it was hard to guess what it would be that closed the book on Detective Elliott's long career.

It wouldn't be retirement.

"Time to go to Encino and see what we can find in Gavin Keller's secret room," I reminded him.

Elliott struggled to his feet. He looked around the squad room with kind of a bewildered expression. When he turned to take his coat from the back of his chair, I saw that his holster was empty again.

I paced myself to stay beside the old man as he shuffled between the desks toward the elevator down to the garage. Every so often he'd reach out to hold something for support, a chair, a cubicle wall.

When we got to the car, he dropped heavily into the passenger seat, leaned his head back and closed his eyes. He didn't open them all the way out the Hollywood Freeway to Ventura Boulevard and Encino.

I wondered if he was sleeping.

When we stopped in front of the house, he opened his eyes and said, "Can I just stay in the car this time? I'm sorry, I know you want some moral support, but I don't think I can make it."

"Sure," I said, reaching over and patting the old man on his knee.

"I can handle this. It's time I grew up."

Elliott started to say something but broke into a coughing spell and shook his head. He waved me to get out of the car, to go on, on to my fate.

502

I left the safety of the car, crossed the sidewalk, and approached the gate, feeling small and alone.

There, in that house in front of me was Val Keller, waiting.

This was the moment I'd been so afraid of, dreaded.

A mixture of fear, fear of what I would be capable of, what I would do when it was just the two of us, Val Keller and I alone in that house.

But I was pretty sure I knew what was coming. I just couldn't help it, couldn't have stopped myself if I'd tried.

No, in fact I was eager for it to begin.

Before I could even push the buzzer for the gate, I heard her cool voice on the intercom.

"Come in. I've released the lock."

The gate shut behind me and I started up the walk to the house. The door opened and there she was, tall, slender, with long brown hair tumbling down over her shoulders. She was wearing a tight, pale blue summer dress, just like the one I recalled Catarina Monreale had been wearing in the picture in Gavin's den, the picture taken of the Monreale family in Bermuda.

"Where's your partner?" Val asked, standing aside to usher me in.

"He's waiting in the car in case we get the call we're expecting on the two-way."

She gave me a quick look and pulled the door shut behind us.

Just as before, it was very quiet inside the house.

The drapes for the windows overlooking the valley were pulled almost shut, giving the dimly lit interior a feeling of being remote, removed from the world outside.

"I'd offer you a drink, but I assume being on duty precludes that small pleasure," she said.

"Yes ma'am, it does."

Another look from Val.

She led the way through the house. "If you'll recall," she said over her shoulder, "the entrance to Gavin's downstairs room was through the bookcase in his bedroom."

"Yes ma'am," I replied.

She paused at the doorway to the bedroom, turned and looked at me.

503

"Yes ma'am?" she said.

She was standing close.

Too close.

"After all we've been through together, it's still, "Yes ma'am?" she asked softly.

She pretended to brush something off my lapel. I felt awkward, clumsy and all too aware that we were alone.

Being this near to her was going to be my undoing.

She was nearly as tall as me. Looking directly into her brown eyes, her face, her lips, there seemed no alternative but to lean forward and kiss her.

She put her arms through mine and around my back and pulled me to her, hungrily returning the kiss, pressing her firm slim body hard against me.

I forgot my hesitation.

I forgot my awkward uncertainty.

I forgot my resolve.

I forgot I was married.

She broke away, stepped back and reached behind her neck. With one hand she grabbed the blue dress and pulled it up and over her head.

Now she was naked. With her other hand she grabbed me by my necktie and pulled me onto the bed and on top of her.

Fumbling, but with her help, I got my jacket and shirt off, undid my belt releasing my shoulder holster and pants and was on her and in her.

Oh God, she was hot, and wet, firm and tight and wild.

Afterwards, I sat up and reached for my pants.

"Why don't you just leave those here," she said.

"After all, we are going downstairs to look at porn." She pressed her body against me. "You might just want to take them right back off again."

Her logic was unassailable.

She got up from the bed and reached to the bookcase to touch the volume of Shakespeare.

504

The bookcase opened.

Naked, with her back to me she was spectacular. I reached out to touch her, caress her.

I was ready to go again.

She led the way through the opening and pulled the hidden door closed behind us. The landing and the stairway to the downstairs room were almost completely dark, lit only by a faint glow of light from below.

When we reached the bottom of the stairs she turned and said, "These films were made seven or eight years ago, and there are dozens of them. I've already set one of them up, so all I have to do is start the projector and the show will begin."

She gestured to a big leather chair. "Why don't you get comfortable in the seat of honor? I'll just kneel in front of you, between your legs," she said softly, slowly drawing her finger down my chest. "The film starring Gavin Keller, Dick Schmitt, Connie, Sandi and Michelle is about to begin."

The cool, smooth leather of the chair felt sensuous on my naked skin.

She reached across me and turned on the projector.

On the screen, a scene appeared. It looked like it had been filmed in a hotel or motel room. In the center of the room was a large bed. On the other side, a big dresser with a mirror tilted showed the scene from another angle. The light from a small lamp, a pair of red panties thrown over the shade, gave the setting a defused, erotic look.

Nude, leaning against the headboard, his face in shadow was a male that I was pretty sure had to be Gavin Keller. There were two beautiful naked girls, one on either side of him. The red head must be the one called Sandi and Michelle the brunette.

At the foot of the bed, also naked, was a young Dick Schmitt.

Facing him, her back to the camera was a very sexy, shapely young blond, the blond called Connie, the blond that Dick Schmitt swore killed the motel manager.

She turned to reach down to pull the covers up from the floor. Now I could see her face, see who she is.

No, the blonds name isn't Connie.

505

This film was made seven or eight years ago, back before I married her, but she hasn't changed much.

It was Sharon, my wife.

CPSIA information can be obtained
at www.ICGtesting.com
Printed in the USA
BVHW020920021222
653294BV00013B/192